Kings & Corruption

Aventine University Book One

Sadie Hunt

Blackthorn Press

Kings & Corruption

Aventine University Book One

Sadie Hunt

All rights reserved. No part of this book may be reproduced in any form or by any electronic means, including information storage and retrieval systems, without permission in writing from the author, except by a reviewer who may quote brief passages in review.

This is a work of fiction. Any resemblance to actual persons, living or dead, events, or locales is entirely coincidental. Any trademarks, service marks, product names, or named features are assumed to be the property of their respective owners, and are used only for reference. There is
no implied endorsement if any of these terms are used.

Copyright © 2022 by Sadie Hunt aka Michelle Zink and Zink Media
All rights reserved.

Dear Reader,

I've written over 60 books and not one of them is like this one.

I don't mean that in a this-book-is-special kind of way — although I think it is because I've been obsessed with it in a way I haven't been obsessed by one of my projects in a long time — but in a this-book-isn't-for-everyone kind of way.

Neo Alinari, Oscar Drago, and Rock Barone aren't bad guys — but they aren't good guys either. All of which is to say, please DON'T CONTINUE READING if you like your books sweet with a side of angst and a generous helping of equality in your power dynamic.

That is... not this book. You've been warned!

Content warning: bullying, stalking, peeping, stepbrother, violence, one attempted SA (foiled by the "good" guys), and other themes and situations you may find uncomfortable.

For those of you who choose to continue...happy reading!

Xo,
    Sadie

Chapter 1

Willa

This was a mistake.

That's what was going through my mind as I watched everyone milling around the reception venue. Some things never changed. It was pretty much the same crowd that had been at every wedding, baptism, and funeral since I was born: dark-haired men packing heat under their suit jackets while their overly made-up wives gossiped, holding champagne glasses carefully so they didn't mess up their freshly manicured nails. The men were talking business — they were always talking business — but they were also watching the younger women in the crowd while they pretended like they weren't.

Probably scoping out a round of new mistresses.

Ew.

I caught the bride watching me and forced a smile. She smiled back, but it wasn't happiness I saw in my mother's eyes.

It was relief.

I guess that's what happened when your ex-husband informed to the Feds and you got a chance to redeem your name with the biggest Mafia don on the East Coast.

That would be Roberto Alinari, the man standing at my mom's side. I had to admit, he looked handsome and elegant in a tuxedo, more like a trust fund billionaire than a Mob boss notorious for his brutality.

I suppressed a shiver when I realized he was staring right at me, regarding me coolly while pretending to engage in conversation with a couple I didn't recognize.

"How are you holding up, Willa?"

The voice came from my shoulder, and I turned to find my best friend, Mara, standing next to me.

"Oh, you know," I said, "my sister's still missing, my disgraced mother just married the most infamous Mafia boss in the country, and thanks to my dad, I'm a social pariah, but otherwise, life's just grand."

"Oooookay," Mara said. "Someone needs more champagne." She plucked a glass from a passing tray carried by one of the uniformed waitstaff and handed it to me.

I drank greedily, even though I'd promised myself I was going to be responsible at the wedding. I'd done enough partying in the year I'd been traveling to last a lifetime.

What could I say? Everyone processed grief differently. My mom had barely been able to get out of bed when it became clear that my sister, Emma, was really missing, and I'd run for the nearest airport the second I'd turned eighteen.

I felt ashamed of it now. I probably shouldn't have left my mom alone, even though she'd seemed more than happy to let

Roberto Alinari help her pick up the pieces, but at the time, I'd been drowning in my own grief.

Grief and the deeply felt sense that something very bad had happened to my sister at Aventine University.

Running, leaving it all behind in a trail of jet fuel and far-flung beaches, had seemed like the best way to forget. It had worked too — until my mom's engagement to Roberto Alinari had broken through my party-til-you-forget haze.

Mara scanned the crowd, her curly brown hair brushing against her shoulders, which were bare under her violet off-the-shoulder dress. She hadn't changed at all in the year I'd been gone, and I could still see shades of the apple-cheeked kid she'd been when we became best friends in first grade.

She froze, her brown eyes lighting with interest. "On the plus side," she said, "you now have the hottest stepbrother in town."

I followed her line of sight to the guy standing against the wall, his murderous gaze trained on me.

"Gross," I said. Antonio Alinari — otherwise known as Neo — might have been beautiful, but he was also the biggest dick in our extended crime family.

And not in a good way. At least, not that I knew of.

"You have to admit it's true," Mara teased. "I'm wet just watching him watch you."

I scowled. "That's all kinds of fucked up."

I would never, and I did mean never, admit Neo was hot. Not out loud anyway. It was bad enough before our parents were married when he was just a garden-variety douchebag.

Now he was also my stepbrother.

Secretly, though? That was another story. In the privacy

of my own screwed-up mind, I had to admit he was gorgeous, with dark hair that shone under the lights in the country club and a muscled physique that strained the seams of his tailored suit.

A tattoo snaked up his neck from under his dress shirt, and I knew from a "family" pool party that what looked like snakes were actually strands of hair streaming from the elaborate angel inked onto his chest.

Mara shrugged. "You're not even blood-related."

"It's not about that," I said. "He's a dick. I refuse to give him a pass because he's good-looking."

"So you admit he's good-looking," she said triumphantly.

I sighed. "It doesn't matter. He's a total douchebag, remember?"

She turned her eyes on the two guys standing next to Neo. "What about Rock and Drago? Do they get a pass?"

"No," I said, glancing at Neo's sidekicks.

Rocco Barone studied the crowd, his gaze casual and curious. His blond hair was an anomaly we shared. My "uncles" had been commenting about my fair hair since I was a kid, making jokes about the mailman even though my mom was a natural blonde.

I wondered if Rocco had been the subject of the same kind of teasing or if that was yet another thing only the women in our world had to endure.

Oscar Drago (I couldn't remember when we'd all stopped calling him Oscar in favor of his last name) stood on the other side of Neo. His hair was black as a raven, his eyes nearly as dark as he surveyed the crowd with something like hunger.

"More for me," Mara said. "I'll be the bologna in a Neo, Rock, and Drago sandwich any day."

That would be stupid.

They're not just jerks, they're dangerous.

They might have something to do with Emma's disappearance.

I forced myself to swallow the words. Mara was just dreaming, and who could blame her? In spite of their personality deficits, Neo, Rock, and Drago had been the three hottest male commodities in our little world since they'd turned sixteen, started marking their bodies with ink and piercings, and developed muscles that took the focus off their vacuous brains.

Okay, that wasn't fair. I actually didn't know them well enough to know if they were stupid, but it made me feel better to think so, because being smart and *that* hot? Well, that would be the ultimate injustice.

Besides, there was no proof Neo, Rock, and Drago were involved in Emma's disappearance. She'd last been seen on the Aventine campus, but no one had copped to any information about why she'd been there, three miles from Bellepoint Academy, the all-girls college she'd attended.

The police had looked at all the security footage and interviewed Aventine's entire student body, but none of it had turned up a thing. All of which meant absolutely nothing. I'd learned a lot of things as the daughter of Frank Russo, but the most valuable was that everyone could be bought.

Lesson number two? Loose lips sink ships, and the rats

get dropped into a deep body of water with cement blocks around their ankles.

It made me sick to look at Neo, scanning the crowd like a fox with access to every henhouse in the Northeast, while my sister was missing.

Probably dead.

No. I couldn't afford to believe that. Emma couldn't afford for me to believe that.

"I'm going to the bathroom," I said to Mara.

"I'll be here," she said, her eyes still on the three tools across the room.

I wove my way through the crowd, smiling and waving at the people who made up my extended family by virtue of their involvement in the criminal underworld, even though I knew they talked shit about my family behind our backs.

I didn't trust a single one of them.

I'd vowed to someday be free of this world, to make my own way without stealing and hurting people. But first, I had to find Emma, and that meant attending Bellepoint when school started again in two weeks. I needed to get cozy with the people who knew Emma, people who weren't part of a world where telling the truth could mean getting your tongue cut off.

The fact that Bellepoint and Aventine were both on the outskirts of Blackwell Falls was a bonus. Emma had told me the two schools partied together all the time, so I'd be able to do some low-key digging in both places.

I hadn't told Mara I was going to Bellepoint yet — she had her heart set on my new stepdad pulling strings for a last-minute admission to Columbia so we could go to school together like we'd always planned — but I would.

I just needed to get through this stupid wedding.

I turned the corner from the noisy dining room and entered a long wide hall. The line for the ladies' room came into view. Of course, it was a mile long.

"What a surprise," I murmured.

I eyed the line, then looked under the sign for the men's room.

Not a man in sight. Typical.

I pushed through the door. I was glad to find it empty, but that wouldn't have been a deal-breaker. Money had been tight since my dad bailed on us, so I'd chosen the cheapest hostels I could find during my year of travel. I'd also found myself with my ass poised over fallen leaves in a Costa Rican forest and squatting over a ditch in the fields of Nepal. Using the men's room at a tony country club in Long Island was a piece of cake by comparison.

I stopped at the mirror and verified that my long blonde hair was still wound into the complicated knot insisted on by my mom. A few tendrils had escaped during the long day, but it worked. My makeup was still mostly intact, in part thanks to the semi-natural look I'd nailed with light eye makeup that highlighted my green eyes and the sheer lip gloss I'd chosen.

Satisfied, I used one of the stalls to pee and was working to rearrange my emerald green dress without letting it fall into the toilet when I heard the bathroom door open.

I hurried to finish, then unlocked the door, stepped out of the stall — and came face-to-face with Neo Alinari.

Chapter 2
Willa

He wasn't alone. Rock and Drago leaned against the counter on either side of him, all three of them in tuxes like gangsters on their way to the prom.

Hot ones.

"Well well well," Rock said. His hair was a shade too long, more surfer than favorite mafia son, and his ice-blue eyes twinkled with something not altogether unfriendly. He'd taken off his suit jacket, which only made his perfectly cut physique more obvious under the snug white button-down. I hated myself for the heat that rose to my cheeks. "If it isn't Willa Russo, the prodigal daughter."

I was surprised he knew the word "prodigal" but figured now wasn't the best time to lob the insult. I was outnumbered, and while I didn't know exactly what that meant, I wasn't eager to find out.

"Looks like your little sis didn't want to wait in line." Drago licked his full lips, and light glinted off the stud in his tongue as it clicked against the small ring in his lip, a match to the ones piercing his left eyebrow. There was something predatory in the way he focused his gaze on me, like a falcon eyeing a mouse. I forced myself not to squirm.

I was no mouse.

"Excuse me," I said, staring right back at them. I needed to get to the sink to wash my hands, but they were blocking the long run of counter with their hulking bodies.

"I don't think so," Neo said.

I narrowed my eyes. "You don't think so?"

"I don't think I will excuse you." Jesus, his biceps were huge, like primordial tree trunks, and his eyes were like chips of amber, hard and unyielding as they pinned me in place. His dark hair was cut short, and the shadow of a bruise darkened his left cheekbone.

Rock had always seemed like a friendly dog that could turn rabid, and Drago was a stereotypical bad boy, but it was Neo who'd always scared me most.

Not that I would ever give him the satisfaction of knowing.

I couldn't put my finger on why he made me want to steer clear of him, which was part of the problem. I was pretty good at reading people, at figuring out what they were about, what they wanted. I knew when mean girls were insecure or just bitches. I knew when a guy lacked confidence or when he might actually be dangerous.

Neo was... blank. He had a vacuous energy that felt like a black hole. There was nothing there, but I knew instinctively it was the kind of nothing that could kill you.

"Good thing I was just being polite," I said, advancing on them. "I don't actually need you to excuse me for anything."

"I think you do," Neo said. I stopped a couple of inches from the wall of his chest, his broad shoulders blocking my view of myself in the mirror behind him. "I think you need me to excuse you for being the daughter of a traitor and a gold-digging whore."

I stared up at him. "You're wrong. I don't need you for anything at all."

Drago's dark laughter filled the room. "Someone's got claws."

Anger flared in Neo's hazel eyes. He took a step toward me and I got a whiff of expensive cologne and the tang of male sweat. It made me a little giddy with lust, and I silently cursed myself.

Apparently my body was a traitorous slut.

"I think you're going to find you're wrong about that," Neo said, a satisfied smile settling on his full lips.

It was a smile that said he knew something I didn't, something I wasn't going to like.

He ran a callused finger down my arm and goosebumps rose on my skin. My nipples hardened under my dress, and I was glad the fabric was thick enough that they wouldn't be visible.

He stared into my eyes as his finger traveled down one of my legs and under the skirt of my dress. A shiver snaked up my back when his fingertips brushed my thigh — and not the bad kind of shiver either.

I didn't bother to hope Rock or Drago would say anything. Where one went, so did the other two. Figuratively anyway. Although there had been rumors they shared everything.

And I do mean everything.

It should have scared me. Instead, a swell of need expanded from my center at the thought of them all naked and —

Nope. Not going there.

I jumped as the door flew open. Mara stuck her head in and looked from me to the boys and back at me again, a ton of questions in her eyes.

Neo didn't even bother to pull his hand back from its position on my thigh, perilously close to the cleft between my legs, which was now embarrassingly wet.

"Uh... your mom's looking for you," Mara said, clearly aware she'd interrupted something. "They're getting ready to cut the cake."

"Exactly what I came to tell you," Neo said, close enough that I felt his breath on my cheek. He dropped his hand and moved toward the door. Rock and Drago peeled off the counter after him.

"See you out there, tiger," Drago said.

"Nah," Rock murmured, dragging his thumb over his full lower lip as he walked past me. "I bet I could make her purr like a kitten."

Goddamn.

Mara lifted her eyebrows but I just shook my head and washed my hands. By the time we returned to the reception, my mom and Roberto were already at the front of the room behind the table that held the towering wedding cake.

"Ah, there she is," Robert's voice echoed through the

microphone as he caught sight of me. Everyone turned to follow his gaze. "My new daughter. Come on up here, Willa. You too, Neo."

I followed Neo to the front of the room, watching as the crowd parted for him like he was Moses standing in front of the Red Sea. Must be nice to be a favored son of the most revered kingpin in the family instead of the daughter of a traitor.

I stood next to my mom, and I was relieved when Neo took up position next to his dad. I could feel his eyes on my face, but if I focused on the crowd, I could almost pretend he wasn't there.

Fuck. Who was I kidding? He was an asshole of the highest order, but there was never any pretending Neo Alinari wasn't there.

"I want to thank you all for joining us on this special day," Roberto began. "As you all know, family is everything. We sacrifice for it. We steal for it. We bleed for it."

My stomach turned, but I kept my expression impassive. I didn't want to bleed for these people. I didn't want Emma to bleed for them either, but I couldn't help wondering if she already had.

Aventine U was a private college, one that accepted applicants almost exclusively from crime families like mine and the Alinaris'. Not that it was an official policy or anything.

Technically, the admission process was wide open.

Except everyone knew it was where families like Roberto sent their kids. Aventine's MBA program was quietly second to none (running a criminal organization in the modern era required knowledge of the law and economics, of global supply chains and international markets), and their chess room had once been a breeding ground for alliances and rivalries.

Their frats were even named after chess pieces: Kings for the Italian faction, Knights for the Russians, Castle house for the Irish, and Bishops for the cartel families, although I'd heard everyone called them the Saints. There were so few women that there was only one sorority, and of course, they lived in the Queens' house.

But while chess had always been the official game of Aventine, it was the after-hours lessons that made you or broke you within your family.

Or so I'd heard.

The games played at Aventine, games designed to prepare us for the world in which we'd been born, made secret societies like Yale's Skull and Bones look like PTA meetings.

Participation wasn't optional.

It was one of many reasons I'd chosen to attend Bellepoint instead of Aventine. The fact that Emma had last been seen at Aventine, that she'd been the outcast daughter of a traitor, made me wonder if she'd become part of the game.

And if she'd paid the highest price of all for losing.

"Today, in the spirit of that family, we commit to joining our lives together, but more than that, we commit to joining our families in every way." Roberto took my mom's hand. Something was coming. It crackled like the electricity that charged the air before a summer thunderstorm. I felt Roberto's eyes on my face and turned to look at him as he continued. "Which is why I'm thrilled to announce that this fall, Willa will be attending Aventine University with Neo."

The bottom dropped out of my stomach as a murmur of surprise rippled through the crowd, followed by a polite smattering of applause.

I found Mara in the crowd, her face white, then turned to look at my mom.

How could she do this to me? How could she send me to the school where Emma was last seen alive? The school where, more than anywhere else in the world, I would be a pariah? The school attended by people who'd been trained in the art of making others suffer?

Looking at the polite smile on her face, I felt a surge of hatred for her. She couldn't even look me in the fucking eyes.

Guess being a traitor ran in the family.

The decision had been made, probably by Roberto, and I knew my mom well enough to know she wouldn't fight it. She was the perfect Mob wife. Always had been. Her father had been part of the family, and his father before him. It was why she hadn't followed my dad into Witness Protection, why she'd opted to stay to prove her loyalty to the family.

My face heated and I turned to find Neo watching me, a cruel smirk twisting the corners of his luscious mouth.

He'd known. My mom hadn't bothered to tell me, but Neo had known I would be attending Aventine with him, Rock, and Drago.

Resolve hardened in my stomach. If there was no

changing it, I would use it. Going to Aventine meant even closer proximity to the people who'd last seen my sister.

It meant proximity to their secrets.

Their lies.

I met Neo's gaze and returned his smile.

You want to play, asshole?

Let's play.

Chapter 3

Willa

I watched through the back seat window as we pulled through Aventine's iron gate. It was purely ornamental: there was no keypad that I could see, which meant it was probably always open.

There was, however, a security camera mounted to one of the stone pillars that flanked the driveway. I watched it as Roberto drove past, its red light blinking like an alarm, and made a mental note to keep my eyes open for others on campus.

If I was going to snoop around trying to figure out what happened to Emma, I needed to be sure I wasn't caught on camera.

"It's so pretty up here," my mom breathed from the front seat. She'd made similar exclamations during the entire three-hour drive from Long Island.

I've always loved Upstate.

I can't wait to come visit you when the leaves change.

I'm envious, Willa!

Kings & Corruption

It was all bullshit designed to keep me quiet. I'd always been the family wild card, and after the stunt I'd pulled taking off to travel for a year, the title felt more earned than ever.

My mom didn't know what I would do, didn't know what I would say, and since she was officially rowing a boat with Roberto Alinari, it was imperative that I kept from rocking it.

Or sinking it.

"Don't you think so?" my mom asked, turning around in the front seat to look at me. She was still beautiful, with thick blonde hair and symmetrical features that made her look like a doll.

"What?" I said, trying to focus on her face and not the fact that I was moments away from being abandoned in the last place Emma had been seen.

"That it's pretty!" Her green eyes were falsely bright, like she had a fever or something.

"Oh... uh, yeah. It's super pretty." I wasn't sure she bought my forced smile, but it didn't really matter. The whole charade was about appearances anyway.

"I've told Neo to keep an eye on you," Roberto said, meeting my eyes in the rearview mirror.

Maybe it was meant to sound nice, protective even, but it sounded ominous coming from him. The last thing I wanted was Neo Alinari and his two mountainous minions all up in my business, and I was glad they'd driven up on their own.

Which, of course they would, because whatever would they do without their expensive cars on campus?

"I'm sure I'll be fine," I said.

I wasn't sure, but I would have to be, wouldn't I? For

17

Emma and myself.

I looked through the front seats at the stone and brick buildings rising from pristine lawns in the distance. As we got closer to the heart of the Aventine campus, students walked alone and in groups, carrying books and bedding and plastic bins.

There were very few parents, which was no surprise. Surviving in our world meant demonstrating you could handle yourself, and everything about Aventine was a proving ground for the lives that awaited us. Having Mommy set up your dorm room wouldn't do you any favors in the street cred department.

Plus, most of the kids at Aventine had taken at least one gap year to work in the family business, something that was seen as critical context for our formal education. I doubted there were many terrified freshmen here.

We passed a road leading to several brick buildings — dorms, I assumed — and circled around a fountain with a statue of some old white guy in front of an imposing stone building with wide front steps.

"I'll check you in," Roberto said.

"It's fine. I can — "

"Nonsense." His voice was crisp. "I'd like to say hello to Dean Giordana, and you have a long few days ahead of you."

Right. Welcome Week.

Dumb, right? And not just because it was, well, dumb, but because it wasn't a whole week. Just four fun-filled days of orientations, meet and greets, and awkward encounters with people who would probably treat me like a leper as soon as they learned my name.

Kings & Corruption

"Thanks," I said weakly, sinking back into the seat.

"You're just the best," my mom gushed, squeezing Roberto's arm. "Thank you."

He leaned over and kissed her full on the lips, long enough to make me squirm. "You and Willa deserve to be taken care of properly."

The way he said it, I wasn't sure if he meant pampered or dumped at the bottom of Long Island Sound.

With Roberto, either was possible.

He got out of the car and started for the steps leading to the stone building. My mom watched him go, then turned around to glare at me.

"You could try being grateful, you know."

"For being forced to go to the school where Emma went missing?" I asked.

My mom set her jaw in a tight line, the way she did when she'd made her mind up about something. "She didn't go missing here."

"It's the last place she was seen," I said.

She sighed. "Did it ever occur to you that Emma ran away? That maybe she wanted something else?"

Like your father.

The words were left unsaid but I could almost hear them. They hurt because somewhere deep inside, when I was all alone at night with the worst of my demons, I'd asked myself the same question.

Maybe Emma had just wanted out. Maybe she didn't want to be Frank Russo's exiled daughter anymore, trying to fit in at Bellepoint, afraid to tell any of the guys at Aventine her last name.

"Emma wouldn't do that," I said. "Not this way. She would have told me."

My mom's eyes flashed. "Because you were so close?"

Ouch. Okay, that stung. Emma and I weren't close, not when she disappeared. But we'd been close, once, after we'd grown out of the childhood get-out-of-my-room phase, just before Emma went to college.

Back then, we'd lie on her bed and stare at the stars projected onto her ceiling, talking about where our dad was, what he was doing, if he ever thought of us.

And then, when we were feeling really honest, whether he was still alive at all. There had been rumors in the family, rumors that he'd been killed, and since he'd never actually shown up on the witness stand at trial, they weren't impossible to believe.

They were things we could only say to each other, and it had been a relief to let it all out in the dim glow of Emma's bedroom before she went to Bellepoint and the weeks afterward when she'd started to feel like a total stranger.

"Because we were sisters," I said.

"Maybe you should start entertaining the possibility that you don't know everyone as well as you think, Willa."

Another low blow. I had been the holdout in our family after my dad disappeared, the one who didn't believe he'd turned to the Feds until I saw it on the news.

The one who'd always believed he was going to come back.

Roberto had stepped out of the glass doors at the top of the stone steps with a middle-aged man wearing a dark suit.

Dean Giordana, I presumed.

"Or maybe I'm not in such a hurry to move on that I'm willing to sell my soul to the devil," I said, watching as Roberto put his hand on the other man's shoulder.

My mom flipped down the Mercedes's visor. I caught her eyes as she checked her makeup in the tiny mirror. "Women in our world only have a couple of tools available to them, Willa." She suddenly sounded tired. "Beauty, youth. We have to use them when we can. While we can. You'll find that out soon enough."

Roberto climbed down the stairs with athletic grace and got back in the car.

"All set?" my mom asked.

"All set." He put the car in gear and used the circular drive to come back the way we came.

Nervousness twisted my stomach as the dorms came into view. After a year of being anonymous in my travels, I wasn't at all ready to be an outcast in my new living quarters.

But when we reached the road leading to the dorms, Roberto kept on driving.

"Where are we going?" I asked.

"Come now," Robert said as he pulled out of the gates and onto the road, "you didn't think we'd let you live in the dorms alone after what happened to Emma."

"I won't be alone in the dorms," I said. "Besides, where else would I live?"

A bubble of hope floated through my chest. Maybe they'd gotten me an apartment off campus, somewhere I could be alone, away from the judging eyes of everyone at Aventine who would know I was Frank Russo's daughter.

"Roberto has made special arrangements with Dean

Giordana," my mom said. "And with Neo."

I sat up straighter. "Neo? What does he have to do with anything?"

My heart thumped like a trapped bird in my chest as we pulled onto a long driveway sheltered by trees on either side.

I had a bad feeling. A very bad feeling.

"Neo is the one who decides who lives in the Kings' house," my mom said as a sleek modern home made of glass came into view in the clearing up ahead. "So of course, Roberto had to speak with him about allowing you to live here."

"Wait... you expect me to live in the Kings' house?" I caught the note of hysteria in my voice but couldn't do anything about it. "With Neo?"

"Neo will keep an eye on you," Roberto said crisply, opening the car door.

I looked to my mom for help, but she was already halfway out of the car. I sat in the back seat in silence, my mind frantically searching for a way out. It didn't take long to find the answer.

There wasn't one.

If I wanted to help Emma, I needed to be near the place where she was last seen. That meant I needed tuition, and thanks to my dad's abandonment of our family, that meant Roberto Alinari.

My mom hadn't said it, but the reality was pretty damn clear: his money, his rules.

All of which meant I wasn't just attending the same school as Neo, Rock, and Drago — I would be living with them too.

Chapter 4

Willa

Less than twenty minutes. That's how long it took my mom and Roberto to leave.

Not that I was complaining. My mom and I had been close once, I think. I have vague memories of her laughing and dancing around the house, of her gentle touch on my forehead when I was sick.

But that was all so far in the past it felt like a dream. Now when I thought of her, I thought of the angry, bitter person she'd been in the years before my dad turned on the family, and the distant, imperious one she'd become since she'd started seeing Roberto Alinari.

We'd gone through all the stages of grief after Emma's disappearance, had countless fights about whether Emma had run, like my dad, or whether something had happened to her.

What more was there to say? Especially with Roberto hanging around the edges of every conversation, his eyes alert like he was some kind of robot recording our conversations with a microchip in his brain.

So it was actually okay with me when they left after dumping my stuff in the foyer of the Kings' house. My mom still couldn't meet my eyes. She'd just given me a stiff hug and waited while Roberto handed over a platinum American Express card for my "incidentals."

I didn't want to take it, but I wanted to argue about it even less, so I slipped it into the pocket of my shorts and let him kiss me stiffly on the cheek before leaving.

I watched through the big glass doors as they drove away, then turned to look at the house.

I don't know what I'd expected. I guess some beat-up old place with beer-stained carpets and thrift store furniture. Wasn't that what most frat houses looked like? I didn't actually know, but that's what they always seemed to look like on TV and in the movies.

But this place was... wow. I mean, gorgeous didn't even begin to describe it. It looked expensive from outside, but inside, it was even more obvious that the place was worth a fortune.

The foyer had triple-height ceilings and opened right onto an enormous sunken living room with a massive TV and several sofas. The sofas were sleek and modern, but they also looked comfortable, and they coordinated perfectly with the eclectic side tables and lamps, not to mention the modern fireplace under the TV.

This did not look like a place decorated by three gym bros whose combined decorating knowledge probably weighed less than a five-pound dumbbell.

I edged into the room, feeling almost guilty for wearing shoes on the pristine wood floors.

No beer-stained carpet here.

A wide staircase with a cable railing led upwards, and the place was filled with light, entire walls made of windows, all of them looking out onto a grassy clearing that led to banks of trees on every side.

What the actual fuck?

I started down a central hall, aiming for the kitchen at the end of it, then stopped when I heard voices coming from one of the closed doors.

I froze, listening, then rapped softly on the door. No one answered, and the voices continued unabated from inside, so I reached for the doorknob and opened the door.

Gunfire assaulted my ears as it swung open, and I instinctively cowered before realizing it was coming from another huge TV mounted to the wall in front of several rows of seating.

A figure popped up from one of the seats, popcorn flying in every direction as he turned to look at me standing in the doorway.

"What the...?" He stopped moving. "Oh, it's you."

"It's... me?" I shook my head. "Who are you?"

He held up a finger and fumbled around one of the seats, then pointed his phone at the screen. The volume was muted on whatever action movie he'd been watching, and a second later the lights came on in the room.

The guy standing in front of me was probably about my age, with dark hair and brown eyes. He wore basketball shorts and a tank top that showed off the sculpted arms of someone who spent a lot of time in the gym.

"Sorry," he said, "I didn't think anyone was coming until tonight."

I moved into the room. "I'm Willa."

"I know." I raised my eyebrows and he continued. "Uh... Neo told us. That you were moving in, I mean."

"Us?"

"Me and the other guys." He grinned and an adorable dimple dented his chin. "I never expected to live with a girl at the Kings' house, but I'm down."

I stifled a sigh. I hadn't even thought about the other guys, but of course they would be there. As luxe as the Kings' house was, it was still technically a frat house — and that meant a bunch of college boys, or more accurately, sons of Mafia dons with something to prove.

This was going to be worse than I'd imagined. Then again, maybe it was good there would be other guys in the house. It would make it easier to avoid Neo and his band of merry morons.

"Sorry, I should introduce myself." He wiped his hands on his basketball shorts and advanced on me with his hand out. "I'm Matt."

I shook his hand and felt the grit of popcorn salt, but I couldn't be mad. He seemed nice. I wondered who his parents were but didn't want to be obvious by asking his last name.

"Nice to meet you," I said.

"You too." He looked around nervously. "You want a tour of the house or something?"

"That's okay," I said. "I should get settled. You wouldn't happen to know where my room is, would you?"

He grinned. "I can guess. Come on."

I had no idea what he meant, but I followed him into the kitchen I'd seen from the hall — one of the biggest freaking kitchens I'd ever seen — and up a set of stairs at the back of the house.

"The front stairs go to the second and third floors too," Matt said. "These are closer if you're not in the living room."

"Got it." The stairwell was surrounded by glass and made me feel like I was climbing into a giant tree house.

We passed the landing for the second floor and continued up another flight of stairs.

"What's on that floor?" I asked.

"Those are our rooms. You know, the other guys."

I heard the words that were left unspoken: *guys like me, guys who aren't Neo and Rock and Drago.*

We stepped onto the third-floor landing and emerged into another hall, and if I thought the first floor was incredible, I was *not* prepared for this one.

One entire side of the wide hall was made of glass. It looked out over the back of the house where a huge swimming pool glimmered in the sun. A jacuzzi was positioned to one side of the pool, and the patio included an outdoor kitchen and lots of upscale outdoor furniture.

Beyond the patio, the trees at the back of the house swayed in the September breeze. They felt close enough to touch, almost like the third floor was nestled in their branches, and I was surprised to feel my shoulders drop as calmness settled over me.

"Wow," I said. "This is amazing."

I was glad Matt was the one showing me to my room. I didn't want to give Neo and his boys the satisfaction of knowing I was impressed.

Matt turned to give me a grin as he continued leading the way down the hall. "Right? So much better than the other houses."

I could only assume he meant the other frat houses at Aventine, just like I could only assume they sucked in comparison to the modern marvel that was my new home. The only research I'd done on the school had been related to Emma's disappearance, which had consisted of reused file footage of Aventine's entrance and the main building where Roberto had checked me in.

Matt stopped in front of a door at the end of the hall. "This must be you."

"How do you know?" I asked.

He shrugged. "I don't, but the other three rooms on this floor belong to Neo, Rock, and Drago, and all the rooms on the second floor are assigned to guys like me."

I looked up at him. He really was cute, with perfect teeth and that chin dimple that managed to be both sweet and sexy.

The cut biceps didn't hurt either.

"What do you mean, guys like you?" I asked.

He shifted on his feet. "Just... you know, normal guys."

I laughed a little. "Is anyone at this school really normal?"

His smile widened. "Good point."

"Besides," I said, smiling up at him, "normal is underrated."

Was he blushing? Just when I thought he couldn't get any cuter.

"You think so?" he asked.

I nodded. "I do. So, uh... do you think it's okay for me to go in?" I asked, looking at the closed door.

"Sure," he said. "I mean, Rock told us to make you comfortable, so..."

I opened the door, then forced myself to hold back a gasp of shock as the room came into view.

First of all, it was huge. Like, massive, with enough room for the king-size bed that dominated one wall plus a sitting area with a sofa, side tables, and a ginormous TV hanging on the wall over a modern fireplace, not to mention all the other furniture, like the dresser and nightstands.

Even with all that stuff, there was plenty of room to move around, but the thing that really got my attention was the wall of glass that overlooked the trees at the back of the property. At first I thought it was a giant window, but when I walked toward it, I saw the almost-invisible seam of a door. The balcony that jutted beyond it was so well integrated it was almost invisible from inside the house.

"This opens?" I asked.

"Yeah, the third-floor rooms all have balconies," Matt said.

"Wow." I felt a little dumb. I'd probably said the word more times in the half hour since my mom and Roberto had left than I had in the previous year.

Matt chuckled behind me and I turned to smile at him. "It's nice," he said. "I don't blame you for being impressed."

"Let's just keep that between us, okay?" I asked.

He nodded. "Trying to play it cool, huh?"

"Something like that." In our world, everything was power.

Pleasure. Pain. Knowledge.

Everything.

"You got it." His gaze lingered on my face, and I felt the familiar pull of sexual tension. "I'm really glad you're going to be here this year."

"Me too." I kept my voice friendly but neutral. It wasn't hard. Every woman I knew was practiced at the technique. It was essential when trying to set boundaries with strange men, and as attractive as Matt was, I didn't know him at all.

More specifically, I didn't know if he would be friend or foe, and I couldn't afford to find out the hard way.

Besides, I was here to find out what had happened to Emma. The last thing I needed was to get involved with one of the criminals-in-training who might have had something to do with her disappearance.

"The campus is big," Matt said. Had he stepped closer? He seemed closer than he'd been a couple minutes ago. "And there's Blackwell too. Maybe I could show you around. We could grab some dinner and — "

"What the fuck to do you think you're doing?"

Matt froze, then spun toward the voice that had interrupted him. I had to step aside to see past his body, but I already knew who'd spoken.

It was a voice I'd know anywhere.

My stepbrother. Neo.

Chapter 5

Willa

"I was looking for my room," I said.

Neo's eyes drilled into mine, but his expression was totally unreadable. "Not you." He bit out the words like shattered glass, like he hated even speaking to me, then turned to look at Matt. "You."

"Uh... Willa wanted to get settled. I thought—"

"What's rule number three?" Neo asked him.

"Don't think unless we're told to," Matt said.

"Exactly. Now fuck off," Neo said.

Poor Matt scrambled from the room without a backward glance, and as much as I hated to admit it, I understood why. Neo, now inside the doorway and walking slowly toward me, was a menacing presence.

And jesus, he really was huge. I'd had to look up at Matt, but if I'd been outside with Neo, I would have been tempted to shield my eyes from the sun.

The sleeves were rolled up on his black button-down to reveal a tattoo of a crown with a snake on his forearm. His shoulders and biceps were so huge it looked like the shirt was going to split open, Hulk-style, and my gaze was drawn to the tendrils of his angel tattoo, snaking over the base of his throat where his shirt was unbuttoned. Gray pants hugged his muscled thighs, accentuating the significant bulge between his legs — a bulge I was trying desperately not to look at even though my body had gone all kinds of rogue and wanted nothing more than to take it in.

Figuratively, not literally.

Fuck. Who was I kidding? Probably literally too.

I realized too late that I'd crossed my arms over my chest on reflex. It was a defensive habit, and the last thing I wanted was for Neo to think I was afraid of him, although even fear was better than lust.

I could not, under any circumstance, let Neo Alinari know that he made my panties wet.

"You couldn't wait downstairs?" he asked.

I lifted my chin. "Why should I? I live here now, remember?"

His eyes flashed, shifting from brown to amber in the afternoon sunlight. "Maybe, but this is my house, and that means I make the rules."

"It's the Kings' house. That means it belongs to the fraternity," I said.

He pinned me with his eyes. "And the fraternity belongs to me."

I didn't have the energy to debate the truth of it. In any other school, I'd call bullshit, but this was Aventine. It was a world unto itself, a world with rules patterned after the ones in the world our parents occupied, the one they expected us to join when we graduated.

Was it possible Neo had incorporated the fraternity as a nonprofit under a shell company that couldn't be traced to him or his father?

Hell yes. Literally anything was possible here.

"Whatever," I said. "If you didn't want me to wander around, maybe you should have been here to show me yourself. Matt was just trying to be nice. No need to be a dick."

Neo leaned in, and I caught the scent of something musky and male that went straight to my now-soaking pussy.

"Let's get something straight, *Jezebel*. I do what I want, here and everywhere. You can find that out the easy way, or the hard way." He dropped his eyes to my cleavage, inconveniently displayed by my tank top and the fact that my boobs were shoved up over my crossed arms, then continued down to my bare legs, which suddenly felt way too exposed in the short-shorts that had seemed like comfortable moving day attire when I'd put them on. When he returned his gaze to my face, he lingered on my lips, a knowing smirk lifting the corners of his mouth. "Then again, maybe you like it hard."

Fuck me. Lust was roaring through my veins. I was desperate to get away from him, to save myself from myself, but no way was I going to let him know that.

"Jezebel huh?" I affected a bored tone, even though the nickname stung a little. "How original."

His jaw twitched, the only sign of emotion on his perfect face. "If the shoe fits."

"Except it doesn't," I said.

"We live in a *sins-of-the-father* world," Neo said, his voice like chips of ice. "I figured you knew that."

"Maybe I just don't buy it," I said.

He stared me down. "Well, you better start."

He was an asshole, but I knew what he meant. I was at Aventine now. Everyone here would think I was a traitor, and that meant I was enemy number one.

Fear clenched my chest like a vise. What was I doing?

"Hey, do you know when—" The voice, coming from behind Neo's colossal body, broke the tension that had been lying like a spell between us. Rock stepped into the room. "Oh, you're already here," he said to me.

"Yep," I said, still staring at Neo.

"I thought maybe Neo was checking to make sure your room was ready," Rock said.

It seemed like an impossibility. Neo doing something — anything — nice for me? The Jezebel of Aventine?

Fat chance.

"Matt showed me up actually." I didn't take my eyes off Neo. "He was very *welcoming*."

The tic in Neo's jaw jumped. Why was I getting off on pushing his buttons?

"Good," Rock said. He looked at Neo. "Did you ask Willa if she was hungry?"

Neo tipped his head and cupped his right fist in his left palm like he was trying to keep from putting it through something. I caught the glint of a gold ring on one of his fingers, the faint shine of black stone. "Now why would I do that?"

Rock's blue eyes flashed. He raked a hand through his

shaggy golden hair, and I realized he wore a ring too. He moved too fast for me to be sure, but the rings looked the same — crowns with snakes, like Neo's tattoo — except for the stone. Rock's had a diamond, and I was betting the black stone on Neo's was onyx.

"Did you at least show her the kitchen?" Rock asked.

I searched his eyes for the hatred I'd seen in Neo's but didn't find any. "He didn't."

Rock sighed. "What are you? A fucking savage?" he asked Neo before returning his attention to me. "Come on, I'll show you around the rest of the house and get you fed."

I forced a smile. No one who hung around Neo Alinari could be called a good guy, but if I had to choose, I'd take the hot one who wanted to feed me over the hot one who wanted to feed me to the wolves. "Thanks."

I moved past Neo, making a point to crowd him a little just to prove I wasn't scared of him. Except when my upper arm brushed against the warm skin of his forearm, the contact zinged through me like a freaking electrical current.

That move was obviously what Nana Russo would have called *cutting off my nose to spite my face.*

My head cleared as I headed for the door behind Rock, like I'd been under the influence of some kind of intoxicant and someone had finally opened a window. I was going to have to be a lot smarter when it came to Neo if I didn't want to end up as a puddle of goo at his feet begging for the D.

No way in hell was I going to let that happen.

Chapter 6
Willa

The house just got better and better. Every bedroom had a private bath, although the ones on the second floor were less elaborate than the ones on the third floor.

Rock's bathroom was luxe, with a marble walk-in shower, a soaking tub (I admit to being surprised by that; it was hard to imagine him cramming his giant body into any tub, let alone enjoying a soak), a toilet and bidet, and a double vanity, one side of which was stacked with feminine toiletries.

That last part left me with disappointed, which was dumb. I wasn't interested in romantic entanglements at Aventine, and I was less than interested in a romantic entanglement with one of the Kings.

And if it was possible to be less than less than interested, well, that's how I felt about Neo, Rock, and Drago.

I was obviously just tired and sex-starved, which made sense given that my last orgasm with anything other than my vibrator had been almost six months earlier, a less-than-satisfying encounter with a fellow traveler I'd met in Berlin.

Mental note: fix that stat, preferably in a non-messy way.

I needed to be clearheaded with Neo and his boys, and Rock was no exception, even though so far he'd been a lot nicer than I'd expected.

Rock didn't show me any of the other rooms on the third floor. He just pointed to each of the two closed doors, indicating that Neo and Drago were the only other residents, and explained that all the rooms were similar except for their furnishings. Apparently I had an en suite bathroom too, something I hadn't had time to discover in my rush to leave Neo behind.

The second floor had eight smaller bedrooms with private baths, all of which were assigned to other members of the Kings' house, Matt included. It also had a large, well-equipped gym, sauna, and steam room.

By the time we got to the ground floor, I was coming around to living in the Kings' house. Sure, it meant being up close and personal with the Kings of Kings, but I was starting to think it might be worth it for all the amenities. I'd just avoid the guys.

How hard could it be?

Rock took me through a posh game room (high-end ping-pong and pool tables, fully stocked bar, couches, big-screen TVs), a guest room, and three more bathrooms, then opened the door to the media room before I had a chance to tell him I'd seen it.

Matt jumped up from his seat, spilling his popcorn for the second time in less than an hour.

"Fuck!" he said before seeing Rock and composing his face into a welcoming smile. "Hey, Rock."

"I was showing Willa the media room," Rock said.

"I saw it when I first came in," I said. "Matt was the only one here."

Rock scowled and looked around the room, taking in the spilled popcorn and empty beer bottles next to Matt's seat. "Clean this shit up. Drago will have your head."

Matt was already moving as Rock shut the door.

"Is Drago a neat freak?" I asked.

"Only in the media room," Rock said.

We continued into the kitchen, a sea of marble and dark wood that somehow managed to be both modern and inviting. I was surprised to see that the commercial-grade range showed signs of use, its stainless surface marred with dark spots that softened the showroom effect.

Two canvas bags sat on the island, two baguettes and a bunch of celery sticking out of one of them.

"Have a seat," Rock said. "I picked up some groceries to tide us over."

I slid onto one of the chairs at the island, not sure whether I was more thrown by the image of Rock grocery shopping or the fact that he'd used the pronoun *us*, like we were roommates by choice or something.

He walked to the designer fridge and removed two beers, uncapped them both, and handed one of them to me.

He took a swig of his beer and studied me. "Are you one of those girls who knows they're super hot or one of those girls who doesn't?"

"Uh..."

He snapped with his free hand and pointed at me, then threw back his head and laughed. It was deep and sexy and ran through me like wildfire. "You don't know!"

I shifted on the chair. "I mean, I wouldn't say I'm—"

"You're hot," he interrupted. "Super hot." He rubbed the blond scruff at his jawline. His eyes roamed over my face and continued appreciatively down my body. "That face, that body, all that hair..."

I swallowed and realized I was twisting a lock of my blonde hair. It was a nervous habit, and I was hella nervous, both because I hated attention and because my body felt warm all over, like a chicken that had been turning in one of those rotisserie ovens in the grocery store.

I was relieved when he set down his beer and moved to unpack the groceries. "Don't mind Neo," he said, thankfully changing the subject.

I lifted my eyebrows. "Don't mind that he's an asshole?"

For a split second I wondered if I'd gone too far. Neo, Rock, and Drago had been inseparable for as long as I could remember, way back when we were all snot-nosed kids running around at various birthdays and graduations and everything else our families celebrated together.

But Rock just grinned. "Yeah, that."

"Why shouldn't I? Mind that he's an asshole, I mean." I didn't ask for any of the shit my dad had done, and I sure as hell hadn't asked for my sister to go missing right before I graduated high school. "Is this where you tell me he's all bark and no bite?"

Rock shook his head. "No, Neo is definitely all bite."

The shiver that ran up my spine wasn't just fear. Thank god Rock was too busy unpacking groceries to see that my nipples had hardened at the words *Neo* and *bite* in the same sentence.

"Then I don't see why he should get a pass for being a dick," I said.

Finished with the first bag, Rock set it aside and removed the baguettes and celery from the other one. "Because he doesn't mean it. Not with you."

I doubt I did a good job hiding my surprise. "Not with me? In my experience, it's *especially* with me."

"Yeah well, looks can be deceiving," Rock said. "Trust me."

Damn. I wanted to. He wasn't at all what I'd expected when I'd watched him, Drago, and Neo swinging their dicks like primates at every family event.

Plus, he was beautiful, his cheekbones sharp enough to cut glass, his blue eyes the exact color of the water off the coast of Bali. His jeans were worn, hanging on his athletic muscle like he'd just stepped off the runway. He had the same tattoo as Neo on his forearm and I searched for signs of more ink under his snug white T-shirt, didn't find any, then wondered what he looked like naked.

Fuck my mind and its stupid imagination.

"How's grilled cheese and salad?" Rock asked, pulling me from my lustful reverie.

"Sounds great," I said. "Can I help?"

He shook his head. "This is my domain."

I looked around as he pulled a skillet from a deep pullout drawer next to the range. "The kitchen?"

He nodded and set the skillet on top of the stove, then grabbed a wicked-looking serrated knife from the gourmet knife block on the counter.

I was still processing that little revelation when Matt came into the room. "Grilled cheese?" he asked hopefully, eyeing the bread and three kinds of cheese sitting on the island.

"You know it," Rock said, slicing through the baguette.

"Is this a tradition?" I asked as Matt went to the fridge.

"Rock makes the best grilled cheese in the state," Matt said. "Mind if I have a beer?" he asked Rock.

"Help yourself and get the rest out of my car," Rock said.

Matt grabbed a beer, opened it, and took a swig. "Be right back."

He left through a door that I assumed led to a garage, and I watched as Rock grabbed an onion and started slicing.

"Onions?"

Rock held up his hands like he was offended. "Just... trust me on this, will you?"

I smiled. "If you say so."

"I do." He smirked. "And if you're worried about bad breath, don't. I don't mind kissing a girl with onions on her breath after I've cooked her an amazing meal."

I laughed. Rock Barone *definitely* knew he was super hot.

Cocky bastard.

Over the next twenty minutes, a stream of guys appeared in the kitchen, all of them arriving for the first semester at

Aventine, all of them members of the Kings' house and presumably occupants of the second floor.

There was Luke and Ricky, twins with matching dimples and shaggy dark hair. David's hair was bleached-blond, and his hazel eyes didn't hide their appreciation as they took in my body. Enzo had short dark hair shaved close to the head and a viper tattoo that wound the length of his arm around a crown on his bicep.

Someone was proud to be a King.

All of them except Enzo seemed happy I was there, quick to start a conversation and make me feel welcome. Enzo just nodded a greeting, grabbed a beer from the stash stocked in the fridge by Matt, and made a quick exit.

It was whatever. I felt lucky the rest of the guys hadn't given me an equally cold reception, given the whole traitor thing.

And Rock was right about the grilled cheese. I almost had an orgasm biting into the gooey three-cheese mixture topped with caramelized onions. The buttery grilled bread even had little pieces of fresh rosemary stuck to it. A little moan might have escaped my mouth, which prompted Rock to lift his eyebrows suggestively from across the island.

I was finishing up my second sandwich when Drago entered the room through the garage door. His black jeans accentuated the lean muscle of his thighs, and his vintage *Fight Club* T-shirt was just loose enough to be sexy rather than sloppy. His forearm was tattooed with the same image inked onto Rock and Neo.

His dark eyes flickered over the room, then lit with interest when they landed on me. His gaze was appreciative, and the stud in his tongue clicked against the ring in his lip. I couldn't help wondering what they would feel like against my increasingly needy pussy.

"Hey there, tiger. I see you made it," he said.

There was way too much hot-guy testosterone in the room for my own good, but I nodded anyway. The nickname didn't sound unfriendly, and his gaze was more curious than critical. Was it possible Neo was the only true asshole of the bunch?

"Yep," I said, sliding off my chair. "And thanks to Rock's amazing grilled cheese and the two beers I downed while he cooked, I'm stuffed and tired. I'm going to head up and get settled."

"Matt," Rock barked. Matt had just been about to bite into his sandwich but he jumped to his feet like a new recruit in basic training. "Take Willa's bags to her room."

I started to protest — I'd traveled alone for a year with nothing but a backpack, which I'd hauled myself — but Matt was already moving toward the front of the house where I'd left my bags.

"Sure, no problem."

"I could have gotten them," I said.

"I know," Rock said. "But why should you?"

"Well... thanks." I must have been even more tired than I thought. Rock Barone seemed *chivalrous*.

"I'm heading up too," Drago said. "I need a shower. I'll walk with you."

"Um... yeah. Okay."

Rock scowled. "Don't take advantage. She just got here."

"*She* is right here," I said dryly. "And the fact that you

think anyone can take advantage of me is just proof you don't know me very well."

Drago surprised me by laughing and throwing an arm around my shoulders. "Told you," he said to Rock. "Tiger."

I caught Rock's suggestive smile as we turned toward the back staircase. "We'll see about that."

Chapter 7

Willa

"Did someone show you around?" Drago asked behind me on the way up the stairs.

"Rock," I said, all too aware that Drago probably had a choice view of my ass in the short-shorts as we climbed the stairs. "No one but Matt was home when I first got here. He showed me to my room and then..."

I thought of Neo and the disgust that had been on his face when he'd stepped into my room.

"And then?" Drago asked, cocking a pierced eyebrow as he joined me on the third-floor landing.

"Neo came home."

Oscar Drago's physique was lean and defined as opposed to Neo's sheer mass and Rock's athletic muscle, and he had sex appeal that was all his own. Something about those dark eyes, all the piercings. and the thick black hair made me think about closing my fingers around it while he fucked me to next Sunday.

Ugh.

"Why do I sense there's more to this story?" he asked.

It took me a sec to banish the image of Drago between my thighs and remember what we'd been talking about. "It's just... Neo."

He rubbed a thumb over his lower lip, and a flash of gold caught my eye. Yep. It was a ring just like the ones Rock and Neo wore, only Drago wore it on his thumb, and the stone in his looked like a ruby.

"You'll get used to it," he said.

"I don't want to get used to it," I snapped. This was good. Drago blowing off my issues with Neo was what I needed: a reminder that no matter how nice Rock and Drago seemed, they were still on Neo's team.

And that meant I couldn't trust them.

He nodded. "I get that. Thing is, we've been like brothers since we were kids."

"I know," I said. "I remember."

"There's no changing Neo, but he's... not what he seems."

"An asshole who hates me?"

Drago laughed. and when he shifted his shirt moved enough to give me a glimpse of washboard abs and a trail of dark hair leading under the waistband of his jeans.

Don't look, Willa. DON'T LOOK.

"Okay, he's an asshole a lot of the time, but he doesn't hate you," Drago said.

"Could have fooled me," I muttered.

"You just have to get to know him." He leaned down so that his face was just a couple of inches from mine. My pulse hammered out a beat in my veins, and it was suddenly a whole lot harder to breathe. "And I don't care what Rock says, I know there's a tiger in there. You can handle Neo."

He straightened and started down the hall. I knew from Rock that Drago's room was two doors down, with Rock's on one side and Neo's on the other (next to mine, of course, because if you were already in hell you might as well turn up the heat).

"Get some rest," he said without turning around. "It's going to be an interesting few days."

I watched him disappear into his room, then opened the door to my own. I stepped inside and closed the door, then stood with my back to it for a minute.

Interesting was one word for it. And not just a few days — the whole year.

Matt brought up my bags and I spent the next two hours unpacking and checking out my new room. The meager amount of clothes I'd brought with me barely put a dent in the space offered by the dresser and the deluxe walk-in closet I'd found behind one of the doors, but it was nice to have everything out of my suitcases.

The room was perfect, the king-size mattress nestled inside an ice-blue upholstered velvet frame with expensive sheets and a pretty blue, white, and gold bohemian comforter that was exactly my stye. The sofa in the sitting area was plush and covered in a crisp linen-colored fabric. I could already imagine how nice it would be to read there with the trees swaying beyond the wall of glass.

Had the room always been furnished this way? It must have been, because the alternative was that it had been decorated for me, and that seemed too considerate for the three Kings, grilled cheese and bellhop service aside.

I couldn't figure out how to open the glass doors leading to the balcony — there was no knob and no control panel that I could see — so I settled for standing next to it, staring into the trees and wondering why, for the first time in a long time, I felt relieved.

I should *not* be feeling relieved at Aventine. *Especially* in the Kings' house.

I would have to be careful. I needed to remember that I was here to find out what had happened to Emma, if Neo, Rock, and Drago might know something about her disappearance. I couldn't afford to get comfortable.

The bathroom was every bit as amazing as I'd imagined, almost identical to the one attached to Rock's room, soaking tub included. I was surprised to find an extensive selection of high-end toiletries on the marble vanity, although I probably shouldn't have been. I'm sure the few girls at Aventine were all vying for a spot in one of the Kings' beds.

Or all of them.

The guys probably kept the stuff around for their many conquests. The fact that it all looked new and unused just spoke to the fact that it was the beginning of a new school year.

Probably bought a value-size pack of condoms too.

The tub was tempting, but exhaustion was starting to weigh on my shoulders. I just wanted to get clean and fall into the giant bed waiting in my new room, so I grabbed the shampoo, conditioner, and bath wash, which combined cost more than a ticket to Costa Rica, and headed for the shower. I promised myself I'd christen the giant bathtub soon, but it felt heavenly to wash the day's stress away under the hot water pouring from the high-powered, full-body shower jets.

By the time I finished, I was relaxed and beyond ready for bed even though the sun had barely started to sink behind the trees. I slathered on a layer of the silky lotion that matched the shower gel and breathed in the scent of coconut and vanilla, then put on a pair of underwear and the *Ciao, Baby!* T-shirt I'd bought in Rome.

Sex is amazing but have you ever slid into one-thousand-thread-count sheets fresh from the best shower of your life while wearing nothing but panties, a well-worn T-shirt, and body products that cost as much as a car payment?

I sank into the down pillows with a sigh.

Chapter 8

Rock

"It wouldn't kill you not to be a dick you know." I stood with my back to the counter, arms folded over my chest as I stared at Neo. Motherfucker was tearing meat off a store-bought rotisserie chicken and pretending he wasn't all kinds of agitated, but I knew better.

"Just being myself," he said.

"Exactly," I said.

"I don't want her here," Neo said, carrying the chicken carcass to the trash can.

"Don't put that—" I sighed and scrubbed my face with one hand as he dumped the bones into the bin.

He pulled the bag and knotted it even though it was almost empty, then carried it to the door leading to the garage. "Enzo!" he barked.

Enzo appeared from the living room, and I gotta say, I didn't love the look on his face. No one liked being a new recruit, but everyone knew you sucked up. You did what you were told — with a smile — until there was some other rookie to boss around.

Enzo walked around the house like he owned the place.

"Take out this trash," Neo said. "Now."

Note to Enzo: You don't own the place.

I thought the asshole — Enzo, not the other asshole, Neo, who I loved like a brother — might be clenching his jaw, but I could't tell. His expression always looked like a piece of fucking granite.

For a second I thought he might refuse, and I was almost eager for the chance to watch Neo put a fist through his face. But Enzo bent over to pick up the bag like a good fucking soldier and headed for the back door leading to the outside trash cans.

"We're going to have to watch that guy," Neo said.

"No shit," I said, "but that has nothing to do with Willa."

He was avoiding the subject even though she was the one subject he wanted to talk about most. It didn't matter that Drago and I were the only two people in the world who knew that, it was a fucking fact.

"Nothing to say about Willa fucking Russo," Neo grumbled. He washed his hands in the sink and grabbed a handful of paper towels to dry them off.

"I know you don't want her here," I said, "but she probably doesn't want to be here either. Have you thought about that?"

"Doesn't matter what she wants." He said it coldly, matter-of-factly.

I couldn't blame him. It was true. What any of us wanted was so far in the rearview it wasn't even worth talking about.

But that didn't mean we needed to make it harder on each other, a position which, I admit, was informed at least a little bit by my soft spot for Willa Russo. Who could fucking blame me?

"I'm just saying... lighten up," I said. "Give her a break."

He turned to stare at me. "I don't take orders from you, from anyone."

He'd always been a giant, but he'd bulked up over the summer, and I started to rethink my desire to see Enzo push Neo too far.

It'd be a fucking bloodbath.

I sighed and shook my head. "Not an order, brother. Just a suggestion."

"Don't need it," he said, heading for the back stairs.

I didn't say what I was thinking, that Neo wouldn't know what he needed if it snuck up behind him and held a knife to his throat. No point.

"I know you have a lot of baggage with her," I said to his retreating back. "Just don't punish her for the things that aren't her fault."

He flipped me off and kept walking.

"Fucking perfect," I said to the empty room. "Good talk."

It was going to be one fucker of a year.

Chapter 9

Willa

Sun was streaming into the room when I woke up the next morning. It took my sleep-addled brain a minute to figure it out — the wall of glass faced west, and there were no windows on the east side of the room, which faced the hall — but then I looked up and saw the blue September sky through the ceiling.

Skylights.

I stretched happily, then froze.

I was in the Kings' house at Aventine U, less than half a mile from the last place Emma had been seen, and today was the start of Welcome Week, which might as well have been called Hell Week for all the fun it was going to be.

Ugh.

My phone dinged from the bedside table. I reached for it and smiled when I saw Mara's name.

How many times have you banged Neo since yesterday?

I grimaced and typed back. **Thanks for making me sick before breakfast.**

The words came easily. They were a reflex. But the memory of Neo looming over me the day before? Of his cologne and male pheromones or whatever it was that made me want to tear off his clothes even though he was a total dickhead?

Those things were something more primal I didn't want to think about.

Rock? Drago?

None of the above, I typed.

What a waste. Want to trade? You can hang out with a bunch of ambitious Ivy frat boys and I'll take your place in a sexy Neo/Rock/Drago cocktail.

I wish.

I didn't really. Columbia didn't sound any better than Aventine. College just hadn't been on my radar, probably because Emma went missing my senior year of high school, when I was supposed to be figuring out my future.

How's the dorm? I typed while getting out of bed.

I went to the bathroom and started brushing my teeth.

My roommate's from Georgia. I can't decide if the accent is cute or annoying af.

I spit out the toothpaste and smiled as I replied. **I vote cute.**

You would.

Going down to find coffee and breakfast. Talk soon?

She gave the text a thumbs-up.

I started for the door, my mind already on coffee, then remembered I was still in panties and the tiny pink *Ciao, Baby!* T-shirt that rode above my belly button when I moved.

Whoops.

I debated putting on sweats, then pulled on a fresh pair of shorts instead. I hardly ever wore sweats, and it was still hot out, which was why I'd worn shorts to move in. I hadn't asked to live in the Kings' house, and I wasn't going to spend the next eight months tiptoeing around them and covering up my body so they didn't have to act like grown-ups capable of controlling themselves.

I pulled my long hair into a high ponytail and started for the door, then backtracked for the Aventine welcome packet Roberto had handed me before he and my mom left.

I'd had zero time and even less of an inclination to dig into the Welcome Week festivities. It was all going to suck, and I was only here for Emma. I'd do what I had to do to give myself cover, but I really couldn't care less about a bunch of forced social "opportunities."

Folder tucked under my arm, I cracked open my door and found the hall empty, the house as quiet as a tomb. I had no idea if everyone had left or if the house was just so well insulated I couldn't hear anything beyond the isolated third floor.

Time to find out.

I chose the back staircase, hoping the guys were busy in the living room or not home at all. Maybe I'd get lucky and be able to have breakfast alone with the stupid orientation packet.

I was halfway down the stairs when I realized I'd been too optimistic. Deep murmuring voices traveled up the staircase, followed by a louder exclamation I couldn't make out and the crash of something hitting the floor.

"Asshole!"

I stepped into the kitchen just as Matt bent to retrieve his phone from the floor. Enzo, the guy who'd stared me down the day before, stood over him. They both wore basketball shorts and no shirt, and as much as I hated to admit it, Enzo was built.

There were plenty of downsides to living with a bunch of big headed bros, but this was an upside I hadn't expected, even if it was just off-limits eye candy.

"Morning," I said, setting the welcome packet on the island next to two boxes of gourmet donuts.

Matt startled at the sound of my voice and hit his head on the underside of the island's marble counter. "Ow! Fuck!"

I winced. "Sorry." He straightened, rubbing his head, then smiled when he saw me. "You okay?"

"I'm fine." He scowled at Enzo, who was glaring at me like I'd just taken his favorite rack at the gym.

"I think I owe you two buckets of popcorn and a trip to the emergency room," I said, heading for the coffee pot calling my name from the counter.

"Nah, it's fine," he said.

I opened a couple cupboards looking for the mugs, pulled one down when I found them, and inhaled the heavenly scent of semi-fresh brewed coffee while it brewed.

"You owe us all a lot more than that," Enzo muttered.

I spun to face him. "Try that again. To my face."

Surprise flickered over his features before he drew himself up a little taller. "I said you owe us all a lot more than that. Because of your dad, some of our parents will probably go to jail."

It took a long time for the other shoe to drop in RICO cases. My dad had been gone for three years, but the family was still holding their breath, waiting for the repercussions of his betrayal.

"I'm not my dad," I said, picking up my coffee.

"You might as well be," Enzo said.

I studied him over the rim of my mug. "Your last name is Capaldi right? Enzo Capaldi?"

He shifted. "Yeah, so?"

"So isn't your dad the guy who got caught giving bribes to Congressman Mellon last year?" I asked.

The congressman had gotten off on a technicality, but it had still exposed the family to a lot of heat.

Enzo shrugged. "That's how our business works."

"The bribes, sure. Getting caught?" I took a drink of coffee. "Well now, that's just stupid."

He fisted his hands at his side and opened his mouth to say something, then stopped when Drago walked into the room. I'm not going to lie, adrenaline was coursing through my veins from the altercation with Enzo, but if it hadn't been, it would have started the second Drago came into view.

Because a rumpled, just-rolled-out-of-bed Oscar Drago? Way yummier than those donuts I'd been salivating over a few minutes before.

"What's up?" Drago asked, looking from me to Enzo and back again.

I'd been playing with fire and I knew it, but I also knew the law of the land, which was not to take any shit. Because the second you took shit from one person in our world, you could count on a having a truckload dumped on you every damn day.

I was *not* having that for the rest of the school year, especially from the guys I was living with.

"Not a thing," I said, setting my cup on the counter.

Drago studied Enzo with narrowed eyes before walking to one of the cupboards. He took down a stack of plates and handed me one.

He was standing so close I felt the brush of his shirt against my boobs. I hadn't bothered with a bra, and my nipples immediately hardened under what now felt like the criminally thin fabric of my T-shirt.

He grinned like he knew exactly what I was thinking, like he knew he'd made my panties wet just by standing next to me. "If you say so... *tiger*."

He smelled like clean sheets and coffee, and I wanted nothing more than to peel off his loose *Kill Bill* T-shirt and lick his body like one of the jelly donuts I'd spotted in the big pink boxes. His dark hair was tousled, and I could almost feel it between my fingers, could almost feel his smooth, cool piercing against my lower lip.

What the fuck was wrong with me?

"Thanks," I mumbled, taking the plate and sliding out from where he'd trapped me next to the counter.

I pulled one of the jelly donuts out of the box.

"There's juice and milk in the fridge," Matt offered, the

first thing he'd said since Enzo had rudely interrupted our pleasant exchange.

"Thanks. Anybody else?" I asked.

"I'll take juice if you're offering," Drago said.

I found the glasses and pulled down two of them before turning to the giant fridge. The top shelf was filled with yogurt, fruit, and eggs, and I remembered Rock and his grocery bags.

The guy knew how to shop for food.

Any other day I would have been all over the fruit and yogurt, but Enzo had soured my mood. I was in need of a serious sugar hit, preferably with more caffeine.

I scanned the contents of the fridge until I spotted a carton of OJ on the bottom shelf. I bent to get it and turned around with it in my hand just in time to see Enzo shift his eyes away from where I was standing.

Motherfucker had been looking at my ass while Drago poured himself a cup of coffee.

"Enzo!"

I don't know who jumped more, me or Enzo, but when Neo walked into the room, shirtless and glistening with sweat, it was Enzo who looked scared.

And from the furious expression on Neo's face, I didn't blame him one bit.

Chapter 10

Willa

"Uh, yeah?" Enzo choked out, all his earlier bravado gone.

"Keep your eyes in your head where they belong," Neo growled, his eyes flaming. He looked like a god in gray sweatpants. "Unless you prefer them swollen shut?"

Enzo's jaw hardened.

"Yes? No?" Neo pressed.

Enzo shook his head.

"Good." I had about a millisecond to appreciate Neo defending my honor before he gave me a look of disgust. "Maybe if your ass wasn't hanging out, Enzo here wouldn't be drooling all over the kitchen floor."

"And maybe if Enzo wasn't a Neanderthal, I could wear whatever I wanted without being objectified like a piece of meat when my back's turned." I smiled sweetly and held up the container of OJ. "Juice?"

Enzo stormed from the room and I made a mental note to

put him at the top of a new list I would title *Enemies at Aventine*, a list that was sure to be long and distinguished.

Neo stalked to the coffee machine and poured himself a cup while Drago pulled some glasses down from one of the cupboards.

I poured juice into the two glasses, pushed one of them toward Drago, and slid into one of the chairs at the island with my donut, juice, and coffee.

"Uh... I'll check you guys later," Matt said, clearly reading the tension in the room and deciding he wanted no part of it.

Smart guy.

"See you," I said, just before taking a bite of the jelly donut.

I moaned and closed my eyes as the soft dough and sugary filling hit my tongue. I'd missed American donuts while I'd been traveling. The French might have killer croissants and the Italians definitely had killer cannoli, but sometimes you just needed a good old-fashioned donut.

When I opened my eyes, both Drago and Neo were staring at me like I'd been masturbating in the kitchen.

"What?" I asked, my mouth still partially full of jellied goodness.

But I knew. Their expressions said it all. Drago teased his lip piercing with his thumb, his eyes dark and liquid with lust, and Neo, for all his bluster, didn't seem immune. Not according to the way he devoured me with his eyes, his gaze trained on my lips like he wanted a bite of me instead of one of the donuts in the box on the island.

"Don't let this go to your head, tiger, but if you could see yourself eating that donut, you'd get a hard-on too," Drago said.

I rolled my eyes, but he was so good-natured I couldn't keep the smile from my face.

Neo just stalked to the fridge, where he removed a carton of Greek yogurt and some blueberries. I watched as he dished everything into a bowl.

"Doing a little reading?" Drago asked, eyeing the welcome packet on the island next to my plate.

"I haven't had a chance to look it over."

"Does that mean you don't know about the ball tonight?" Drago asked.

"Shit... is that tonight?" I asked, my heart sinking. Everyone knew about the welcome ball. It was tradition, part of Welcome Week. I just hadn't known it would be so soon.

Neo finished dishing his fruit and yogurt and put everything back in the fridge, then pulled his phone from his pocket and set it next to mine on the island.

"Is that a problem?" Drago asked.

"Um, no, it's not a problem." I mentally ran through the clothes I'd brought, hoping I was wrong, but nope, I was right: I hadn't packed a fancy dress. I hadn't even packed much makeup. I'd gotten out of the habit of wearing it while I'd been traveling, and I'd been angry and in a hurry when I'd packed my stuff for Aventine.

I silently cursed myself for not reading the orientation packet sooner.

Neo slid my phone toward me and pocketed his. He started for the hall with his bowl in his hand. "Be ready at nine."

"Wait... what do you mean?" I asked.

He stopped and turned around, the hate in his eyes burning through me. "You're here so I can *look out for you*, remember?" The words were laced with bitterness. "That means you're coming with us."

He left the room before I could say anything else, and what would I say anyway? We lived in the same off-campus house, and I didn't have a car. Sure, I could call an Uber, but it made more sense to ride with the guys, even if I didn't love the idea.

I'd just focus on Rock and Drago, who so far weren't nearly as bad as I'd expected, and try to ignore Neo.

"Chin up," Drago said. "It's a dance, not the guillotine."

He was right, except I was pretty sure the welcome ball was going to be an entirely different experience for me. Everyone else on campus would party and dance and regroup with the friends they hadn't seen since last year while I was scrutinized like a bug under glass and probably squashed by someone's shoe.

I took a drink of coffee, mentally flipping through the clothes I'd brought, desperately searching for something that would work for a dance where everyone would be dressed to the nines.

Drago grabbed a donut from the box and leaned against the counter to take a bite. And man, it was one sexy lean, his jeans slung just low enough on his hips to give me another glimpse at the tempting trail of hair leading to the bulge between his thighs. I suddenly wanted to be wrapped in those sculpted arms, pressed against all that lean muscle.

I shifted in my seat and pressed my thighs together as my pussy pulsed with need.

Down, girl.

"Is Neo some kind of health freak?" I asked, hoping to redirect my suddenly raging sex drive.

He lifted his shoulder. "Off and on."

Hmmm, cryptic.

I finished off my donut and picked up my phone.

Except it wasn't my phone.

It was a newer model, the newest actually, sans case.

I stood. "This isn't my phone. Neo must have taken mine on accident."

Drago shook his head. "It's yours."

I looked down at it again to be sure. "It's not. I think I know my own phone."

"We bought you a new one," Drago said, walking to the sink to rinse his hands.

Anger flared in my chest. "I don't *want* a new one. I want mine."

"Relax, tiger. This one has all the bells and whistles, plus it gives you access to the house's security system and the electronic features, like that glass door to the balcony in your room." He walked over and took the phone from my hand, then scrolled to an app I'd never seen before. "It's all here. Your old photos and contacts too. Neo just synced it for you. I'll text you the codes to the security system."

I didn't bother asking how he had my number. "In the future, I'd appreciate being asked if I want something new."

A low chuckle vibrated from Drago's throat. "You'll have to take that up with Neo."

"Yeah, good luck with that," Rock said, stepping into the room with a wide smile. He looked like a blond Adonis in faded jeans and another white T-shirt that set off his tanned skin and chiseled features. He hooked a thumb in the direction of the hall. "But speaking of Neo, what's got his panties in a twist?"

"What doesn't?" I asked.

He cocked his head. "You make a good point." He scowled at the crumbs on my plate. "Don't tell me these animals let you eat *donuts* for breakfast."

He said the word *donuts* like they'd been laced with arsenic.

"They didn't *let* me do anything," I said. "I'm an adult. I ate a donut for breakfast because I wanted to."

Rock tugged on my ponytail with a grin. Somehow the sensation went straight from the top of my head to my pussy, which was clawing like a hungry animal toward the package in Rock's perfectly fitted denim. "Easy, kitten. Just looking out for you."

Fuck me. I had two gorgeous guys calling me adorable nicknames. I didn't know whether I would be a tiger or a kitten if I ever got them naked, but damned if I wasn't itching to find out.

Rock walked to the fridge and removed a kombucha, then cracked the cap. Of course someone so perfect wouldn't drink coffee and eat donuts in the morning.

Drago used the sink to rinse the remnants of his donut from his fingers. "So what's on tap for today?"

I sighed. I didn't have the energy to fight about the new phone. It was done, and I had to admit, the new one was super nice. "I guess I'll go into town."

I had a black maxi dress that I could probably dress up for the ball, but I was definitely going to need more makeup.

"Sounds good," Drago said. "I can be ready in five minutes."

I scowled. "That wasn't an invitation."

Rock laughed. "You'll figure out that Drago doesn't need an invite. Anywhere."

I crossed my arms over my chest. "What if I don't want company?"

Drago walked toward me and leaned down, close enough that his cheek briefly brushed mine, his scent filling my nose.

"Give it a chance. You might just like it."

His voice was low and sexy, a whisper against my ear that sent a shot of lust rushing straight to my pussy, which had clearly gone all kinds of rogue.

"Fat chance." I could only hope he couldn't read the lie in my words, that he couldn't tell I very much believed I'd like it, that I was a fraction of an inch from giving *it* a try.

He chuckled and I jumped in surprise when he patted my ass on the way out of the room. "Get dressed. We'll leave in half an hour."

Chapter 11
Willa

A half hour later I was sliding into the passenger seat of a shiny black Porsche Boxster.

Because of course, Oscar Drago drove a Porsche.

He'd been waiting in front of the house, wearing black jeans and boots and leaning sexily against the passenger door of the car, when I'd emerged. Now I couldn't help wondering what other cars lurked in the massive garage attached to the sleek modern mansion that was going to be my home for the school year.

He closed my door and I caught sight of an expensive-looking camera in the back seat while I was buckling my seat belt.

"Nice camera," I said when he slid into the driver's seat.

He shrugged and the car sprang to life with a sexy roar.

"Someone got access to the trust fund," I said.

He looked over with a grin, and I almost fell into his dark eyes. "Try again, tiger."

I didn't have time to take another guess about how Oscar Drago had come into enough money to buy such an expensive camera. He hit the accelerator and I was pushed back in my seat as he sped down the driveway.

The car rode like a dream, and with the sunroof down and the wind in my hair, I could almost imagine I was somewhere else, with someone other than one of the guys who might know something about Emma's disappearance.

The thought tied a knot in my stomach.

Dammit. I was starting to *like* them. Rock and Drago anyway. But that was a mistake. A dangerous one, for me and for Emma.

The streets leading to town were crowded with students, most of them in groups or couples. They looked happy and carefree, and I couldn't help being envious. The weight of Emma's disappearance had been hovering over me for two years. It had been there even when I'd been traveling, shadowing me like a ghost I couldn't quite shake.

Before that, my dad's abandonment had loomed over our lives. We'd been one of the most powerful families in the country before he turned traitor, then suddenly, we were outcasts, barely scraping by on the little money my mom had found hidden in the house and offshore accounts, moving to a smaller house, pretending like we didn't notice the cold shoulder given to us by so many of the people we'd once thought of as family.

Not just business family, but real family.

That had hurt the most, and I knew I was in for more of it at school, especially at Aventine, where everyone would be looking for an edge, some way that they were better and more powerful than everyone else.

Drago slowed the car as we came to an intersection.

"Where to?" he asked, the engine revving down enough that I could actually hear him.

"I'm not sure," I said. "Is there a drugstore or something?"

I'd only been to the town of Blackwell Falls twice, when my mom and I had driven up to see Emma at Bellepoint. She'd shown us around campus and taken us to her favorite bistro in Blackwell Falls. The town was well-appointed, with a tree-lined main street, cute little shops, and expensive eateries, but I doubted they had a Sephora.

"You got it." Drago took the corner so fast I grabbed the door handle.

He parked on a side street and turned off the engine. I reached for the door but was surprised when he ran around to open it for me.

Oscar Drago, a gentleman?

I wasn't sure I could take many more surprises.

I stepped onto the curb and waited while Drago shut the door to the Porsche. I didn't know when it had started to seem normal that we would go into town together, but sometime between the annoying interaction with Neo and our arrival in Blackwater Falls, I'd let the baggage between us fall away.

It was still there, lurking in the shadows — I didn't trust Drago or his two gorgeous and annoying bros — but being in the Kings' house meant I needed them.

For now.

Plus, the closer I got, the more access I would have to their secrets.

"Let's go," Drago said.

"Your camera..." It was in full view in the back seat, just asking to be stolen.

"No one's going to mess with my camera." There was a threat in his words, but I didn't have time to analyze it, because a second later he reached for my hand. He chuckled when I tensed, the sound as smooth as expensive Scotch. "No Willas will be harmed in the making of this field trip, I promise."

I didn't tell him that being harmed had moved to the number two position on my list of Things to Worry About — right behind being sucked in by Drago's sexy af smirk and Rock's sea-blue eyes.

As for Neo Alinari, fuck him.

"There's a Walgreens on the next block," Drago said, his big hand still wrapped around mine as we started down the street. "We can take you to the city sometime if you want legit shops, but this should do for now."

The pedestrians milling around us were mostly students — obvious from their age and attire — and I tried to ignore the ones who stared as we passed.

Which was most of them.

I had no idea if they were staring because they knew I was the traitor's daughter, because they knew I was Emma Russo's sister, or because I was holding hands with Oscar Drago, one of the three most desired men on Aventine's exclusive campus.

It didn't matter. I just wanted to buy what I needed and get back to the house, which was already starting to weirdly feel like a refuge from the real world. After a year of anonymity, I was going to have to ease into this whole notoriety thing.

"You should be able to find what you need here," Drago said as we stepped into an upscale Walgreens. Typical for a town like Blackwell Falls to try and pretty up its drugstore, like there was something unseemly about a store that carried literally everything you needed for basic survival.

"Thanks." I looked around until I found the makeup section. "I can take it from here if you want to go have a beer or something."

He shook his head. "I'm good."

I stared up at him. "No offense, but I don't need a babysitter."

"Think of me as your private security detail." His biceps bulged as he crossed his arms over his chest, and there was a glimmer of amusement in his dark eyes as he stared down at me. "Would a bodyguard go *have a beer* and leave the person he was protecting to fend for herself?"

"Except I didn't hire you," I snapped. "And I don't need you."

I thought about all the people who'd stared as we walked through town, about the anonymous hate mail my mom had gotten after word got out that my dad had turned informant.

My peers at Aventine would play rough. No doubt about that. But I didn't need a bodyguard to go to Walgreens.

He rubbed his thumb along his lower lip in a gesture I was beginning to recognize as one he used when he was considering something. "Tell you what, I'll check out their anemic DVD section. Scream if you need me."

"There's a movie section at Walgreens?" Why was I

keeping this convo going? I should be happy to send him on his way, not making small talk and looking up at him while my heart fluttered in my chest like some kind of Victorian heroine about to swoon.

"It's not comprehensive by any means, but it'll keep me busy for a few minutes while you pick out some mascara and lip gloss," he said.

He turned around and walked away before I could say anything else.

I sighed and headed for the makeup aisle. Whatever. Everything I did here was about Emma. Drago was just being nice by giving me a ride into town. Once the school year started and the guys got busy with their own lives, they wouldn't have time to follow me around.

Chapter 12

Willa

I formulated a plan as I headed for the makeup aisle. I'd dug into the welcome packet while I'd gotten ready to leave for town and discovered that the welcome ball was held in Aventine's ballroom, which happened to be on the ground floor of the administrator's building.

Dean Giordana's office was upstairs on the second floor. There would probably be some commotion when I first arrived, especially since I would be arriving with Neo, Rock, and Drago, but if there was one thing I knew about my peers, it was that they were inherently self-absorbed.

Eventually, everyone would go back to reuniting with their friends, sharing stories about their summer, getting drunk, and hooking up.

Slipping away after that would be easy, and I'd have plenty of time to do some exploring in the administrative offices upstairs to see if I could find out anything about Emma. I didn't know what I was looking for, but I had to start somewhere.

I wasn't all that surprised to find the makeup section empty. Most of the girls at Aventine and Bellepoint had all summer to plan for their return to school. They'd gone to Bergdorf or Bloomingdale's in the city, or had bought makeup online or in Paris on their summer vacations.

All the better for me.

I scanned the brands as I made a mental note of what I needed and stopped in front of the foundations and CC creams. I was testing one of them on my jawline to make sure the shade was right when a voice sounded behind me.

"It's too dark for you."

I turned to find a pretty girl about my age with red hair and sparkling hazel eyes studying my face.

"Excuse me?"

"That shade," she said, walking toward me. "It's too dark."

I hadn't been sure looking at the picture I'd taken of myself on my phone. I watched as she plucked another shade off the shelf.

She handed it to me with a smile. "Try this one."

"Thanks." I unscrewed the cap on the test bottle and rubbed a little on my jawline, then took another picture. She was right. It was so seamless I couldn't even tell where I'd rubbed it in. "Wow, you're good."

She laughed. "I'm a makeup whore. And you're Willa Russo."

I sucked in a breath and braced myself. She seemed nice, but lots of people *seemed* nice in our world — right before they cut off your tongue and dumped your body in the Atlantic.

"Guilty," I said. "Of being Willa Russo. Nothing else, despite what everyone seems to think."

She grimaced sympathetically. "That bad huh?"

"To be honest, I'm not exactly sure," I said. "I guess we'll find out tonight. I've been kind of hiding out for the past year, and I haven't seen too many people on campus yet." I studied her. "Actually, how did you know I was at Aventine?"

"Oh, it's all over school," she said with a laugh. "That was inevitable, especially once it got out that you're living with the Kings."

Right. The other guys at the house. Even if Neo, Rock, and Drago had kept quiet, the other guys probably wouldn't, not necessarily out of malice but because we were all young, and some of us were way too eager for drama.

"I didn't really have a choice on that one," I said. "Also, I feel like I'm at a disadvantage. You know my name but I don't know yours."

"Right! Sorry about that. I'm Claire," she said. "Claire Byrne."

I smiled. "Nice to meet you."

"Same! I live in the Queens' house." She scanned the shelves and started pulling products and handing them to me. Taking them was a reflex.

"How is that?" I asked. She seemed to know what she was doing so I just went with it. Plus, her own makeup was on point.

She barked out a laugh. "If you want drama, just put a bunch of Italian, Russian, Irish, and Latina Mafia princesses together under one roof."

I winced. Living in the Kings' house was weird, but I was

starting to see that the benefits might extend beyond the eye candy and luxurious digs. "Yikes."

"Yeah." She sighed. "It's fine. You get used to it."

"Get used to what?" a voice asked behind us. "Hanging out with traitorous sluts?"

Claire rolled her eyes like she already knew who was talking, then turned around to face the owner of the snide voice, who turned out to be a gorgeous brunette with amazing boobs and legs for days extending from a skirt that made the most of them.

"Oh look, an unoriginal insult from Alexa Petrov," Claire said, her voice emitting boredom. "What a surprise."

"Like I'm worried about being considered original by *you*." The girl named Alexa turned her nose up at Claire, then looked me up and down with a sneer. I suddenly wished I'd put more thought into my appearance. My shorts and T-shirt weren't exactly high fashion. "I'm actually glad you're here."

I narrowed my eyes. Somehow I didn't think so, and I let it show in my response. "Thanks?"

She took a step closer and I caught a whiff of her cloying perfume. "No, really. Even the games get boring after a while. It'll be fun to have a fresh — "

"Victim?" Claire interrupted.

Alexa's smile was patronizing. "Let's call it a... diversion."

Drago came into view behind her.

"What's a diversion?" His eyes had turned a shade darker, and I saw the shadow of something menacing in his expression. He glanced at Claire. "Hey, Claire."

"Hey," Claire said weakly. I didn't know if she was scared

or if she wanted to get in his pants, but honestly, I wouldn't blame her for either.

Alexa spun on her heels. "Drago! Hey!" She hurried toward him and stood on tiptoe to kiss his cheek. "How was your summer?"

I'm not going to lie, watching his response was satisfying. He stood rigidly, not bothering to bend to give her easier access to his cheek. He was *not* happy to see her and it showed.

"I asked what you were talking about," Drago said. "Because I know you weren't talking about Willa here, who's living in the Kings' house and is therefore one of us."

Alexa tried to smile but it didn't quite cover the fear in her eyes. "Just a little joke, Drago. Don't get all serious on me *now*."

Drago rubbed the whiskers shadowing his jaw. "I'm glad to hear that, Lex, because if someone fucks with Willa, they'll be fucking with us." He stepped toward me and took my hand, then looked at Alexa. "Spread the word."

Lex, huh? Did everyone call her that or was there some kind of history between her and Drago?

Claire hurried toward me as he pulled me away. "Wait! Your makeup."

She dumped all the makeup she'd collected off the shelf into my hands. It was a surprisingly complete assortment. "Thank you."

"Sure!" she said. "See you tonight at the ball?"

"I hope so."

"Have everything you need?" Drago asked. I nodded and he started walking with me to the cashier. "What a twat," he said, before we were out of range, loud enough that Alexa definitely heard.

I glanced back and saw Alexa staring after us, her face murderous.

"Yeah, uh, that might not have been the best way to call off the dogs," I said nervously.

He bent down and kissed me right on the mouth. I widened my eyes in surprise before he pulled away.

"Relax, tiger. Lex is the biggest gossip on campus. She'll tell everyone and their mother that if they fuck with you, they'll be fucking with us. It won't stop them from fucking with you, but they'll have to be more careful, and at least they can't say we didn't warn them."

I was still in shock over basically everything when it was our turn to pay. Drago slapped down his credit card over my protests, paid for all the makeup, then took my hand to lead me out the door.

"Hungry?" he asked, slipping on a pair of shades as we stepped onto the busy sidewalk.

I thought about the altercation with Alexa Petrov and suppressed a shudder. "Yeah, but I'll just grab something back at the house."

"Come on," he said. "I got you."

Chapter 13

Willa

We walked a couple blocks to a cute little deli where Drago ordered sandwiches, salt and vinegar kettle chips, and a couple of bougie-ass sodas. Then we stopped at the car so he could get his camera.

"Is that a hobby of yours?" I asked. "Taking pictures?"

"You could say that," he said cryptically.

He slung the camera around his neck and led me off Main Street and down one of the side streets. He pointed things out as we went: an old-fashioned barber shop with one of those red-and-white twirly things out front, a smoothie shop he liked where the graffiti changed every month, a used bookstore with a quaint brick storefront and a green awning. His expression darkened when I pointed to the side of town I'd never visited.

"What's down there?" I asked.

"Nothing you need to see. Just don't go past the deli on this side of town."

My brain was telling me to protest. I'd been traveling the

world alone for a whole year, and I had been as indoctrinated into our world of violence as he was.

Okay, that wasn't entirely true. Organized crime was a world still ruled by men. Daughters were raised to live with the dangerous men they married, not become like them.

But still. I *had* traveled alone. I'd fended off my share of unwelcome advances from men, not to mention one near assault at a hostel on the outskirts of Vienna, which I'd evaded by stabbing the offender in the hand with my metal nail file.

In any case, I didn't have time to register a protest. The next thing I knew, we were at the edge of town, standing at a trailhead leading into Blackwell National Park, which bordered the town on one side.

"I didn't wear shoes for hiking," I said, looking down at my sandals.

"No hiking required," he said. "There's a good picnic spot right off the trail. It's not too far."

We started down the trail, the trees thick and tall on either side of us. I felt my shoulders drop, and a sense of calm drifted over me as we left town behind. Maybe the trail was more crowded on the weekend, but it was a Thursday, and most of the student arrivals were busy stocking their dorms and meeting up with old friends.

Here there was no one to stare and whisper about me or my family. There was just the rush of wind in the trees, the sound of birds chirping overhead, and the rustle of small animals in the forest beyond the trail.

We didn't speak while we walked and I was surprised by how comfortable the silence was between us. Oscar Drago was turning out to be not at all what 'd expected, and I still wasn't sure what to do with that.

Then again, maybe he planned to murder me, cut me into a million pieces, and bury me in the forest.

Who knew?

After about fifteen minutes, Drago stopped at a narrow offshoot of the trail. He shifted the takeout bag in one hand and reached for me with the other. "Come on, just a couple minutes this way."

Taking his hand felt way too natural, but I did, because I obviously wasn't nearly as immune to his quiet charm as I wanted to be.

The trail ended at a small clearing of long grass and wildflowers on the bank of a rushing river. We stood there for a second, taking it in. Sunlight glinted off the water and made the meadow look like a field of gold.

"It's so beautiful here," I said.

His tongue snaked out to touch his lip piercing as he looked down at me with smoldering eyes. "It's nothing compared to you."

I rolled my eyes, but my face heated anyway.

Dammit.

"Can we eat?" I asked. "I'm starving." I was always hungry, and the single jelly donut, as orgasmic as it had been, hadn't taken me very far in the fuel department.

He smiled down at me. "You're going to have to get better at taking compliments, tiger. But yeah, we can eat."

Drago stripped off his jacket for me to sit on and we settled on the bank of the river, shaded from the sun but close enough that we could still feel its warmth through the branches of the trees.

"This is one of my favorite spots," he said, unpacking the food. "I come here when I need quiet."

"Must be a lot given your roommates," I said, unwrapping my sandwich.

He laughed. "You're actually funnier than I remember."

I stared at him, my sandwich halfway to my mouth. "What do you mean?"

"What? You think I don't remember you?" He uncapped both our sodas and nestled them in the dirt. "We've been around each other since we were kids."

"Yeah, but you could say that about half the kids at Aventine. Do you remember them all?" I asked.

"They aren't all like you," he said.

My face grew hot and I took a bite of my sandwich to hide my embarrassment. Emma had been the center of attention in our family. Tall and willowy, beautiful and funny, Emma had been like a shining star. I'd always been the quiet sister, always reading in a corner by myself, studying everyone else, wondering how they made it all look so easy.

Until my dad turned traitor, I'd always assumed I'd been invisible to Neo, Rock, and Drago.

To everyone.

We talked about everything and nothing while we ate: about Drago's love of movies and photography, about his friendship with Rock and Neo ("they're my brothers in every sense of the word"), my year of travel.

"I'm sorry about Emma," he said as I balled up the paper

that had been around the turkey and avocado sandwich I'd devoured. "She's good people."

I stiffened, remembering that Drago could know something about my sister. It seemed impossible after our afternoon together. He seemed so normal.

So nice.

But I couldn't afford to take anything for granted. Even if the Kings hadn't been responsible for Emma's disappearance, I knew how it worked, how the people in our world protected each other, especially the men.

"Thank you." I looked out over the river, watched as it tumbled over the slick rocks that protruded from its surface. "I miss her."

He nodded. "I bet you do."

He sounded like he meant it, and I remembered that he had an older brother who'd died when we were in middle school. My parents had told me he'd gotten sick, but I heard later that he'd committed suicide.

My chest felt tight and I rose to my feet. "I'm going to rinse my hands."

I walked to the riverbank and crouched, swirling my hands in the water, turned amber by the light. I forced myself to breathe through my grief, waiting for it to subside before standing. I had a lot of practice. I knew the drill. How it could hit me like a rogue wave, knock me off my feet, pull me under if I wasn't careful.

When I felt steady, I turned back to the picnic spot and stood over Drago. "Should we go?"

He reached out a hand. "Come here."

I should have said no, should have said I wanted to leave.

But his voice was gruff, his eyes warm and concerned, and right then? Well, right then, all I wanted was to be held.

I let him pull me to the ground and he laid back on the grass and nestled me into the crook of his arm so that my head was against his chest.

"I'm sorry," he murmured, dropping a kiss on my head. I was stiff in his arms, still debating the merit of letting Oscar fucking Drago comfort me. He chuckled, and the vibration of it moved through my stomach like an earthquake, setting all kinds of things on fire along the way. "Relax, tiger. I won't bite... unless you want me to."

I laughed and shook my head, but I also nestled a little deeper into his magnificent chest. Because I was only human. And Oscar Drago? Well, Oscar Drago was starting to look like a gift I hadn't known I wanted.

I rested my hand on his chest and my fingers froze when they brushed over something hard under his T-shirt.

He laughed again. "You can ask. I know you want to."

"You have nipple piercings?" I asked, cursing my body for the flood of desire that rushed between my thighs.

"I have a lot of piercings." His voice was suggestive, and my pussy clenched at the thought of Oscar Drago with a pierced dick.

I forced myself to breathe, grateful when he didn't say anything else. I had the sense that the situation was getting away from me, that it was spinning into something I couldn't control.

Attending Aventine with three douchebags who were very obviously the enemy?

That I could do.

Living with three thirst traps who were varying degrees of nice and sexy as fuck?

I was not prepared.

We lay like that for a while, the sound of the river and the forest around us calming me down and soothing my sadness about Emma.

And yeah, okay, the hot guy under me didn't hurt either.

"It doesn't fit," I finally said.

"What doesn't fit?" Drago asked.

"Your nickname."

He lifted his head to look at me. "Oh yeah?"

I craned my neck to stare at his face. It was still a shock how gorgeous he was with those bottomless eyes and sculpted cheekbones, the full lips that made me want to lick his piercing and find the other one on his tongue.

Oh, for fuck's sake. I really needed to stop.

"Oscar Drago," I said softly. Names were good. Names were safe territory. "I'm just going to call you Oscar."

He grinned. "You can call me whatever you want, tiger. Or, you know, scream it while we're in bed."

I smacked his chest, but the suggestion sent a fireball of heat to my pussy. "Down, boy."

He stretched. "It's all good. I'm a patient man... as long as I get there first."

I sat up and stared with my mouth open, but I couldn't help laughing. "What's that supposed to mean?"

"Oh come on, you have to know we're all vying for your attention in the house. Well, Neo, Rock, and me anyway. The others better not fucking dare."

I shook my head. "Not Neo."

"Don't be naive." I didn't have time to process that little firebomb before he sat up. "We should head back."

Reluctance was heavy in his voice. I knew the feeling, but I got to my feet anyway. He was right. I needed to get ready for the ball and figure out how I was going to make my cotton maxi dress, meant for casual summer nights out, work for the formal kickoff to my school year at Aventine.

Because hot or not, Oscar Drago had been at Aventine when my sister went missing. And tonight I started the hunt for what had happened to her.

Chapter 14

Willa

Oscar parked the Porsche in front of the house and we headed for the door. Except once we got there, we could barely open it for all the boxes crowding the entry.

"What *is* all this?" I asked, edging past them.

Oscar looked at a couple of the labels. "Looks like they're all for you."

"I didn't order anything," I said.

But he was right. They *were* all for me.

Wtf...?

"Let me see your keys," I said.

He chuckled. "I don't have any keys."

I did a double take. "What do you mean you don't have keys?"

He shrugged. "Cars have fobs. House has keyless entry."

I hadn't even thought about the fact that he'd punched a code into an access panel to get into the house, but he was right: I hadn't seen him use a key once.

He opened a drawer in the console table that sat against one wall in the foyer, then handed me a pair of scissors. "This should do the trick."

I cut open one of the boxes and found a giant white box with an *SL* monogram. "This must be some kind of mistake."

Saint Laurent was way out of my league.

Lifting the lid on the box, I was greeted with a half inch of thick tissue paper. When I dug through that, I found a gorgeous black silk cocktail dress with a sheer panel across the chest.

"I didn't order this," I said, wishing I could have.

Wishing I could.

Oscar was already halfway up the stairs. "Looks like it's yours anyway."

"Hey," Rock said, entering the room from the hall. Damn, those faded jeans really were made for him. "Let me help you get these upstairs, seeing as how *Drago* can't be bothered. I hope you didn't let him fool you on your little field trip today. He's actually a selfish bastard."

Oscar's laughter drifted down the stairs. "You're just jealous because I got Willa alone first."

"I'm jealous as hell, but that doesn't supersede you being a self-centered prick," Rock said.

"I'm so confused," I said. Was I talking about the dresses? Because there was definitely more than one given the labels on the shipping boxes. Or was I talking about the guys, who were starting to seem just *a little* bit endearing?

Both?

I looked up at Rock. "Did you do this?"

He held up his hands. "Wasn't me."

Kings & Corruption

I sighed, feeling suddenly tired. It was almost four, and I was really hoping for a nap before I had to get ready for the ball. "Can you just... help me?"

He wagged his eyebrows suggestively. "I can help you with a lot of things, kitten."

"With the dresses," I specified, picking up one of the boxes.

He flashed me a wide smile. "No problem."

He stacked three of the remaining boxes in his arms and followed me up the stairs to my room, where he set them on the sofa in the sitting area.

I started for the hall but he put a hand on my arm to stop me. "I got it."

"I can help," I said.

"You stay. I'll take the elevator this time."

I stared up at him. "Wait... there's an elevator?"

He shrugged. "Sure. I assumed someone showed you."

"They didn't." What else did the house have? A robotic butler?

"It's tucked away. I'll show you sometime," he said.

Great. Just what my ass needed, an elevator. I made a mental note to keep taking the stairs, and maybe visit the gym on the second floor too. I'd spent the last year carrying twenty pounds on my back and walking all over the world. I was going to have to replace the exercise with something.

I started going through the boxes while Rock brought up the rest. There were nine in total: six designer dresses that together probably cost as much as a reliable new car, plus shoes, a handbag, and a gorgeous Fendi coat.

"Need anything else?" Rock asked when he was done. "A hand opening the rest of them? A bath? An orgasm?"

I rolled my eyes. In any other scenario the over-the-top flirting from Oscar and Rock would have been smarmy, but they were so good natured it was easy to get sucked into their banter.

"I'm good." I turned him around — my god, these guys really were enormous — and shoved him toward the door before I caved and took him up on his orgasm offer. "Thanks for the help."

He chuckled knowingly. "Anytime."

I pushed him into the hall and closed the door in his face.

His perfect, beautiful face.

Then I let out a breath I hadn't known I was holding. I was starting to wonder if I could be trusted around my new roommates.

Well, Rock and Oscar anyway. I'd rather take a bath in simmering oil than fuck Neo Alinari.

But really, I couldn't afford to think about fucking any of them. So why did my body feel tight, coiled with tension that I was absolutely certain could be banished by a little naked playtime with Rock or Drago?

Or Rock *and* Drago.

Now that would be interesting.

My pussy pulsed at the thought and I hurried to one of the nightstands to look for something to open the boxes. I'd only been at Aventine for twenty-four hours and I was already losing my shit. I needed to clear my head and focus.

First: pick a dress.

Next: take a nap.

Lastly: a hot bath and a self-administered orgasm.

I needed to get these boys out of my dirty fucking mind (emphasis on *fucking*).

And fast.

Chapter 15

Willa

Four hours later, I leaned toward the mirror in the bathroom and studied my finished makeup. Claire had been right: she'd given me everything I'd needed at Walgreens, and I'd done a decent job of shellacking my face with it considering I hadn't worn heavy makeup in over a year.

The nap had helped. The masturbation session in the bath had helped more.

I felt calmer and more clearheaded than I had since I'd arrived, and I was ready to face my new peers at the ball and start figuring out what had happened to Emma.

Happy with my makeup, I left the bathroom and walked to the closet where I'd stored all the dresses after unpacking them and trying them on. They were all stunning, from the black Saint Laurent to a fluffy white cocktail dress with a feathered skirt by Andrea and Leo.

In the end, I'd gone with a red two-piece by Tom Ford. Made of deep scarlet silk with a cropped one-shoulder top and a simple drapey skirt that brushed the ground, even in the sky-high heels (Louboutins of course) I'd found in one of the boxes, it was not for the faint of heart.

I'd hesitated over it for at least twenty minutes, studying my reflection in the mirror, my desire to stay under the radar warring with the fact that this dress?

Well, this dress made me feel amazing.

And I kind of needed to feel amazing when I walked into the lion's den tonight. Plus, the more I thought about it, the more it seemed important not to let everyone at Aventine think I was afraid of them. Ours was a world built on three things: honor, reputation, and sheer balls.

I couldn't do anything about the first one. My dad had fucked that for me. I wasn't much of a contender on the second either. I mean, I'd run away a year after Emma's disappearance, and I was absolutely sure my social media posts hadn't done me any favors.

My pictures from the past year depicted a young carefree girl having the time of her life, not someone broken and grief-filled, struggling with the question of whether her sister was still alive. That had been by design. Who wanted to post a bunch of pics of themselves curled into a ball, sobbing into their pillow?

In any case, my year abroad hadn't exactly gained me any street cred. I'd have to fix that — starting with the killer dress that would make it clear I didn't intend to hide in shame at Aventine.

And there was no way I was hiding in the Tom Ford dress. One tanned shoulder (thank you summer sun) was revealed while the other was encased from shoulder to wrist in shimmering red silk. The top stopped just under my boobs, offering a clear view of my stomach above the fitted skirt, which barely covered my navel and skimmed my curves in all the right ways before dropping to the floor in a simple waterfall.

I turned around in front of the full-length mirror in my room, checking the view from behind, satisfied by the fact that it revealed a good portion of my back and hugged my ass just enough to leave a little to the imagination.

I'd styled my hair in a long blonde braid over one shoulder, pulling loose a few wavy tendrils around my face. The effect was sleek but just a little sexy, a perfect accompaniment to the smoky eye and glossy nude lip I'd created with the makeup Claire had picked out for me.

I wished I had some bling to go with it all, but the only jewelry I'd packed were the earrings I'd bought in India. They were ornate and dangly, and without any other jewelry, that would do.

I grabbed the black clutch that I'd found in one of the boxes — Gucci — and took it into the bathroom, where I dug through my stuff until I came up with a hairpin. I tucked it inside the bag with my lip gloss and powder.

Heading back into the bedroom, I was reaching for my phone when it dinged.

I furrowed my brow as I read the text from Oscar in a group chat someone had set up on my new phone under the label THE FOUR BEST FRIENDS THERE EVER EVER WAS.

I exhaled a puff of laughter. Fuckers.

Get your fine ass down here, will you?

Great. As if living with the Kings wasn't enough, I was apparently going to have to deal with them on my new phone too. I wondered who'd set that up, then decided it had probably been Neo, who seemed to have a special gift for getting on my nerves.

Whatever. Better than having them banging on my door.

I left my room and used the front staircase to get to the main floor. I'd been right in assuming they would all be waiting in the living room, and whoo boy did they look good in their suits and tuxes.

In fact, I was pretty sure there was no finer sight than Rock in a fitted navy velvet tux and Oscar in tailored black pants and a vibrant red and black floral jacket, his black shirt open enough to reveal a patch of smooth skin between his throat and chest.

Except maybe Neo, which I hated admitting, even to myself.

Still, there was no denying it. Sure, he was staring up at me with something like hatred, but somehow it only made him sexier in a steel-gray suit and charcoal shirt, the buttons open even further than Oscar's. His broad shoulders strained the seams of his jacket, and his pants hugged his thighs like gloves.

I felt the slide of dampness between my thighs and tried to tell myself it was because of Rock and Oscar. I didn't even want to think about when *they* had become the safe option in my sexual fantasies.

"Fuuuuuuck," Rock said, his eyes glued to me as I came down the stairs. He'd used some kind of product to push his blond hair back from his forehead, which only made the perfection of his face more obvious. "I might need a few minutes in a cold shower before we leave."

Oscar came toward me as I stepped off the staircase. He put a hand possessively on my arm, then bent to murmur in my ear. A lock of his dark hair brushed against my cheek. "I don't want to embarrass you," he murmured in my ear, "but he's right. You're looking very..."

"Nice?" I offered.

He laughed. "I was going to say fuckable, but I thought it might be inappropriate."

"We need to go," Neo said, his voice icy. "If you're both done drooling over Jezebel here, I mean."

I was tempted to bite back, but forced myself to ignore him. It was what he deserved, and denying Neo Alinari attention was the worst punishment of all.

Besides, some of the other guys were there too, and Matt came up to me with a sheepish grin. "You look unreal."

I returned his smile. "You're looking good too."

He ducked his head and I could have sworn his cheeks flushed. "Thanks."

"Salvatore!" barked Neo. "Out."

Matt shifted his eyes away from me and hurried for the door.

A couple of the other guys walked past, murmuring nice things about how I looked, and I was suddenly flush with pleasure. There were worse things than living in a houseful of gorgeous guys who lavished me with compliments.

Except for Enzo. He was wearing his I-Wish-Could-Murder-Willa face, and I wondered again why he hated me so much. Neo made sense. We were unwilling family now that our parents were married..

I resisted the urge to gag as I remembered it.

Gross. Neo Alinari really was my stepbrother. That actually happened.

But Enzo? The only explanation was that it had to do with my father. Some of the kids were more identified with the family business than others, and Enzo obviously took it very seriously.

"Got something to say?" Oscar asked, staring Enzo down.

Enzo's mouth turned down in a frown as he shook his head. "Not a thing."

"Good," Oscar said, his arms folded over his chest. "You should probably keep it that way."

Enzo followed the other guys out of the house and a series of car engines fired to life outside.

"Let's move out," Neo said, heading for the door to the garage.

"No coat?" Rock asked as he moved into step beside me.

I'd opted to skip the coat, not wanting to cover up the dress. Plus, it was still warm enough that I didn't think I'd need it. I'd be wearing the shit out of it when the weather cooled off though.

"I'm good," I said.

He nodded and slung an arm over my shoulders. "All the better for me to keep you warm."

I shook my head. "Has anyone ever told you that you're incorrigible?"

"I have no idea what you're talking about," he said.

"She's talking about you being a brutish fathead," Oscar said. He offered me his arm. "My lady."

I stifled a smile and took his arm. I was liking these two way too much.

"I'm hurt, babe," Rock said. But he was smiling as we stepped into the garage. "You can make it up to me later."

Neo was already making his way through the massive space, the motion sensor lights coming on as he walked past several expensive cars and three motorcycles.

"What the...?" I didn't finish my statement. I couldn't. I was too stunned by the series of cars in the garage, which included the Porsche, a BMW convertible, two Audis, and a sleek red Maserati.

Oh, and at the end of the row? A massive black Hummer.

"Man, I was really hoping we were taking the Beamer," Rock said.

"You should know better," Oscar said.

I had no idea what they were talking about. I was still trying to do the math on the hundreds of thousands of dollars of horsepower in the garage. Where the fuck were these guys getting their money? I mean, yeah, our families had money. Or theirs did anyway. We'd lost all of ours.

But this was like... yacht money. Some of our parents had it. Neo's dad probably did — our parents were experts in hiding money offshore and investing dirty money in real businesses that made them legitimately rich — but it was hard to believe Roberto Alinari would give his son the kind of money necessary to fund this lifestyle.

"Get in," Neo said, opening the Hummer's passenger side door.

I ignored him and moved to the back seat.

"I'll take shotgun," Rock said, climbing into the car.

I got into the backseat, careful not to let the skirt of my dress drag on the ground. When I looked up I was surprised to find Neo standing there, waiting for me to get settled.

His eyes met mine in the moment before he shut the door without a word. A few seconds later, he was starting the Hummer and backing out of the garage.

Oscar reached over and linked his hands with mine. "You okay?" he asked softly.

Like he knew. Like he knew how hard this was going to be for me.

"I'm good," I said.

I should have pulled my hand away. I'd been in the Kings' house for a little over twenty-four hours and I was already slip-sliding into a dangerous place, a place where I saw as friends the men who might know something about my missing sister.

But damn if that wasn't getting harder to believe.

Chapter 16

Willa

I held my head up and tried not to notice everyone staring when we stepped into the ballroom. To be fair, it was entirely possible they were only looking because I happened to be accompanied by three of the most gorgeous men on the planet.

Sure, Neo lost points for his personality, but I doubted any of the thirsty bitches at the ball cared about that.

Music thumped from several speakers as a DJ mixed tunes from a high-tech setup at one end of the room, and I wasn't surprised by the bar at the other end. Aventine wasn't exactly a rule-following institution, despite the brochures that made it look like any other expensive private college on the Eastern seaboard.

We came here to learn how to break the rules, not follow them.

Besides, thanks to the customary gap year or four, most of Aventine's students were over twenty-one anyway. Neo, Rock, and Oscar had been three years ahead of me in high school and taken time off to work with the family, and they'd already been at Aventine for two years.

"Willa!"

I thought I was imagining the sound of someone calling my name through the beat of the music and the murmur and laughter of the crowd, but then Claire was in front of me, looking gorgeous in a short purple dress with feathers on the sleeves and skirt.

"Hey!" I was more than a little relieved. All the D in the Kings' house was nice to look at, but I was in serious need of a woman friend. "You look amazing!"

I had to shout it over the music, but I knew she'd heard me when her smile widened. "Thanks! But look at you!" She looked me up and down. "Someone came to play."

I laughed and she looked up at the guys, who had somehow closed ranks around me, creating a wall of manchest and shoulders.

"Oh look, it's the big, bad Kings," she said playfully.

"Claire," Rock said. "When did you...?"

"We met in town today," Claire shouted over the music. "And we're going to be best friends, so get used to seeing me around." She grabbed my hand. "Let's get drinks and dance."

She tugged me toward the bar. Weirdly, Neo moved to follow and was only stopped by Oscar, who put a hand on his arm. They started to argue, but I couldn't hear anything, and a second later, I was standing at the bar, accepting a clear drink with a faint purple cast in the bottom.

I wasn't quite twenty-one yet — that would happen in November — but no one here cared.

I leaned toward Claire. "What is this?"

"Huckleberry Twist," she shouted back. "Just drink it!"

I took a sip and smiled approvingly.

Yum.

I spotted Alexa Petrov holding court on the dance floor at the center of a group of mountainous men. She really was beautiful, her dark hair and tan skin set off by a white dress that hugged her perfect body.

It really was too bad about her personality.

The song that had been playing ended and a new one started.

"I love this song!" Claire squealed. I had a feeling she was ahead of me by at least three drinks. "Finish that so we can dance."

I downed the rest of the drink and left the glass on the bar, then followed her out onto the dance floor. I started moving slowly, but the drink had been *strong*. It only took a couple minutes for the music and alcohol to work their magic.

My hips loosened, and I started really moving, the way I had at techno clubs in Paris and beachside parties in Thailand. It felt good. For the first time since I'd come home, I felt free.

Like myself.

Not Frank Russo's daughter or Emma's sister or Roberto Alinari's new stepdaughter.

Like Willa.

We danced hard. I lost track of time, but at some point a couple of Claire's friends joined us. I caught their names after several attempts to be heard over the music — Quinn was the most beautiful girl I'd ever seen, with a halo of curly black hair and big brown eyes, and Erin was as tall and slender as a model, with a short brown pixie cut that highlighted her delicate features — and we proceeded to dance our asses off.

I was pretty sure half the crowd was amped up on Molly or coke, but that was no surprise. I wasn't into it, but I'd seen plenty of it during my travels with kids my age from all over the world. Everyone wanted to party. Everyone wanted to let go.

Everyone wanted to forget something.

A couple of times I caught sight of Oscar, Rock, and Neo, but they were never dancing. Instead, I'd see them skulking around the edges of the dance floor looking like bodyguards in a Fashion Week runway show. I had no idea what they were up to, but when I spotted them huddled in a group in one of the ballroom's corners, talking to a tall guy with black hair, I saw my opportunity.

"Going to the bathroom!" I shouted at the girls.

They nodded and kept dancing.

I checked to make sure the guys were still distracted, then slipped out of the ballroom, the music fading to a dull thump as I started down the long hall.

There were a few stragglers outside the ballroom — a couple of guys, heads bent as they exchanged something between them, and one couple having an argument — but it was otherwise empty, everyone obviously happy to be partying with their friends again.

I started down the hall, my eyes drawn to the cameras at the corners of the ceiling.

Fuck. I hadn't thought about cameras. There were only four of them, one in each corner, but still.

Shit, shit, shit.

I slowed my steps, debated turning back, then decided I could get away with a look on the second floor where Dean Giordana kept his office. If there were cameras upstairs, I could always turn back and pretend like I'd gotten lost.

I moved to the back of the building, guessing there would be a stairwell that was less visible than the fancy curved staircase at the front of the building. That one was too visible. Anyone who entered the building would see me headed to the second-floor administrative offices.

I found what I was looking for tucked behind a door near a janitor's closet. I opened it and started up the stairs, suddenly creeped out by the confines of the dim stairwell and the fact that no one knew where I was.

I'd made the switch back to the second floor and was halfway up the last run of stairs when I thought I heard footsteps behind me. I paused, my heart hammering in my chest, but when I looked over the railing at the stairs below, no one was there.

I continued up to the door on the second-floor landing and stepped into another hall. This one was less luxurious than the one downstairs. It could have been any hall in any corporate building in America, with utilitarian linoleum and tacky oil paintings of the campus.

I looked for cameras, didn't see any, and guessed they'd opted out of them on the second floor to protect the privacy of administrators like Dean Giordana.

Seemed lazy, but who was I to judge?

I started down another hall with a row of closed doors

adorned with brass plaques. I didn't recognize any of the names — until the last one.

Stephen Giordana
DEAN

Bingo.

I turned the knob, hoping to get lucky, and found it locked.

Opening my clutch, I dug for the hairpin and looked around to make sure the hall was still empty. It was so quiet up here the music had faded to nothing but a vibration under my feet.

I bent the hairpin a bit wider and leaned down to stick it in the lock, silently thanking Helga, a girl I'd met at a hostel in London. She'd taught me to pick a lock with a hairpin, a consequence of an argument she'd had with a hostelmate, who'd proceeded to lock the door of our shared room.

The trick wouldn't work with a complex lock, but this wasn't complex. I closed my eyes and felt for the locking mechanism, waiting for it to catch on the hairpin. When it did, I turned the knob, and voilá.

I was in.

I closed the door quickly and looked around. The room was nicer than the glass-fronted offices I'd seen on my way down the hall. Those had been simply furnished with outdated wood furniture, a few potted plants, and lame art.

This one had gleaming wood floors that were covered by an intricate (and obviously expensive) area rug. Bookshelves dominated one entire wall in front of a sitting area with a sofa and two chairs.

Nice, but uninteresting for my purposes.

I looked at the carved wood desk that sat in front of a generous window offering a view of the grounds in front of the admin building.

That's where I needed to look.

A faint glow emanated from a lamp on the desk, and I hurried to the window, careful to stay to the side as I drew the drapes. The last thing I needed was for someone down on the quad to look up and see me rifling through Dean Giordana's shit.

I was eager to check out the contents of the computer, but that probably involved passwords and a whole lot of digging — digging I didn't have time for, not with the entire Aventine student body partying downstairs and the Kings circling the ball like guard dogs.

I started with the top drawer of the desk instead.

I didn't know what I was looking for. That was the problem with Emma's disappearance. The trail had been cold from the beginning. There was just her roommate and friends at Bellepoint saying she went to a party at Aventine, then that last image of Emma on Aventine's security cam.

Then... nothing.

No one at Aventine would cop to seeing her at the two parties on campus that night, which meant she hadn't made it to either one or everyone on campus was keeping a secret.

But I had to look. I had to try. The detectives assigned to Emma's case had interviewed anyone at Aventine who'd known Emma even a little, and that had to be almost everyone if she had been regularly partying there. Maybe there was something about the investigation in one of Dean Giordana's files or something.

The top drawer of the desk wasn't helpful: a few pens, some Post-it notes, a tube of lip balm, and some paper clips. I reached to the back of the drawer, just to be sure I wasn't missing anything, and closed my hands around a couple of foil packets. When I pulled them out, I saw that they were condoms.

Gross. Was Dean Giordana married and having an affair at work? Or did he and Mrs. Giordana get nasty on his desk when she met him for lunch?

I didn't want to know, and I opted not to sit in the chair as I opened the drawers on the left. There were some old-school hanging files in the larger drawer, but they were all empty. Wherever Dean Giordana kept his records, it wasn't here.

I turned my attention to the drawers on the right. The top two were almost entirely empty, but the third?

The third was locked.

I chewed my lip. It wasn't incriminating in and of itself. Everyone was entitled to privacy.

But I wanted in. I wanted to be sure.

I opened my clutch and dug for the hairpin. I was bending to insert it into the lock when the door flew open.

I stood on reflex, pulse racing — and found myself staring at my stepbrother.

Chapter 17

Willa

He shut the door behind him and leaned against it, his eyes glinting in the dim light of the room. He squeezed one of his fists in the other palm. "Do you have any idea what you're doing?"

The implication was clear: that I was stupid, that I *didn't* know what I was doing. It pissed me off, because while I didn't want to be here — at Aventine, in the Kings' house, in the dean's office after hours — I had to do it for Emma.

"I'm doing what no one else has been willing to do," I said sharply. "What no one else cares enough to do. I'm looking for my sister."

He pushed off the door and stalked toward me.

I tried to back away from him but came up against the curtained window behind Dean Giordana's desk.

Neo was almost on top of me when he finally stopped moving, his chest brushing against mine as he stared down at me, his eyes spitting fire. "You don't know anything about Emma's life here."

My mouth dropped open. I didn't know what I'd expected him to say, but it wasn't that. It wasn't Emma's name, familiar, even... *intimate* in his mouth.

"What do you know about Emma?" I asked, staring up at him.

He leaned closer, his cheek brushing against mine. "What do you *think* you know?"

He spoke the words right into my ear, his lips grazing my earlobe. The sensation went straight to my pussy, the scent of his sweat and cologne filling my head like some kind of drug.

"She was here," I managed to say as he shoved his knee through the silky fabric of my skirt. He wedged it between my legs, and I had to fight the urge to grind on it as my clit sought friction. "She... she came for a party. Her roommates said she came... they said she came for a party."

Fuck me. Why couldn't I get the words out like an intelligent human being?

He brushed his nose along my jaw and I felt his hand close around my throat.

He squeezed. Not hard. Just enough to make me wet.

"What else?" he murmured against my neck.

"N... nothing else. She was at Bellepoint. Then she was here. Then she was gone."

The horror of it broke through my lust. I felt it as a sharp pain in my chest, a vise that threatened to crush me in its grip.

Neo kissed my throat and I cursed myself as a sigh escaped my mouth.

"Drago thinks you're a tiger," he said, kissing his way up

my neck. "Rock thinks you're a kitten. You know what they both have in common?"

"What?" I barely managed to choke it out as he dropped a feather-light kiss at the corner of my mouth.

"They're both cats," he said against my lips. "And you know what they say about curiosity and cats."

He crushed my lips under his, and I admit it: for a split second, I forgot.

I forgot why I was in Dean Giordana's office, why I'd come to Aventine.

I forgot that I despised Neo Alinari. That he might know something about Emma.

Because that kiss? That fucking kiss *destroyed* me.

He still had his hand around my throat as he claimed my mouth, his tongue thrusting against mine like an invading army that intended to leave no prisoners, and his chest flattened my boobs, making my nipples ache for his hands, his mouth.

And all the while his hard dick was pressed against my stomach, sending wet heat to the center of my body, clamoring for him like some kind of wild animal.

I moaned into his mouth and his free hand fished frantically under my skirt.

And thank god, because it was the heat of his palm on my thigh that brought me back to reality.

What the *fuck* was I doing?

I bit his lip. Hard.

"Ow, fuck!" He stepped back, a look of shock on his face.

His eyes were cloudy, and I felt a surge of triumph. He'd

Kings & Corruption

obviously been working some kind of twisted power play on me. The sick fuck.

But he'd lost track of his agenda — whatever it was — as much as I had.

He lifted a couple of fingers to his bleeding lip, then looked at them with surprise. "You fucking bit me."

I gave him a sweet smile. "There's more where that came from if you want it."

I expected him to be pissed. Instead an evil smile lifted the corners of his mouth.

"Don't make promises you can't keep, Jezebel." His voice was low and dark. He started for the door. "Security will be patrolling the second floor in less than three minutes. And you won't find what you're looking for here."

I hesitated, wondering how he knew about the security guards and their patrol schedule, how he knew there was nothing about Emma in the dean's office.

Then I wondered how Neo Alinari managed to make me so hot when he was such a colossal asshole.

He reached the door and turned back to me. "You coming?"

Chapter 18

Willa

Rock grinned at me from across the kitchen island. All the guys had taken off their jackets the second we walked in the door, and Rock had unbuttoned his dress shirt. He looked tousled and sexy as hell. "I should have known our kitten would be curious."

"I think stupid is a better word," Neo said, slamming the fridge shut.

He uncapped a beer and drank half of it in one go.

We'd left the ball shortly after Neo and I had returned to the first floor. And he'd been right: the security guard had been heading for the stairwell when we stepped back into the ballroom.

Neo had filled Oscar and Rock in on the way home while I'd sulked in the backseat. I didn't know what pissed me off more — the fact that Neo was treating me like a child or the fact that he'd made me want him so fucking bad in the dean's office.

I glared at him. "It's not stupid to want to know what happened to my sister."

"It's not," Oscar soothed, taking the seat next to me at the island.

"Yeah, Neo," Rock said, cutting a glare at Neo. "It's not."

"Fucking suck-ups," Neo said, shaking his head.

"Can you blame me?" I shot back. "What would you do if someone you loved went missing? Buy another Hummer? Add a wing onto your house?"

His gaze hardened and that nerve jumped in his jaw. "Wanting to know isn't the problem. You broke into the fucking dean's office. If I hadn't come in when I did, the guard would have caught you. You would have been expelled. How would you have helped Emma then?"

My face heated with shame. He was right. I had to be more careful.

"What'd you think you'd find?" Oscar asked.

I looked down at the island and traced the veins in the marble with my index finger. "I don't know. I was just hoping for something... Dean Giordana's office seemed like the best place to start."

"Well, it wasn't," Neo said.

I shot daggers at his stupid gorgeous face. "I'm getting that."

Rock leaned over the island and tugged on my braid. "You should have asked us for help."

I couldn't hide my surprise. "I didn't think that was an option."

And also, I don't trust any of you as far as I can throw you. Even if you are stupid hot.

"Of course it's an option," Oscar said. "You're staying with us so we can look out for you."

I crossed my arms over my chest. "Right."

"Why else would you be staying with us?" Rock looked genuinely confused.

My eyes slid to Neo. "Probably so my new *stepdad* can keep an eye on me through stepbrother dearest here."

"That's not why," Neo said. He was standing with his feet apart, his humongous arms crossed over his equally humongous chest, all of it stretching the seams of his expensive shirt like he was a bouncer at some high-end club. "And don't call me your stepbrother."

"Isn't that what you are?" I asked, staring at him.

"Technically." His voice dripped with disgust.

"Well, there you go," I said. "And trust me, I'm not any happier about it than you are."

"The point is, you need to be smarter," Neo said.

I ignored him and looked at Rock. "What would that look like? Asking you for help?"

He shrugged one shoulder. "Just ask, dollface."

I narrowed my eyes at him. "That's it? No strings?"

A wide smile cracked his face. "I wouldn't say no to a shot at making you scream my name, but it's totally not required."

I looked at Oscar. "What about you?"

He met my gaze. "I'm all in, tiger. Whatever you need."

I took a deep breath and looked at Neo. "Let me guess, you don't help traitors."

"Normally," he said, his eyes cold. "But if you get caught snooping around while you're living here, it makes us all look bad. So..." He shook his head. "I'm in too."

His reasons made sense, but I almost couldn't believe it. I looked from Neo to Oscar to Rock and put my finger on what was still bothering me.

"Why didn't you do this before?" I asked.

"Do what?" Rock asked.

"Look for Emma," I said. "See if you could find out what happened to her." I pinned Neo with my eyes. "You made it sound like you knew her. If that's true, why haven't you been trying to find out what happened to her?"

Rock straightened. "Come on, Willa, we said—"

"Answer the question," I said, turning my attention on him and Oscar. "That goes for all of you, any of you. If you're willing to help me now, why haven't you been doing it all along? She's been missing for two years. Why didn't you do anything before now?"

"Who says we haven't?"

The words came from Neo, but when I turned to look at him he was already walking out of the kitchen.

"What do you mean? Did you look for her?" I called after him. "Did you find anything?"

"Sounds like you already have it all figured out, Jezebel," he said without looking back.

I exhaled my frustration and looked at Rock and Oscar. "What the fuck?"

Oscar walked toward me and tucked a loose piece of hair behind my ear. "We'll do what we can. I promise."

I watched him leave the room.

Rock's giant arm dropped onto my shoulder. It should have been annoying, but the weight of it was oddly comforting.

"I'll walk you up," he said. "It's been a long day."

The force of it hit me all at once. It had been a long day.

A long fucking day.

I let him pull me against his side and walk me toward the stairs.

I was glad we didn't talk on the way up. I was exhausted. I didn't have the energy to banter with Rock, and I definitely didn't have the energy to resist him if he made a move. Snuggling against him sounded like the nicest thing ever, which was just evidence of how totally fucked my head was at the moment.

"Everything will be okay," he said, his voice surprisingly gentle when we reached my door.

He gave me a quick hug and headed for his room down the hall.

I stepped into my room and took off the heels, sighing with relief when my bare feet hit the wood floors. I removed the dress carefully, not wanting to smear it with makeup, then padded into the bathroom in my bra and underwear to remove my earrings and makeup.

Except when I got to the mirror and reached for my earrings, I froze, my brain refusing to process what I was seeing.

It couldn't be...

But the truth was right there, staring me in the face.

One of my earrings was gone, and less than two hours earlier, I'd been snooping in Dean Giordana's office.

Chapter 19

Willa

I flipped my pillow to the cold side and turned over in bed for the thousandth time as moonlight streamed in through the wall of glass in my room. I'd been tossing and turning for hours, replaying the night in my mind.

I was a mess, my mind flitting from my missing earring to the things Neo had said in the dean's office (*you don't know anything about Emma's life here*) to the fact that the guys had offered to help me find out what had happened to my sister.

I remembered the way they'd reacted when I asked why they hadn't done anything to look for her before.

They'd been *uncomfortable*.

Or had I imagined it?

Was it because they knew something? Or because they felt guilty for *not* doing something sooner?

Ugh. These guys were turning out to be a bigger mystery than I'd expected. I'd figured by now it would be obvious we were mortal enemies, we'd steer clear of each other for the next nine months, and that would be that.

Instead, I had two charmers on my hands, plus one dickwad, none of whom I trusted even though they'd offered to help me figure out what happened to Emma.

I exhaled and punched the comforter down with my fist. Not trusting people who were supposed to be helping me was a problem, but having no one to help at all was a bigger one, as evidenced by the fact that Neo had caught me in the dean's office.

If we'd been working together, I would have known about the guard's patrol schedule. I could have had someone watch the door from the hall. I probably would have known not to bother at all.

So... yeah. I didn't trust them. But I still had a better shot of finding out what happened to Emma if I worked with them.

And then there was the problem of my missing earring. I told myself I could have dropped it anywhere — on the dance floor or by the bar in the ballroom or even in the Hummer — but I kept seeing myself in the dean's office, bending over his desk, digging through his files.

I sat up in bed with a sigh. This wasn't working. This whole sleep thing.

I tapped my phone on the nightstand.

3:32 a.m.

Dammit.

I got up and briefly considered putting on more clothes — my panties and the *Halt deinen Mund* shirt I got in Berlin didn't cover much — then headed for the door.

Fuck it.

It was the middle of the night. I was just going to make a cup of tea.

Assuming these savages had tea in the house.

I stepped into the hall and headed for the back stairs. The house was still quiet when I got to the kitchen, and I put the kettle on and opened several cupboards until I found a surprisingly varied assortment of tea.

Rock's doing, no doubt. I needed to stop underestimating him.

I poured boiling water over a bag of lavender chamomile and dipped the tea bag in and out of the water before picking up the steaming mug and wandering into the hall. This was the perfect opportunity to take a closer look at the rooms on the first floor.

I was making my way down the hall when I heard voices coming from the closed door of the media room.

I obviously wasn't the only one who couldn't sleep.

I opened the door and was greeted with a grainy image on the big screen: a blonde woman with poofy hair and smoky eye makeup.

"Can't sleep?"

I followed the voice to Oscar, slumped over in one of the cushy chairs facing the screen. He was shirtless over flannel pants, and I had to force my eyes away from his sculpted chest, the corded plane of his abs.

I shook my head. "You either?"

He raked a hand over his face. "No, but that's not unusual." He patted the seat next to him. "Want to join me?"

"What are you watching?" I asked.

He lifted his dark brows. "Does it matter?"

"I guess not." I stepped into the room and made my way to his row of seats.

I settled carefully next to him and took a drink of my tea before setting it on the little table next to my seat.

"It's *And God Created Woman*," Oscar said. Goddamn. He smelled like rumpled sheets and sleep. "The black-and-white version is better. I hate the way they fucking colorize everything now."

"She's pretty," I said about the woman on the screen.

"That's Brigitte Bardot," he said. "She changed cinema."

His face looked younger and more vulnerable with the lights of the movie flickering over it.

"You like movies," I said.

His tongue snaked out, and I heard the now-familiar click of his piercings clashing. "You could say that."

"Is that why you take pictures?" I asked, leaning back in the plush movie seat.

He hesitated. "I like stories."

"Have you ever thought about going into film?" I asked.

He snorted. "Right."

It was a dumb question. The son of a mafioso becoming a *filmmaker*?

It would never happen. Not with the blessing of any of our parents. Too much attention. Too many nosy fans and journalists.

I bit my lip. Why had I assumed I was the only one imprisoned by the expectations of the family?

I stifled a yawn and Oscar raised the armrest between us. He lifted his arm. "Come here. Get comfortable."

I hesitated. Hadn't I just lectured myself about not

trusting these guys? Hadn't I been lecturing myself since I got to the Kings' house about not letting my hormones get in the way of good sense?

And yet...

I edged closer to him and rested stiffly in the crook of his arm.

He laughed and my pussy clenched at the sound of it. It was a late-night laugh.

A tousled sheets and all-night-sex kind of laugh.

"Relax," he said, dropping a kiss on the top of my head. "I'm not going to ask you to marry me, I promise. Just consider us two insomniacs looking for safe harbor for a couple of hours."

I slumped against him, giving up what little resistance I still had. I tried not to think too hard about the casual way he had of kissing me.

Like it was normal. Like we'd known each other forever.

I tried even harder not to think about the fact that I liked it.

That I liked him.

His scent did all kinds of things to my body, running straight from my nose to my pussy until I wanted to rip off his clothes and rub against him until I had that smell on every inch of my skin.

I focused on the movie instead. It was in French, but there were English subtitles. I tried to follow along for a few minutes but eventually just gave in to the images playing across the screen.

My eyelids were heavy, the weight of Oscar's arm around me making me feel safe.

This was bad. Like, really bad.

I couldn't let myself feel safe with the Kings. Any of them. At least not until I knew what had happened to Emma.

But it was one thing to tell myself those things. It was another to fight the pull of sleep tugging at my eyes, the way my body molded against Oscar's side like I was right where I belonged,

I closed my eyes. I just needed to rest. Just for a second...

My eyes flew open. I looked around, feeling disoriented, then remembered.

The media room. Oscar. The movie.

The screen was blank now, the room still dark. But Oscar was still there.

In fact, he wasn't just *there*. He was under me on the row of seats, and I was nestled into the crook of his arm like we were fucking lovers.

But that, as insane as it was, wasn't the kicker.

The kicker was Rock, who was slumped over my legs like one of those weighted blankets.

What. The. Fuck?

I tried to sit up and Rock shifted. His baby blues flickered open, gazing at me sleepily over a blanket that had somehow been thrown over me in my sleep.

"Morning, gorgeous," he drawled. "You look good enough to eat."

"Feels even better," Oscar said. "Not that you would know."

Rock shot flaming arrows at his friend over my body. "Fucker. If I'd known Willa might be up in the middle of the night, you know I would have gotten here first."

"Oh my god," I groaned. Were they really fighting over me? As if I could ever be anything but reluctant allies with either of them? "It's way too early for this... whatever this is."

I sat up and pushed Rock away so that I could extricate myself from the blanket of magnificent man-meat that had somehow ended up snaked around my body in the middle of the night.

"Aw, leaving so soon?" Rock asked, staring up at me. "I was hoping to play with our kitten."

Oscar laughed. "She'll eat you alive, bro." He looked up at me with a sly grin and sleepy dark eyes. "We can go to my room and go back to sleep if you want to be alone."

I laughed. I couldn't help it. They really were unbelievable.

But if I went to Oscar's room right now, there was no way we'd be sleeping. Ditto if I was alone with Rock.

Basically, I couldn't be trusted with either of them, and looking down at their sexy man-bodies, all warm with sleep, I was beginning to believe I *really* couldn't be trusted with both of them together.

"I'll pass. Thanks for helping me sleep though." I started for the door, suddenly aware that I was in nothing but panties and my Berlin T-shirt.

Oh well. Too late now.

I thought of something and turned around only to find both of them staring at my ass, which, okay, was for sure hanging out of my underwear. I rolled my eyes. "Can I help you?"

"Not unless you want to give me a piece of that beautiful ass," Rock said with a grin.

"Stop," I said. "I was going to say thank you. Don't make me regret it."

Oscar's brow furrowed. "Thank you for what?"

"For the clothes last night. I don't know which of you did it, but... it was really nice. So thank you," I said.

Rock surprised me by laughing.

I crossed my arms over my chest. "What's so funny?"

"Those weren't from us," Rock said.

"They weren't?"

Oscar shook his head. "I hate to break it to you, tiger, but they were from Neo."

Chapter 20

Willa

I spent the day reviewing my class schedule and ordering books online. I loaded up with pre-reqs, because let's be honest, I had zero interest in a degree from Aventine U and even less interest in the business classes that made up most of their curriculum.

The name of the game was getting through this year to find out what happened to Emma. I didn't know what would come after that, but if I decided to go to school somewhere else, I could always transfer the credits from my prerequisites.

I went down to the kitchen to forage for food at lunchtime and was told by Matt that there was a party that night at the quarry. In any other situation, I would have been eager to skip it, but apparently it was a big deal. All the other houses would be there, which meant it was a prime opportunity to do some digging on Emma's disappearance.

I'd exchanged phone numbers with Claire before leaving the ball the night before, so I texted her for the dress code.

She quickly fired back "slutty casual," which made me laugh out loud.

With that in mind, I chose a pair of frayed denim cutoffs that barely covered my ass and an off-the-shoulder floral crop top. I paired the outfit with platform sandals and hoped for a trail leading to the quarry.

Rock and Oscar were already in the back seat by the time I got to the Hummer. In the few seconds I spent trying to decide whether to cram myself in next to Rock or deal with riding shotgun next to a surly Neo, Rock growled and pulled me onto his lap.

I spent the next twenty minutes bouncing over potholes with his hard dick under my ass while Neo drove up the mountain. By the time we reached the clearing packed with cars, I was soaking wet, the impulse to turn around and ride Rock's dick like a prize-winning cowgirl almost impossible to resist.

Somehow, I managed. But damn. It actually hurt.

"Thank Christ," Rock muttered in my ear when Neo pulled the Hummer to a stop. "My dick's about to explode."

At least I wasn't the only one in need of a fire hose to put out the inferno raging through my body.

"I call Willa for the ride home," Oscar said.

"Jesus," Neo muttered. "You're both a bunch of babies."

I noticed that his knuckles were bruised and hoped someone, somewhere, had gotten sick of his shit and landed a few punches before he hit back.

"Don't be a hater just because you don't have a shot in hell of having Willa's sweet ass bouncing all over your dick," Rock said.

"Fuck you," Neo said darkly, pulling blankets and chairs out of the back of the Hummer.

I should have protested being treated like a piece of meat, right? Wasn't that what a good feminist would do?

I didn't though. I told myself it was because it wasn't worth it, because I didn't have the energy, because they were just having fun.

But deep down I knew it was because I *liked* it.

No, *like* was too mild a word.

I fucking loved it.

What girl wouldn't love having two hot guys vying for her attention? I mean, I was only human.

I tried to help carry the blankets, chairs, and cooler, but the guys wouldn't have any of it. They just picked everything up in their giant arms and started down a path that wound through the trees, carrying everything easily, as if they weren't loaded up like pack mules.

The sun was setting, a bonfire raging in a wide clearing surrounded by trees on three sides. The fourth side was nothing but sky, clearly some kind of cliff.

The clearing was thick with bodies, my peers talking and laughing and dancing to music that thumped from a big speaker. Several coolers were set up around groups of chairs, and I looked around, trying to get a handle on who was who.

It wasn't hard. The Saints — members of the Bishops' frat — were easiest to spot, congregating near a group of chairs and blankets at one side of the bonfire. The men were dark and sensual, with hooded eyes, lush lips, and sculpted cheekbones, their beauty rivaled only by the women in their midst who were a tangle of curves and long dark hair.

A group of enormous men with angular features and sharp eyes had gathered to their right. Their shoulders were like brick walls, and I would have pegged them as members of the Knight's house even if Alexa Petrov hadn't been with them, glaring at me with pointed hatred.

She was gorgeous, I'd give her that. She'd poured herself into a pair of tight black jeans, and her perfect boobs spilled out of an off-the-shoulder sweatshirt that had been artfully arranged to look sloppy.

"You're staring, gorgeous."

I looked up to find Rock grinning down at me. I was getting used to the fact that he was almost always in jeans and a white T-shirt, but Rock in faded jeans and a white T-shirt did not look like your average guy in faded jeans and a white T-shirt.

He looked good enough to eat, the cut planes of his chest obvious through the thin fabric of the T-shirt, his shaggy blond hair falling across his face until he gave a sexy a toss of his head.

"Sorry," I muttered.

"I'm guessing you've gotten a handle on the crowd." He handed me a beer. "Don't take one of these from anyone but us."

Duh.

"The Saints are over there," I said, looking at the cartel kids, before letting my eyes slide to Alexa and the Knights. "Russians over there."

"Keep going," he encouraged.

I looked at the group next to the Russians, but my work

was done for me when I spotted Claire, Quinn, and Erin. "Castle house, obviously."

I knew Claire's dad was big in the Irish mafia.

"That one's easy," Rock said, swigging on his beer.

I looked up at him. "Because of Claire?"

"And all the gingers."

I laughed. They weren't all redheads, but they had more than their share, in keeping with their Irish heritage. "Fair."

"That leaves the Queens, but it looks like they've been assimilated into the frats, for the party at least. What a surprise," I said dryly.

He draped an arm across my shoulders. "Aw, is our kitten a feminist?"

I shrugged off his arm. "Well, yeah. Aren't you?"

He looked offended. "Babe... seriously? Of *course* I'm a feminist. I want you in my bed of your own free will, begging for my dick and telling me exactly what you want. Because I'm sex positive and shit."

I laughed. Fuck me. Why were these guys making it so impossible to keep my distance? And why were my panties wet?

Again.

"So the girls congregate with the men in their families," I said. "Do the frats mix with each other at all? Because this is lame."

"Give it time," Rock said. "And a lot more alcohol. Everyone will be mixing like a dirty cocktail in about an hour."

"If you say so."

"I'm going to check on a couple of things," Rock said. "Stay where we can see you."

"I'm not a baby," I said.

"Just looking out for you." He kissed me on the mouth before I could protest, then swaggered over to where Neo and Oscar were talking intently about something.

It said a lot about my life that in the last forty-eight hours I'd gone from despising the three guys I was living with to letting two of them fight over me and kiss me on the mouth. It seemed the only one I'd been right about — at least in the asshole department — was Neo.

I flashed to the designer dresses piled in the hallway before the ball and pushed the image aside. He'd probably wanted to make sure I didn't embarrass the Kings' house by showing up in something lame.

I took a drink of my beer and looked around. Everyone was with someone — friends, boyfriends or girlfriends, housemates.

I was alone, like I'd been ever since Emma disappeared. Even when we weren't close, I'd known she was there. I'd known that when push came to shove, she had my back.

Now I felt like I was walking a tightrope with no safety net.

It was only a matter of time before I fell.

I looked at the edge of the cliff and walked carefully toward it. When I looked past the ledge, I saw the quarry glittering dark and bottomless in the light of the setting sun.

The bottom dropped out of my stomach. I was pretty adventurous, but I'd always been terrified of heights, and the quarry was huge, a black mass that could hide a multitude of secrets.

Was Emma down there? Was this a dumping ground for Aventine's secrets? The Long Island Sound of upstate New York?

My stomach rolled over, and I backed away, irrationally afraid of turning my back on the yawn of empty space, like it might reach out and snatch me over the edge.

Chapter 21
Willa

The next couple of hours passed in a dizzy mix of alcohol, names I'd probably never remember, and dancing, thanks to Claire, who found me standing awkwardly in the Kings' area and pulled me into her orbit with Erin and Quinn.

She introduced me to everyone at Castle house, then dragged me around to the members of the other houses and did the same. Most of the people were nicer than I'd expected, although each house seemed to have at least a couple members who glared at me like I'd killed their grandmother.

It wasn't as bad as I'd expected. Maybe it was just because Claire was with me and the minute I was alone, I'd be fed to the wolves, but I was daring to believe I might survive a year at Aventine.

After a couple of hours, everyone had loosened up, and the clearing around the bonfire was filled with people dancing and partying without regard to the origin of their families. The sun had set behind the quarry, the bonfire was blazing, and someone had hooked up a couple of battery-operated party lights that swung multicolored light over the scene like it was some kind of rave.

Everyone was buzzed, myself included, and I spotted some of the guys from Kings' house dancing with girls from each of the other houses.

Except Rock, Oscar, and Neo, who stayed at the edges of the party, watching the crowd like they expected a bomb to detonate any second.

It was weird. I mean, not so much for Neo, who always had a stick up his ass, but definitely for Rock and Oscar, who'd proven they could be fun and seemed to want to prove it to me privately even more.

I shivered at the thought. I definitely had the hots for two of my housemates. I didn't like it, and it didn't mean I trusted them, but there was no point lying to myself.

I was tempted.

Claire was a godsend, sticking by my side most of the night. I was already starting to see her as someone I might trust, so I was relieved when we finally caught a couple of minutes alone and I was able to bring up the subject that had been caught in the back of my throat all night.

"Can I ask you something?" I asked her.

She pulled her eyes from the crowd — she'd been scoping out one of the Saints for the better part of the night — and looked at me. "Sure."

My stomach fluttered with nervousness. What if I was wrong about her?

I took a deep breath. It didn't matter. I was never going to be a hundred percent sure I could trust anyone at Aventine. I had to take the plunge sometime.

"Did you know my sister?" I asked. "Emma?"

Something shuttered in Claire's face. "Oh, Willa... you shouldn't..." She looked around like she was afraid someone might have overheard. "You shouldn't ask about her here."

"Here at the party or here at Aventine?"

"Anywhere really, but especially not here," Claire said.

"Because there are so many people?" I asked.

"That's one of, like, a million reasons." She chewed her lip, like she was trying to decide what to say next. "Look, I knew her, okay? She came here a lot. But I really can't... I can't talk about her."

Dread bloomed like a stain in my stomach. "Do you have a sister?"

"Two of them," Claire said. "Both younger."

"Well, Emma is my sister. I can't not ask about her life here. I'm not looking for anything serious." It was a lie, but clearly I was going to have to ease into my mission to find Emma. "I just... I just want to know what her life was like. We were kind of... not talking as much when she went away to school."

Claire's expression softened. "That sucks, Willa. I'm sorry. I didn't know her well, but I'm not kidding when I say we shouldn't talk about this here." She looked scared, her eyes darting around the crowd like she expected to be attacked by one of them any second.

"Will you talk to me later?" I asked. "When we're alone? Tell me everything you remember about her?"

"Will you promise not to keep asking questions like this if I do?" she asked.

I felt bad about all the lies I was about to tell, but I nodded anyway. I liked Claire. I badly needed friends, and she seemed like someone I might be able to call a friend someday.

But finding Emma came first.

Claire sighed. "Ask me again when we're alone. And for the love of Mary and Joseph, don't mention Emma's name to anyone else at Aventine. That's the last thing you need."

I wanted to ask what she meant, but I didn't have time. A second later, Quinn joined us with two of the Saints and I tried to pretend like I had nothing on my mind but flirting with the seemingly never-ending supply of ridiculously hot guys at Aventine.

It wasn't easy. I kept hearing Claire's voice, her obvious warning that talking about my sister was a dangerous topic of conversation ringing like an alarm in my mind.

Chapter 22

Willa

I'd been hanging with Claire, Quinn, and the two gorgeous Saints for almost an hour when a cheer suddenly went up from the Knights. I looked over to see that they were doing shots, and a few seconds later, Alexa and an enormous dark-haired guy started making the rounds with a bottle of vodka, offering shots to members of the other houses.

We watched as each of the groups did shots with Alexa and the Russian giant, and I braced myself as they made their way toward us.

"Don't look now but the Queen of Mean is on her way," Claire said.

"Alexa?" I asked. "Don't give her that power. She's no queen. Just a bully in designer clothes."

Claire laughed. "Ouch."

"Oh, look," Alexa said when they reached us, "it's our resident charity case."

It stung a little because it was true. I was only here

because of Roberto Alinari. But also, you literally couldn't have paid me to come to Aventine if it hadn't been for my need to find Emma.

"Oh, wait..." I said. "Do you... do you think I actually wanted to come here?" I laughed. "You're adorable. I spent the last year walking the streets of Paris and lying on beaches in Thailand. This is a little... pedestrian by comparison."

Her eyes flashed. "Then why are you here?"

I shrugged. "Apparently it's an Alinari family tradition. I'm just playing along."

"I bet you are," Alexa said. "*Playing along* with *all* the guys at the Kings' house."

Nice try to slut shame me, but this wasn't the 1950s.

"Don't be jealous," I said sympathetically. "There's plenty to go around, and I've never minded sharing my toys."

That was a lie. The thought of Alexa with Rock or Oscar made me want to claw her eyes out — a feeling I was not eager to explore — but she didn't need to know that.

"Is that, um, vodka?" Claire asked, clearly trying to get us onto safer ground.

Alexa rolled her eyes and handed us some shot glasses. I watched her pour her own from the bottle before taking the glass she'd poured for me. I didn't trust this bitch as far as I could throw her.

We did our shots with the guy next to her, a man of few words who more than made up for it with his massive biceps and never-ending cheekbones.

"Hear ye! Hear ye!" A deep voice boomed through the crowd, and I turned to realize it was Neo standing near the bonfire. "We have some business to attend to. Everybody gather round."

The music cut off, and a strange hush descended on the group as everyone crowded around the fire.

"What's going on?" I asked no one in particular.

Alexa smirked. "Didn't anyone tell you it was Game Night?"

She flounced off — gorgeous sidekick in tow — toward the rest of the group.

I looked at Claire and tried not to panic. "The game starts now?"

I'd heard about them of course. Everyone in our world had. But I didn't know exactly what they entailed, and I wasn't eager to find out. I had a feeling playing games with the kids at Aventine was going to be less Spin the Bottle and more Russian Roulette with a Loaded Gun.

Claire smiled. "Not exactly. Come on."

I followed her to the fire and waited while everyone found a place to stand where they could see Neo. I hated the bastard with a white-hot passion, but even I couldn't deny that he looked like a god standing in front of the fire, his dark eyes like lava over his prominent cheekbones.

And I was afraid to get started on his body, which looked just as hot in jeans and a black long-sleeve T-shirt as it had looked poured into his tux for the ball.

"Thank you all for coming," Neo said. I couldn't get over how hushed the crowd was. It was reverent. And a little off-putting. They looked at Neo like he was an actual king, and I couldn't think of anything more dangerous than a guy like Neo with a little power.

"As you know, tradition dictates that tonight we kick off this year's games. You all know the rules, and if you don't, you should: four games, each assigned to a two-month period." He paced in front of the fire, looking like a general ordering his troops into battle. It was all a bit much, but I wasn't immune. My breath was shallow, my heart racing. "It's up to each house to assign players to each game. The houses that complete each game get the points for that round. Points are cumulative throughout the semester."

"Here we go," Claire said. The fear in her voice made my stomach do flips.

"But before we start, a reminder." Neo paused, and I waited for whatever order or edict he'd issue next. Instead he shouted something I didn't understand. "*Sangue oltre la famiglia!*"

The crowd roared the words back to him, some of them raising their fists, others throwing in a whoop of excitement.

"*Sangue oltre la famiglia!*"

Wtf kind of cult had I walked into?

I leaned over so Claire could hear me over the riled-up chatter around us. "What does that mean?"

"Family beyond blood," she shouted back. "It's like... a reminder."

I raised my eyebrows. "A reminder?"

"That even though we compete in the games, even though we're all from different families, we're a family too," Claire said.

I searched her face for some trace of humor, but she was serious as a heart attack.

Okay, then.

"And now, let's get down to business," Neo said. "Game number one, to be completed no later than the Bad Ball. Steal all six medals from the admin lounge..." A murmur rolled through the crowd, and I was glad Neo paused so I didn't miss what was next. "... Without breaking the glass."

"Oh my god," Claire said next to me before the crowd erupted in a roar.

"What's the Bad Ball?" I asked Claire. "And what medals?"

"The Bad Ball is the Halloween dance," Claire said.

Quinn appeared next to her, breathless, her eyes bright. "Can it be done?" she asked Claire.

"Sure, if you can get the key," Claire said. "If you can even find it."

"Dean Giordana?" Quinn asked.

I was trying to follow their conversation, trying to figure out what it all meant,

"Maybe?" Claire bit her thumbnail. "Although..."

"Seems too easy?" Quinn asked.

"Kind of."

"Let's go!" Neo clapped his hands and the crowd quieted. "House leaders, come up here and pick your team of two."

"Two?" someone protested from the crowd.

Neo's eyes turned hard as he sought the offending voice in the crowd.

"Damn," Quinn said.

"Is that bad?" I asked.

"It's not good," Claire said.

"The more people, the better for a challenge like this," Quinn explained. "Two people means only one person to

Kings & Corruption

stand watch while someone else breaks into the lounge, and that's after you find the key."

She was obviously thinking out loud, but I was starting to see what she meant, even if I didn't know what the medals were or how hard they'd be to steal.

Four people joined Neo around the fire, including Alexa. Because of course Alexa was house leader of the Queens.

"Fuck," Claire said next to me.

"What?"

"She hates me," Claire explained.

I laughed. "You don't try very hard to get her to like you."

Claire sighed and went back to chewing her thumbnail. "I know. She's just *such* a bitch. I can't help myself."

Quinn laughed. "You're your own worst enemy."

"Don't I know it," Claire said.

The Russians went first, and a guy I'd never seen before chose himself and the guy who'd been making the rounds with Alexa.

"A hundred bucks says Alexa appoints herself observer for the Queens to get some face time with George," Claire said, her eyes on Alexa's drinking buddy.

"No way am I taking that bet," Quinn said. "She's been dying to get into George's pants since he showed up on Wednesday. It'd be a waste of time anyway. No one actually watches the game go down. They just lie and say they did."

"Poor George," Claire murmured. "He has no idea what's coming for him."

"They don't know each other?" I asked. George was obviously the guy Alexa had been dragging around all night.

They'd seemed so friendly when they'd made the rounds with their bottle of vodka.

"He's a freshman," Claire said, her eyes on George as he made his way back into the crowd.

Right. I kept forgetting that our ages were all mixed up at Aventine. George looked too... manly to be a freshman in college, but he could have been anywhere from nineteen to twenty-five.

How much time the Mafia kids took off before going to Aventine was dependent on a lot of things. Some of them took a year to work with their dads. Others took more time and worked in different cities, and sometimes even different countries, which was what I'd heard Neo, Rock, and Oscar had done by working with one of the Sicilian families.

George might have been new to Aventine, but he was all man, and I couldn't help wondering (hoping?) if Alexa had bitten off more than she could chew.

I watched nervously as the Saints chose two beautiful men with dark hair and eyes, followed by the Knights, whose leader chose twins from their ranks.

The Queens and Kings were all that was left, and I wasn't surprised when Neo called Alexa up to appoint the participants for the Queens' house.

The bastard was an attention whore. He would save himself for last.

"Here we go," Claire muttered as Alexa took her place next to Neo by the fire.

Alexa paused dramatically, firelight flickering over her perfect features.

"As head of the Queens' house," she finally said, "I appoint myself and Mila to the first challenge."

"Or course," Claire said.

"What's going on?" I asked. Being at Game Night made me feel like I'd just stepped out of the airport in an unfamiliar country and was trying to negotiate for a taxi.

"The challenges get harder," Quinn explained. "But our *fearless leader* would look weak if she didn't do at least one of them herself."

Now I understood why it sounded like Quinn put the words *fearless leader* in quotes. "So she chose the easiest one."

"Exactly," Quinn said. "And she chose Mila because they're BFFs."

"She's probably saving me for last," Claire said.

"What's the point of all this?" I asked. "I mean, I get the whole pissing contest thing. But is that it?"

"That's the biggest thing," Claire said. "But the winners also become the school's unofficial leaders, and they get to choose next year's games."

"Plus, they get to wear the rings," Quinn added.

I remembered the rings winking on Neo's, Oscar's, and Rock's hands, a match to their tattoos. So they'd won last year. Except...

"But the rings have crowns on them," I said. "Isn't that the Kings' symbol?"

"The gold in those rings is older than the school," Claire said. "Every year, the winning house has them melted down and remade their way."

The other house's leaders had stepped aside, and everybody grew quiet again, all eyes on Neo.

"The Kings choose Rock for the first challenge," he said. "And Willa."

I didn't register that he'd said my name until I heard the murmur roll through the crowd. My mind was short-circuiting, trying to figure out what it meant.

"Well, it could be worse," Claire said. "At least Rock knows what he's doing."

Her words did absolutely nothing to calm the boiling of my blood.

I met Neo's eyes from across the fire, and it was safe to say I wasn't imagining the smirk on his stupid mouth. "I'm going to kill him."

Chapter 23

Willa

I was still fuming the next morning. I hurried down to the kitchen for a cup of coffee, glad the guys were all outside, and returned to my room.

We'd left the bonfire shortly after the games announcement, and I'd stalked to the Hummer without a word to the guys. Rock sat up front with Neo on the way home and I sat in the back with Oscar.

Next to him, not on his lap, even though he gave me puppy dog eyes with his ridiculously long eyelashes.

I'd barely waited for Neo to pull all the way into the garage before opening the door and storming to my room, and I'd tossed and turned all night, contemplating all the possible scenarios for my probably ill-fated attempt at committing a crime.

I felt trapped. At Aventine. In my life as Frank Russo's daughter and Emma's sister.

And definitely as Neo Alinari's stepsister.

Just saying it made me want to throw up in my mouth.

I needed to get a car. Or a bike. Anything that would allow me to escape the confines of the giant house and all its giant men.

I settled for the balcony after figuring out how to open the door with the app on my new phone.

The balcony was cute, with a couple of chairs and a little side table, but instead of enjoying some peace and quiet with my book and coffee, I just got more annoyed listening to the sound of the guys having fun by the pool out back.

Music blared from the outdoor speaker system that was part of the smart house, and a chorus of deep voices and laughter wound its way through the warm September day.

I was rereading the same paragraph for the third time when my phone pinged.

Thank god. I could really use some Mara time.

Except it wasn't Mara, it was Rock in the group chat.

Stop pouting and pour your gorgeous body into a swimsuit.

I ignored it, but a second later another text came in from Oscar.

Or better yet, forget the swimsuit.

Dumbass, Rock texted. **You want all the guys in the house to drool over our girl?**

I stabbed at my phone. **First of all, I am NOT your girl. Second of all, I'd rather stick ice picks through my eyeballs than be near any of you right now.**

It's one of the last nice days of the summer,

Oscar texted. **Why miss out on some sun just because you're mad at us?**

I stared at the words on the screen. It was getting warm on the balcony. Sweat had started to trickle between my boobs and down my back, and the sound of splashing from the pool out back was more than a little tempting.

I heaved a sigh and stood to change. The only thing worse than a couple of insufferable bros was a couple of insufferable bros who were right.

I threw on a red crocheted bikini I'd picked up in Mykonos, braided my long hair, and grabbed my sunglasses. Outside my room, I paused at the wall of glass in the hall to get a read on what I was getting myself into.

Several muscled, glistening guys — including Matt, Luke, and Ricky — were in the pool, batting around an inflatable ball with the seriousness of a pro volleyball match. I couldn't see Rock and Oscar, but I assumed they were under the overhang created by the house's modern second story, which hung like magic at a perpendicular angle over the first floor.

I headed for the back stairs and emerged into the kitchen, stopping cold when I spotted Enzo looking in the fridge.

He straightened, and for a split second, I could see his appeal. He had the kind of dark good looks and muscled bod women craved. Then he realized it was me, and his mouth curled in a familiar sneer. Unfortunately for me, his obvious disdain didn't translate into a lack of interest in my physical attributes, and I watched as his eyes roamed my body.

"I guess it's too much to expect you to wear some clothes," he snarled.

"I'm going swimming," I said. "Not that I owe you an explanation."

"You owe me — and everyone here — a lot more than an explanation," he said.

I opened my arms, still holding my phone and book in one hand. "What do you want from me? A pound of flesh?"

He cracked open a beer and took a long drink, then stared at me with narrowed eyes. "That would be a start."

"Fuck off."

My heart had started drumming in my chest, adrenaline flooding my bloodstream. I half expected him to lunge for me as I left, but a few seconds later I was stepping out of the glass doors in the kitchen and into the blinding sun and warm breeze of a perfect September day.

I forced myself to exhale slowly. Enzo was a bully, and like all bullies, he just needed to know I wasn't going to take it.

My mood lightened. The scene around the pool was pure fun, not to mention pure fire with all the half-naked hot guys lounging around and hitting the ball in the water.

And speaking of hot guys...

Holy damp panties, Rock and Oscar were lying side by side in lounge chairs, their muscled bodies glistening with suntan oil and sweat. Rock's bright blue Speedo matched his eyes and gave me a view of his dick that made my mouth go dry, and Oscar's board shorts hung low enough on his hips that I got a prime view of his tantalizing V and the line of hair that started at his navel and disappeared under his waistband.

And don't get me started on the nipple piercings.

My pussy clenched with lust as I imagined their slick skin against mine, their hands roaming my body as they —

What the actual fuck? Was I daydreaming about fucking not one of my douchey roommates, but two of them?

At the same time?

Ugh.

"There's our tiger," Oscar said, getting to his feet. He stood to scoot his chair away from Rock's and my gaze stalled on his back, or more specifically, on the massive tattoo inked on his skin.

It was amorphous and dark, like a shadow come to life, a featureless angel promising doom. I wondered why I'd never noticed it before, then realized this was the first time I'd seen his naked back. I swallowed the lump in my throat, wondering why I felt sad.

I tried to recover my composure as he maneuvered another lounger between his and Rock's. "It's fine." I waved at the extra lounge chair. "I can just sit somewhere else."

Rock looked seriously offended by the possibility. "And let all these thirsty bastards flirt with you all day? No way."

I stood over him. "You do know I'm not your girlfriend right?"

I don't even like you.

The words got stuck at the back of my throat. As much as I wanted them to be true, they weren't. Worse, I knew they would hurt Rock's feelings and I didn't want to do that.

I was glad my sunglasses hid my eyes. It was embarrassing enough to know I was starting to like these two. The only thing that would be worse was letting them know it.

"Yet," Rock said. "You're not my girlfriend yet. Wait until you taste my beef bourguignon."

Oscar handed me a black towel almost as thick as my comforter back home. Being in the Kings' house was like living in a five-star hotel, and I had to admit, I was enjoying that part of it.

"Thanks," I said, spreading the towel out on the lounge chair.

I got settled, leaned back, and closed my eyes. I had to stifle the sigh of pleasure on my lips. It was childish, but I didn't want them to know how nice it felt to lay poolside next to the two of them.

"Still mad?" Oscar asked next to me.

"Don't touch that!" Rock's urgent voice made me open my eyes just in time to see him leap from the lounge chair and hurry toward Neo, who had emerged from the house carrying a platter of raw chicken and steak.

And unless Rock had a tattoo on his ass, my instinct had been right — other than the crown tattoo on his forearm, his skin was unmarked by ink.

Neo scowled. "I know how to grill."

Unlike everyone else around the pool, Neo wasn't wearing a swimsuit, but that didn't stop him from looking like a thirst trap in slouchy jeans that hung low enough on his hips that I was practically rooting for them to drop an inch lower. His sculpted chest glistened like a model who'd been oiled up for the camera, the angel tattoo on full display, her hair seeming to float in waves around her face, and fuck me if his bare feet only added to the whole "casual god" look he had going on.

Kings & Corruption

"Uh, right," Rock said, taking the platter out of Neo's hands. "I know. I just enjoy doing it."

It was clear from the nervous way he moved away from Neo that he didn't trust Neo to cook the meat.

Neo's gaze slid over the scene around the pool and came to rest on me. For a split second, I almost thought he looked happy to see me. But I must have imagined it, because his eyes immediately hardened as he took in my bikini-clad body stretched out on the lounge chair.

Still, he couldn't hide the lust in his eyes, which made me feel a bit better about my own. When you got right down to it, humans were just high-functioning animals.

We wanted to eat. We wanted to sleep. We wanted to mate.

It was pure biology. If I'd been a leopard in the wild, it wouldn't have mattered at all that I wanted to fuck a big-dick douchebag. My brain was just trained by society to feel guilty for things that were natural.

It was all true, but I was still annoyed as fuck at myself.

"So?" Oscar said next to me. "Are you? Still mad?"

"Just because I live here doesn't mean I'm part of the Kings' house," I said, turning to look at him. "I don't want to play your game, so you can tell Neo to fuck right off."

Oscar exhaled a breath that sounded a lot like frustration. He swung his legs over the side of the lounge chair and took off his sunglasses to stare at me. I almost fell into his dark bottomless eyes in the few seconds it took him to speak.

"Neo isn't the only one in charge here, tiger." He stood and looked down at me. "And he wasn't the only one who decided you'd play. We all did."

Chapter 24

Willa

I was almost relieved when Monday came around. I was here to find Emma, not get a degree, but at least class was an excuse to leave the house.

And the house, well, the house had gotten very confusing.

My three most annoying housemates were enigmas — well, Rock and Oscar anyway. Neo was still a very obvious asshole — and I was tired of walking the tightrope of affection and distrust.

Getting dressed for the first day of school felt easy by comparison, and I chose a short floral romper from my closet, paired them with my platform sandals, and curled my hair into long loose waves. A quick application of makeup finished the job, and I grabbed my bag and went downstairs.

Rock and Oscar were already in the kitchen with Matt. They looked up when I entered and eyed my bare legs appreciatively.

"Morning, Willa," Matt said with a smile.

"Morning." He really was cute, but after hanging with Rock and Oscar, it was hard not to think about Matt like a little brother.

"Morning, tiger," Oscar said. "You're looking gorgeous as usual."

I scowled. "Compliments will get you nowhere."

It was a lie — I loved the appreciation he and Rock showered on me every day — but I was still mad about the game. I'd been so sure Neo was the one who'd decided I would play. Rock and Oscar had started to feel like allies, and I couldn't help feeling betrayed that they'd been in on it too.

It was a good reminder not to trust them, a reminder I'd obviously needed.

I started to hunt in the cupboard for one of the travel mugs I'd seen there.

"What are you doing?" Rock asked.

"Getting coffee before we go." I'd already resigned myself to riding to campus with the guys.

"Don't bother," Rock said. "We'll stop on the way. Tradition."

"Thank god," I muttered.

"That hurts," Rock said, sounding genuinely wounded. "If you want a different brand coffee, just ask and I'll buy it. Or better yet, come with me to the grocery store and you can pick it out yourself."

"It's not that." The house had all the amenities, and Rock bought the best quality food — and coffee — available, but I was starting to get cabin fever. I missed coffee shops and restaurants and people who didn't look like Calvin Klein models. "I've just been wanting to see more of Blackwell Falls."

"We'll get out more now that school has started," Oscar said, plucking a set of keys from one of the hooks by the garage door. "Let's go."

"Wait," Rock said, opening the fridge. He handed me a plastic container and got a plastic spoon from one of the cupboards. "You need breakfast."

"What's this?" I asked.

"Yogurt parfait," he said as if it was obvious. "With fresh fruit."

My stomach grumbled a little. I'd always had a big appetite, and I'd been avoiding the kitchen. The more I saw the guys, the more complicated things became.

"Thanks."

We headed to the garage and I made a beeline for the Hummer, but Oscar stopped in front of the Audi R8. It was a beautiful car — sleek, black, and low to the ground with windows so dark I couldn't see the interior through anything but the windshield.

"We're taking the Audi?" I asked.

"Have to take advantage of it when Neo's not around," Rock said, opening the passenger side door and cramming his giant body in the back seat.

I slid into the passenger seat and inhaled the scent of expensive leather and men's cologne. "Neo doesn't like the Audi?"

"Neo doesn't like little cars," Oscar said, firing up the engine as the garage door slid silently open.

"Where is that ray of sunshine?" I asked.

"Driving separately," Oscar's tone made it clear that was all he was going to say on the subject.

He put the car in reverse and backed out of the garage. A second later we were careening down the driveway at what felt like warp speed.

We turned away from campus and headed into town where Oscar parked next to the curb outside a coffee shop called Cassie's Cuppa. It was small and adorable, with a striped green awning and a handful of tables inside that were already packed with college students.

We ordered coffees and Rock introduced me to Cassie, the owner of the store. She was surprisingly young and extremely beautiful, with long red hair tied into a ponytail and sparkling hazel eyes.

We chatted for a bit while the barista made our coffee, then headed back to the car.

"She's so young to have her own place," I said as we took off toward campus.

"Yeah, well, it helps when you're Bram Montgomery's little sister," Rock said.

"Who's Bram Montgomery?" I asked.

Oscar glanced in the rearview mirror, and I was almost positive he gave Rock a metaphorical kick under the table.

"Townie," Oscar said, a hint of warning in his voice. "One you don't want to mess with."

I sipped my coffee and chewed on that little tidbit.

"So how are we going to get that key?" Rock asked from the back seat.

Right. I was still on the hook for the game.

"How should I know? I have no idea how any of this

works. I've never even seen these medals everyone's talking about." Maybe if I played dumb, they'd consider me a liability for the games and never, ever assign me to one again.

"We need to find out who has the key first," Oscar said. "Neo's making a list of all the possibilities. We'll start there."

Ugh. I'd been so busy avoiding the guys over the weekend that I'd allowed myself to slip into denial. Now the reality came crashing back. The guys had clearly been working out preliminary details over the weekend, and they weren't going to give me a pass.

I was going to have to play their stupid game.

"What about Emma?" I asked. "You said you'd help me find out what happened to her."

"And we will," Oscar said without looking at me.

"Yeah? Well, it seems to me we're doing a lot of talking about a pissing contest while my sister is still missing. I'm only here to find out what happened to her."

"We're working on it," Rock said from the back seat.

I turned around to look at him. "You are?"

He nodded, meeting Oscar's eyes in the rearview mirror again. "Yeah."

They obviously had some kind of secret communication going on, communication that didn't involve me. "What have you found out?"

"Nothing we can talk about yet," Oscar said.

"Just trust us," Rock said.

I looked out the window. "Trust you. Right."

"Have we given you any reason not to trust us?" Rock asked.

I floundered for an example and couldn't find one, which

just made me more annoyed. I focused on the scenery outside instead of answering, until I remembered something.

"Hey, did you guys go out last night?" I'd heard a car outside just before midnight. When I'd looked out the window, it had been just in time to see the Hummer's taillights disappear down the long driveway.

Oscar pulled through the gates at Aventine. "Uh, yeah. We had an errand."

"An errand? At midnight on a Sunday?" I asked.

"Yep." The answer was curt, a clear signal that he wasn't going to say any more about it.

I couldn't see his eyes because of his sunglasses, but he was definitely hiding something, and Rock, who was usually good for a steady stream of cheerful conversation, was quiet.

Interesting.

We passed the admin building and kept going toward a cluster of matching stone buildings that dotted the rolling lawn.

My mom had been right. It was a stunning campus, like a real-life Hogwarts but with criminals instead of wizards. The sweeping lawns gave way to a ring of trees that acted as a natural barrier against the outside world. The sidewalks were dotted with kids walking their way to their first day of classes, most of them in couples or groups, all of them looking a lot more relaxed than I felt. If I hadn't known better, I might have believed Aventine was just like any other college on the first day of a new year.

"You have Psych first right?" Oscar said.

I narrowed my eyes at him. "How did you know that?"

He shrugged and somehow made the gesture look sexy as hell instead of apathetic. "I know a lot of things, tiger."

He pulled into the parking lot at the center of the stone buildings that housed classes and lectures. The lot was almost full, but Oscar slid the Audi into one of three empty spots up front.

We got out of the car and Oscar lifted a hand. "See you back here after class."

I started toward the cluster of buildings up ahead, then stopped walking when I realized Rock had fallen into step beside me.

I stopped walking. "What are you doing?"

"Going to class."

I narrowed my eyes. I was definitely getting paranoid, but who could blame me? "Where is your class?"

He sighed like I'd caught him stealing a cookie from the cookie jar. "Okay, it's back that way," he said, gesturing toward Oscar's retreating back. "But I'm going to walk you to class. I have plenty of time."

I glared up at him. "I don't need an escort to class."

"I know you don't need it, but it's something I want to do," he said.

"What if I don't want you to do it?"

Something hardened in his face, and I was reminded that for all his easygoing charm, he was still Rocco Barone, son of a notorious Mafia boss, criminal in training.

He was still dangerous.

"Too bad," he said, draping an arm around my shoulders. "Now let's go. You're going to be late."

Chapter 25

Willa

I would never admit it to Rock or Oscar, but I was glad Rock came with me to class. When we got to the lecture hall, every person in the room turned to stare, and they definitely weren't all friendly.

I watched in real time as some of their expressions shifted from malicious to neutral when they spotted Rock at my side. I was hoping for a spot in the back, one where everyone might forget about me, let me fade into the woodwork, but Rock clearly had something else in mind, and I forced myself to keep my head up as he led me down the stairs of the amphitheater-style lecture hall to the front.

"Maybe I should sit in the back," I muttered under my breath.

"No way," Rock said. "Our girl doesn't sit in the back. Our girl doesn't hide. She doesn't need to."

I didn't have time to debate his use of the phrase *our girl*. It was so certain, so... possessive. It should have annoyed the shit out of me. Instead, my pussy pulsed with hunger and I had to resist the urge to climb Rock like a tree.

He led me to the front row and waited while I got settled in one of the seats.

"See you after class," he said.

"What? No. You don't have to walk me around like a five-year-old on the first day of school." He'd swung his dick around enough to make it clear I was with him, with the Kings. I wasn't looking for a 24/7 escort.

He leaned down and kissed me on the lips before I knew what was happening. He even lingered there, the bastard, and I felt my mouth opening to him, felt the slide of his tongue on my lower lip.

My brain forgot we were surrounded by other students while my body screamed *MORE!*

He pulled away, grinning like he knew exactly what I was thinking. And he probably did. My face was hot. Hell, my whole body was on fire. I was surprised I didn't melt into a puddle of goo then and there.

"See you after class, kitten."

He walked away. No, *walked* wasn't the right word. The fucker *swaggered*, like he'd just added another notch to his belt buckle right in front of everyone.

I sighed and sunk lower in my seat, my face flaming. I felt like I'd been picked up by a tornado. Like Dorothy, I'd been dropped into a world where nothing made sense, where a new threat was around every corner and they didn't all look like threats.

Because Rock? Rock did things to my body that made me

feel like I couldn't trust myself any more than I could trust anyone else.

The side door to the lecture hall opened and a youngish guy walked across the stage toward a long desk where a laptop and projector were already set up. He was cute, with shaggy brown hair and enough scruff to look a little devilish.

He set down the stack of books and notebooks he'd been carrying. Then he took off his navy blazer and laid it across the table before scanning the lecture hall.

I watched as his gaze skimmed the crowd before coming to a stop on me. We locked eyes for a second, and I resisted the urge to squirm. Normally, I'd assume he was just a slightly older dude who saw something he liked.

It wasn't unusual, for me or any girl my age.

But the fact that we were at Aventine made me wonder if he had some kind of stake in the criminal world too, if he knew who I was, knew what my dad had done.

Great. The last thing I needed was to be worried about the teachers hating me too.

"Good morning," he said. "My name is Professor Ryan and I'll be your teacher for Psych 101."

He continued by explaining the curriculum and directing us to the Aventine portal to download the syllabus, and I spent the rest of the class focused on its requirements.

It felt good to think about something besides my family, besides Emma and what had happened to her, and I was surprised when he announced the end of class.

Everyone got up, gathering their stuff and talking as they made their way up the stairs and out the door. I took my time.

Rock had clearly escorted me to class as a warning to the other kids — a warning I appreciated even if I did pretend to hate his and Oscar's insistence on acting like my private security detail — but that didn't mean I wanted to test its effectiveness.

My plan for the first few days was to fly under the radar, get the lay of the land.

That, and get some alone time with Claire so we could talk about Emma, because no way was I trusting my search for answers to the Kings, no matter how appealing Rock and Oscar were.

"How's your first day going, Ms. Russo?"

I looked up and found Professor Ryan sitting at the edge of the lecture stage. He looked young and approachable, but I didn't miss the way his eyes briefly roamed my body before returning to my face.

"This is my first class," I said, "but so far, so good."

He nodded. "I'm glad to hear it." He hesitated. "I'm sure it's... difficult."

"Difficult?"

"Being here." He didn't say whether that was because of Emma or my dad, but either way, he was right. It was difficult.

"I'm managing," I said.

He smiled. "I'm happy to help if you ever need it. Just say the word. You can find my email on the portal."

"Thanks," I said.

"Willa." My name was spoken in a bark behind me, and I realized Rock had entered the lecture hall. He looked angry, but his gaze wasn't trained on me.

It was trained on Professor Ryan.

"Let's go," Rock said, his eyes still on the professor.

I was annoyed, but pride made me act like it was normal, like I was choosing to have Rock follow me around like a Rottweiler instead of being forced to endure it.

"See you Wednesday," I said to Professor Ryan.

I glared at Rock, then brushed past him and headed up the stairs.

Chapter 26

Willa

It was like that all day: Rock showing up at every class to walk me to the next one, staring down any guy who showed even friendly interest in me. By the time I reached my last class, I was more than annoyed, and I was relieved when the professor dismissed us early so I could head to the admin building on my own.

Turns out, my sociology professor was a bore. The only thing I was going to get out of a year with him was a nice daily nap. It had taken me all of fifteen minutes to decide to switch it out for anthropology, and for that I needed to go to the admin building.

Walking across campus on my own felt almost subversive after having Rock as my shadow all day. I second-guessed my decision to leave without texting the group chat — Rock was going to be pissed when he came to pick me up and realized I wasn't there — and felt a burst of frustration.

At myself.

Why did I care what Rock — or any of the Kings —

thought? Why did I care if they were mad because I broke one of the rules I never even agreed to follow?

I took a deep breath and headed across the lawn using the walkways that connected the buildings. The sun was shining, the temperature perfect. The trees that ringed the campus were just starting to change color, a few of the leaves tipped with yellow, and I was suddenly excited for fall, when everything would turn gold and the air would get crisp and cool.

Passing by other students on their way to and from class, I could almost believe I was just like everyone else at Aventine. I'd be thinking about whether it was too soon to start wearing boots and sweaters, about the cute guys in my class — the ones who weren't acting like wardens in a maximum-security prison.

But it was a fantasy. I was Willa Russo, daughter of a traitor, sister of a missing girl everyone seemed to have forgotten.

Except I wouldn't let them. I would do whatever it took to find out what had happened to Emma. I would pretend like I was here for school like everyone else while I quietly hunted for answers.

I would even play the Kings' stupid game.

But that didn't mean I had to like it.

I reached the admin building and followed the signs to the registration office. After ten minutes in line and another ten dropping sociology, I was on my way out of the building when I decided to double back to the second floor.

This was one of the few occasions when I actually had an

excuse to be "lost" in the admin building. I might as well use it to get the lay of the land.

The ground floor was a hub of student activity. I passed the ballroom where the welcome ball had taken place, then glanced into the cafeteria, a large high-ceilinged room with wood floors and round wood tables. It looked more like an upscale corporate dining room than a college cafeteria, but other than that, it was a surprisingly normal scene, with students talking, laughing, and goofing off while they ate.

I thought I spotted Claire and Quinn and hurried past the room. I wasn't looking to draw attention to myself and that was something I seemed to attract at Aventine without even trying — and not the good kind of attention either.

I passed a closed set of carved double doors with a gold plaque announcing the room beyond as the chess room. I'd been taught to play chess by my dad, but it wasn't something I'd kept up with, and the days of legendary chess matches at Aventine had faded with the advent of video games and social media.

Still, I was curious about the room rumored to be a breeding ground for rivalries and alliances that sometimes followed the students of Aventine for decades. My own father had been mortal enemies with a cartel boss named Felix Jiménez because of a particularly sly checkmate back when they'd gone to school here.

I continued past the bursar's office to the back stairs, and the noise fell behind me as I stepped into the stairwell and climbed my way to the second floor.

I emerged onto the familiar landing still clutching my drop form in case someone asked what I was doing. Then I remembered that the best way to avoid being asked questions when you were somewhere you didn't belong was to act like you do.

I marched down the hall like I knew where I was going, trying to take it slow enough that I could get a handle on all the different offices. There were a couple of people I'd never seen before at desks in the smaller offices, but Dean Giordana's office door was closed.

I hooked a left at the end of the hall, and the top of the main staircase came into view. It was busier here, with a handful of people coming and going on the wide curved staircase that started in the grand entry hall of the ground floor.

Note to self: use the back staircase unless you want to be seen.

I passed the staircase and made another left. This hall was almost empty, with a closed door labeled *Supply Closet* and two restrooms with signs that read *Staff*. I was reaching the end of the hall when murmuring voices caught my ear. They grew louder as I came closer to the place where I would either have to turn back or make another left, which would take me to the back staircase where the loop would start all over again.

I slowed my steps as I came to the open door that was the source of the noise.

It was a large room with several sofas and a couple tables surrounded by chairs. Light shone in from the windows on one wall, casting the room in a cozy afternoon glow that made it look like a nice place for teachers to relax between classes.

Which made sense, because this was obviously the professors' lounge.

The handful of people congregated in the room were too old to be students at Aventine, and I spotted my philosophy professor talking to an older woman near a coffee bar and refrigerator.

I did a quick scan of the room, practically slowing to a stop when I spotted Professor Ryan leaning forward in an oversized lounge chair, studying his iPad like it held the secrets to the universe.

And behind him? Well, behind him was a glass case, a row of gold medals lined up and on display.

I stepped into the room almost without thinking, then regretted it a second later when it grew silent.

"Thank god! I'm so glad you're here!" I said. Professor Ryan looked up from his iPad, and I started going through my bag as I came toward him, trying to act the part of flustered first-year student. "I just had a question about the syllabus."

"Young lady, you are not supposed to be in here," said the older woman who'd been talking to my philosophy professor.

"Oh... I'm sorry!" I said. "Dean Giordana told my stepfather, Roberto Alinari, that I shouldn't hesitate to ask the administration if I needed help."

The Alinari name worked like magic. The room grew even more quiet, the tension as thick as pea soup.

Professor Ryan jumped to his feet. He really was attractive for a professor, his dark eyes earnest, that stubble on his jawline bringing to mind rumpled sheets and breakfast in bed.

"This will only take a minute, I'm sure," he said to the

older woman before turning to me. "What can I do for you Ms. Russo?"

I scrolled through the syllabus on my iPad, scrambling for something that represented a valid question.

"Um... this says that class participation will be worth a third of our grade." I pointed to the screen. "But I'm not sure what that means exactly? Is that asking questions? Or just, like, listening?"

I hated myself for sounding stupid, but this was an emergency. The way to keep the Kings on my side was to play their game, and to play their game, I needed to help with the first challenge.

I'd been given a golden opportunity to do recon. No way was I passing it up.

I shoved my iPad at Professor Ryan and tapped at the place where it described the breakdown for grades, counting on the human inclination to look at something when someone pointed even when you knew what you'd see.

It worked. He leaned in, his gaze trailing over the screen to my index finger.

I used the time to look at the glass case, willing my mind to calculate every detail in the short amount of time I had in the lounge. I couldn't make out the words on the medals, but there were six of them, each with a photograph of two people shaking hands handing behind it.

My mind snagged on the other details, including the fact that there were no cameras. Then Professor Ryan was looking up at me and I realized his lips were moving and he was answering my question about class participation.

"Okay, got it," I said, registering the answer, which was

basically the answer any person of average intelligence would have guessed: an informal calculation of how engaged you are in class.

God, he must have thought I was a massive dipshit.

I wanted to die of embarrassment, but I was still glad I'd made the move. Now I knew where the medals were, and I knew something else about them too, something the Kings would want to know.

I thanked Professor Ryan profusely for taking the time to talk to me — noting the way he stared at me super hard, the way guys stare when they're willing themselves not to look at your boobs — and apologized to the other professors for barging into their lounge.

Then I got the hell out of there and booked if for the entrance to the admin building, my mind turning over what I'd seen and what it meant for the game.

It said a lot about how much my life had changed in the last few days that I wasn't even surprised when my phone dinged with a text from Oscar.

Where the hell are you? Oscar texted. **We had a deal.**

I typed as I crossed campus to the parking lot by the lecture halls. **YOU had a deal. I never agreed to anything.**

You didn't even wait for me after class.

That was from Rock, and I could almost hear the disappointment in his text.

We got out early.

Why was I explaining myself to them? I didn't owe them

anything. The only reason I was stuck to them like glue was because I didn't have a car and the Kings' house was in the middle of nowhere.

I spotted them way before I reached the parking lot: Oscar leaning against the Audi like some kind of fucking supermodel and Rock pacing like a mountain lion.

"I can't believe you ditched me," Rock said, shaking his head sadly.

I rolled my eyes. "I didn't ditch you. I needed to drop a class so I went to the admin building."

Oscar held the passenger door open, then stepped closer when I went to slide into the car. He smelled fantastic, like cologne and sweat and old books, and it went straight to my pussy like a thunderbolt.

"Don't do that again, tiger." He leaned closer, murmuring in my ear. "You might just earn yourself a spanking."

I suppressed a shiver and slid into the car, clamping my thighs together and ordering the lust galloping through my veins to stand the fuck down.

Oscar closed the door and walked around the driver's side. The car started with a sexy purr and Oscar backed out of the parking space.

"You're both making a big deal out of nothing," I said. "You're going to be thanking me in a few minutes."

"Why would we thank you for blowing us off?" Rock said from the back seat.

"Because I talked my way into the teachers' lounge while I was in the admin building and now I know who has a key to the case," I said.

"How can you know that just from visiting the lounge?"

Oscar asked, pulling onto the main road that ran through campus.

"Because I got a look at the case. There's no dust." It was a glass case, so I expected it to be cleaner than an open shelf. But not that clean. "I'm talking not a speck of dust, not even a smear on the glass."

For a few seconds, nobody said anything.

Oscar broke the silence. "The cleaning crew."

I nodded. "The cleaning crew."

Chapter 27

Willa

I was still thinking about the possibility of taking keys from the cleaning crew when we stepped into the kitchen from the garage and found an older woman bent over and studying the contents of the fridge.

She straightened when she heard us come in, her long gray hair a mass of waves around her lined face, a printed tunic flowing over her jeans. If her arms hadn't been stacked with an assortment of bracelets, some of them colorful and others clearly made of gold, I might have thought she was displaced and looking for food, which was why I was surprised when Rock's face broke into a grin, his arms opening for a hug.

"Reva!"

She came toward him with a grin. "There are my boys!"

She walked into his arms and I stood awkwardly by while she exchanged hugs and greetings with the guys.

"Reva, this is Willa," Oscar said when things calmed down. "Willa, Reva manages the house."

Now I understood. I'd been wondering how the Kings kept the house clean and in good repair. I couldn't imagine Neo cleaning a toilet or even calling for a plumber.

I smiled and held out my hand. "It's nice to meet you."

She laughed and pulled me into a sandalwood-and-patchouli scented hug. "I gave up handshakes with my Southern roots many moons ago, darlin'."

I heard the remnants of an accent in her voice when she said it.

Maybe I should have been annoyed to be hugged so enthusiastically by someone I barely knew, but I found myself squeezing her back. It had been a long time since I'd been hugged by a woman. My own mother wasn't a hugger. She was a fixer, a judger, someone who showed her love by telling me all the things I did wrong, all the ways I was making life harder for myself.

I almost didn't want to let go when Reva pulled back to look at me. "Wow! You are a beauty," she said. "No wonder these boys want you here."

"That's not why," Neo grumbled, heading for the fridge.

Reva lifted a mischievous eyebrow and turned to Oscar as he asked about her summer.

I headed for the back stairs, not wanting to intrude on their reunion, and spent the rest of the afternoon going over my notes from class and organizing my homework.

Later that night, I sat at the kitchen island while Rock made dinner (some kind of pasta with chicken and sun-dried tomatoes that made my mouth water). We'd been talking about the key and the cleaning crew, and I didn't know why I was surprised when the guys went from zero to sixty by suggesting we break into the house of the cleaning lead.

"Can't we just lift them off the crew while they're cleaning?" I asked. I was not down for a B&E charge, or for scaring some innocent person half to death if they found us digging around their house.

"Cameras," Neo said.

It was how he always talked to me. Short. To the point. Not an ounce of friendliness.

I hadn't seen him all day, and I'd almost forgotten how much his attitude toward me got under my skin. The fact that he looked good enough to eat in gray sweats and a white tank top that showed off every one of his stupid muscles only made it worse.

"Only on the first floor," I pointed out.

Rock turned off the heat under the skillet and reached for the plates he'd stacked on the counter. "They'll pick us up on the way in. It's too risky after hours when the rest of the student body isn't there to give us cover."

"Right." I chewed my lip.

"We can figure out who's cleaning the building by staking it out at night," Oscar said.

"Yeah, but then what?" I asked.

"Whoever it is will probably be asleep during the day," Neo said, opening the fridge. "You and Rock can be in and out and have the keys back before they wake up."

"Except that means breaking and entering." I eyed the pasta Rock was piling on three plates. "And stealing the medals during the day."

Neo shut the refrigerator door and set an already prepared salad with chicken on the island. "Yep."

"But that's... that's crazy," I said, remembering all the people milling around the admin building. The second floor was quieter for sure, but it wasn't empty.

"It's doable," Neo said, digging into the salad as Rock set plates of pasta in front of Oscar and me.

"You don't like pasta?" I asked Neo. He had me skittish as a cat, afraid he would rip my head off every time we interacted, but I wasn't going to let him know that.

"He likes pasta," Rock said. "Just not tonight."

I thought about the Hummer's disappearing headlights the night before, Oscar's cryptic answer when I'd asked if they'd left the house at midnight.

What the fuck were these three up to?

"Think any of the other teams are close?" Oscar asked just before shoving a bite of pasta into his mouth.

Neo shook his head. "Nah. It's only been two days since Game Night. Even if the other teams have figured out who has the keys — and I don't think they have — they're going to be pussies about breaking in to someone's house to get them."

"Pussies are strong and resilient," I said.

Neo looked at me like I had two heads. "What the fuck are you talking about?"

"You said they would be pussies, implying they're weak, but pussies are strong and resilient," I said.

"She's right," Rock said, taking his first bite of food.

The way Neo glared made me second-guess giving him a lesson in feminism, which was why I was pretty fucking shocked when he nodded.

"Point taken." He stared at me for a beat longer than was comfortable, and my panties dampened between my thighs before he pulled his eyes away from mine and looked at Rock and Oscar. "So we need to plan a stakeout, figure out which member of the crew has the keys."

I finished chewing the bite in my mouth and looked at Rock. "This is amazing."

The pasta was perfectly cooked, with a tiny bit of chew and a creamy sauce that contrasted with the bite of the sun-dried tomatoes and minced olives in the dish.

He grinned. "Glad you like it. Gotta keep our girl properly fueled." The innuendo was clear in his voice.

I rolled my eyes. "Do you think Dean Giordana has an extra set of keys?" I asked. "Maybe that will be an easier way to get in."

Neo looked at me, his eyes cold. "Would you rather break into the dean's house or the house of some exhausted off-campus custodian?"

I sighed and stabbed another bite of pasta with my fork. "Fine."

I spent the rest of the meal listening to them plot the stakeout of the cleaning crew, grateful for a second helping of Rock's pasta, which gave me an excuse not to participate.

Maybe I was still in denial about the fact that I'd have to participate in the game, but I'd had enough talk about it for one day. I was groaning by the time I was done, but it was worth it for both the amazing food and the pleasure on Rock's face when I finished the second plate.

"Finally!" he said. "Someone who appreciates my cooking."

"I'm going to appreciate my way out of my jeans," I said, standing.

He took my plate, then unabashedly squeezed my ass. "Fine with me."

I had a weird feeling he meant it. That he... *liked* me? And Oscar too.

My world really had turned upside down.

"I have homework," I said, starting for the back stairs. The other guys in the house were playing video games in the living room, and another string of insults from Enzo was the last thing I needed.

On my way out of the room, I noticed a black duffel bag on the floor next to the garage door. I tried not to make a big deal of it even though it was unusual — the guys worked out at the house in the fully equipped gym on the second floor — but when I got upstairs I stripped out of the shorts and T-shirt I'd put on after school.

I dug through my drawers in a hurry, searching for something practical, and came up with artfully ripped jeans and a cropped black T-shirt. I grabbed my chunky black ankle boots and set them by the door, then pulled my hair out of the messy bun I'd thrown it into after school, opting instead for a high ponytail that wouldn't get in the way.

I had no idea what the guys were up to at night, but I intended to find out.

I listened by the door and felt victorious when I heard the Kings' voices in the hall outside my room. I'd guessed they weren't leaving right after dinner. Neo had been wearing sweats, and it didn't seem like his style to leave the house in them.

The stick up his ass wouldn't have allowed it.

Their voices disappeared as they went into their individual rooms. I waited another minute. Once I was pretty sure they weren't going to burst back into the hall, I picked up my boots and slipped out of my room, feeling like a thief as I hurried down the back stairs.

Chapter 28

Willa

I'd never been more grateful for video games in my life. The guys were still playing, some kind of shooter game, and the noise gave me all the cover I needed to slip into the garage in my socks.

I blinked when the light nearest the door came on by itself.

Fuck. I hadn't thought about the fact that the lights were on a motion sensor. I would have to hurry and get settled well before the guys came into the garage.

I took a few seconds to slip on my boots and hurried past the smaller cars. I was betting whatever the guys were up to at night, they were up to together.

That meant the Hummer, even though I had no idea why Neo didn't like the smaller cars.

I opened the hatch and cursed when I realized there was nothing to give me cover. All the blankets from Game Night had been taken into the house. There wasn't so much as a gym bag back there, which made sense when I thought about the fact that it seemed to be Neo's car. Like everything in his life, the Hummer was immaculate.

I reconsidered my plan, my eyes darting to the other cars. I could try to follow them, but that seemed stupid. The house was isolated, and Blackwell Falls wasn't exactly a metropolis. Plus, I had zero experience tailing someone. I wasn't dumb enough to think I'd be any good at it.

I climbed into the back of the Hummer. I would have to take my chances and hope they didn't open the hatch.

I curled up in the back and exhaled my relief when the lights in the garage went off a minute later.

I settled in to wait, the garage quiet, a perfect cocoon isolated from the rest of the house. I was starting to think I'd made a mistake — maybe the guys weren't going anywhere after all — when one of the lights came on.

I heard Rock's voice first. "I'm just saying, we're going to have to tell her eventually."

I froze, wondering what they were talking about, and this time it was Neo who spoke, his voice louder now that they were closer to the Hummer.

"We've been over this. It's too soon," he said.

They were right on top of the Hummer now, and I held my breath, willing them to just *get in the fucking car already*.

Except that's not what happened next. What happened next was that the hatch flew open, and I had a front row seat to the brief expression of surprise on Neo's face before it turned murderous.

"What the *fuck?*"

"What?" Rock's voice was distant, but a second later his face appeared next to Neo's, followed by Oscar's, his camera in one hand.

I sat up, more annoyed by my loss of dignity than the fact that I'd been discovered. "You won't tell me anything!"

Oscar looked mildly disappointed, which bothered me more than it should have. "That's no excuse, tiger. This could have been dangerous for you."

"I'm not some kind of fainting virgin who needs to be kept safe from the world," I said. "I've actually been out in it. Alone. And I did just fine."

Rock held up a finger. "One, glad to hear about the virgin thing. I prefer a girl with experience." He held up another finger. "Two, we know you're a strong person, Willa. But you have no idea what you could be getting into sneaking into one of our cars, especially this time of night."

I crossed my arms over my chest. "Then why don't you tell me?"

"Out," Neo said, standing back to give me room to exit the Hummer. He'd changed into black track pants and a black T-shirt, and he looked even bigger and more menacing from my position on my ass in the Hummer. "Get out and go back in the house."

"No," I said. What was he going to do? Murder me? "I'm not yours to order around."

His face turned red, the nerve in his jaw jumping until I thought his head might explode. "So help me, Jezebel, if you don't get out of the car, you're going to feel my hand on your ass when I throw you over my shoulder and carry you back into the house."

The threat should have scared me — he really did look like he was on the verge of violence — but instead I had a flash of Neo's hand on my ass.

Spanking my ass, that is.

I didn't hate the image. Like, at all. In fact, my panties were wet, and a persistent throbbing had started in my pussy.

"Either you explain where you're going, or you take me with you," I said.

Neo squeezed his fist in the other hand and turned away, pacing to the garage door while he muttered a string of curses.

"You should go inside," Rock said. "This isn't a good night for him to lose his cool. Not yet anyway."

"What's that supposed to mean?" I asked.

Neo stalked back toward me. "Get in the back seat, *Jezebel*. You want to come, you can come. Don't say we didn't warn you."

The threat sent a flutter of nervousness to my belly, but there was no backing out now.

I climbed out of the Hummer and Neo threw the black duffel into the back.

Right. The duffel. I should have known he'd open the hatch.

Oh well. It didn't matter. I'd wormed my way into this... whatever this was.

Neo got into the driver's seat and Oscar climbed in next to me while Rock took shotgun. I was surprised when Oscar took my hand, and I was even more surprised when I didn't pull away.

Was it my imagination that he looked worried?

Sadie Hunt

I tried not to think it, tried not to think about the warning in Neo's voice as he backed out of the garage and started away from the house.

Don't say we didn't warn you.

Chapter 29

Willa

At first I thought they'd just been trying to scare me. We entered the town of Blackwell Falls, which looked as cute as ever after dark. The old-fashioned street lamps that lined Main Street cast cozy light on the upscale brick storefronts, and there wasn't another car in sight.

But we kept going, and the town suddenly started looking a whole lot less cozy.

Here the buildings looked seedy and rundown, more than a few of them vacant. People loitered on the corners and in the shadows, all of them casting a long stare at the Hummer as Neo drove past.

I was suddenly nervous, and I had to remind myself that the windows were tinted and it was unlikely anyone could see me in the back seat with Oscar.

A few minutes later, even that part of town seemed nice. This part of Main Street didn't even look like the same town as the one where Oscar and I had grabbed sandwiches last week, where I'd gone with Rock and Oscar to get coffee at Cassie's Cuppa that morning.

Here, the buildings were all abandoned, most them made of crumbling brick. They rose two and three stories into the night sky, and I wondered if Blackwell Falls had been a manufacturing hub at some point. The buildings looked like old factories, large window frames empty or filled with broken glass.

"What is this place?" I asked.

"This is the part of town I warned you about," Oscar said next to me.

"Just remember," Neo said from the front, "you asked to come."

"I know," I snapped. I didn't need Neo Alinari thinking I was scared. "It's fine. I'm just asking."

Neo slowed the car, and I realized that I'd been wrong: not all of the buildings were abandoned. More often than not, I could spot faint light behind the people standing around on the sidewalk.

"Are these underground clubs?" I asked. "Raves?"

"Something like that," Rock said.

We slowed to a stop in front of a glass-fronted building with a large marquee: an old movie theater.

The marquee was empty, but an unlit sign loomed above the place announcing it as the Orpheum. Through the glass, I could see people moving inside, shadows in the darkened interior.

Neo shut off the car. "Let's go."

I reached for the door handle to get out, but he beat me to it, opening my door from the outside.

Kings & Corruption

"Thanks," I said, getting out of the car.

He didn't say anything, but he grabbed my arm hard enough to pinch.

Hard enough to make me wet.

He glared down at me. And honestly? I wouldn't have been surprised if someone watching would have seen flames leaping from his eyes.

And not just flames of hatred either. He was as attracted to me as I was to him, and he obviously hated it just as much.

"Stay with Rock and Drago," he said coldly. "No matter what."

I wrenched my arm away. "Okay."

He stared me down. "I mean it, Jezebel. You shouldn't be here."

"So you've said." I tried to flounce away, then realized I had no idea where I was or what we were doing here.

Luckily, Rock came to my rescue by taking my arm and guiding me toward the glass doors. He laughed. "You should just fuck him already and get it over with."

I looked up at him in surprise. "You wouldn't care?"

I wondered if it was my imagination that his jaw tightened a little. "I mean, don't get me wrong, I'd like to get there first — or even at the same time — but that's your call."

At the same time...

The words caused all kinds of dirty, filthy, *hot* images to fill my mind. I shoved them down as we pushed through the glass doors of the old movie theater, because this was clearly not the time for erotic fantasies about fucking the three Kings.

"Well, you don't have to worry, because I hate Neo

Alinari with the fire of a thousand suns. Not only would I not fuck him first, I wouldn't fuck him if he was the last man on earth."

Rock's laughter was a low sexy rumble. "If you say so, kitten."

By the time we stepped into the theater, Oscar and Neo were on our heels, and I have to say, I was glad even though I wouldn't have admitted it.

Colored lights swept the lobby, music thumping from somewhere beyond it. It would have been cool if not for the people staring at me with a combination of hatred and hunger.

Correction: the men staring at me with a mixture of hatred and hunger.

There were a few women in the mix, but it was mostly men, and these men did not look like college boys, not even like college boys from Aventine, who admittedly weren't like most college boys.

Most of the men inside the theater were older, their clothing a mix of jeans and leather jackets and combat boots that looked like they'd already stomped more than a few heads.

They had the weather-worn faces of men who'd seen a lot of bad things — who'd done a lot of bad things — and most of them were bearded on a scale from obvious scruff to biker Santa Claus.

Rock nodded at a few people as we weaved our way through the crowd, and it wasn't lost on me that Neo and Oscar stayed close at our backs.

We were past the old concession stand and on our way

down a long hall that led to the old theaters when a leviathan of a man stepped in front of us to block our way.

"Is there a problem, Bear?" Rock asked good-naturedly.

"Do I need to frisk you?" the other man asked. His dark beard was thick and full, his face creased with lines that might have been from the sun or age or both. I had no idea if he was a weathered thirty-five or an edgy, well-preserved sixty.

"Fuck no," Rock said, shouting a little to be heard over the music. "We know the rules."

The man named Bear crossed his giant arms over a chest that was at least twice as wide as my body. "Did you know the rules when you sent Tex to the hospital last time?"

"That wasn't our fault," Rock said. "He threw the first punch. I just happened to have a bottle in my hand. It wasn't meant to be a weapon."

Bear narrowed his eyes. "Are you saying he ran into your beer bottle?"

"I'm saying we don't have any weapons, but feel free to frisk us if you want," Rock said.

The man turned his attention to me, his eyes roving my body. "Maybe I should frisk your new toy."

Before I knew what had happened, Neo had inserted himself between me and Bear. I couldn't see Neo's face, but I heard the threat in his voice. "Touch her and you die."

I heard the man laugh. "This one must be special."

My brain was misfiring. Neo Alinari threatening someone to keep me safe? Probably some kind of pissing contest where Neo wanted to prove that like everything at Aventine, I belonged to the Kings.

"You going to frisk us or not?" Neo asked. "I have to get ready."

"Go ahead," Bear said. "But don't start any trouble. You're already on thin ice."

"Restitution is supposed to wipe the slate," Oscar said, coming up on my other side. The camera around his neck did nothing to make him look less intimidating and a whole lot to make him look sexy af.

I was flanked by the Kings now — Neo in front of me, Rock still holding my arm on my left, Oscar on my right — and I have to say, it felt damn good. It felt safe, even though there was nothing about this situation, nothing about trusting the Kings, that was safe.

"It does," Bear said. "On paper. In reality, you three are always a fucking hurricane."

"Hurricanes are necessary," Oscar said. "They clear the air."

"Yeah? Well they also leave a fucking mess." Bear stepped aside to let us pass and I watched as he looked at Neo. "Good luck." His gaze swept to me. "And keep an eye on your pet. The other boys might want to play."

He laughed as we continued past him and I resisted the urge to give him the finger. I was getting really fucking tired of being treated like some kind of trust fund princess when I'd faced more shit in the past five years than the Kings ever had.

I wasn't a swollen giant, and I wasn't packing heat, but I was fairly confident I could take care of myself if a situation went bad.

We continued down the hall, past the entrance to several

old auditoriums. People came and went from them but we were clearly headed for the large double doors open at the end of the hall.

The music grew louder, a vibration I could feel in my feet and chest. We were almost to the doors when Neo peeled off.

"Where's he going?" I shouted up at Rock.

"Change."

I didn't know if that meant he was going to get change or if he was going to change his clothes — under the circumstances, either scenario was weird — but the music was too loud to ask any more questions.

I was glad Rock still had my arm in his hand as we stepped through the door. I might have stopped in my tracks otherwise. As it was, I had no choice but to be propelled along by Rock's momentum as I took in the massive theater.

The seats had all been removed, and people stood around in groups talking and drinking and dancing on the slightly sloped floor while *Casino* played on the screen at the front of the theater.

I knew it was *Casino*, because I'd watched it with my mom more than once. She'd always laughed at the scene where Sharon Stone ties her kid to the bed so she can go party.

The volume on the movie was off, replaced by the ear-shattering music thumping from speakers next to a DJ booth next to the screen. As with the lobby, multicolored lights swung around the big space, and somehow a bar had been set up along one wall.

"What is this place?" I shouted up at Oscar.

He shook his head, indicating that he couldn't hear me,

and I gave up and soaked it all in as people came up to shake hands with him and Rock. The crowd was more varied than it had been in the lobby. There were still a bunch of biker dudes, but there were also quite a few people who looked like townies, and a handful I would have bet were students from Bellepoint or Aventine trying and failing to fit in.

I was scanning the room, taking it all in, when my gaze snagged on a guy leaning against the wall in the shadows. He was covered in ink, his muscled arms adorned with full sleeves, visible in his sleeveless black shirt. He had dark hair and high cheekbones, but his expression was completely blank.

And he was staring right at me.

He was gorgeous in an animalistic sort of way, but looking into his dark eyes left me cold.

I felt a ripple of fear and turned away, glad to be next to Rock and Oscar.

I bounced along to the music, feeling the vibe. I'd been to lots of underground clubs when I'd been traveling, and I'd always loved how insulated I'd felt from the rest of the world. Out of time. Like there was no place else in the world but that room and those people. In a room like that, I wasn't Emma's sister or Frank's daughter.

I wasn't even Willa.

I was nobody, and sometimes it was really liberating to be nobody.

I looked over and spotted Oscar pointing his camera at me. I smiled, and a second later, he lowered the camera. His eyes met mine through the darkness, the lights sweeping over his face, and I felt the pull of his body, a gravitational force I wasn't sure I even wanted to resist.

Then someone came up and leaned in to talk to him and the spell was broken.

I was debating the wisdom of grabbing a drink from the bar — when in Rome — when a groan went up from the crowd. The movie had glitched, the image warping before the screen turned black.

"I got this," Oscar said. He took my hand. "Come on, tiger. You're with me."

Chapter 30
Willa

Oscar pulled me through the crowd back into the hallway. It was packed, and it seemed like everyone was moving toward the big theater at the end of the hall, migrating in one direction like a pack of wolves.

We came to a black door about halfway down the hall. Oscar opened it and ushered me through, then shut the door behind us.

It was quieter in here, a tiny vestibule and a set of long narrow stairs leading upward, the music just a beat beyond the painted black walls.

"After you," Oscar said, gesturing to the stairs.

I narrowed my eyes. "I feel like you either want to look at my ass or you're planning to cut me into a million pieces while everyone dances out there."

He grinned. "It's the ass, for sure."

I sighed and started up the stairs. When I reached the

top, I stepped right into a large messy room. I knew right away what it was.

"This is the projection room," I said, walking toward the wall of glass.

"Yep," Oscar said, heading for the machinery in front of the big window.

The music was louder here than it had been in the vestibule, but still muted, and the crowd I'd been part of a few minutes before looked like ants as they moved through the lights crisscrossing the theater.

"You guys don't get in trouble for using this place?" I asked.

"No."

Typical. Getting information out of the Kings was proving to be a challenge.

I wandered the room, picking up dusty black cases marked with the names of movies from the 90s and setting them back down, inspecting old schedules that listed movie times, while he worked on the projector.

By the time I made my way back to the big window, *Casino* was back onscreen, a small plane landing on a lush green golf course, Joe Pesci trying to hit it with golf balls while two men in suits ran away.

"Do you pick the movies?" I turned around and found Oscar pointing the camera at me again. "Why are you taking pictures of me?"

He took another, lowered the camera, and stared at me. "Because you're beautiful. And because I like looking at you."

It had been a mistake, coming to the projection room with

Oscar Drago. The air was charged with the chemistry that had been crackling between us, the muffled music making it feel like we were in a world of our own.

There was no one else around. No witnesses to pressure me into making good decisions.

He set down the camera and stalked toward me, his combat boots thudding ominously on the old floors, his dark eyes a well of lust I was already drowning in.

There was no preamble. No buildup.

He plowed into me, shoving me back against the glass of the projector room, his mouth closing over my mine while his hands snaked into my hair.

He dove into my mouth, the smooth metal of his stud sliding against my tongue as he twisted his hand in my hair, yanking my head back to take the kiss deeper. He was already hard, his dick pressed against my stomach, and I whimpered into his mouth as his hands traveled down my neck and over my chest until he found the hem of my cropped T-shirt.

Thankfully, it didn't take long for him to lift it, exposing my boobs, because I was on fire for him. The part of my brain that should have objected — that would no doubt give me a nice long lecture tomorrow — had officially left the building. At that moment, there was literally nothing in the world I wanted more than Oscar Drago's mouth on my tits and his cock in my cunt.

He complied a second later — on the first one at least — tearing his lips from mine and yanking down the cups of my bra, which was right about the time I realized I was up against the glass.

"We can't," I said. "The window…"

Kings & Corruption

"It's tinted," he muttered. "No one can see a thing."

It was all I needed to hear. My head dropped back against the glass as he closed his mouth around one of my pebbled nipples, using one of his free hands to tease the other one between his fingers.

I moaned long and low as the smooth metal of his tongue and lip piercings warred for attention with the suppleness of his lips. The contrast against my skin was so erotically charged I could already feel the orgasm building in my pussy, helped along by the fact that Oscar's thick cock was pressed against my thigh, a reminder that he was only inches from being inside me.

He scraped his teeth lightly over my nipple, then sucked hard to draw it into his mouth. I gasped with pleasure and he slid a hand into the waistband of my jeans. The heat of his palm against my hairless pussy sent a shudder of greedy need through my body, and a second later I sighed as he sank his finger inside me.

"You're so fucking wet," he murmured, lifting his face to mine. His breath was a whisper against my cheek, his eyes glazed with the same mindless hunger roaring through my veins. "I knew you would be."

His finger was working magic on my pussy, his thumb making rhythmic circles around my clit. I was desperate for more skin on skin contact, and I reached for the button on his jeans, ready to feel his dick in my hand.

He grabbed my wrist. "Not this time, tiger."

"I want to feel you," I demanded. "I want you to fuck me."

A low chuckle rumbled from his mouth. "I'm going to

take my time the first time I fuck you. It's not happening like this. Just enjoy it. Let me watch you come."

I should have been disappointed. Instead, it was like I'd been granted a permission slip, and I rocked my hips to the rhythm of his finger moving in and out of my soaking pussy, seeking the friction of his thumb against my clit, climbing toward the promise of release.

I thought it was as good as it could get until he added another finger to the one already inside me, his thumb still working my clit.

I closed my eyes and rode his hand, letting the pressure build at the center of my body.

"Good girl," Oscar coached, adding a third finger to the two already occupying my pussy. "Now come for me."

The words released the last of what little control I had left. I came *hard*, my pussy clamping around his fingers, my body shuddering as the waves of my orgasm washed over me again and again.

A string of filthy words erupted in my head.

Or were they actually coming from my mouth?

I might have said he was so fucking good. I might have said I'd kill him if he stopped. I might even have told him I was going to suck his cock next time.

I wasn't quite sure what was in my head and what I actually said out loud. All I knew was that I was out of my mind, drunk on pleasure, every filter I'd cultivated to keep Oscar Drago at bay obliterated by the ecstasy rolling through my body.

I came to with my head against the glass, Oscar dropping kisses on my jawline.

I slowly opened my eyes as I became aware of what had just happened. I'd let Oscar Drago finger me into oblivion in the projector room of the Orpheum, and I'd made absolutely no secret about the fact that he'd rocked my world with nothing but his mouth and his fingers.

I felt the vibration of his knowing chuckle through my own chest. "Don't start regretting it yet."

Dammit. How did this fucking guy know me that well already?

"I'm not," I lied. Well, it wasn't totally a lie. A girl would have to be crazy to regret such a mind-blowing orgasm. It was the stuff that went along with it I was worried about.

He kissed me on the lips. "Give me a sec."

The music was still thumping in the theater below, and I watched while he searched the room for something. A few seconds later, he came up with a roll of those hard brown paper towels used in public bathrooms.

"Sorry these aren't softer," he said, tearing off a sheet.

I wondered if he kept them up here for his sexual escapades, if I wasn't the first girl he'd ever fingered or fucked in the projection room, then forced myself not to think about it. The thought made me want to rage, and I didn't have the time to lecture myself about how ridiculous that was.

The only thing worse than letting Oscar finger me into oblivion was catching feelings for him. I could forgive the primitive needs of my body, but my mind knew better.

"May I?" he asked, holding up the piece of paper towel he'd ripped off the roll.

"I got it." I took it from his hand and cleaned myself up. I was crashing back into reality hard, and what was the first thing on my mind? My sister and how this would complicate my work with the Kings to find her?

No, Rock Barone and how this would complicate *that* situation.

"Is there a...?" I looked around for a trash can.

"I got it." Oscar took the paper towel from me, folded it neatly, and slipped it into his pocket.

I straightened my clothes and found him staring at me. "What?"

He grinned. "Just thinking about how good it's going to feel to finally fuck you."

"Why didn't you then?"

He looked offended. "Because you're not some mindless hookup, tiger. I thought you knew that."

I didn't like how the words made me feel, all warm and fuzzy.

He walked toward me and held my face in his hand, then came in for a hot, demanding kiss. I was already weak in the knees from Oscar's magic fingers, but that kiss? That kiss just about finished the job. I was surprised I hadn't melted onto the nasty-ass protection room floor.

"When I fuck you, it's going to be someplace we can both enjoy it, someplace I can take my time, not up against a window at the fucking Orpheum," he said, his voice raw and husky.

"What if I change my mind and don't let you fuck me at all?" It suddenly felt important to remind him — to remind myself — that this wasn't a done deal. I wasn't going to ride off into the sunset with Oscar fucking Drago.

He stroked my lower lip with his thumb while he stared into my eyes. His gaze was mesmerizing, and I fought to stay coherent. "Is that what you want? To change your mind?"

"What about Rock?" I regretted the question as soon as I asked it — this wasn't about Rock — but it was the thing that came out of my mouth while I was trying to avoid the other conversation I was trying not to have.

Oscar stepped away, and I have to admit, I hated it. I wanted him close again, preferably on top of me — or under me — while we were both naked. "What about him?"

I tried to formulate the words to explain my concern about Rock. I wasn't committed to him. I wasn't committed to anyone. I could do whatever I wanted and whoever I wanted.

But Rock had been nice to me, and there was a big part of me that was just as eager to be naked with Rock Barone as I was to be naked with Oscar.

I decided honesty was the best policy. Whenever possible anyway.

"I like him," I said. "I don't want him to think I went behind his back with one of his best friends."

"No need to keep this a secret," Oscar said. "We're big boys, and you don't have to worry about me asking you to marry me for at least a year."

I rolled my eyes but he actually didn't look like he was joking.

"And if I decided to... pursue things with Rock?" I asked.

"Go right ahead," Oscar said. "I'll be jealous as hell, but if I have to share you, I'd rather it be with Rock or Neo."

I grimaced at the mention of Neo. "Ew. I'll pass on Neo."

Oscar laughed and reached for my hand. "Never say never, tiger. Come on, we're going to be late."
"Late? For what?"
He pulled me toward the stairs. "The fight."

Chapter 31

Willa

I didn't have time to ask questions. We were down the stairs and back in the hall leading to the theater with a crowd that had tripled in size since we'd made out way upstairs to fix the movie.

The music was still loud, *Casino* back onscreen as we stepped into the dark theater. We couldn't have been gone for more than half an hour, but the mood in the room had changed. Before, it had felt like a party, everyone dancing and drinking and making eyes at each other.

Now, the room felt tense in spite of the music and lights, and everyone was moving toward the front of the theater while leaving an empty space between the crowd and the screen.

Oscar held on to my hand and led me to the front where Rock was talking to a skinny guy with a mohawk and more hardware in his face than a Home Depot.

Rock leaned in and said something to him and the guy looked nervously around before slipping into the crowd.

Rock turned to face us, took one look at me, and shook his head. "I fucking knew it," he shouted over the movie.

I slapped Oscar's arm. "Jesus! Did you text him on the way down the stairs?"

He looked wounded. "I don't kiss and tell, tiger."

"I know a post-orgasm face when I see it," Rock shouted over the music.

I looked around, but no one was paying attention and it was doubtful anyone would have been able to hear the exchange over the music anyway.

Rock lifted his hand in the air and Oscar slapped it with a grin.

"Are you *high-fiving* because Oscar just made me come in the projector room?" I shouted.

They didn't have a chance to answer. A second later, Neo appeared next to Rock in nothing but shorts and sneakers, the angel on his god-like chest already glistening with sweat. I had to force myself to yank my eyes away from the trail of dark hair that led under the waistband of his shorts.

"You ready?" Rock asked him.

Neo bounced on his feet a little. "Ready."

"Remember, Marvin wears those fucking boots when he fights," Rock said. "Watch his legs and feet."

"Fucking dumbass," Neo said. "The boots make him slow."

"Yeah, well, they'll also make your ears ring if he lands a kick to the head," Rock said, looking at something past Oscar's head. "Here he comes."

I followed Rock's gaze and saw a giant barreling through

the crowd, parting it like the Red Sea as he came toward the front of the theater.

"Who is that?" I asked Oscar. I'd gotten used to shouting over the music.

"That's Marvin," Oscar said. "But he fights under the name Mayhem."

I looked back at Neo, who suddenly seemed vulnerable in nothing but shorts when the monster lumbering toward him was wearing jeans and a T-shirt with some savage-looking combat boots.

"Here?" I asked. "Where are the gloves? Where's the ring?"

"Street fight," Oscar said simply.

Oh my god... these dumb assholes were going to get killed. Or more accurately, Neo, the original dumb asshole, was going to get killed.

I should have enjoyed the thought of Neo being chewed up and spit out like prime ground beef, but I was suddenly nervous for him. Marvin's body wasn't the only thing that was enormous — his feet looked to be the size of Neo's head.

Rock was right: one blow with those boots and Neo might never remember his name again. Don't get me wrong, I was all for a Neo Alinari personality adjustment, but strangely, I didn't want to see him drooling out of the side of his mouth.

The music dropped a couple hundred decibels and Rock and Oscar moved into the space the crowd had created near the screen. Safe to say this wasn't the first time a fight like this had happened at the Orpheum. I remembered the bruise on Neo's face at the wedding, the dried blood on his knuckles a few days before, and it all made sense.

A woman stepped from the crowd and everybody stopped talking all at once. The mood in the theater turned reverent, all eyes on her.

She was about my mom's age, but where my mom took pains to hide her age behind artfully applied makeup and a figure that reflected hours at the gym, the woman standing in front of the screen had done nothing to hide the creases in her face or the roundness of her body.

Her hair was bottle blonde, and she was at least a foot shorter than Marvin, who had a couple inches on Neo. There was something hard about her face, something that scared me a little. I understood why she commanded the attention of everyone in the room even though this particular crowd didn't exactly seem soft.

"Welcome to the Orpheum!" Her voice was a raspy echo in the large room. "Tonight's match is between pretty boy Neo here and our very own Mayhem. Usual rules apply."

"Tell 'em, Marge!" someone yelled from the crowd.

She looked from Neo to Marvin, and I waited for her to explain the rules. Instead she only said one thing. "Don't be dicks."

She stepped back and the crowd seemed to do the same, making more room in front of the screen, still playing *Casino*, as Neo and Marvin moved into the empty space.

They started circling each other, the crowd already cheering and shouting. I glanced up at Oscar, who had lifted his camera to take a picture of the scene.

"What are the rules?" I asked.

"There aren't any," he said without lowering the camera.

I was wrapping my head around the answer when

Marvin landed a fast hard punch to the left side of Neo's face. After that, everything moved quickly, a flurry of hands and feet and grappling that I struggled to see as the crowd got more worked up, surging the arena, shouting and cheering with every punch and kick.

I'd never been into boxing, which was fine, I guess, because this wasn't boxing. Oscar was right: there were no rules, just two men trying to beat each other bloody any way they could.

I couldn't have articulated technique or anything, but as I watched, I started to pick up on some of the nuances. Neo had been right about Marvin being slow. He was massive, and he had trouble keeping up with Neo's footwork.

And there was a lot of footwork. Neo wasn't quite as enormous as Marvin, but he was still a big guy, and I was impressed with how light he was on his feet. It was obvious he was trying to tire Marvin out, forcing him to work around Neo's constant movement.

Blood dripped down Neo's left cheek from the first punch, but he looked otherwise undamaged, unbothered, despite the flurry of kicks and punches that were exchanged between him and Marvin.

I could tell Neo was trying to avoid Marvin's feet and the combat boots. It worked for a while, but then Neo went in for a punch to Marvin's kidney. Marvin winced when it landed — he was obviously already tired from moving his hulking body around Neo's lighter one — but a second later his leg came up in a savage kick to Neo's chest.

Neo stumbled backwards. I couldn't hear anything over the roar of the crowd, but the expression on his face made it seem like he might be wheezing, struggling to catch his breath.

The crowd shifted, and I lost sight of Neo as they cheered even louder.

Oscar was still taking pictures, so I tugged on Rock's arm. "Is he okay?"

I thought maybe he hadn't heard me when he didn't answer, but a split second later, he lifted me onto his wide shoulders like I was a kid at the country fair.

Now I could see that Neo was fine, and not only that, but the pressure of Rock's head against my pussy revved me up in spite of my recent orgasm with Oscar.

I didn't know what it was about these guys that was turning me into a sex fiend, but I forced myself to ignore the throb in my pussy and focus on the fight.

Neo and Marvin exchanged punches, Marvin trying to get another kick into Neo's body while Neo forced him to move, sneaking in punches Marvin didn't expect, ducking under his arms to avoid the boots.

Neo had another cut above his right eyebrow that dropped blood down his cheek, but Marvin wasn't unscathed. His face was already swelling, one eye starting to close, and it looked like he had a broken nose. He was slower now too. All the work Neo had done to keep him moving was wearing on him, making his feet look plodding, his punches lethargic.

Which was probably why he tried to use the boot trick again, this time aiming for Neo's face when Neo got closer to try and land another punch.

But instead of taking the hit, Neo grabbed Marvin's foot

and drove him hard and fast against the screen where Joe Pesci was turning framed photographs over while he tossed jewelry into a bag.

"Not the screen!" Oscar yelled over the crowd.

The screen shook but didn't break as Marvin slammed into it, and I gasped along with the crowd as Neo grabbed a fistful of Marvin's beard, twisting hard and punching him in the kidneys until he fell to the ground.

Neo was on him like an animal taking down prey, straddling his chest and using his legs to keep Marvin's hands at his sides while Neo landed punch after ferocious punch to his face.

At first Marvin flailed, trying to free his hands, but it only took a few seconds for him to realize it was futile. Neo's muscular legs were locked around Marvin's arms and chest like a vise. His face was a mask of cold tranquility, like he was taking out the trash instead of beating a man two inches taller and fifty pounds heavier to within an inch of his life.

The crowd roared its approval and I started to worry Neo was actually going to kill Marvin, that the crowd was going to let him do it, when the woman named Marge stepped next to Marvin's bloodied head.

"Calling it!" she shouted.

"He didn't tap out," Neo grunted, hitting Marvin again. Blood sprayed against the concrete floor.

"You have his arms in a lock," she pointed out.

Neo paused, then jumped to his feet with the agility of a cat. He looked unbothered in spite of his bruised and bleeding face. He didn't even seem to be breathing hard.

Marge grabbed Neo's hand and tried to lift it in the air but only got about halfway there because she was so short.

"Neo takes it!" she shouted.

Someone cranked the music and a wave of noise rolled through the crowd. I tried to get a read on how much of it was approval and how much of it was disdain. It was almost impossible to tell, but if I had to guess, I'd give the edge to disdain. Clearly most of the people at the Orpheum didn't like Neo, didn't like any of the Kings.

So why did they do this?

I looked at Oscar, but he was taking pictures, not with his camera this time but with his phone.

Marvin was stirring on the floor, a couple of big bikers at his side, when Neo started through the crowd. Most of them gave him a wide berth, but a few of the girls who looked like students moved toward him, trying to catch his eye.

I couldn't blame them. With his shirt off and his inked chest on full display, the angel tattoo glistening with blood and sweat, he elicited carnal fantasies even from me.

I was glad when Rock eased me off his shoulders and onto the ground. I had no interest in watching girls fawn over my douchebag of a stepbrother.

I looked up at Rock. "Now what?"

Half the crowd had started for the bar and the other half had started dancing like Neo hadn't just beaten the shit out of a man called Mayhem, now being helped to his feet by his biker buddies in the middle of their party.

"Now we wait for Neo to finish his pussy tour," Rock shouted over the music.

"His pussy tour?"

Rock grinned and nodded toward the girls falling all over themselves to get Neo's attention. "He can take his pick tonight."

I rolled my eyes and looked at Oscar, but he was looking at something across the theater. A second later he shoved his camera at Rock, his eyes still on something — or someone — across the cavernous room. "Hold this."

I watched as he made his way through the teeming mass. It didn't take long to see that he was headed for a guy leaning against the wall in the shadows — the same inked-up guy who'd been staring at me earlier.

Oscar leaned in and said something to him, and he pushed off the wall to walk with Oscar toward the theater exit.

I felt like Dorothy in *The Wizard of Oz*, except instead of going from black and white to color, I'd done the opposite: gone from a world that made sense to one that was shadowed with gray.

The Kings were nothing like what I'd imagined. They were obviously into some dark shit and some very shady people. Now I just needed to figure out what it all meant — and whether it had anything to do with Emma.

Chapter 32

Willa

I thought about the fight all day at school the next day. I had questions, but none of them were formulated enough to actually ask, so I kept quiet on the way to campus, this time in the Hummer with all three guys.

Neo's face looked better than I'd expected. He'd still been bleeding when he got in the car — surprisingly single — after the fight, but now it was just bruised, the cut above his eye closed with a butterfly bandage.

Still, he didn't say a word to me the whole way, and I was unsurprised when he got out of the car and walked off without a word.

"He's chipper today," I said. It was hard not to admire the span of his shoulders as he walked away, especially now that I'd seen him shirtless and in action at the Orpheum.

I remembered the flex of his muscles when he'd punched Marvin, how easily he'd moved on his feet, and clenched my thighs to stop the need that screamed to life in my pussy.

"He's replaying the fight," Rock said. "Making notes for next time. It's what he does."

"Why does he do it?" I asked, watching his retreating back.

"To prove he's the baddest motherfucker around," Oscar said.

"Prove to who?" I asked.

A wall of secrecy slammed down over his eyes. "You'll have to figure that out for yourself, tiger."

Rock glanced at his phone. "You good?"

I narrowed my eyes. "You're not walking me to class?"

"You made it clear you don't want that," Rock said.

"That didn't stop you yesterday," I pointed out.

Rock grinned and looked at Oscar. "I think our girl actually likes us."

I sighed. "I'm not your girl. And I don't need you to walk me to class. I just don't understand the sudden change."

"We made our point," Oscar said.

I lifted my eyebrows. "The point being?"

"That you're with us." Oscar's voice was steely. "That if anyone messes with you, they're messing with us. And they don't want to mess with us."

"So I'm free?" I asked. "I can just... go to class?"

"Sure," Rock said. "Just text us when you leave one class and again when you get to another. So we know you're safe."

"I knew there was a catch." I rubbed my forehead, trying to contain my frustration. "I'm not leaving campus. I don't even have a car."

"It's for your own safety," Rock said. "Or I could walk you to class instead...?"

I sighed, hearing the threat loud and clear. "Fine. I'll text."

"Cool." Rock leaned down and kissed me on the lips. "Have a great day, babe."

I looked at Oscar to see if he was feeling territorial, but he just grabbed my hand and kissed me too.

"See ya, tiger." His voice was a sexy purr, and I gotta say, if this was a dream, it wasn't a bad one.

I watched them swagger off and wished someone was around to pinch me. A second later, I remembered that I wasn't supposed to trust them. Even if they were being straight about Emma, about being willing to help me find her, there was still a whole lot I didn't know about the Kings, as evidenced by the scene at the Orpheum.

My second day at Aventine was surprisingly ordinary. I felt a little guilty when Professor Ryan was overly friendly — he'd picked up on all the right signals when I'd barged into the lounge — but I was at Aventine now. I couldn't afford to worry about being nice. I had to find Emma, and I had to keep myself in one piece at the same time.

That meant playing by their rules, which meant being willing to break the usual ones.

I sat with Claire in the cafeteria, but she was already with Quinn and Erin, so I didn't get to call in her promise to talk in private about Emma. It was nice to feel like I already had a few friends, even if Alexa Petrov did glare at me from across the room while she whispered and laughed with her posse of Russian dolls.

I followed orders and texted the group chat every time I

Kings & Corruption

left one class and arrived at another, but only because I didn't want Rock to show up and babysit me for the rest of the day.

By the time I finished with classes and started toward the parking lot, I was feeling pretty good about the upcoming year at Aventine. Then I spotted my roommates at the Hummer and remembered they might actually be the death of me, or at least the death of everything I'd ever believed about myself.

Neo was leaning against the driver's side, his bruised face only making him look more menacing as he glared at my approach, while Oscar lay on the hood of the Hummer, his faded T-shirt riding up just enough to give me a glimpse of the hard abs that had been teasing me since day one.

Rock sat on the roof, looking off into the woods surrounding campus like he didn't have a care in the world, his jeans tight around thighs that looked like they could crack a walnut.

Jesus. How was any mortal girl supposed to resist?

"Fucking finally," Neo said when I got within a few feet of the Hummer.

I gave him a saccharine smile, grateful for the reminder that he was a royal dick. "Aw, the King of Aventine isn't used to being kept waiting by a girl?"

He glared at me and slid into the driver's seat while Rock hopped off the roof of the Hummer with surprising ease for a guy his size.

"Have a good day?" Oscar asked.

My stomach fluttered when he took my hand and gave it a squeeze. "I did."

I climbed into the Hummer and squeaked when Rock squeezed my ass under my skirt. "You were a good girl today."

"Only because I had no choice," I said, settling next to him in the back seat.

"I'd be happy to make the hardship up to you later," he said. "In my bed. Or yours."

I ignored the innuendo, still not sure how to navigate the whole wanting-to-fuck-two-friends thing, especially when they were both right there in the car. I hadn't had a chance to talk to Rock alone since my orgasm in the projector room with Oscar. That conversation needed to happen sooner rather than later, because I was beyond confused about how to handle them both in a way that wasn't gross or hurtful.

The guys talked about the stakeout to figure out who had the keys to the glass case in the staff lounge. They decided on Saturday, figuring the admin and teaching staff would be less likely to work extra hours over the weekend.

My stomach churned with nerves as I listened to them plan. I kept hoping they'd let me off the hook, but then Neo met my eyes in the rearview mirror and asked, "Saturday good for you, Jezebel?"

"Fine," I said, turning my face to the window. I didn't like the way he looked at me, a confusing blend of hate and hunger that was a mirror to my feelings about him.

By the time we got home, I just wanted to escape into my room. The late night at the Orpheum had taken its toll in more ways than one, and I was eager for some comfy clothes and a whole lot of alone time.

I jumped out of the car first and headed into the house, hoping to miss the other guys. I'd noticed Matt's Civic parked out front, plus a Corvette I worried belonged to Enzo, and I had no desire to make chitchat with the former or field insults from the latter.

The guys talked in low voices behind me as I climbed the steps to the house, but when I stepped into the kitchen, it wasn't Matt or Enzo who was there but Reva, humming as she wiped down the counters with vigorous strokes.

"Hello," I said.

She looked up and broke into a smile when she saw me standing there. "Hey there darlin'. How goes it?"

I smiled. "It... goes."

She laughed and I felt my smile widen. "Better than the alternative, I suppose. That's what my mother used to say anyway."

She looked genuinely happy to see me, and it probably said a lot about my relationship with my mom that her use of the word *darlin'* made me feel all warm inside.

I didn't have time to say much though because Rock stepped into the kitchen behind me, took one look at Reva, and sighed dramatically. "Thank god. Someone needs to clean up after these pigs."

I had a hard time hiding my skepticism — the Kings were the cleanest men I'd ever met, and I'd stayed with men all over the world in the hostels I'd occupied during my trip — but the way Reva blushed with pleasure made me think Rock just wanted to make her feel useful.

A year ago. I wouldn't have believed any of the Kings would do something just to make someone else feel good. Now it seemed they were all capable of being nice at least occasionally, and quite often in the case of Rock and Oscar.

I had to remind myself that I'd only been at Aventine for a couple weeks, and one thing I knew to be true about our world was that everyone had secrets and no one was really what they seemed.

"Stop it now," Reva said to Rock. "You're all neat as pins, and you know it. You hardly need me here."

"You underestimate yourself," Oscar said. "We'd fall apart without you."

"Don't blow sunshine up my ass," Reva said. "I know you don't need me for much, and I know this one here," she hooked a thumb at Rock, who was looking through the fridge, "is the chef in the house, but sometimes even the chef needs a break." I wondered why Oscar looked stricken but didn't have time to ask about it before Reva continued. "And I know how much you boys like my lasagna, so I put two trays of it in the fridge for you today. All you have to do is put it in the oven for an hour."

Rock was standing behind her looking like she'd just issued his death sentence.

I was so confused.

"'That's...... great!" Oscar said. He laughed nervously. "You know how we love your lasagna."

Reva beamed and turned to Rock who hurriedly replaced his expression of panic with a smile. "Totally! Your lasagna is my favorite. It's way better than mine."

"It's no trouble at all," Reva said, moving toward a tote bag leaning against the wall. "It's nice for me to have people to take care of."

She sounded wistful, and I suddenly wanted to know more about her.

She crossed the kitchen and surprised me by planting a kiss on each of my cheeks. "Don't let these big lugs push you around."

I smiled. "Not a chance."

I already liked her and hoped she'd be around the house more often. She said goodbye to the guys and let herself out the front door.

Oscar hurried to the living room, obviously intent on something, while I stood there feeling lost.

"Is she gone?" Rock asked.

Oscar returned a minute later. "Gone."

Rock exhaled and hurried to the fridge.

"Why do I feel like I'm missing something?" I asked.

"Oh you're missing something all right," Rock said, removing the two trays of lasagna from the fridge. "You're missing a little E. coli, maybe even some botulism."

I watched in horror as he took a spatula out of the drawer and dumped the lasagna from the first tray into the trash. "Oh my god... what are you doing?"

Oscar took the empty tray from Rock's hand and went to rinse it in the sink while Rock started on the other one.

"Trust us," Oscar said. "We're saving your life."

"Or at least your palate," Rock said. "Reva is literally the worst cook in the world."

Now it all made sense, all the glances between Rock and Oscar, Rock's terrified expression when Reva mentioned cooking for them.

I couldn't help laughing. "Are you telling me you hate her cooking but pretend to eat it because you're afraid to tell her the truth?"

I thought of all the times they'd been brutally honest with me and couldn't help laughing that Reva had them wrapped around her finger.

"We don't want to hurt her feelings," Oscar said.

Rock looked at me accusingly. "Yeah, Willa. Reva is the nicest lady I've ever known. Do you want us to hurt her feelings?"

"Of course I don't want you to hurt Reva's feelings. I'm just saying, it's a shame to waste all that food, not to mention all the time she put into cooking it."

"She likes cooking for us, so we let her," Oscar said. "No harm in that."

I shook my head and headed for the back stairs. I needed to get away from the whole scene before I forgot that the Kings were dangerous.

That I couldn't like them.

And I still didn't trust them.

Chapter 33

Willa

I spent the next couple of days trying to focus on school. Not just the work, but the social scene, which was ten times more interesting. Everyone still treated me like I might have a communicable disease, but I made an effort to be friendly anyway.

If I was going to figure out what happened to Emma, I needed friends, and that meant I had to send the signal that no one was going to get their limbs ripped off by the Kings if they talked to me.

By Thursday, I was settling into the routine of driving to campus with the Kings — sometimes with Neo and sometimes without — and going to class, eating in the cafeteria with Claire, Quinn, and Erin, driving home with the Kings, doing homework in my room until dinner, which was always something amazing either cooked by Rock or ordered from one of the restaurants in town.

I was in the middle of an Econ paper Thursday night when my phone pinged with a text from Mara.

Please tell me you've fucked at least one of those boys.

I grinned. **I have not. Sorry. What about you?**

Nothing but preppy fuckboys here.

And the Kings aren't fuckboys? I texted back.

Our fuckboys are better than their fuckboys.

I laughed out loud. She wasn't wrong. When you grew up around a bunch of big-dick criminals, polo-wearing trust fund boys didn't hold much appeal.

Fair. How are you otherwise?

Bored af. You?

I considered my answer. I'd only been at Aventine a week and my other lives — the one where I hung out with Mara after school, the one where I hopped on a plane on a whim — seemed light-years away.

Getting used to it here.

There was a pause, and I wondered if Mara was holding back too. There was only so much you could say via text.

You okay? she finally texted back.

I'm good. I was surprised that it wasn't entirely a lie. **It was weird at first but it's getting less weird.**

Except for the part where I was seriously considering fucking two of my roommates. And the part where I had to force myself not to fantasize about my stepbrother. And the part where I was going to have to break into someone's house and then steal the stupid medals.

It was too much. Too much to tell her via text and maybe too much to tell her ever.

I'm glad, she texted back. **FaceTime soon?**

Yes please.

She sent me some kissing emojis and I sent some back before setting my phone down. I tried to refocus on my Econ paper, but my mind was scattered. I was almost relieved when my phone pinged again.

I picked it up, expecting it to be Mara, but it wasn't. It was a text from Rock in the group chat.

This meatloaf isn't going to eat itself.

I stared at my phone and briefly considered passing and going down later after everyone else had eaten, then sighed and got to my feet. I told myself it was because I was hungry, but the truth was, I'd started to enjoy the nightly routine.

I liked the other guys in the house, except for Enzo, who still looked at me like dog shit on his shoe. I enjoyed the banter and laughter and camaraderie, probably too much, and as much as I hated to admit it, the house was starting to feel a little like home.

Everyone but Neo was already there, piling meatloaf and garlic mashed potatoes on their plates, when I got to the kitchen. The other guys moved aside a little as I came into the room, something I'd noticed they always seemed to do, like they were afraid to get too close to me.

Except for Rock and Oscar, who continued to kiss me and pat my ass and do all kinds of other things I would have broken anyone else's hands for doing. I couldn't get my head around why I allowed it — why I liked it — but I'd put that particular question aside for the time being.

"Want a beer, tiger?" Oscar asked, standing in the open door of the fridge.

"Sure." I still had to finish that paper, but one beer wouldn't kill me.

I was spooning mashed potatoes onto my plate while Luke and Ricky fought over the last piece of meatloaf when Neo swaggered into the kitchen. His hair was damp from the shower, which meant he'd probably been training in the gym on the second floor. I ordered myself not to stare at the defined cut of his biceps in his tank top and *definitely* not at the bulge on display in his gray sweatpants.

Except that left me nowhere to look but his face, and that didn't help either.

He really was fucking beautiful. The cut on his face was healing, the bruise turning yellow, but somehow it only made him look more dangerous.

More appealing.

"Can I help you?" Neo asked, looking right at me.

Fuck. I'd been staring.

"The cut above your eye looks better." It was in direct violation of my don't-be-nice-to-assholes rule, but it was all I could think of to say.

He stared into my eyes and everyone else in the room seemed to recede in the moment before he looked away to grab a plate. "Thanks."

I exhaled a breath I hadn't been aware I was holding. Being around Neo was like dancing across a field of land mines. That singular "thanks" might have been the only un-insulting thing he'd said to me since I'd been at Aventine.

"Stop acting like Neanderthals," Rock said to Luke and Ricky, shoving them aside to set two more platters of meatloaf on the island. "There's always enough food."

The other guys waited around for a couple of minutes after dishing their food, clearly waiting to see if the Kings would claim the living room. There was another media room on the second floor, which was where the other guys in the house hung out to watch TV and play video games when Neo, Rock, and Oscar claimed the downstairs living room.

It seemed like an unspoken rule that the other guys weren't allowed to take up space around the Kings unless they were invited. Maybe I should have felt sorry for them being treated like second-class citizens, but I'd learned the hard way that you got what you thought you deserved, what you demanded other people give you.

The other guys had signed up to be members of the Kings' house and all that entailed. They had to have known what it meant.

"Beat it," Neo finally said without looking at them.

They scattered for the front stairs.

"Love or Money?" Rock asked me, dishing his own plate of food.

I lifted my eyebrows. "Excuse me?"

"We're behind on Love or Money," he said. "Want to stay and watch?"

"I feel like you're speaking another language right now," I said. "It's like you're saying words but I don't understand what any of them mean."

"It's that show where people have to find someone to be in a couple with and then at the end they get offered more and more money to break up," Oscar explained.

"You've never seen *Love or Money*?" Rock looked mildly horrified.

"I've been traveling, remember?" I'd come home because of my mom's engagement to Roberto Alinari and we'd spent the whole summer planning the wedding. I hadn't had time to catch up on all the shows I'd missed while I'd been angling for the cheapest plane ticket from one country to the next.

"Riiiight," Rock said. "Well, grab your plate and get settled on the sofa, because Amanda is about to dump Marcus and set her sights on Daniel."

"Still feel like you're speaking gibberish," I said. I glanced at the stairs, thinking about the half-written paper in my room. "And I have homework."

"It'll wait," Oscar said. "We'll just watch two episodes."

"For fuck's sake," Neo said, "stop begging like puppies. If she wants to go, let her go."

That settled it. I guess my truce with Neo was over.

"Sounds great," I said.

Neo scowled and I had to suppress a triumphant grin. I had no idea why getting under his skin was so much *fun*.

I followed Oscar and Rock to the living room, hoping they'd make it easy for me to pick a seat. I really needed to talk to Rock about what had happened between Oscar and me at the Orpheum. They sat at opposite ends of the sofa, which didn't make my seat selection any easier, so I sat between them, trying to be diplomatic.

Neo came into the room carrying his plate. He took a seat in one of the overstuffed chairs facing the TV and Rock cued up *Love or Money*, which turned out to be super cheesy, with obnoxious graphics and dramatic music that acted as a backdrop to all the maneuvering and fighting and making out between the couples.

I was hooked within the first half hour, and I tried not to be annoying as I asked Rock and Oscar questions about the contestants, trying to catch up on the things I'd missed in earlier episodes.

I devoured my meatloaf, mashed potatoes, and the green beans Rock had sautéed with loads of butter and little almond slivers, then leaned back against the sofa with a groan.

Rock patted the spot next to him and I glanced at Oscar, trying to get a read on how this was going to work. His answer came in the form of a suggestive grin that I took as a sign of approval, so I leaned into Rock with a sigh, tucking my feet under me and resting my head against his chest.

If someone had told me a week earlier that I'd find myself sitting on the Kings' sofa, watching reality TV after a gourmet dinner, cuddling with Rock Barone, I'd have said they were high.

But here I was, doing all of those things and feeling like I'd landed in paradise.

Except for Neo, who still acted like I was stinking up the place.

Still, two out of three wasn't bad, and I had to stifle a moan when Oscar reached for one of my bare feet and started rubbing. His fingers were magic against the soles of my feet, putting just the right amount of pressure on my skin while Rock's fingers absently stroked my bare shoulder.

Fuck.

I was getting turned on watching TV, my pussy wet as I imagined Rock and Oscar naked.

Together.

With me.

I was glad Neo was there. I didn't trust myself to be alone with Rock and Oscar, and I was almost relieved when my phone buzzed with a text.

I reached for it on the coffee table and smiled when I saw it was Claire.

Sleepover at my place tomorrow night?

I remembered our conversation at Game Night, Claire's promise to talk to me about Emma when we were alone. The Queens' house probably wasn't super private, but I was guessing Claire had her own room, which meant it was the best shot I had at getting answers.

Sure, I texted back.

It would be good for me to get out of the Kings' house for a while anyway. I was on hot-dick overload, and my annoyingly ravenous pussy was becoming less trustworthy by the second.

Chapter 34
Willa

"I need a car," I mused, looking out the passenger side window of the Audi.

I still wasn't sure which car belonged to which King, but when Rock had offered to drive me to Claire's on Friday night, he'd gone straight for the Audi.

He'd just pulled up in front of an old mansion on the outskirts of Blackwell Falls, and I was feeling more than a little embarrassed to have needed a ride to the Queens' house.

"We don't mind driving you," he said.

I looked over at him, sexy as fuck in his trademark white T-shirt and jeans that showed off his muscled thighs. "Did it occur to you that maybe I mind? That maybe I don't like being dropped off at the Queens' house like a kid being driven to a sleepover by her parents?"

His grin was lazy and sex-filled. "If you want me to be your daddy, just say so."

I laughed in spite of myself. "I'm not used to being dependent on other people."

He reached over and slid a hand under my hair and onto the back of my neck. "I get that, but it's no trouble. We like taking care of you."

"And I like being independent," I said, trying not to be distracted by the soft stroke of his thumb at the base of my neck.

"I like your independence. I like everything about you." His sea-blue eyes were hooded with desire. "But I'd like it more if you were grinding on me right now."

I thought he was being his usual flirtatious self, but his expression was serious, the air charged with tension as his gaze dropped to my mouth. He was going to kiss me, and that was going to make things hella complicated... but that didn't mean I didn't want him to kiss me.

I was fucking *desperate* for Rock Barone to kiss me, and I had the throbbing pussy to prove it, but I wanted to clear the air about Oscar first.

"You don't... mind?" I asked. "About Oscar?"

"Oh, I'm jealous as fuck that he got the privilege of making you come before I did," he said. "But we're all adults, and I'm happy to share. *More* than happy."

His looked into my eyes, his emphasis on the word *more* making his meaning clear.

Fuck me. I was more than a little worried that fucking Oscar and Rock separately would permanently alter my brain function, turning me into some kind of sex-crazed zombie, but fucking both of them at the same time?

My panties were instantly wet, need beating out a drumbeat in my veins.

"And this is something you've done before?" I asked. "Shared?"

An unfamiliar swell of jealousy threatened to claw its way up my throat, but I forced it down. I had no right and I knew it.

His thumb was still working its magic on the back of my neck and I imagined what it would feel like to feel his fingers inside me.

My breath quickened, and I pressed my thighs together to stop the throbbing in my pussy.

Down, girl.

"We don't need to talk about anything that's happened before. You're different. If we share you, it won't be just for fun." He laughed, low and sexy. "I mean, don't get me wrong, it'll be a hell of a lot of fun, but not just that."

"What then?" I wasn't looking to get married, but I was curious. I wanted him to verbalize the attraction that had developed between us, attraction that had morphed way too quickly into actual affection.

"I don't know," he murmured, staring into my eyes. "But I'm ready to find out."

I barely had time to register the words before he leaned in and captured my mouth in a languid kiss that sucked all the air out of my lungs.

I sighed into his mouth, opening to him as light exploded behind my closed eyelids, and turned my body to get better access as our tongues sparred, threading my fingers into his long blond hair.

He groaned and slid his hand into the hair at the back of my head, angling my face to take the kiss deeper, sweeping my mouth with his tongue until he let out a groan of frustration against my lips.

"Not enough," he grunted, using his left hand to slide the driver's seat farther back. He put pressure on the back of my neck, making it clear what he wanted. "Get your sweet ass over here, kitten."

I climbed over the console and straddled him with the steering wheel at my back, totally oblivious to the very real possibility of someone walking by and seeing me dry humping Rock Barone in the front seat of the Audi.

"That's more like it," he murmured against my lips.

And this time, there was nothing languid about the kiss. It was bruising and demanding, his tongue occupying my mouth as his hands traveled over my shoulders and tits, down to the hem of my blouse.

"Fuck, you taste good," he muttered, sliding his hands up under my shirt. "Like strawberries and cream."

"Are you thinking about food while you kiss me?" I asked, holding his face in my hands.

His chuckle was so fucking sexy a fresh surge of wetness dampened my panties. "It's not food I'm thinking about eating."

The words sparked a fire between my legs and I settled more firmly on top of the thick, granite-like bulge between his thighs, moaning into his mouth as he thumbed my nipples over my bra.

I was damn near ready to strip right there, residents of Blackwell Falls be damned. My pussy was clamoring for his cock, so close and yet so far away as he moved his hips with only our jeans between us.

He lifted my shirt and closed his mouth around one of my nipples, sucking it through my bra. The heat of his mouth was so close to my bare skin it sent shudders of ecstasy through my body, and I slid my hands under his shirt, letting my fingers map the peaks and valleys of his muscled chest as he sucked and licked my nipple.

He clamped his hands around my ass and scooted me even harder against him. I moaned as his dick pressed against my throbbing core, and I rocked my hips against him without thinking, my body seeking out the orgasm promised by his mouth and hands.

"That's it," he coaxed, lifting his mouth from my tit. "Grind on me, kitten. Use me."

I was going to come right there in the car, and I didn't give a single fuck who might see it. Rock's cock was wedged into the perfect spot between my thighs, rubbing against my clit as I rubbed against him, giving me a taste of what it would feel like to have him inside me if it weren't for my stupid jeans.

For fuck's sake, *why* did I wear jeans instead of a skirt or dress that would have given him easier access?

One hand was still wrapped around my boob while he sucked on the other nipple. His other hand cupped my ass, pressing me hard against him, his fingers teasing the crack of my ass and making me wonder what it would be like to be fucked in the ass by Rock Barone.

I moved faster against him, a battle warring inside me between wanting to come and wanting to hold out, wanting to make it last.

"Do it, kitten," he coaxed. "Use me to make that sweet pussy come."

The words sent me over the edge. I came hard, shuddering as I gripped his shoulders. He sucked harder as I cried out in the car, dirty words falling from my lips as I tried to articulate how fucking good it felt to come against his engorged cock, even through our jeans.

Finally, I dropped my forehead against his shoulder and gasped for breath, drifting in that post-orgasm space that was a little like the moment when I first woke up from sleep.

My mind gradually cleared, and I lifted my head to look at him. His blue eyes were sharp and glittering as he reached up to stroke my lower lip with his thumb.

"Watching you come is so fucking hot," he said. "I deserve a goddamn medal for not creaming my jeans."

"It was pretty amazing for me too." I bit my lower lip. "Thanks for letting me... use you?"

His laughter filled the car. "You can use me like that any fucking time, kitten. *Any* fucking time."

He pulled down my shirt and reached up to hold my face in his hands. "The next time I make you come, it's going to be with my face between your thighs."

The words sent a white-hot bolt of need straight through my body and my pussy tightened in response. He could have done it then and there and I would have come in under a minute despite the fact that I was still recovering from orgasm number one.

I was glad when he pulled my head down to kiss me. There was no thinking while Rock was kissing me, nothing but his soft lips on mine, his tongue invading my mouth.

Thinking was starting to feel like the enemy.

Because if I thought life in the Kings' house was complicated before, what was it going to be like when I was fucking around with not one but two of the men who were supposed to be off-limits?

Chapter 35
Willa

I wasn't thrilled about having Rock walk me to the door of the Queens' house, but he insisted. On the plus side, I was able to ask him to look at my ass and make sure I didn't look like I'd wet my pants, a very real possibility given how soaked my pussy felt at the moment.

Cleanup in aisle one.

Standing on the porch with Rock, waiting for someone to answer our knock, I felt like a kid all over again. Then Claire opened the door with a wide smile and I forgot about being embarrassed as she gave Rock an appreciative head-to-toe scan before pulling me into the house.

I laughed when she shut the door in his face without a word.

"Boys!" she said dramatically. "Am I right?"

I smiled. "You're right."

She lifted her eyebrows suggestively. "Although I have to say, yours look like they're worth the trouble."

"The Kings are not *mine*," I said, ignoring the flutter of excitement in my stomach at the thought.

She studied me, a smirk lifting the corners of her mouth. "You're either lying or you're an idiot."

"Wow, tell me how you really feel, Claire."

"Seriously," she said, "Rock looked like he was about to eat you whole."

I remembered his comment in the car about what he wanted to *eat* and felt my cheeks heat. "You're imagining things. He's just looking out for me because I'm Neo's stepsister."

I felt bad about lying to her — and I had to literally force the word *stepsister* from my mouth — but the last thing I needed was everyone at Aventine gossiping about Frank Russo's daughter sleeping with the Kings.

"If you say so." She didn't sound like she believed it, but she linked her arm with mine and dragged me through the high-ceilinged foyer toward a staircase. "Come on, I'll introduce you to everyone."

She led me up the stairs and into her room on the second floor. At first, I was a little worried — the room had two double beds and was clearly occupied by two people — but Claire explained that her roommate was out for the night.

That was a relief, because I was determined to talk to Claire about Emma, something that would have been difficult with a hovering roommate given Claire's caginess on the subject at Game Night.

We dropped my bag in her room and she showed me around the house, which was a beautiful old Victorian with original moldings, polished wood banisters, and a large renovated kitchen. It was more like what I'd imagined the Kings' house would be, minus the beer-soaked carpet.

She introduced me to other residents of the Queens' house as we went. Erin and Quinn were there, plus a few other girls I'd seen at Game Night or around campus. I hadn't realized how much I'd gotten used to seeing the different crime families separated into groups, but even after only a week at Aventine, it felt strange to see the Italian girls I'd grown up with laughing and talking with members of the cartel, Irish, and Russian families.

It was nice, like a big family, complete with two girls who were having a loud fight over leftovers in the fridge. It made me realize how much I missed Mara. The Kings had been nicer than I'd expected, and other than Neo and Enzo, the other guys in the house had been welcoming, but I'd missed hanging with a bunch of girls.

Every now and then, I'd catch one of the Queens staring at me, but it was mostly friendly curiosity, and they asked questions about how I was settling in at Aventine and my year of travel instead of my family.

Claire and I spent time talking to a few of them in the kitchen, then settled into the living room.

The next two hours flew by. I learned more about Claire, like the fact that her family was a high-ranking one in the Irish Mob out of Boston. She had five brothers, and she talked about all but one of them fondly. Apparently three of them had already been at Aventine, one had chosen not to attend college, and the fifth had been working in Dublin and was due to start next year.

According to Claire, they were annoying and

overprotective, which sounded about right for any family in our world. There were more women in positions of power than there used to be, but protecting us seemed to be coded into the male Mafia DNA.

Claire's phone buzzed and she looked at it, then widened her eyes in surprise. "It's after eight! Let's order Chinese. Unless you want something else?"

"Chinese is good," I said.

She ordered online and we wandered into the kitchen to talk to some of the other girls while we waited for it to be delivered. This time Alexa was there, holding court with the two girls who seemed to be her main sidekicks. We'd been introduced at Game Night, and I was pretty sure the blonde was Anya and the brunette was Natalie.

They were both gorgeous of course, although not gorgeous enough to take the focus off Alexa, which was probably the point.

Alexa's cool gaze flickered over me as I came into the room with Claire. I forced myself not to shrink under her icy analysis. I didn't consider myself a shrinking violet, but she had a way of making me feel about half an inch tall.

No way was I letting her know that though.

"Leave it to you to bring Judas into the house," Alexa said to Claire.

Claire just gave her a patronizing smile. "Aw, where's your hospitality, Lex? Willa is our guest. You don't want everyone saying the Queen of Queens' house is a royal bitch, now do you?" She put a hand over her mouth and widened her eyes in mock surprise. "Oh wait... too late!"

I shifted uncomfortably, half expecting Alexa to subject

Claire to some kind of medieval torture right there in the kitchen.

Instead, Alexa just rolled her eyes. "No talk about the game."

"Duh," Claire said.

I already knew the rules. Rock had been very clear on the ride into town, right before he'd delivered my earth-shattering orgasm in the car: absolutely no discussion with the Queens about the game. Claire and I could be friends, but in the game, our houses were competitors, and the competition wasn't all in good fun.

Whoever won would hold the power over the game next year. Plus, they'd get the rings, something that was apparently a very big deal.

I exhaled my relief when Alexa flounced off with her minions in tow. I had zero interest in trying to win her over, but I also didn't love being her target, if only because it drew attention. Finding Emma meant blending in, being just another student at Aventine.

My dad had already made that difficult. My sister's disappearance made it next to impossible.

The last thing I needed was to become a source of amusement for Alexa Petrov.

We talked to the other girls while we waited for our Chinese food, but one by one, they peeled off to other parts of the house. I understood why a little while later when the sound of multiple blow dryers drifted down the stairs, the scent of body wash and perfume lacing the air: it was Friday night, and that meant everyone was going out.

I thought fleetingly of Rock and Oscar, wondering what

they'd do while I was gone for the night, if they'd bring another girl back to the house, to their beds, but an answering roar of jealousy forced me to shut down the thought.

I didn't own them, and I couldn't afford to be attached to them.

Our Chinese food finally arrived, and Claire and I piled our plates high with lo mein, General Tso's chicken, and egg rolls before heading upstairs to her room.

She put on some music and we settled on the floor with our food. We talked about our classes and the guy in the Saints' house Claire had her eye on, but I was happy to keep it light while we ate. I genuinely liked her, and I didn't want her to think I was just using her to get information.

"Oh my god," she groaned, leaning back against her bed and pushing away her plate. "I'm so full of noodles and MSG."

"Same," I said. "And egg rolls. So. Many. Egg rolls."

"I eat way too much takeout during the school year," she said. "You're so lucky to have Rock. I've heard he's an amazing cook."

"He is," I said. "I didn't expect it to be honest."

She sighed. "It's enough to make me want to spring for a personal chef."

I laughed. "It's definitely been an unexpected perk."

She grinned slyly. "I'm sure there are a lot of *unexpected perks* to living in the Kings' house."

"Unexpected perks and a whole lot of temptation."

She studied me. "Don't tell me you haven't given in. I'd be *all* over that."

I chewed on my thumbnail, trying to decide how much to tell her. "It's complicated."

"Because of Emma?"

I didn't even try to hide my surprise at the mention of my sister. I'd started to wonder if Claire was going to avoid the topic or wait for me to bring it up. "Among other things, but... yeah. Emma is the biggest." I hesitated. "Did you know her?"

"I wouldn't say I knew her," Claire said carefully. "I saw her around, you know? At parties and stuff. In town a couple of times."

"Did she hang out with anyone from Aventine? Anyone specific?" I asked.

"Not that I remember, but it's a haul to get over here from the Bellepoint campus. The girls, they come and go. Rockview is closer for them."

Rockview was another private college. Like Aventine, but minus the criminals and closer to the Bellepoint campus. I could see why the girls might decide to cast their nets there.

"Were the kids at Aventine nice to them?" I asked. Claire looked down, her cheeks flushed, and I reached out to take her hand. "Whatever it is, you can tell me."

She glanced at the closed door to her room.

"I'm not going to tell anyone," I said. "I promise. This is just for me."

"The boys were nice to them," Claire said. "They called them fresh meat, made a game out of it. But they're dumb that way, always showing off. You know how they are."

My stomach turned as I imagined my sister being used and thrown away. Had the guys at Aventine taken special

Kings & Corruption

pleasure in using someone like Emma, someone they saw as a traitor?

Had she known? Or had she thought they really liked her?

"The Kings too?" I couldn't stop myself from asking. I had to know. "Did they use the Bellepoint girls?"

"The Kings are careful," Claire said. "Quiet. They keep to themselves. I don't think I'd know even if they *had* fucked around with the Bellepoint girls." She squeezed my hand. "Is that why you're being careful with them? Because you think they're involved in Emma's disappearance?"

"I don't have any reason to believe that," I said truthfully. "But honestly, I think you might be the only person I trust here."

Her mouth turned down in a frown. "I'm so sorry, girl."

I saw the sympathy in her eyes and knew it was genuine.

"Thanks," I said. Something was scratching at my mind, but it took me a minute to figure out what it was. "You said 'girls' plural. Did the Bellepoint girls come in groups?"

"Not always groups," Claire said, "but usually in pairs at least."

"What about Emma?" I asked, practically holding my breath. "Did she come with someone?"

"The first two times she was with someone, a girl named... Nikki, I think? Brown hair, big blue eyes?"

"Nikki." It was all I could manage to say. Because Nikki? Nikki had been my sister's roommate at Bellepoint, and she'd sworn to the police she didn't know a thing about Emma and Aventine.

Chapter 36

Willa

I thought about what Claire had said as I followed Rock through the woods the next night, my mind struggling to come up with a reason Nikki would have lied. I mean, yeah, Bellepoint had a curfew. As an all-girls college in the middle of nowhere, it was a no-brainer for them to have those kinds of rules in place, even if everyone knew they were broken on the regular.

But getting caught breaking curfew — something Emma had laughed off by saying everyone did it — didn't seem like a good reason to lie to the police, especially when it came to something as big as your missing roommate.

"You okay?" Rock asked.

He'd stopped a few feet in front of me, his brow furrowed as he studied me in the residual glow of the flashlight on my phone.

"Fine, why?" I asked.

"Just checking. You haven't said anything in a while." He nodded at my phone. "Keep that light down."

I pointed it at the ground. "Sorry."

He'd told me I could use it to keep from tripping in the woods surrounding Aventine, but only if I kept it aimed at the ground so no one would see it.

He walked back toward me and used his thumb to rub gently at my cheek. "You've got a little dirt here."

"Must have been from that branch that smacked me in the face a while back," I said.

His hand was warm against my cheek, and I swam through his blue eyes while he rubbed, trying to ignore the spark that flared between my legs.

Orgasmic muscle memory, I guess.

We'd both worn black — I wasn't an experienced criminal or anything, but it made sense in this scenario — and his black sweatshirt only made him look even more like a blond god.

I was glad I'd braided my long hair. In the darkness, it would have been like a beacon despite my black sweatshirt, jeans, and boots.

"No blood at least," he murmured, dropping his hand.

"Thanks," I said.

"No problem. Let's keep going. We're almost there."

The trail was wider here than it had been when we first parked the car and stepped into the woods, and I fell into step beside him.

"Why is there a trail here?" I asked.

"No cameras," he said.

I thought about my sister. Was this how she'd avoided being caught on camera when she was at Aventine? Had she accessed the campus through the woods?

The thought sank to my stomach like a stone. If the trail

gave girls like Emma access to campus without being seen, it also gave anyone else a way to leave without being seen.

I tried to remember if the police had said anything about searching the trail but couldn't. The days immediately following Emma's disappearance were a blur of panic, police interviews, and phone calls from Bellepoint's dean to my mom.

Another branch almost smacked me in the face, and my hand went up reflexively to swipe it away.

"Ugh. This isn't what I imagined when we agreed to stake out the admin building," I muttered.

Rock glanced over his shoulder. "What did you imagine?"

"I don't know," I admitted. "Snacks and sitting?"

He chuckled and the sound of it in the dark tickled my belly. "We have to be able to see inside the admin building. Can't do that from a car."

I didn't love the thought of sneaking into the admin building, but he was right: there was no way to see who cleaned the lounge unless we were inside. "What about the cameras in the building?"

"We can work around them for this," he said.

"But not to take the medals?" I was still hoping for a way to steal the medals that didn't involve taking them in broad daylight on a school day.

"No," he said. "That hallway has cameras at either end, and we can blend into the crowd during the day. All we need to do tonight is see who goes in to clean the lounge. We can stay hidden for that."

"Right," I said miserably.

He slowed his steps and I came up beside him. I'd always known the Kings were big guys, but I hadn't expected how it would make me feel. Standing next to Rock in the woods, getting ready to enter the admin building when we were definitely not supposed to be there, I felt completely safe.

There was something about him — about all of them if I were honest, even Neo, who I still fantasized about suffocating in his sleep — that was solid and reassuring. Maybe it was their sheer size, or maybe it was the way they swung their dicks like they owned everything and everyone. I didn't know, but I felt untouchable when I was with them, and for someone like me, someone who'd been anything but safe for a long time, it was a nice fucking high.

Light had started to seep in through the woods, and I realized we'd come to the edge of the forest. We walked for another minute and came to the tree line. Beyond it, the campus' streetlights shone, illuminating the roads and pathways.

We stopped walking, and I saw that we'd emerged from the woods right behind the admin building. "The trail leads right here?"

I was thinking about Emma, about all the students — from Bellepoint and Aventine — who used the trail to sneak on and off campus. Why make it to the admin building? There were more cameras there than anywhere else, plus the possibility of being seen by someone working late.

"This one," Rock said.

I looked up into his blue eyes and my heart stuttered a little. Fuck, he was gorgeous. "There are other trails?"

"Quite a few of them," he said.

My heart sank. Emma could have come and gone on any of them.

I didn't say anything and he looked down at me, his expression softening like he knew what I was thinking.

He reached out and touched my face. "The cops searched all the trails," he said. "More than once. We all did, even the townies."

I knew it was true because I'd been there during a couple of the searches that had been conducted for Emma, taking my place in a sea of people with flashlights at night, all of us walking only a few feet apart in a grid pattern to make sure we didn't miss anything.

"All of them?" I said.

"All of them," he said. "Dean Giordana knows they're here. Everyone does. It's a way for staff to look the other way when it's best for them to look the other way."

I nodded. Aventine was populated with students from notorious crime families. Being here wasn't about following the rules — it was about learning how to break them.

The heat of his fingers made me remember the way he'd squeezed my tit in the car, the feel of his hot mouth on the other one while he licked and sucked my nipple.

I squeezed my thighs together to force myself to focus. "Now what?"

"Now we go in."

It wasn't as hard to get in as I'd expected, mostly because Rock knew where the cameras were positioned and how to avoid them. We approached the building in a blind spot and slipped in through the door leading to the dumpsters behind the building — propped open, just like he said it would be, so the cleaning crew could dump trash without worrying about being locked out.

Clearly the Kings had done recon without me.

Once we were inside, Rock opened the door leading to the back stairwell, careful to press the metal bar quietly in case someone was making their way up or down the stairs.

But it was empty, and we continued up the stairs, pausing in the second-floor vestibule to peek into the hall to make sure no one was there. I waited while Rock opened the door, sweat slicking the back of my neck, breaking out on my hairline as I thought about the possibility of being caught.

I wouldn't be expelled — not as Roberto Alinari's stepdaughter — but it would be humiliating and disappointing for my new stepdad. He would make me pay for that, and it wasn't like Neo would come to my rescue by admitting the Kings had roped me into the game.

"Come on." Rock waved me forward and I followed him into the hall, my heart pounding like a parade drum in my chest.

The hall was empty, but I could hear the clatter of someone working in one of the rooms as we crept toward the juncture leading to the next hall. Every time we passed an open door to one of the rooms, I felt dizzy with panic.

Except for my travel rebellion, I was the good girl in the family. I didn't break the rules, especially not the big ones. That was Emma's job. Beautiful, wild Emma, who'd never thought the rules were for her, who'd left Bellepoint to party with the people who hated us most and probably never in a million years dreamed they didn't want her here.

We'd reached the bend in the hall, the final stretch leading to the lounge, when Rock shoved me back into a tiny vestibule leading to one of the rooms.

It happened so fast — one second we were walking side by side and the next we were crowded into the narrow vestibule, Rock's body pressed so tightly against mine I could feel his muscled chest through his shirt, not to mention his hard dick pressing against my stomach.

Adrenaline flooded my body — and not because of the hard dick, although I was more than aware of it — but he just smirked.

"Someone's coming," he whispered.

He turned around, his wide shoulders blocking my view, and a minute later I heard the rattle of something I assumed was a cleaning cart.

"Did you get the bathrooms?" The voice belonged to a guy, someone under forty by my guess.

"Yep. And I got them last time too," a woman replied. She sounded young-ish, maybe even around my age. "Those are on you next time."

Rock shifted and I caught a heady whiff of his cologne that went straight to my pussy. I didn't know what was worse, standing there in the vestibule praying we wouldn't get caught or standing there in the vestibule realizing I wanted nothing more than for Rock to turn around and finish what he'd started in the car outside the Queens' house.

"Fuck that," the guy said. "You're the rookie."

"Are you seriously pulling rank on this shitty cleaning

job?" the girl asked. There was an easy camaraderie between them, like they'd known each other forever.

"Seniority rules, baby." The guy's voice was right on top of us. I couldn't see past Rock's gargantuan body, but I wouldn't have been surprised if the guy was right in front of the vestibule.

"Do you know how much it sucks to have someone say that to you every day of your life for twenty-two years?" the girl asked.

Every day of your life? So they were siblings. Had to be.

"I don't make the rules," the guy said. "I'm going to hit the lounge. You start on the first floor."

"Fine," the girl said. "But if I have to do another set of bathrooms, you owe me breakfast when we're done."

His laughter echoed through the halls, but he was farther away now, probably heading for the lounge.

The cleaning cart's squeaky wheels rattled down the hall, the sound getting more distant. A few seconds later, I heard the ding of an elevator. I hadn't even realized the admin building had one. It must be tucked away somewhere.

Rock turned around to look at me. "It's just the two of them. We need to get to the lounge, make sure the guy has the keys to the case."

"What?" I hissed. "No! We know he's the one who cleans the lounge. Let's just... I don't know, wait here or something."

"No way." Rock's voice was resolute. "We've come this far. We have to make sure he's actually got the keys. Plus we'll get a better look at him up close."

I couldn't refute the logic. As much as I didn't want to get up close and personal with the guy cleaning the lounge, I didn't want to have to go through this again either.

I swore. "Fine."

He flashed me a grin, then lowered his mouth to mine, capturing my lips in a kiss that made me forget all about the fact that we were trespassing. By the time he broke away, I was breathless, my underwear wet and sticking to my jeans.

He lifted his eyebrows suggestively like he knew exactly what my body was up to. "Let's go."

I followed him out of the vestibule and down the hall, surprised that such a big guy could move so silently. We passed several open doors, then slowed our steps as we came to the lounge.

The sounds coming from the room made it easy to guess what was going on inside: the running water in the sink by the microwave and coffee pot, the bang of trash cans being emptied.

Rock crept closer. My stomach turned with nervousness, but I followed him anyway.

I was in it now.

We used the open door as cover, partially hiding our bodies behind it. I was terrified to look, sure the guy inside would be looking right at me the second I dared, but when I finally peered out from behind Rock's body, the guy had his back to us.

He stood next to a cleaning cart near the display case and was using a long-handled duster to get the walls and the corners of the ceilings. He had dark hair and broad shoulders under a black T-shirt, his arms flexing as he dusted, and he was tall enough that he didn't have to stretch to reach the room's high ceilings.

We ducked back behind the door before he turned to make his way around the room.

I dared to look again and saw that he'd circled back to the cart in front of the display case. He bent to put the duster away and I caught a glimpse of his profile — strong cheekbones and full lips.

Rock lifted his phone to take a picture, and a second later the guy straightened. Except this time he had a smaller duster in his hand — and a set of keys.

I held my breath as he flipped through them and inserted one into the lock on the display case.

It opened.

Rock looked down at me and mouthed one word.

Bingo.

Chapter 37

Willa

We spent the rest of the weekend talking about how to get ahold of the keys.

Well, the Kings spent the rest of the weekend talking about how to get ahold of the keys. I was in denial, pretending my role in the game was over, that I wouldn't have to break into some guy's house while he was sleeping to steal his keys.

But that's what it came down to, because the only time we could be sure he wouldn't need the keys to the admin building was during the day when he wasn't on the job. That meant breaking in, stealing the keys, hurrying back to Aventine to steal the medals in broad daylight, and returning the keys before the cleaning guy knew they were missing.

We knew who he was now, and where he lived: Daniel Longhat, a townie from Blackwell Falls who had a sister named Samantha.

It took less than twenty-four hours for the Kings to

identify Daniel from Rock's picture. I didn't bother asking how they'd done it. I remembered the scene at the Orpheum, the weird unspoken language that seemed to exist between the Kings and the townies.

There was obviously a whole lot more going on in Blackwell Falls than the average college town, and whatever it was, it was obvious the Kings were playing some kind of part in it.

By Monday I was glad to get back to classes and the routine of driving to school with the guys, meeting up with Claire and Quinn in the cafeteria, trying not to give Professor Ryan any encouragement when he stared at me in Psych.

But it wasn't the game and my impending B&E arrest that preoccupied me the most. It was my sleepover at the Queens' house and Claire's mention of Emma's roommate, Nikki. I spent the week stewing over what she'd said, wondering why Nikki would lie to the police, to my mother and me, when Emma's life was at stake.

By Thursday I couldn't stand it any longer. I waited until after dinner when Neo was in the gym, Rock and Oscar were in their rooms, and the other guys were piled into the downstairs living room playing video games.

Then I snuck into the garage and scanned the key fobs that hung on the pegboard. I passed over the Hummer, the Audi, and the Porsche. It was weird that they'd become old news, but I'd ridden in them all enough to be ready for something new.

My gaze landed on an upside-down M that looked liked Poseidon's trident.

That would work.

I plucked it off the board and headed for the sleek metallic candy-apple-red Maserati parked next to the Porsche. I'd admired the car in passing every day for the past two weeks, but sliding into the driver's seat was a whole different experience.

It smelled like leather and men's cologne.

Like sex and money.

It was a fucking work of art, and I felt giddy at the prospect of driving it.

My pulse quickened. Was I really going to do this? Steal one of the Kings' cars and drive to Bellepoint? It's not like I expected it to stay a secret. The car had twin turbo V-8 engines according to the spec stamped on the steering wheel.

It was going to make some noise.

Fuck it. I'd been a good girl since I'd gotten to Aventine. I'd followed the Kings' stupid rules. I'd even played — was still playing — their stupid game.

They, on the other hand, hadn't said another word about Emma since they'd agreed to help me find her, which meant I was on my own again. Might as well have some fun while I was at it.

I pressed the engine button and the car came to life, its initial roar settling into a sexy purr.

I clicked the button to open the garage and waited impatiently while the door slid open. As soon as there was enough room for the Maserati to make a clean exit, I shifted into reverse and punched it.

All the tension let loose inside me as the car glided out of the garage, and I laughed as I sped backwards onto the driveway. Adrenaline surged through my veins, although I couldn't say whether it was from the power of the car or the fact that I'd stolen one of the Kings' beloved cars right out from under their noses.

I glanced at the garage, half expecting to see Neo racing after me. But there was no one there, just the other cars lined up like expensive soldiers, the Maserati's glaringly empty spot staring at me like an accusation.

The door was already closing and I shifted into drive and sped down the driveway. I kept my eyes on the rearview mirror all the way down the tree-lined drive, but no one followed.

I was still in the clear when I turned onto the main road, and I breathed a sigh of relief as I opened up the engine, giving it some serious gas on the straight stretch of asphalt leading away from the house.

I rolled down the windows and opened up the sunroof, then cranked the stereo, which had auto-paired with my phone. Music filled the car, and I glanced at the GPS I'd preset on my phone to give me the best directions to Bellepoint.

I was still learning my way around Blackwell Falls, and I didn't want to waste time getting lost.

The weather had changed in the two weeks I'd been at Aventine. The leaves on the trees were tipped with red and orange, and the wind had the subtle bite of cold in spite of the golden light that blanketed everything.

Driving through the winding, sun-dappled roads leading

to Bellepoint, I could almost forget where I was going and why I was going there. Then I felt disloyal, like I almost always did when I felt good or happy or peaceful — anything but sadness about Emma.

The car was a high-performance animal encasing me in steel and leather, and I thought about the men who owned this car, men I increasingly wanted to bang. It was perfect for them, powerful and sexy as fuck.

Did I trust them? Hell no.

But in the privacy of my own thoughts, there was no denying that I wanted them.

Except for Neo. Sure, he was pretty in a hard, mean kind of way, like a piece of black granite that couldn't hide its darkness in spite of its polish. But I preferred my men with at least an eyedropper's amount of warmth, not to mention a heartbeat.

I glanced at the GPS, which cited my ETA at Bellepoint as less than ten minutes. I was settling back into the rest of the drive when movement caught my eye in the rearview mirror.

Another car was gaining on me on the otherwise empty road, the howl of its engine rising above even the music blaring inside the Maserati.

It was big and black, with tinted windows.

It was the Hummer.

Fuck.

I tried to see who was driving — that would give me some insight into how much trouble I was in — but the windows were tinted, the sun shining at an angle that obscured the driver's face.

I looked at the speedometer and contemplated trying to outrun him, but I was already going way too fast — faster than I'd ever driven before — and the backroads were twisting and unfamiliar.

I kept at my normal speed instead. I was at least making it to Bellepoint. If the Kings wanted their precious car back, they could take it. I'd call an Uber or something to get back to the house.

But one way or another, I was going to talk to Nikki about my sister.

Except the Hummer didn't stay at a safe distance, it sped up, riding the Maserati's bumper.

Too close at this speed. Way too close.

The blood rushed in my ears, my heart hammering as my body went into fight-or-literal-flight mode. I glanced at the GPS and saw that my ETA at Bellepoint was a little over five minutes.

I didn't bother thinking about what I would say to whoever was driving the car (Rock? Oscar? Neo?) when we both arrived there. It didn't matter. I'd be on the Bellepoint campus where they couldn't talk me out of going, where they couldn't distract me from the goal of finding out what happened to Emma.

I eased off the accelerator as I approached a curve in the road, a yellow sign on the side of the road screaming a warning.

Unfortunately, whoever was driving the Hummer didn't do the same. They actually sped up as we entered the curve, crossing the double yellow line and roaring past me while I stared in shock, the sharpness of the curve demanding every bit of my reduced speed and attention.

I held my breath, expecting the Hummer to crash into another car coming in the other direction or topple off the side of the road, but there were no other cars, and the Hummer cleared the front of the Maserati, then gunned the engine, putting space between the two cars.

What the fuck? Why chase me down just to leave me behind?

I understood a few seconds later when the Hummer skidded to a stop sideways, blocking the road in front of me.

Slamming on the breaks, I kept the steering wheel in a death grip as the car started to fishtail. I steered against the skid like I was taught to do in driver's ed, and I had to force myself not to close my eyes and brace for impact as I gained on the Hummer, straddling the double yellow and blocking my way.

The car came to a stop without a sound, no squeal of brakes or anything, and for a second I wondered if I was dead. But then I opened my eyes and saw that I was sideways next to the Hummer, no more than three feet away.

I was dizzy with adrenaline, the blood rushing in my ears.

I sat there with my breath coming in short gasps, my hands still tight around the steering wheel.

I jumped when the driver's side door opened, then barely had time to register a murderous Neo staring down at me in the second before he leaned into the Maserati to reach across my body.

I wondered if I'd hit my head without realizing it, if I had a concussion, because Neo looked like he wanted to kill me and all I registered was the musky scent of cologne mixed with the sweat, the scruff on his jaw, the press of his body against mine as he unclipped my seat belt.

He didn't say a word as he dragged me out of the driver's seat like I was no heavier than a feather. I barely had time to register that he was wearing a tank top and basketball shorts, which meant he'd left the house in a hurry, because Neo never left the house looking anything less than perfect.

I stumbled when my feet hit the asphalt and he shoved me up against the car, the driver's side door still open next to us, and placed one of his hands on either side of my body, locking me in place.

"What the *fuck* do you think you're doing?" His voice was dangerously low, his face only inches from mine, his eyes spitting fire. "You could have been killed."

I was still breathing hard, although now I wasn't sure if it was adrenaline from the car chase and near collision with the Hummer or the fact that my stepbrother was so close I felt the press of his thighs against mine.

"Me?" I countered. "What do you think *you're* doing? If I'd been killed, it would have been because *you* chased me like a maniac!"

"Because you stole my car!" he roared. I fought against the instinct to shrink away from his anger, which I couldn't have done anyway since I was smashed up against the car. "And you're not supposed to be out alone. Do you have any idea how dangerous it is for you to leave and not tell anyone where you're going?"

"I'm not your prisoner!" I screamed at him. "I don't have

to follow your orders! You're the most annoying, obnoxious—"

"And you're the most oblivious, stubborn— "

I was still going, but now he'd started in with his own insults, both of us talking louder, trying to make sure we were heard over each other. I didn't even know what I was saying anymore. The words were just falling out of my mouth, my voice so loud on the empty road I only caught snippets from Neo.

Stupid...

Naive...

Cocktease...

The last one stopped me in my tracks.

Cocktease?

"Cocktease?" I was practically shrieking at him now. "The 1950s called, they want their insult back. And besides, you're obviously only mad because you know I would never — not in a million years, not for a million dollars — touch your cock!"

I was breathless with rage, but the barb had landed. The road felt strangely silent in the vacuum of our earlier shouting, no sound at all except for the birds chirping in the trees by the side of the road.

Neo's face was red, his eyes wide and bulging, and for a second, I almost thought he would hit me. He kissed me instead, slamming his mouth down on mine, pushing me back against the Maserati.

My arms didn't know what to do with themselves, and they hung helplessly at my sides while Neo's tongue dove into my mouth, his hands still braced on either side of my body like he was afraid to touch me.

My brain was misfiring, reason trying to grab hold amid the fireworks exploding in my brain, the tidal wave of lust building between my thighs as Neo's rigid, clearly huge dick pressed hard against my stomach.

It was useless. There was no room for reason in the raw hunger that had roared to life in my body. My erect nipples rubbed painfully against his T-shirt, begging for his mouth and hands, and my pussy was slick with need. I was already grinding against his cock, trying to get myself off through our clothes while he fucked my mouth with his tongue.

I slid my hands under his shirt and gasped against his mouth when he did the same, tugging my bra down and squeezing my tits, rolling my nipples between his fingers.

His kiss was an invasion, an occupation. I couldn't fucking get enough of it.

I opened my mouth wider to him, meeting every stroke of his tongue with my own while I mapped his muscled chest with my hands, his skin hot and smooth under my fingertips.

He broke the kiss, leaving us both gasping for breath, and I caught a glimpse of his face — expression tortured, eyes glassy — in the moment before he closed his mouth around one of my nipples.

I moaned as he sucked and licked, and I shifted position so that I was riding his thigh, working the friction on my clit to stoke the orgasm that had been building since the second his mouth had slammed into mine.

I was on fire, every nerve ending in my body screaming for

him to fuck me senseless right there in the middle of the road. I slid my fingers into his hair, still grinding on his cock, my pussy soaking wet as I became more desperate for him to fuck me.

"Neo," I gasped. "Fuck me."

He growled and spun me around to face the Maserati. I braced myself on the car's roof while he yanked down my jeans and underwear. A split second later, his dick was against my ass, so close to my pussy I could almost feel him pushing into me.

It was massive, almost thick and long enough to make me hesitate.

Almost.

He slid his cock between my thighs, and I groaned as his head bumped against my clit, settling against my entrance.

He scooped my hair away from one shoulder and draped it over the other, then lowered his mouth to my shoulder. I thought he was going to kiss me until I felt the sting of his teeth, hard enough to bring tears to my eyes, to send a fresh wave of moisture to my cunt.

I was delirious, out of my mind with need. I pushed back against him. "Do it," I gasped. "Fuck me."

He grabbed ahold of my hips, then froze as a horn cut through the air.

What the...?

It sounded again and I lifted my head, trying to clear my mind enough to figure out what was going on.

Then I saw the truck idling on the other side of the Maserati. The driver was a younger guy, and he was gesturing wildly, clearly annoyed that the Maserati and Hummer were blocking the road.

Neo was still behind me, his dick right up against the opening of my pussy.

The guy in the truck honked again and Neo waved him off. I should have felt exposed, but the Maserati blocked everything but my head from the front, and Neo's body was still pressed against mine from behind.

He lowered his mouth to my ear. "Just remember, Jezebel. You asked for it."

Chapter 38

Willa

The windows of the Hummer were rolled up, the interior of the car silent except for the soft ticking of the cooling engine. Neo had insisted on driving me to Bellepoint. I'd resisted — how fucking humiliating after what had happened, and had almost happened, on the road — but he wouldn't take no for an answer, and we'd left the Maserati parked at the side of the road so Oscar could come pick it up.

My face was still burning with humiliation. I could only hope he wouldn't tell Oscar, or anyone, what had happened between us.

I looked around the parking lot outside the dorm where Nikki was living in her final year at Bellepoint, something I only knew because Claire had done some digging with other girls she knew at the school.

"Do you want to talk about that?" I finally asked.

"Nothing to say," Neo said, staring straight ahead.

I don't know what I wanted him to say. That he didn't

regret it? That would be stupid, because I was already regretting it.

Liar. You're just regretting that he didn't finish what he started.

I ignored the voice in my head. It wanted to hand me a lighter while I stood next to the grenade that was my attraction to Neo — that was our attraction to each other — and I was apparently already holding a lit match in one hand.

"Fine," I said, reaching for the door, "but you can drop the Jezebel act. If I'm not mistaken — and I'm not — you would have been more than happy to fuck me back there."

He turned to face me, and I was almost surprised to see the hatred still burning in his eyes. "Wanting to fuck you and liking you, *trusting* you, are two very different things, Jezebel."

"You have a lot of nerve talking about trust. It's been two years since Emma went missing. Two years!" Tears stung my eyes. "You've been here the whole time, were here when it happened, and you haven't done anything to find her. And I'm supposed to trust you?" I shook my head. "I don't think so."

His expression turned cold. "I'm not the one who left the country for a worldwide party."

The insult took my breath away, literally sucked all the air out of my lungs.

Because it was true. They were the words that taunted me when I let myself stay still long enough to hear them. I'd spent my last year of high school hanging on every word the police spoke about Emma's disappearance, printing flyers, combing her social media for clues about what might have happened to her.

I should have come to Aventine when I graduated. Instead, I'd bailed. I'd left my mom with Roberto and I'd tried to pretend none of it had happened.

"Maybe," I said. "But what you did was worse. You were there — at Aventine when she disappeared and for two whole years afterwards. And you didn't even bother to look for her." I took a breath. "Stay. Leave. I really don't care. I'm going to talk to Nikki."

I slammed the car door and started across the parking lot, feeling Neo's eyes burning a hole in my back every step of the way.

The Bellepoint campus was old and quaint, with stone buildings and sweeping lawns surrounded by old-growth trees, but Lenape Hall looked like any dorm in any college in America.

I made my way over gray linoleum in the second-floor hall and watched the numbers on the doors, all of them decorated with two names written in glitter and stickers that varied from butterflies to music notes to theater masks.

I'd been surprised to find out that Nikki still lived in the dorms. I'd assumed every college student wanted to move off campus in their last two years, but Claire told me it was hard to find rentals in Blackwell Falls. Its residential makeup consisted of townies who'd lived in their houses for decades — and sometimes generations — and downstate people who owned most of the upscale homes in the area. It was one of the reasons the sororities and fraternities were so popular: living off campus was a huge perk.

Some of the doors were open, and I caught glimpses of the life I might have had if I'd started school as a freshman at a regular college — posters on the wall and rumpled bedding and fairy lights and music and laughter between girls spread out on the floors and beds.

Leaving the country had been a choice, but it hadn't felt like a choice at the time. I'd been drowning in grief, completely unequipped to deal with my mom, who'd spent her days in bed unless Roberto Alinari was paying a visit. Now I felt a pang of loss. I liked to play tough and act like I hadn't wanted to be like everyone else graduating from high school, but I couldn't help wondering what it was like to start college with so much hope and innocence.

I passed a girl with wet hair in boxer shorts and a tank top carrying a shower caddy, continued past three more doors, and stopped at room 238. A glittery green name tag that read MELODY was taped to the wall on one side of the door. The other side spelled out NIKKI in pink.

I took a deep breath and knocked, hoping Nikki wasn't out. I really didn't want to have to come back, especially since I was pretty sure Neo would hide the keys to the cars after today.

The door flew open. A dark-haired girl stood in its frame, her expression distracted, music playing softly in the background.

Her blue eyes widened in surprise.

"Hi, Nikki," I said.

She stared at me for what felt like ages. "You shouldn't have come here."

She sat on her bed after offering me the desk chair. Her roommate — the girl named Melody — was at the library studying with friends, a stroke of luck for me.

The dorm room was standard, and a fresh pang of loss washed over me as I looked around. My mom and I had driven up to Blackwell Falls with Emma to help organize her dorm room. It had been a fun day, full of excited chatter, and for the first time in a long time, I'd felt something like hope.

I'd thought the worst of our bad luck was behind us, my dad either in witness protection or dead. Emma had been excited to start college, to be away from home, and I'd been looking forward to my senior year of high school.

Then she was gone.

"Whatever you have to say, you should say it before Melody comes back," Nikki said.

She was nervous, tapping her bare foot on the linoleum, her eyes darting to the door like she expected Melody to burst in at any second.

"You were with Emma at Aventine," I said. "Not the night she went missing, but before."

"So?"

"You lied," I said. "To us. To the police."

She picked at a thread on the comforter on her bed. "Like you said, I wasn't with her that night. I didn't think it mattered."

She was lying. I could see it in the way she wouldn't look me in the eyes, in the manic tapping of her foot. "If it didn't matter, why did you lie?"

She looked up at me, her eyes cold. "You came up to visit Emma, what, twice?"

My skin prickled with the need to defend myself, my guilty conscience about the distance that had grown between Emma and me roaring back to life. "I was a senior in high school," I said. "I didn't even have a car."

"Still," Nikki said, "you have no idea what it's like here."

"So tell me."

"You just started at Aventine this year right?" she asked.

"How did you know that?"

She shrugged. "Blackwell Falls is a small town. The campuses here are even smaller. The daughter of Frank Russo and sister of Emma Russo at the college where she went missing? Word gets around."

Great.

"What does my attending Aventine have to do with Emma?"

"The year just started," she said. "You don't know what they're like there, what they do."

"I know about the games," I said.

She rolled her eyes. "The ones they talk about," she said under her breath.

"What's that supposed to mean?" I asked.

She met my eyes, really looked at me, for the first time. "Did you know Emma was the fourth girl to go missing from Bellepoint in the past four years? And that another girl went missing last year?"

I felt like I'd been slapped. "What are you talking about?"

I'd basically lived online the year after Emma went missing. I'd spent more hours doing research on Bellepoint and Aventine — although I admit the latter was buttoned up pretty tight — than I could count. I'd even dug into the history of Blackwell Falls.

"Every year one girl from Bellepoint goes missing. It's why I stopped going to Aventine with Emma," Nikki said.

The words spun through my mind. I was opening my mouth to ask another question when the door flew open. A tiny redhead burst into the room wearing a backpack, carrying a takeout bag with a logo I couldn't make out, and staring down at her phone.

"Oh. My. God. If I ever see that tool — " She stopped cold when she saw me sitting in Nikki's desk chair. "Oh! Sorry! I didn't know you had company."

"Could you give us, like, five minutes?" Nikki asked.

"Uh... sure. Let me just drop my stuff."

Clearly this was Melody, Nikki's roommate. I watched as she dropped her bag on the other bed in the room. She set the takeout bag on the second desk and I caught a whiff of cooked meat and onions.

She glanced sideways at me as she hurried back out the door.

I refocused on Nikki. I needed to cut to the chase. "I did a lot of digging after Emma went missing. On Aventine, but on Bellepoint too. I never saw a single news article talking about missing girls."

"They call them runaways," Nikki said.

"Runaways are kids," I said. You couldn't be classified as

a runaway if you were over eighteen. I knew because it was one of the excuses the police had used when Emma went missing.

"I'm using the term loosely," Nikki said. "Point is, they always look like they left on their own. Their purses and phones are always missing. Their bank accounts are empty. Their parents file missing persons reports, but it never goes anywhere because no one really looks. Until Emma."

"I'm confused." I hated to admit it, but the pieces weren't coming together the way I needed them to.

Nikki's gaze slid to the door. Her foot was tapping faster now. "The girls who went missing before Emma, they were girls that don't get sympathy on the news. Two black girls. A Native girl."

I sucked in my breath. She didn't need to explain. I knew how it worked, knew that some girls got more media attention than others because they were white and considered pretty. It was a statistical fact, one I'd learned in the immediate aftermath of Emma's disappearance.

"No one even looked for them?" I asked.

There had been justified outrage when Emma's case hit the news, pictures of other girls her age who'd gone missing without any fanfare, questions about why there was so much attention on Emma and so little on others.

I'd felt guilty that Emma was getting special treatment, but I hadn't had the luxury to dwell on it while my sister was missing. Now, the guilt came rushing back. Was Nikki telling the truth? Had three other girls gone missing from Bellepoint with so little attention that they hadn't even come up in the research I'd done online?

"Not really," Nikki said. "I mean, the parents put up posters and stuff, but the police said they couldn't do anything, not when it looked like they'd chosen to leave."

I chewed my bottom lip, hesitant to ask the next question. "Is there any possibility they did?"

Nikki looked at me — *really* looked at me — for the first time since she'd let me into the room. "Three of them?"

I exhaled. She was right. It was too much, too many girls to be a coincidence.

"Why didn't you go with Emma that night?" I asked. "You'd gone with her before."

"Honestly? The place creeped me out," she said.

"Aventine?"

She nodded.

"Why?" I asked.

"It always felt like something else was going on, like everyone at Aventine was in on some joke that we weren't part of." I thought about the game, our families that were impossible to explain to anyone outside of the criminal underworld. "And it wasn't the game," she added, as if reading my mind.

"So what was it then?" I asked.

She went back to picking at the thread on her comforter. "I don't know, but it felt like..." She took a deep breath and met my eyes gain. "You know how the douchebags in high school pick on one kid, except they pretend to be the kid's friend so that kid never quite realizes they're being picked on? And everyone else is kind of embarrassed and humiliated for them?"

I nodded. Who didn't? High school was savage.

"It was like that," Nikki said. "Except we were those kids, invited to parties, targets for hookups with the Aventine guys, but secretly laughed at... or something." She shook her head. "I can't explain it. I just picked up a vibe I didn't like. I didn't feel safe there, and neither did Emma."

That got my attention. "What do you mean?"

"We talked about it. I begged Emma to stop going, but she wouldn't. She felt it too," Nikki said.

"Then why did she keep going without you?" I asked.

"Because," Nikki said, looking up at me, "she wanted to find out what was going on."

Chapter 39

Willa

"Why didn't you tell me about the other missing girls?" I asked, storming into the kitchen from the garage.

Neo had asked me how it went with Nikki when I got back in the car, but I hadn't wanted to say anything until I had all three Kings together. I wanted to ambush them, to prevent Neo from warning Rock and Oscar so they could keep bullshitting me. I'd spent the drive home sulking in the passenger seat, replaying everything Nikki had said and trying to figure out what the actual fuck was going on.

Rock was standing over a pot of soup, wearing an apron and holding a wooden spoon.

He set the spoon down and glanced at Oscar and Neo.

"Don't look at them," I said. "Look at me."

Oscar crossed his arms and leaned against the island. "Listen, tiger, if you just sit down and —"

"Don't you dare condescend me, Oscar Drago." I glared at him. "I want answers. Now."

Rock dared another glance at Neo, a *what-the-fuck* look in his eyes, but rather than say something rude or patronizing, Neo just shook his head. I wondered if he was feeling guilty about what had happened between us on the road, because somewhere under my anger and fear for Emma, that's how I was feeling.

I didn't owe Rock or Oscar anything in terms of an explanation — we weren't exclusive or anything — but it still felt like a betrayal.

I hated that.

"We don't think it had anything to do with Emma," Rock said, setting down the wooden spoon.

I laughed, but it came out more like a bark. "How can you say that? All the missing girls were from Bellepoint, and they all had a habit of coming here to party."

I'd found out that last part later, after Nikki told me Emma had known something was going on at Aventine.

"A lot of girls from Bellepoint come here to party," Neo said calmly. "Only four of them have gone missing."

I spun on him, still standing near the garage door. Somewhere beyond the kitchen, I could hear the sound of a football game on the TV in the living room.

"*Only*? Only four girls?" Tears had sprung to my eyes, and sorrow warred with rage in my body. "How can you say that? Every one of those girls had people like me who loved them."

"I'm sorry."

I almost passed out from shock. Neo Alinari apologizing? To me?

"That came out wrong," he said. "I'm making the point

that the percentage of girls who came here to party and went missing is statistically small, not to minimize their disappearances, but to keep us from focusing where we shouldn't."

I was still recovering from the fact that Neo had apologized, that he'd even sounded sincere for the first time in his life. I wanted to go back to just hating him, but between the memory of his mouth on my boob, his cock throbbing against my stomach, and his almost-human disposition, he wasn't making it as easy as I'd hoped.

"It seems like we should be focusing on the detail that girls from Bellepoint are going missing at Aventine. What do they have in common?" I asked.

"No offense," Rock said, turning off the burner on the stove, "but you're looking at this wrong."

"What are you talking about?"

"You're focused on what the girls have in common," Oscar said, "instead of what makes them different."

I tried to make sense of what he was saying. "I'm still not following you."

"The other girls were black, Native," Neo finally said from his spot by the garage door. "And they were made to look like they left voluntarily."

The words were coalescing into something that finally made sense. "Whoever took Emma took a risk," I said. "They knew she wouldn't be under the radar." Something else clicked into place. "And they didn't have time to make her disappearance look intentional."

"Exactly," Rock said.

"Are you asking the same question we've been asking yet?" Neo asked, his voice cold.

"You first," I said.

"What was the rush with Emma?" Oscar's dark eyes searched mine. "Why was it so important to make her disappear? Important enough that whoever was responsible was willing to risk all that attention after spending years covering their tracks?"

"So you do think Emma's disappearance is connected to the other girls," I said.

Oscar raked his hand down his face, something he only did when he was frustrated or tired. "We just don't know. The fact that the other girls look like they left voluntarily makes things... complicated."

I glared at him. "It's not complicated. Four girls have gone missing from Bellepoint in four years. They're connected. You knew about it all this time, and from the looks of things, you haven't done a fucking thing about it."

Grief was like a kick to the chest, and I had to force myself to suck in a breath as the reality hit me. No one had looked for the first three girls. Whoever had taken them had a free pass to keep doing it when Emma disappeared.

Oscar reached for me. "You don't understand what's at play — "

"Four years." I interrupted Oscar. "And from where I'm standing, it looks a lot like nobody gave a fuck."

I was drowning in a familiar ocean of grief. No way was I going to lose it in front of the Kings.

I turned and stalked from the room.

Chapter 40

Willa

I paced my bedroom, replaying my conversation with the guys in my mind. I kept snagging on the same detail: Emma was different from than the other girls. Because she was white, and because whoever took her hadn't had time to make her disappearance look voluntary.

But I knew beyond a shadow of a doubt that whoever had taken Emma was responsible for the other girls' disappearances too. Find the person who'd taken one of them, and we'd find the person who'd taken all of them.

I tried to make sense of it. Who would take these girls? And why?

I teased the details. Whoever had taken them was able to get into the dorms, pack the girls' bags without anyone seeing (did Bellepoint have cameras on campus like Aventine? I would have to find out).

I shook my head. None of it made sense. If the other three girls lived on campus (did they? I'd have to check), they would have had roommates. A stranger packing their bags would have been noticed by them and the other students in the dorm.

I sat on my bed and dropped my head in my hands. I'd been at Aventine for over two weeks and was no closer to finding out what had happened to Emma than I'd been the day Roberto and my mom had dumped me at the Kings' house.

I'd been a bitch to the guys, criticizing them for not doing anything to help find Emma when they were obviously the only people who'd even tried. They'd known about the other three missing girls, had already been working the problem of why Emma was different.

You don't understand what's at play...

Oscar's words drifted through my mind. The guys obviously knew more than they were letting on. It bugged me. We were supposed to be working together, and it felt like I was still on the outside, like *they* still didn't trust *me*.

Which was crazy. I was Emma's sister. No one wanted to find her more than me, but it felt like I was earning the trust of the Kings instead of the other way around.

Still, they had been asking questions, and I believed them when they said they wanted to help me find her. Did that mean I trusted them?

Hell no.

We were a long, long away from trust. But it was better for me — better for Emma — if we worked together.

And that meant not acting like a brat when we were on the subject of my missing sister.

Neo couldn't care less about the way I was feeling (I couldn't even think about what had happened between us on the road), and Rock was so easygoing he probably hadn't even registered my insults, but Oscar had been stung by my attitude in the kitchen. I'd seen it in the way he'd blinked when I'd interrupted him, the resignation in his eyes when I'd left the room.

I sighed and got to my feet. I needed to make things right with him. That wouldn't have been a big deal by itself. I needed him, needed the Kings to help me find Emma.

The thing that was really fucked was that I *wanted* to make things right with him.

What was that about?

I didn't know, but whatever it was, it would take more than one night to figure out.

I didn't know how long I'd been stewing in my room, but I was hoping Oscar had already come upstairs to his. Apologizing to him wouldn't be so bad, but I had zero desire to be humble in front of all three of the guys, especially Neo.

I stepped into the hall and turned right toward Oscar's room. The door was usually closed, but this time it was open a crack, music playing from inside.

I knocked softly. "Can I come in?"

There was no answer, so I pushed the door open a little more, thinking maybe he couldn't hear me over the music. The smell of soap and shampoo hit me all at once, the sound of running water coming from the half-open door.

He was in the shower.

Fuck me, the last thing I needed to think about was a naked Oscar all wet and slippery in the shower.

I was preparing to shut the door behind me when

something on the bed caught my eye. I only hesitated a few seconds before stepping into the room.

The room was large and well-furnished, with a modern bed (neatly made) in dark wood, a desk, and two dressers. Across the room, the door to his walk-in closet was open, his clothes hanging like shadows inside it.

But the thing that really got my attention was the TV. It was massive, taking up nearly half of one wall, two bookcases on either side of it with DVDs lined up on their shelves.

The cords from his gaming system were neatly arranged and tied together, and a black leather sofa faced the TV. This must be where Oscar watched movies and hung out when he didn't want to be in the media room or with the other guys.

The water was still running, so I walked over to the bed, focusing on the photographs that had drawn my attention from the doorway. They were spread out across the black and gray comforter, and it only took me a second to realize what they had in common.

They were all of me.

I touched the edge of the ones on top, spreading them out so I could see the ones on the bottom, but yep. Every single one of them was of me.

Some of them were in black and white, and some of them were in color, but they'd almost all been taken when I wasn't paying attention. There was a color photograph of me at the river the day Oscar had taken me into town. In the picture, my head was bent to the river, sparkling in the sun behind me while I rinsed my hands, my hair lit up from behind like a halo.

I slid the pictures aside one by one, watching the first

weeks of my life in Aventine pass before my eyes, seeing them as Oscar had seen them through the lens of his camera.

A picture of me laughing in the kitchen, probably because of something Rock had said, given that his hand was in the frame, the sapphire in his ring flaring in the lights.

My face lit by the bonfire on Game Night, the shot obviously taken from across the fire. Oscar must have been hidden by the shadows when he'd taken the picture.

Me, leaning against the wall at the Orpheum, my hair tousled, lips swollen, clearly taken after our steamy makeout sesh in the projector room.

There was even one of me drying off after a shower. It had been taken from the doorway of my bathroom, my back turned to the camera as I toweled off my legs, water beading my spine.

I should have been pissed — and maybe I would be later — but the picture was good. If it had been hanging in a gallery somewhere, it might even have been considered a work of art.

"What are you doing?"

I spun to find Oscar standing in the doorway of the bathroom.

Completely naked.

It made sense since he probably hadn't expected company, but that didn't stop the raw hunger that roared to life in my body at the sight of him.

"I... uh... the door was open..."

"You didn't answer my question." There was no anger in his voice, just curiosity.

There was no eagerness to cover his nakedness either,

which wasn't a bad thing, because Oscar Drago naked and dripping from the shower?

Well, that was a fucking sight to behold.

His dark hair was tousled, drops of moisture clinging to his sculpted chest and muscled abs, and the massive dick hanging between his legs — make that the massive *pierced* dick —made my pussy pulse with hunger.

I could almost feel him fucking me.

"I was... uh... coming to apologize," I said, forcing the words out around the lust vying for control of my senses.

He walked slowly toward me, and I noticed his dick had gotten hard in the last few seconds even though he'd done nothing but stand a few feet away and look at me.

He tucked a piece of hair behind my ear. "I don't hear an apology, tiger."

"What is all this?" I forced myself to break eye contact and look at the pictures. I didn't trust myself with a naked Oscar Drago. I could hardly trust myself with a fully clothed Oscar Drago.

"What does it look like?" he asked.

"Pictures," I said, stating the obvious. "Of me. But why?"

"I told you I like to take pictures." I could feel his eyes on my face, pulling my gaze back to his against my will.

"But why me?" I asked, looking up at him,

He reached out, dragging his thumb along my lower lip, his gaze never leaving mine. "Because you're so fucking beautiful," he said, his voice hoarse.

He paused, his stroke of my mouth pressing against the seam of my lips. I knew what he wanted, and I knew what it would mean if I let him in, but I didn't have the strength to fight my attraction to him anymore.

I didn't even want to.

I opened my mouth and took his thumb between my lips, sucking until he groaned.

Then he was sliding his hands into my hair and crushing my mouth under his in a kiss so consuming everything else fell away.

Chapter 41

Willa

Kissing Oscar Drago was like being caught in a riptide. At first you thought you were swimming, but a second later — when it was too late to do anything about it — you realized you were drowning,

And it was definitely too late to do anything about it. I was drowning in Oscar's mouth and the stroke of his tongue, his dick at attention and pressing against my stomach, doing all kinds of crazy things to my already soaking-wet pussy.

I ran my hands over his pierced nipples and damp chest, over his stomach, then took his erect cock in my hands.

He hissed at my touch. "Careful, tiger," he warned. "I've been waiting for you to do that for a long time."

He sucked on my neck, and I stroked my way up his thick shaft, running my thumb over the two silver barbells pierced through his swollen head. "Did this hurt?"

"Pain is just a construct," he said, his breath a hot whisper across my neck.

"Very funny," I said, stroking my hand down his cock.

"Nothing about this is funny," he groaned.

"What..." I stopped what I was doing and pulled away long enough to look down at the metal I felt at the base of his dick. I hadn't realized he had more than the piercing on the head of his dick, but now I saw that there was another barbell at the base, below his stomach. "What is this?"

"What does it look like?" he asked with a chuckle.

I rolled my eyes. "I mean, why here?" I'd seen a penis piercing or two, but never at the base.

He cocked an eyebrow in a suggestive expression that was sexy as hell. "Think about it."

I did, and my pussy immediately clenched with excitement. The barbell at the base of his shaft was positioned to stimulate a woman's clit during sex, and I suddenly couldn't wait to give it a test run.

"Jesus, Oscar."

He grinned. "What can I say?" He leaned in to kiss my neck, flicking his hot tongue out to lick my skin. "I'm committed to your pleasure."

I sighed. "I can't wait to test your, er... *commitment*."

He dropped slow kisses at the corners of my mouth, pausing to lick at my lower lip before diving in for another kiss. And this time, there was nothing slow about it. His tongue was feverish, pillaging my mouth with fierce strokes that sent licks of fire through my body.

"No fair," he said against my mouth. "You have too many clothes on."

I bit his lip and he favored me with a lascivious grin as I stripped off my T-shirt.

"Easy enough to fix," I said, wrapping my arms around his neck and pressing against him.

"Not good enough," he said, unclasping my bra with one hand.

It fell away and he pulled it out from between our bodies and tossed it aside.

Then he did the last thing I expected: he leaned back to grab his camera from the nightstand.

I covered my boobs by reflex. "What are you doing?"

He snapped a quick picture and put the camera back on the nightstand. "Don't worry. It's just for me. I want to remember the way you look right before I fuck you for the first time."

I forgot about it a second later when he stretched out on top of me, the sudden skin-on-skin contact enough to send a shiver of ecstasy down my spine.

"I'm not sure I like how easy that was for you that bra removal," I said, tipping my head back as he trailed kisses down my throat.

His laugh was a sexy rumble I felt in my chest.

"Getting jealous on me, tiger?"

"No." It was a lie, but I wasn't in the right state of mind to analyze the fact that I wanted to pull out the hair of any girl who'd ever touched Oscar before me.

"Liar," he said, laughing and pinching one of my nipples between his fingers until I gasped. "It's okay. I want you to be jealous."

"You do?" I was surprised I could say anything around the panting of my breath, the need that was pulsing through my veins like a fucking drumbeat. "Why?"

"Because I'll tell you right now I'm going to annihilate anyone who puts their hands on you after this." He murmured the words against my tit, then sucked my nipple into his mouth.

A strangled moan escaped my throat. "What about Rock?"

Maybe I shouldn't have said it. Not now. Not while Oscar was sucking my tit and preparing to fuck me.

But he didn't seem to mind.

"I'll let him live if we fuck you together."

A fresh wave of desire coursed through my body, and I slid my hands into his hair and tightened my fingers around the silky dark locks. His tongue stud and lip piercing were doing crazy things to my nipple, sending a steady stream of heat to my pussy that made me feel like I was on fire from the inside out.

"Fuck," he said, lifting his head, "I want to look at you."

I gasped in surprise when he shoved me back on the bed.

I fell into the pictures scattered on the comforter. "Your pictures..."

"I have copies," he said, advancing on me.

"What a creeper," I said, grinning up at him.

"When it comes to you, tiger, you have no idea."

Hmmm... that sounded intriguing.

He bent down and unfastened my jeans, then slid them off my hips, taking my underwear along with them. I tried not to think about the fact that only a few hours before, I'd wanted Neo to fuck me on the road against the Maserati.

That had been a mistake.

This felt right, even though I didn't know why.

"Jesus, you're fucking magnificent, you know that?" he asked, staring down at me.

I squirmed under the heat of his gaze. I wasn't exactly shy — I'd visited more than one nude beach during my year abroad — but there was something a little too thorough about the way he was looking at me. Like he was seeing past my body to all the stuff I'd been trying to keep hidden inside.

I cocked my head, wanting to keep things simple. Fucking Oscar was one thing. Getting all up in my feels with him was something else entirely.

"What are you going to do about it?" I asked with a mischievous smile.

He grinned. "If that's a challenge, I accept."

I squealed as he pounced on me, burying his face in my neck. He came in for another kiss, this one long and slow, then ran his nose down to my collarbone and between my tits, across my stomach and down to my cunt.

I heard him inhale and laughed. "Are you smelling me?"

"You smell delicious," he said, kissing his way between my thighs. "I can't wait to taste you."

I sighed. "That makes two of us."

He chuckled and nipped at my inner thigh. A second later, I moaned as he sank two fingers inside my dripping core.

"Oh my god..." I closed my eyes as he lapped at my clit.

"Hmmm..." he murmured. "I knew you'd taste good."

He thrust his fingers in and out of my tunnel while he worked my swollen nub with his tongue.

I sank onto his fingers and mouth, reaching for more of what he was already giving, losing my hold on reality as waves of pleasure washed over me. He stroked the walls of my channel with his fingers and drew my clit into his mouth, sucking until I cried out into the room.

I threaded my fingers into his silky dark locks and tugged, then felt his growl reverberate through my core.

"You're so fucking wet, beautiful." He pushed my thighs open and spread me wide, then ran his tongue all the way through my folds.

I moaned. "You better get up here and fuck me, Oscar Drago."

"Sounds like a threat," he said, pleasure dripping from his voice.

"It is." I looked down and the sight of his dark head between my thighs just about sent me over the edge. "I'm going to come on your face if you don't hurry up."

He looked up at me and grinned. "I've been dreaming about you coming on my face for weeks."

"Fuuuuuck," I moaned as he buried his face in my pussy all over again.

He put his fingers back inside me and sucked on my clit, teasing it with his tongue.

I moved my hips in time to his movements as I rode his face. I was beyond thought, beyond anything but the promise of the earth-shattering orgasm building in my stomach.

"Don't stop," I gasped, grinding against his mouth and fingers, moving my hips faster as release crept closer.

He sucked harder and pressed against the upper wall of my pussy.

That was it. I was a goner. The orgasm flooded my body like a fever, light exploding as my voice erupted into the room, a raw animalistic cry I didn't recognize as my own.

I came *hard*, shudders wracking my body, rolling through me like an earthquake. It went on and on, and I was only vaguely aware that I was begging Oscar not to stop.

Not that I needed to worry about that. His face was buried in my pussy, lapping up every drop until I lay limp and breathless, spread out on his bed, the pictures still spread all around me.

He kissed my inner thigh and kneeled between my thighs.

"Not tired, are you?" he asked, his eyes liquid with desire. "Because we're just getting started."

I lifted my head, the sight of his pierced dick jutting between my thighs sparking my hunger all over again.

I batted my eyelashes sweetly. "That's cute. Now get a condom and fuck me."

He opened his mouth to say something, then startled as the door flew open behind him.

"What the fu—"

It happened so fast I barely had time to register a series of facts: Rock had walked into Oscar's room while I was ass-naked and spread out on Oscar's bed, Oscar's dick literally inches from impaling me.

I didn't even have time to try and cover myself.

"Ah, jesus fuck," Rock said. He pointed at us. "One, sorry for not knocking. Two, you fucking lucky bastard."

Oscar sighed, like it wasn't the first time Rock had walked in without knocking. "What the fuck, Rock?"

"I said sorry." He sounded wounded. "Anyway, as much

as I'd love to have a front row seat to this little show — or better yet, a ticket to ride — there's something you should both see."

"Can it wait?" Oscar gritted out.

"Uh, no, it can't, actually," Rock said. "Hurry up. Neo's waiting in the kitchen."

Chapter 42

Willa

Neo was waiting in the kitchen, and he didn't look happy. Whether that was because Rock had let him in on the, er, situation he'd walked in on in Oscar's room or because of whatever the big news was, I had no idea.

"What's up?" Oscar asked as we entered the room.

I felt like a teenager caught having sex by my parents, and I reached up to try and smooth my tangled hair. We'd thrown our clothes on in a hurry, and I was suddenly worried I'd put my shirt on inside out or had done something else that would give away the fact that I'd just had a mind-blowing orgasm thanks to the magic of Oscar Drago's mouth and fingers. Not only that, but I'd been seconds away from finally feeling his big pierced dick inside me.

Dammit. This better be good.

"This." Neo shoved a manila envelope across the kitchen island.

I reached for it, then saw that it was addressed to me.

And it had been opened.

I glared at him. "You're opening my mail now?"

"We're opening your mail always, Jezebel." He wasn't moved by my annoyance. "And this is why."

I lifted the torn flap and reached inside, then removed what felt like a stack of paper. Except it wasn't a stack of paper. It was a single sheet of paper with letters from a magazine glued to it and a stack of photographs.

Of me.

With my face scratched out.

"What the fuck?" I dropped it like I'd been burned.

"Exactly," Rock said, raking his hand through his hair. "And there's something else in there."

I reached cautiously for the envelope and peered inside, not wanting to take a chance by just reaching into it in case it was full of... I don't know. Pig guts or something?

But it wasn't pig guts. It wasn't even anything gross, just something terrifying.

I reached inside and removed the earring. My earring. The one I'd dropped at the welcome ball when I'd snuck into Dean Giordana's office.

"That belong to you?" Neo asked.

I nodded. "I dropped it in the dean's office during the ball."

I avoided his eyes, both because I knew he was going to be pissed that I hadn't said something sooner and because I didn't want to think about the first time we'd kissed, about the fact that I couldn't stay away from him when we were alone even though I hated him with the fire of a thousand suns.

Emphasis on the word *fire*.

"And when, exactly, were you going to tell us?" Neo's voice was so hard I thought it might crack.

I shrugged. "I wasn't even sure where I'd dropped it. It could have been by the bar or in the ballroom or on the dance floor or — "

"In the dean's office," Rock said.

Oscar scrubbed his face. "You should have told us, tiger."

The criticism from him stung, even combined with the nickname. Probably because he'd had his face buried between my thighs fifteen minutes earlier.

"Yeah, well, I didn't," I said, picking up the photos. "How was I supposed to know some psycho was going to find it?"

The pictures were recent, taken on and around campus. There was one of me walking to class outside and another in the cafeteria, sitting at Claire's table. In one of them, I was standing somewhere unfamiliar, and when I looked closer I realized it was the deli where Oscar had taken me to get lunch when we'd gone into town for makeup.

There was even one of me leaning against the wall at the Orpheum, my surroundings dark, making me appear like I was floating.

They might have been decent pictures if not for the scratched-out faces, clearly done with something sharp that had punctured the photo paper in places.

These were definitely not love letters.

The thought reminded me about the page that had been on top when I'd dropped everything onto the island. I picked it up and a shiver ran up my spine as I saw the disjointed words crafted out of magazine letters.

SNITCHES GET STITCHES. STOP DIGGING.

I felt the threat in my chest, like a physical blow.

"Whoever it is, they've been following me since before I dropped the earring," I said, thinking of the picture from the deli.

"Yep," Neo said. "Which means you're not going anywhere without one of us from now on. And you're definitely not playing the game."

My head snapped up. "That's not your decision."

"The fuck it isn't," Neo growled. "Especially after what happened with the Saints."

I started to protest, then realized what he'd said about the Saints. "What happened with the Saints?"

"They got caught trying to break into the case," Rock said. "They're out."

"Of Aventine?" I asked.

"Of the game," Oscar said. "And they're on probation."

Of course. Dean Giordana — and probably everyone else — knew about the game. They put up with it for the same reason they put up with all the other bullshit pulled by the students at Aventine: because they were scared of our parents and wanted to keep the money flowing.

"Which is why you're out too," Neo said. "Dean Giordana knows the case is our target. They'll be watching it more closely now."

I glared at him. "You don't get to tell me what to do. It's not like you care what happens to me anyway."

His expression hardened. "I care about this house and its reputation, and like it or not, you're one of us right now. You're under our protection. If something happens to you on our watch, we're the ones who lose the cred."

"That's what you're worried about? Your cred?" I didn't want to admit what I was really thinking — that he hadn't corrected me when I said he didn't care about me, that it hurt for a reason I couldn't begin to fathom.

"You just got here," Rock said. "You don't know how things work."

The tone of his voice said he was trying to be nice, trying to soften Neo's words, but all I heard was condescension.

Poor little Willa is so naive, she has no idea how anything at Aventine works. We're just stuck with her until she figures out what happened to her sister and takes off to post pictures on social media from the Maldives or something.

"I don't know why you're throwing such a shit fit," Neo said. "You don't even want to play the game. You should be happy you have an out."

"That's not the point," I snapped. "The point is, I'm not some little girl who needs to be protected, and I'm definitely not someone who's going to be bossed around by three... by three..."

I had several world-class insults on my tongue aimed at Neo, but I couldn't get them out with Rock's big puppy-dog eyes looking at me and my thighs still wet from the orgasm Oscar had given me.

"Three..." Neo looked satisfied by my brain freeze, and I had the sudden urge to tell him why I was so thrown, that I still hated him but was genuinely starting to like Rock, that fifteen minutes earlier I'd been desperate for Oscar to fuck me.

Why did I want to hurt him? And why did I think he'd care anyway?

"Three overbearing, controlling, narcissists playing at being gangsters while they're away at college," I said.

"You think I'm overbearing?" Rock said at the same time Oscar said, "It's only because I care about you."

Neo came around the kitchen island to advance on me, his expression so menacing I had to resist the urge to back up.

"You have no idea what you're talking about, Jezebel." His face was only inches from mine, his breath warm on my face. But instead of making me recoil, I felt a fresh wave of lust rip through my body. "Someday you're going to realize that, and when that days comes, you're going to feel like a world-class dumbass."

I was breathing too fast, too shallow, sure he could see it in the way my chest rose and fell. I could only hope he thought it was anger and not the need that had opened up inside my pussy.

But he was agitated too. I could see it in the flare of his eyes, the tic in his jaw. He got off on our battles of will.

Just like me.

A second later, his familiar mask of indifference slid back into place.

He straightened. "Until then, you can do whatever you want, but we will be watching. And opening your mail."

"Fine," I said, folding my arms over my chest. "When do we get the keys to the case?"

Chapter 43

Oscar

"That went well," I said after Willa left the kitchen. My voice dripped sarcasm.

Neo grabbed three beers from the fridge, which was how I knew he was worked up. He had another fight coming up, and he didn't usually drink unless he had at least a month to train before the next one.

He set two of the beers on the island, twisted the cap off the one still in his hand, and took a swig.

"What do you want me to do?" he asked. "Congratulate her on breaking into the dean's office? Give her a trophy for leaving something identifiable behind?"

I raked a hand down my face, trying to control my frustration. I understood Neo's feelings about Willa — as much as any of us could understand anything about Neo — but his fucked up psychological shit was making things harder than they needed to be.

"Maybe try understanding why she felt like she had to go

it alone," I said. "We haven't exactly been any help in the Emma department."

"That's for her own good," Neo said. "We talked about this."

"Yeah, we did," I said, picking up one of the beers. "I just didn't expect you to be such a monumental dick to her."

"That's on you," Neo said tightly, finishing the rest of his beer in one long drink.

He wasn't wrong. I hadn't felt great about getting Willa into the house under false pretenses — she'd been through enough — but guilt had started really fucking eating away at me. It wasn't that I hadn't been prepared to like Willa. We all liked her, even Neo, emotionally broken as he was.

But I hadn't expected to have, well, *feelings* for her. I hadn't expected to find her funny and interesting. I hadn't expected to want her in my bed for more than sex.

I hadn't expected to want to tear the head off anyone who hurt her.

Even Neo.

Sure, I'd had a thing for Willa for half my life. We all had, and that was a fucking fact, however much Neo wanted to lie to himself. We'd all wanted to protect her, in a wounded-animal-kind-of way.

We owed her that much.

Except my protective instincts were in overdrive now that I really knew her. The girl fucking haunted my dreams. She was a drug I had no desire to quit. I couldn't stay away from her, and I didn't even want to try.

"This is a waste of time," Rock said, leaning against the

counter and folding his arms over his chest. "This is bad. Very bad."

"No shit," Neo said. "But what's done is done."

"So it's damage control time," Rock said.

Neo snorted. "Obviously. I'll call Rafe."

I nodded. Rafe was the security guy. He'd installed the system currently in place at the house, but it obviously hadn't been enough.

And things were only going to get worse.

I looked at the manila envelope on the island and thought about the pictures of Willa, thought about someone following her, scratching her eyes out of the photographs. I was no FBI profiler, but that was some serious rage, and the thought of it directed at Willa made me want to kill someone.

Slowly.

"Tell him to make sure no one can get within half a mile of this place without us knowing," I said. "We should beef up our access to protection inside the house too."

We always had weapons scattered throughout the house. The other guys didn't know anything about them, although I doubted they'd be surprised. Frat life at Aventine wasn't like frat life anywhere else, and we chose our pledges carefully, with an eye toward their usefulness in our off-campus operations.

Every one of the pledges came from a notorious crime family, even doofuses like Matt, who constantly eye-fucked Willa with his puppy dog eyes. The rookies would understand the need for guns in the house.

Especially ours.

"Rafe is defense," Rock said. "So are more guns in the

house — which I agree with, by the way — but we need to play offense too."

"We've sent the message," I said. The message being that Willa was ours, that she was under our protection.

"Not loud enough," Neo said. "Obviously."

I looked from him to Rock, my resolve to protect Willa hardening into stone.

Immoveable.

Indestructible.

"So we send it again," I said. "Louder this time."

Chapter 44

Willa

I lay in bed, staring at the ceiling and replaying everything that had happened in the kitchen for the hundredth time. My mind was spinning, jumping from the package that had been delivered to the house to the fact that the guys were opening my mail to the annoying but undeniable chemistry between me and Neo.

Oscar had said goodnight at the door to my room, leaning in and whispering, "To be continued," in my ear before retreating to his space.

I'd been both disappointed and relieved. What had happened between us was hot, and I definitely wanted more, but that whole pictures-with-your-eyes-scratched-out thing was a real vibe killer.

"Ugh," I muttered, reaching for my phone to check the time.

It was after three in the morning, and I'd been trying to get to sleep for more than two hours. I'd used the lavender sleep spray I'd picked up in France and tried a sleep meditation I'd learned in Goa. I'd even had a late-night text convo with Mara.

I was still wide awake.

I considered knocking on Oscar's door. Maybe enough time had passed that we could pick up where we'd left off. I knew he'd deliver another explosive orgasm, hopefully with his giant pierced dick, and maybe he'd even let me stay in his room and cuddle.

But my pride wouldn't let me. The fact that I wanted it — wanted him — was bad enough.

I sighed and threw my legs over the side of the bed. Time to call it, for now at least.

I slipped shorts over my underwear and considered throwing a hoodie over my tank top, then decided to skip it. The odds of anyone being awake were slim, and if someone was, they'd just have to deal with my braless boobs.

The third floor was quiet as I slipped from my room. I headed for the back stairs and descended to the kitchen. It was empty, and I filled the kettle and got a mug out of the cupboard, then fished through the boxes of tea.

I settled on vanilla chamomile and lifted the lid on the ceramic jar that sat on the counter. Rock had made some killer oatmeal chocolate chip cookies — with walnuts, after I'd told him they were my favorite cookie — and I was hoping there were still some left.

There were, and I gleefully removed two of them and set them on a paper towel to eat with my tea.

I was putting the lid back on the jar when a voice behind me broke through the silence.

"Oh look, it's the house slut, and without her bodyguards too."

I turned around to find Enzo standing across the room, his dark eyes glittering with hatred in the dim light of the kitchen.

A thrum of fear beat through me, but I forced my expression blank, my voice steady. "I know it's late, but you're really going to need some new insults. Slut is so 2004."

I almost wished he was angry or disgusted. The vacant expression on his face was worse than any emotion he might have shown. I felt vulnerable and exposed, and I wished I'd worn the hoodie over my tank top.

"You don't think I can hear you?" he asked. "That we can't all hear you?"

I tried to process his words but my mind drew a blank. "I'm sorry if I woke you. I couldn't sleep."

He advanced on me so fast I barely had time to back up against the counter. "You think I'm talking about tea?"

His body was pressed against mine, his hard dick unwelcome against my stomach. "I don't—"

"My room is under Drago's." His voice was hard and brittle. "I heard you fucking him."

I opened my mouth to correct him — Oscar and I hadn't technically fucked — then remembered that I didn't owe this asshole an explanation.

"That's none of your business," I said, trying to make my voice as hard as his. I put my hands on his chest and shoved. "Now get away from me."

Except he didn't move. His body was like a wall of bricks, and my low-grade nervousness morphed into full-on terror.

He shoved his hand up my tank top, grabbing my right boob. "If you wanted some action, all you had to do was ask."

My solo travel reflexes kicked in all at once. I kneed him in the balls and he doubled over for a second, long enough for me to slip out from between his body and the counter.

"Fucking cunt!"

I only made it a few feet before he caught hold of my tank top.

I went down fast and hard, breaking my fall with my arms, the tile floor slamming into my elbows like a freight train, sharp pain radiating into my shoulders.

I hurried to scramble away, but he was on me too fast, covering my body with his and pinning me to the floor.

"Get the fuck off me!" I shouted.

His hand came over my mouth. "I had a feeling you might like it this way."

He fumbled with his sweat pants and panic tore through my body. I writhed and struggled, trying to put enough room between us that I could roll to my stomach and use my arms to push up, but he was too heavy.

Too strong.

I felt the hot, smooth weight of his bare dick against my thigh and started to cry.

He grabbed ahold of my shorts and tore them away, then fumbled with my underwear, pushing them aside.

Oh god... oh god... oh god.

And then he was gone.

One minute he was there, his weight an oppressive force pinning me to the ground, the next I was lying on the floor alone, gasping for breath, trying to figure out what the fuck was going on.

Then I heard Neo shouting.

"Motherfucker... You think you can touch her? She said get off."

His words were interspersed with the thud of fists meeting flesh, the thuds turning wet as Neo's punches opened up Enzo's face, blood splattering across the kitchen floor.

And he wasn't alone. Rock and Oscar were there too, taking turns kicking Enzo, curled on the tile like a giant baby, while Neo straddled his shoulders to work his face.

I scrambled to my feet, backing away against the wall, too stunned to do anything else while Enzo went limp under the weight of the beating.

The kettle was screaming. I had no idea how long it had been boiling, but it cut through my shock, and I hurried to the stove to turn off the burner before it woke up the whole house.

Then I turned to the Kings, still beating on Enzo even though he was clearly unconscious, blood seeping across the floor under his body.

"Stop!" They froze like a pack of dogs being given a command, and turned their heads to look at me. "You're going to kill him."

"He was going to rape you," Neo said, his voice dripping ice.

"I... I know. But I don't want you to go to jail because of it." I was surprised to find I didn't just mean Rock and Oscar.

I meant Neo too.

"No one's going to jail, tiger," Oscar said, his voice low and threatening.

I didn't know what that meant, but I didn't want them burying a body in the woods because of me.

I took a deep breath. "It's okay. I'm okay."

Rock walked over to me and peeled off his sweatshirt. He slipped it over my head and I put my arms through the holes, sinking into the safety of it. My shorts were still on the floor, but the sweatshirt came to the middle of my thighs.

He pulled me against his chest and wrapped his arms around me. "You sure you're okay?"

I nodded, and he stood there for a minute and smoothed my hair. "If you let me keep going, I'll kill him for you."

I couldn't tell whether he was kidding, but it made me laugh. "I'd rather not have it on my conscience."

"Asshole like this?" Oscar said behind me. "Wouldn't keep any of us up at night after what he tried to do to you."

I pulled away from Rock. "It's okay. I just want to go to bed."

They looked at each other, some kind of unspoken communication seeming to track between them.

"I'll take you up," Rock said.

"What about him?" I asked, looking at Enzo. His face was hardly recognizable.

Neo met my eyes. "Don't worry about him."

"Is he... is he alive?" I asked.

"He's alive." Neo didn't sound happy about it.

I nodded, and Rock put his arm around me and guided me to the stairs.

We climbed to the third floor in silence. Rock hesitated when we reached my door.

"Want me to stay with you?" he asked.

I looked up at him. "Would you?"

"You don't even have to ask." He opened the door to my room, then closed it behind us.

I crawled into bed and he dragged a chair from the sitting area over to the bed and took a seat.

I pulled the covers up and looked at him through the darkness. "You're too far away."

He got up and slid into bed next to me, lifting an arm so I could snuggle up against his chest.

"That's better," I said.

He pulled me tighter against his chest, and I remembered that he'd walked in on Oscar and me earlier.

"About earlier," I said.

He kissed my head. "No explanation necessary." He chuckled softly. "We've got all the time in the world."

I inhaled the scent of him and let my eyes drift closed. I didn't know what he meant, but it sounded pretty good.

Chapter 45

Willa

He was gone when I woke up the next morning, and I could tell it was late even without looking at my phone. The sun slanted in through the wall of windows, heating my room and casting it in warm autumn light.

I checked my phone — after 11 a.m. — and yawned.

Last night seemed like a dream.

Or a nightmare really.

Had it happened? I grabbed the pillow next to me and inhaled Rock's scent to confirm.

Yep, he'd definitely been there, as evidenced by the desire that woke up every nerve ending in my body.

I wasn't eager to greet the day after what had happened with Enzo, but I needed to go down and scope out the situation.

I went to the bathroom and brushed my teeth, then pulled my hair into a messy bun. I tugged on some flannel bottoms, hoping Neo or Oscar had picked my shorts off the kitchen floor before the other guys could see them, and started downstairs.

It was almost noon, so it was no surprise that someone was in the kitchen. Rock for sure — I caught the smell of cooking bacon — and at least one other person. They were talking quietly, their voice a soothing murmur behind the clink of utensils on plates and the sizzle of frying meat.

"Morning," I said, stepping off the stairs and into the kitchen. Rock was cooking while Oscar sat at the island with a plate of bacon and eggs and a pile of toast.

Rock turned around, flipping the dish towel he'd been holding over his shoulder. "Morning, sunshine."

I lifted an eyebrow. "No *kitten?*"

"I've decided to save that for when I'm making you come." He furrowed his brow. "Want me to make you come?"

Yes, please.

I rolled my eyes. "No, thank you."

"Okay, how about some coffee and bacon?" he asked.

"I will definitely take coffee and bacon." I slid onto the stool next to Oscar. "Hey."

He leaned over to kiss my temple. "Hey. How are you feeling?"

"I'm fine," I said.

He looked into my eyes. "Really? Because it's okay if you're not."

"Really," I said. "But thanks."

I didn't love the fact that I was starting to be less surprised when Oscar and Rock were nice. The lines were blurring between us, my suspicion thawing even though I didn't have any proof that they weren't involved in Emma's disappearance. I was forgetting who they were for one reason: they were nice to me.

How pathetic.

Rock set a hot cup of coffee in front of me and I sighed as I lifted it to my mouth. It was nice, being taken care of like this, having people to look out for me. Sure, I *could* do it myself. The incident with Enzo aside, I'd proven that when my dad became an enemy of the family, when Emma disappeared, when I traveled alone for a year.

But it was a relief to let my guard down a little. It was dangerous, but I couldn't deny that it felt good.

Rock set a plate of bacon, eggs, and toast in front of me.

My stomach growled, and I reached for a piece of perfectly cooked bacon and bit into it with a sigh.

"What did you guys do with Enzo?" I asked, reaching for the fork Rock had set on my plate.

"Don't worry about that," Oscar said. "He won't bother you anymore."

He sounded so menacing, the words so final that a shiver ran up my spine. "You didn't... kill him?" I lowered my voice on the last two words, just in case any of the other guys walked in.

"You told us not to." Disappointment shaded Rock's words.

"I know," I said. "Just checking."

"We didn't kill him," Oscar said, finishing his coffee and taking his mug to the sink.

It was obvious he didn't want to say more, so I left it alone and took a bite of perfectly toasted bread with melted butter and the best strawberry jam I'd ever tasted.

"Oh my god," I said around the bite of toast. "Where did you get this jam?"

"I made it," Rock said, like it was obvious.

I almost choked on the toast in my mouth. "You... made it?"

He grimaced at me like it was obvious. "Dumb to buy jam when strawberries are in season in the spring and it's so easy to make."

"Right," I said, making it clear it was not, in fact, obvious to me.

Rock started cleaning up and I suddenly realized how quiet it was. Not everyone-is-in-the-other-rooms-dong-their-own-thing quiet, but silent-as-a-tomb quiet.

"Where is everyone?" I asked.

"Gone."

Neo's voice came from behind, and I jumped a little on the stool.

He walked into the room wearing basketball shorts and a tank top, the hair on his angel tattoo snaking out and up his neck. He'd obviously just finished a workout, and I tried not to stare at his cut biceps and the way his sweat made the tank top cling to his sculpted chest, but it was always hard to tell whether I was actually successful.

I realized all over again that he'd protected me last night, just like Oscar and Rock, and I felt the lines blur even further in my mission to figure out what had happened to Emma.

"Gone where?" I asked, trying to stay focused on something besides the way his muscles flexed when he moved, the way it had felt to have his body smashed up against mine on the road, his tongue invading my mouth while his hands roamed my body.

I squirmed on the stool. Thinking about the moment we'd shared in the middle of the road was not going to help.

"Gone from this house," Neo said, moving around the kitchen as he started to make his post-workout smoothie. "For good."

"For good?" Now I was confused.

"Like it or not, you're a disruption, Jezebel. Can't have a repeat of last night."

My confusion hardened into anger. "So last night was my fault?"

"That's not what he means," Rock said, scowling at Neo. "What he means is that we just want to protect you."

"Nope, I meant what I said. You're a disruption."

He hit a button on the blender and the kitchen was filled with the grating cacophony of the motor mixing berries and protein powder and whatever else the big asshole put in his smoothie every morning.

He looked at me with a satisfied smirk as I stared at him, Rock and Oscar also silent as we waited for the blender to stop.

"You didn't have to make the other guys leave," I said when he finally turned it off.

I was starting to suspect Neo just liked getting under my skin as much as I liked getting under his. I didn't need him to tell me that what had happened with Enzo hadn't been my fault. I'd been around enough entitled douchebags to know that. Some men just thought they had a right to take what they wanted, and nothing made them more desperate to prove it than a woman who dared to tell them no.

"It's just a precaution," Oscar said. "With everything that's going on, it's smartest to close ranks, limit the amount of contact you have with other people."

"The letter was mailed," I pointed out.

"That doesn't mean anything," Neo said. He wasn't wrong. The envelope had been postmarked from the main post office in Blackwell Falls, which meant anyone could have sent it. "And this isn't up for debate."

I thought about arguing the point. Neo wasn't my boss, and it felt important to keep reminding him of that fact. But honestly? I was exhausted.

"Whatever." I slid off the stool and took my plate to the sink, then kissed Rock's cheek. "Thanks for breakfast."

He blinked like he was surprised. "Anytime."

"We leave in forty-five minutes," Neo said as I headed for the stairs.

I flipped him off without turning around. I wasn't in kindergarten. I knew when my classes started.

"And don't forget," he continued, "tomorrow you and Rock are getting those keys."

I didn't need the reminder. I'd been full of big talk when it had been about proving Neo wasn't the boss of me. Now that the moment had passed and I actually had to go through with breaking and entering into Daniel Longhat's house — while he was asleep — I was feeling a lot less brave.

Fuck me. And fuck Neo Alinari.

Chapter 46

Willa

Back in my room, I gravitated toward the jeans and hoodies in my wardrobe, then realized it was because of Enzo. I hadn't been lying when Oscar asked if I was okay. I was, but that didn't mean I wasn't still a little shaken up over the whole thing.

Nothing like some big asshole trying to take what wasn't his to remind you that you weren't invincible.

Fuck that. I may not be invincible, but I wasn't going to shrink because of what Enzo had pulled in the kitchen.

I chose a tight skirt and matching crop top that showed off my increasingly pale stomach — I needed some self-tanner stat — and paired the outfit with heeled booties and a shearling-lined jacket.

I pulled my hair into a high ponytail, then applied light makeup and some gloss before I headed to the car.

Neo was already in the driver's seat, hands on the steering wheel and staring out of the windshield like he was late for the Indy 500, while Oscar and Rock stood patiently next to the car, looking like they had all the time in the world to wait for me to get ready for school.

Oscar looked me up and down, his eyes lingering on my bare legs.

He grinned. "Good for you."

I was pretty sure that was admiration I heard in his voice, and it made me extra glad I'd decided not to play the wallflower just because of what had happened with Enzo.

I rode in the back seat with Oscar while Rock took shotgun next to Neo in the front. Oscar's hand played with my bare leg just above my knee, his long fingers stroking the inside of my thigh, teasing me into a state of low-key excitement that was totally inappropriate for 8 a.m. on a school day.

Not that I minded. The alarm bells that had rung insistently when I'd first realized I was going to be living with the Kings were growing fainter by the day. Deep down, I knew I was in real trouble with Oscar, and probably with Rock too, since they seemed to be agreeable to the idea of my sleeping with them both, but I was too far gone to care.

And honestly, I was tired. Tired of being on guard all the time and tired of being the only one who cared what had happened to Emma. I would take all the help I could get finding out the answer to that question, even if that help came from three of the men I'd hated most when I got to Aventine.

By the time we pulled into the student parking lot I was more ready for Oscar's dick than for psych class with Professor Ryan. If we'd been alone, I would have been tempted to straddle him then and there. I was quickly reaching the point of no shame when it came to my attraction to Oscar, and I could admit — if only to myself — that I was basically desperate for a replay of the moment we'd shared in his room.

Except this time I wanted to finish what we'd started.

I didn't even protest when Oscar kissed me on the lips after we got out of the car or when Rock grabbed my ass under my skirt. I tried to tell myself it was just to get back at Neo, who clearly hated the flirtatious nature of my relationship with his two roommates, but there was no point lying to myself.

I liked it. I liked them.

It wasn't what I'd expected to happen, but here we were.

We parted ways at the car, the three Kings going one way to class while I headed to Psych.

More and more, I couldn't see them in the Aventine ecosystem. They were bigger than life, and they seemed completely out of place with all the other students. It was almost impossible to imagine them taking notes in some lecture hall, but I had to assume they did, since this was their third year at Aventine.

Either that, or they were paying someone to pass them so they wouldn't have to crack a book, but that didn't feel right either.

I shivered as I hurried toward the door to the building. There was a definite bite in the air and most of the trees surrounding campus had already lost their leaves. It wasn't enough to make me regret wearing a skirt, but I would definitely have to start considering the weather when I planned my outfits for the day.

It was a relief to step into the warm building, and I relaxed my shoulders as I headed to class.

I was a little early, only two other kids in the lecture hall, both of them staring at their phones as Professor Ryan worked on his laptop at the front of the room. He looked up when I started down the stairs and his eyes met mine as I slid into a seat halfway up the theater-style seating.

Not long ago, I would have spent the entire class making googly eyes at Professor Ryan, but times had definitely changed. My mind spun between what had happened with Enzo in the kitchen, the fact that Neo had kicked all the other guys out of the house (to protect me?), and the fact that tomorrow I wouldn't be on campus: I would be breaking into Daniel Longhat's house with Rock, trying to steal the keys to the case in the teachers' lounge while Daniel slept, after which we would have to race to campus and open the case during the school day while the admin building was packed with teachers and students.

It sounded crazy because it was.

But Neo had made the point that we couldn't break into the lounge on a Saturday or Sunday. Daniel and his sister would need the keys to clean the building, and he would probably report them missing the second he noticed them gone.

Plus, there was the matter of the security cameras.

Breaking into the teachers' lounge during the week while everyone was on campus meant that we could blend into the crowd in the places where we couldn't avoid the cameras, and since there were no cameras in the lounge itself, they'd never be able to prove we were the ones who'd broken into the case.

It also meant Daniel Longhat and his sister wouldn't be cleaning the admin building. If we could break into the case during the day and get the keys back to Daniel's house before nightfall, he would never know they'd been missing when he used them to clean that night.

The more I thought about it, the more insane it seemed. More than once, I contemplated using the out Neo had given me, but my pride wouldn't let me take him up on the suggestion that I sit this one out.

The Kings already thought I was some kind of weak Mafia princess who couldn't hold her own in the game. For some reason I didn't understand, I was more determined than ever to prove them wrong.

I hadn't registered a single thing during class by the time it was over, and I hurried to gather my things and get to lunch to meet Claire.

I wasn't too worried about missing notes. I'd always been lucky that way. It was one of the only things I had that and Emma hadn't: I always did well in school with minimal effort while Emma had to work extra hard just to get passing grades.

I couldn't take credit for the ability, but with all the distractions I had going on, I was grateful for it.

I was edging my way out of my row in the lecture hall when Professor Ryan called up to me from the front of the hall.

"Everything all right, Miss Russo?"

I stopped in my tracks. "Uh... yeah, definitely. Why do you ask?"

He smiled. "Why don't you come down here so we aren't shouting at each other across the lecture hall?"

I wasn't really in the mood to chat, but I also didn't want to be rude. No reason to piss off Professor Ryan when he was in charge of my grade and I was barely paying attention in his class.

I stuffed my laptop into my bag as I made my way down the stairs.

"That's better," he said when I was standing in front of him. His gaze was appraising, and I didn't think I was imagining the fact that it kept dropping to my cleavage before he quickly remembered I was a student and forced himself to focus on my face.

"You seemed distracted during class today," he said.

"Yeah, sorry about that." Was he going to ding me on the participation portion of our grades just because I wasn't paying attention one day in class?

But instead of scolding me he looked at me sympathetically. "I'm sure it's been quite an adjustment," he said.

"Being here at Aventine?" I contemplated telling the truth, telling him that it actually hadn't been that bad, that I'd gotten used to being at Aventine a lot faster than I'd expected.

But why ruin a perfectly good excuse when — between the game and trying to figure out what happened to Emma, not to mention my three hot new roommates — it was more than likely that I would be distracted in class a lot this semester?

"It's definitely different." I laughed a little.

"Have you been into town at all?" he asked. "Sometimes it's good to get a change of scenery, remind yourself there's more to the world than Aventine."

I forced myself not to roll my eyes. I was pretty sure I'd been on more continents in the past year than Professor Ryan had visited in his entire life.

Still, there was no denying that he was hot, his dark hair just long enough to make me want to slide my fingers into it, the 5 o'clock shadow on his jaw just present enough that I knew it would be scratchy against my thighs.

Which was why I was surprised to find that I wasn't turned on. Like, at all. I mean, I could acknowledge that he was cute and everything, but he seemed almost too nice, too... weak.

The thought sent a thrum of worry through my body. Was I actually getting used to all the alpha-male bullshit in the Kings' house? Was I starting to think nice guys were boring?

I saved those questions for another time and focused on Professor Ryan's question.

"Just once or twice," I said, thinking about my first trip into town with Oscar and the fight at the Orpheum.

He hesitated. "I'd be happy to show you around sometime. I know a great used bookstore tucked away at one end of town and an even better place for lunch."

I guess the invitation shouldn't have taken me by surprise. I was technically an adult, and Professor Ryan had made his interest in me pretty clear. It was unethical, even though I was over eighteen, because he was a professor and I was a student and that was a fucked-up power dynamic, but in any other situation I would've been more than happy to take him up on his offer.

But this wasn't any other situation and I just wasn't interested.

"It's nice of you to offer but I'm super busy getting ready for midterms and everything. Maybe some other time."

I hated myself for adding the last part. It was something all women did at one time or another — try to soften the blow of rejection for the men who constantly hit on us.

I thought that would be the end of it but he picked up a pen, then grabbed a small piece of paper and started writing.

He handed it to me, and I looked down and saw that he'd written a phone number under the name *Josh*.

He smiled. "Just in case you change your mind. Call anytime."

"Thanks." I folded the piece of paper and slipped it into my bag. "See you next week."

I had no intention of ever using the number, but it would be rude not to accept it, and there was always the chance that he was genuinely trying to be helpful, although my experience with men so far told me it was unlikely.

I left the lecture hall and started across campus to the admin building. The cafeteria was humming with students looking for a warm place to socialize, and I grabbed a hot coffee and a bagel, plus two packages of cream cheese, because what was the point in having a bagel if you couldn't slather it with an inch of cream cheese?

I spotted Claire sitting with Quinn and Erin at our table. Claire waved me over and I hurried across the cafeteria, casting a glance at Neo, who was sitting next to some blonde, his hand between her thighs under the table.

He wasn't even trying to be subtle, and I was suddenly mad with a feverish brand of jealousy that made my face feel hot.

It was ridiculous. I didn't own Neo. Just because we'd made out in the middle of the road didn't mean that he owed me anything.

I didn't even *like* the big asshole.

"Hey girl," Claire said as I approached the table. "Have a seat."

I sat between Claire and Quinn, but Quinn didn't notice, too busy talking to Erin about some guy in her sociology class.

"I haven't seen you in a few days," Claire said. "Where have you been hiding?"

I hesitated. Part of me wanted to tell Claire everything, to let down my guard completely and take my chances.

But sitting in the cafeteria made me realize something: the only people who had been at the ball were the students and teachers at Aventine. That meant someone at the school knew I'd been inside Dean Giordana's office, and whoever that person was had also sent me the threatening letter.

It wasn't safe to trust anyone. In fact, the weirdest thing of all was that the people I could probably trust the most at Aventine were the Kings. They'd been at the house when the letter had been delivered and had clearly been surprised by the fact that my earrings were in the envelope.

Even Neo.

Either that or they were very good actors.

"Willa?" Claire was looking at me expectantly. "Are you okay?"

I smiled. "Fine," I said. "Sorry. I guess I'm distracted by all the homework I just got assigned in Psych."

Claire laughed. "By the homework or by Professor Ryan?"

I raised my eyebrows, playing along. "He is pretty hot for a teacher."

I was relieved when Claire took the bait and ran with it, waxing poetic about Professor Ryan's dark hair and blue eyes while I looked around the cafeteria, wondering who was threatening me.

And why they wanted me to stop asking questions about Emma.

Chapter 47

Willa

The house was on a quiet street surrounded by other houses almost exactly like it, all of them small two-story farmhouse-style homes that had probably been built sometime in the early 1900s. The neighborhood was set back from Main Street, and I was grateful that there was hardly any traffic as Rock and I made our way to the side yard that was home to a couple of trash cans and a shovel.

We hadn't talked much about how we were going to get into the house. I assumed he had some kind of master plan, but when we got to the sliding glass door at the back of the house, he opened it like he'd been there a hundred times before.

"How did you know?" I whispered, surprised it was unlocked.

He shrugged. "I didn't. But no one locks their doors around here."

"Oh my god," I muttered, hoping his entire plan didn't hinge on vagaries like no one locking their door.

He opened the door carefully, but it still sounded too loud to me. I stepped into the house behind him fully expecting Daniel Longhat to be waiting for us, but the house was quiet except for the soft hum of the refrigerator that stood against one wall.

Rock left the door open behind us, probably to avoid making more noise when we had to leave, and we stepped into a small neat kitchen, the counters clean, the sink empty of dirty dishes.

We spent a few minutes looking for a hook or bowl or somewhere else Daniel's keys might be kept when he wasn't using them. When we didn't find anything, we moved carefully toward a long narrow hall.

We passed a tiny bathroom on the left and continued toward the front of the house. A cozy living room stood to the right of the foyer, the curtains drawn against the bright October day, and a giant TV was positioned at one end of the room with a stylish sofa in front of it.

House plants lined the shelving units and end tables, and a thick blanket lay on the back of the couch. A textbook sat open on the coffee table, but I couldn't make out the subject from the foyer.

The house was surprisingly orderly, but I had the feeling I was missing something, some detail that was right in front of us that I couldn't quite grasp.

Rock started for the stairs, resting his foot on one side of the first tread.

He leaned down to whisper in my ear. "Old house. Stairs are creaky in the middle."

I grabbed his hand before he could go any farther up the

staircase, and he looked back at me with a question in his blue eyes.

I tipped my head toward the foyer. The house might be occupied by a young bachelor, but it was well organized, and we'd used the back door to enter the house. The keys hadn't been there, but that might be because Daniel used the front door when he got home from work or school.

I let go of Rock's hand and backtracked to the foyer. A piece of wood was nailed to the wall, a series of coats and jackets hanging from a set of hooks. Underneath them, a small table stood empty except for a worn leather wallet and a tiny wood bowl.

I focused on the bowl, or more specifically, on the set of keys inside of it.

Rock followed my gaze and stepped carefully off the tread.

I closed my hand carefully around the keys, trying to keep them from clinking together, or at least hoping to muffle the sound with my palm. It mostly worked, and a second later I had the keys in my hand.

I looked at Rock, who was grinning at me with approval. He gave me a thumbs-up, then turned toward the back of the house where we'd started.

We made our way back down the hall, through the kitchen, and out the open sliding glass door. Rock closed it slowly behind us, making sure to leave it unlocked.

Then we were hurrying back through the side yard, past the trash cans and shovel, toward the car waiting at the curb.

There was no way to know for sure that the key we needed was on the ring in my hand, but I was betting it was, that Daniel's penchant for organization meant that all his keys were in one place.

I exhaled my relief as I got into the passenger seat of the Audi.

Rock slid behind the wheel and looked at me with a massive smile. "I knew you'd be a natural."

Adrenaline was coursing through my body, and I would have been lying if I'd said it didn't feel good. We'd just stolen from someone, had entered their house while they were sleeping.

So why did I feel liberated? Why did I feel euphoric?

"Let's go," I said. "We probably don't have much time."

Chapter 48

Willa

Any sense of victory I felt leaving Daniel Longhat's house with the keys in my hand dissipated the second we stepped into the admin building.

It was packed.

I told myself it was a good thing, that we needed all those bodies to help mask our movements on the way to the teachers' lounge, but it didn't really work. I was back to being terrified, sure that we were going to be caught, I was going to be expelled, and any chance I had of finding out what had happened to Emma would be gone forever.

But it was too late now. I was in it, the keys in my pocket, Rock at my side. We were so close, too close to give up, too close for me to back out.

We strolled casually down the hallway opposite the teachers' lounge, scoping out the crowd as we made our way around the corner and across the back of the building.

I shifted my bag on my shoulders. We'd debated whether it would be a help or a hindrance on our mission but had eventually decided we needed it, both in case we had to explain our presence in the lounge and because we would need a place to put the medals once we removed them from the case.

Now I was glad to have it on my shoulder. It wasn't very heavy, but even its minimal weight felt like an anchor in the storm of rules I was intent on breaking.

We'd sat in the car for twenty minutes after leaving Daniel's house, planning our timing to line up with an hour when most of the teachers would have class: after morning coffee and gossip time but before lunch.

There was still no guarantee the lounge would be empty, but that was where my bag came in. I would slip inside while Rock kept watch, and if someone was in the room, I would remove my notebook and say I was looking for Professor Ryan.

I knew he had a class, so I wasn't worried about him being there. Worst case, someone was in the lounge, and Rock and I would have to try again later.

It wasn't foolproof, and the last thing I wanted was a repeat of our breaking and entering at Daniel's house to get the keys a second time, but we had to play the cards we'd been dealt.

I only hoped we had a good hand.

Chapter 49

Willa

Rock waved and smiled at our fellow students, acting like it was just a normal day as we walked along the back hall and headed for the stairs. I hoped I was doing as good a job acting casual, but I felt like I was about to shit myself.

We didn't slow down as we emerged onto the second-floor landing and into the hall with the teachers' lounge. We'd talked in advance about how important it was to act like we knew exactly where we were going and like we had every right to be there. Acting nervous might not tip anybody off then and there, but later, after the medals went missing and campus security reviewed the tapes, any nervousness on our parts — or should I say my part? — would tip them off that we were the thieves.

I wasn't thrown when, as we came closer to reaching the door to the teachers' lounge, Rock acted excited to see someone and stopped to talk to them. It was all part of the plan. The Kings knew everybody, and it had been a pretty safe bet to rely on Rock using an acquaintance as an excuse to pause outside the door and keep lookout.

I looked up at him. "I'm going to see if Professor Ryan is in the lounge."

It was said for the benefit of his friend — Brady somebody-or-other — but Rock nodded absently and continued talking.

I had to hand it to him: he was a good actor. If I didn't know any better, I would have assumed he was on his way to or from one of the admin building's offices, stopping to compare class notes with a friend.

I forced myself to keep breathing as I opened the door to the teachers' lounge.

It was harder than I'd expected not to hesitate as I stepped inside. Bravado was one thing, but deep down, I knew I wasn't supposed to be here and that went against every one of my pathetic rule-following instincts.

Act like you belong, Willa. Act like you belong.

I closed the door behind me and I breathed a sigh of relief at the sight of the empty room. It didn't last long though.

Now I had to actually steal the medals and hope no one walked in while I was doing it.

I hurried across the room, trusting that Rock would do whatever was necessary to keep anyone from entering the lounge while I was there.

When I got to the case, I reached into my bag and withdrew Daniel's keys. Then I started trying the ones that looked like they would fit the tiny lock on the glass doors.

There were fewer than I expected. The lock on the case was obviously meant for a small key, and most of Daniel's keys were full-size. I was on the third of five small keys when the lock on the case clicked open.

A giddy rush of excitement raced through me as I slid the doors open and came face-to-face with the medals. They were the key to the Kings' win.

And not just their win, but mine.

Once I took the medals, I would have real cred at Aventine, and while I didn't care what anyone on campus thought of me for my own sake, there was no doubt that being trusted would give me access to more information about Emma.

Plus, there was the added benefit of proving Neo wrong about me. I'd never admit it to his face, but that had started to become just as important. I didn't dare examine the reasons why.

With the case open, grabbing the medals was easy. There were six of them spanning two decades, small circular discs in fake gold engraved with some kind of emblem and various accolades, from *Collegiate Teacher of the Year* to *Top Five Private University*.

I pulled them off their hooks and stuffed them into my bag, then quickly shut the glass case. I locked it behind me for good measure, hoping it would be a while before anyone noticed they were gone. The more time that passed, the harder it would be for campus security to narrow the list of potential thieves.

I'd just turned around and started for the closed door, a thrill of victory surging in my chest, when it opened.

I stopped in my tracks, my heart stuttering in my chest as a stern older woman entered the room. I recognized her from my recon visit to the lounge. She'd been the one who looked at me disapprovingly while I'd flirted with Professor Ryan.

She registered a moment of surprise when she saw me standing there alone.

"This is the teachers' lounge," she said. "You're not supposed to be in here."

My brain short-circuited while I fumbled for an explanation. It took me a second to remember the plan.

"I... I'm looking for Professor Ryan?" I reached into my bag and pulled out my notebook. "He said to meet him here to get some work I missed."

The woman's expression relaxed, although she still didn't look pleased. "Well, as you can see, Professor Ryan isn't here. You'll have to wait in the hall."

"Right, sure. Sorry." I made my way to the door brushing past her and hoping her eyes didn't go right to the empty case.

I didn't know what I'd expected to find when I got back into the hallway.

The police? Campus security?

But it didn't matter, because everything was just as I'd left it, Rock still talking to Brady and students crowding the halls, their minds and attention on their own problems.

Rock looked down at me as I rejoined him. "All set?"

"Yeah, he wasn't there." I shrugged. "I'll just come later."

He nodded and said his goodbyes to David and we headed down the hall toward the front of the admin building.

I half expected to be stopped by a shout, but a few seconds later we were out the door and heading back to the car.

"Sorry about the old bat," Rock said. "She got by me too fast while David was running his mouth."

"It's okay," I said. "I told her I was looking for Professor Ryan." Rock didn't look at me as we continued to the car but I could hear the smile in his voice. "Was that before or after you got the medals?"

I looked up at him and grinned, refusing to show any of my earlier nervousness. "After, of course."

He wrapped his arm around my shoulders and pulled me against him as we walked. "That's my girl," he said excitedly, kissing the top of my head.

I was embarrassed by how happy the compliment made me, not to mention the term of endearment.

What the actual fuck was happening?

Chapter 50

Willa

It was afternoon when we got back to Daniel's house. I convinced Rock to stay in the car as lookout while I returned the keys. At this time of day, I was just as worried Daniel might have a visitor as I was about him waking up while I was in his house. Rock would wait outside and text me if anyone showed up while I snuck back in and returned the keys to the bowl.

Whether because of my recent victory stealing the medals or because this was my second time breaking into Daniel's house, I wasn't as nervous as I'd been that morning, and I hurried along the side yard, the keys already balled in my fist to minimize noise once I was inside.

I hesitated next to the sliding glass door leading to the kitchen, listening for running water or any other sound that might indicate Daniel was awake. When I didn't hear anything, I peered through the glass door and found the kitchen as empty as it had been that morning.

I slid the door open and left it that way as I crept down the hall toward the foyer. The house was still quiet, which made sense, given that less than three hours had passed since we'd stolen the keys. If Daniel worked the night shift, he probably slept until late afternoon.

I set the keys in the bowl slowly, releasing my grip a little at a time to avoid making noise as the metal keys hit the ceramic bowl. They clinked a little, but it must have sounded louder to my ears than it actually was, because there were no sounds from upstairs to indicate I'd woken up Daniel Longhat.

I exhaled the breath I'd been holding a little at a time, my gaze straying to the living room and the book on the coffee table. It was stupid, but I couldn't help being curious.

I glanced at the stairs, then stepped carefully over the old wood floors, stopping when I reached the coffee table. I looked at the textbook, its title now visible: **The Associated Press Guide to News Writing.**

Interesting. Daniel Longhat must be a student at the state university one town over. A piece of paper stuck out of the textbook, and I opened it to find a syllabus for a class titled **Journalistic Inquiry: The Written Word** resting between the pages.

I skimmed to the bottom of the syllabus and a section that had been highlighted: *Mandatory participation in the* Gazette *is required. Students must submit a 10,000 word article showcasing investigative journalism skills as their final.*

But it wasn't the assignment that made me catch my

breath, it was the note scrawled next to it in sloppy but bold handwriting: *expose corruption at Aventine?*

Holy fuck... Was Daniel Longhat about to write an article about the games at Aventine? Or did his reference to corruption refer to something darker?

Dread bloomed through my body as I thought about Emma, about how no one seemed to know anything about her at Aventine even though that's where she'd last been seen.

I didn't know how long I stood there before I remembered that I was trespassing, that Daniel Longhat was asleep upstairs. I forced my feet to move, backtracking out of the house and through the open sliding glass door before closing it carefully behind me.

This time my pulse raced not because of any imminent danger but because seeing the words written on Daniel's class syllabus felt like validation. Maybe he was just talking about the games, about the way the administration looked the other way while students at Aventine behaved badly because of their connected parents.

But maybe not. Maybe there was something else going on at Aventine, something that had gotten Emma hurt or killed.

I felt sick as I slid back into the Audi's passenger seat.

"Jesus, I was about to come in after you," he said. "What took you so long?"

"I was just being careful."

Rock looked more closely at me. "Everything go okay?"

I forced myself to smile as I met his gaze. "Everything was fine. I left the door unlocked like we found it."

He leaned over the console and kissed me on the lips. "You did it! You fucking did it."

I wanted to tell him what I'd found inside Daniel's textbook as he started the car and pulled away from the curb. The fact that I didn't was a reminder.

No matter how much I liked Rock and Oscar, we weren't on the same team.

Chapter 51

Willa

I'd expected the crowd at the quarry party to be surly about our win, but everyone was pumped as Neo announced it in front of the bonfire. Maybe it was the sheer amount of alcohol that always seemed to be present at Aventine parties, but they all seemed happy that at least one house had gotten away with the medals, even if it hadn't been theirs.

Word had spread fast once Rock and I got the medals back to the Kings' house, aided by Neo's picture of them on a nondescript background sent to the other houses from a phone that couldn't be traced to him. But that only seemed to have primed Aventine's student body for the formal announcement.

"To Rock!" Neo shouted, almost finished with his speech. He raised the medals, clutched in one hand, into the air. "To Willa, to the Kings, and to *sangue oltre la famiglia!*"

I didn't know what I'd expected — everyone to refuse to say my name maybe? But they didn't. They screamed it right along with Rock's, and I found myself roaring the motto with everyone else like some kind of cult member, carried along by the excitement around the fire.

The acceptance felt good, like I'd taken one small step toward earning everyone's trust. Pathetic? Maybe, but I couldn't deny it was true.

"Now, let's party!" Neo shouted.

Another roar went up from the crowd, the music was cranked, and everyone dispersed to dance, drink, and probably fuck.

I wished fervently I was one of them. On the fucking, that is. The last few days had me wound tight. Between the little gift from my stalker and the harrowing day stealing the medals, I needed some relief, and I'd been too distracted to play with my vibrator.

I eyed Oscar and Rock across the bonfire, their faces beautiful, almost harsh in the darkness, and I felt my underwear dampen. Then my gaze settled on Neo, talking to them both, his expression intense, and they got even wetter.

I had a flash of the moment we'd shared on the road, his mouth on my tit, how ready I'd been for his shockingly big dick when he'd spun me around to face the car.

"Having carnal thoughts about your roommates?" Claire said, suddenly standing next to me.

I looked down at her. "Can I plead the Fifth?"

She laughed. "Sure, but you'll get no judgment from me. You must have lady balls of steel to resist them."

"Yeah, well, I don't know if we can accurately say I've *resisted* at this point," I said.

Her green eyes lit with excitement. "Oh really?" She

grabbed my arm and led me toward one of the coolers filled with ice and alcohol. "Do tell, and I want every detail."

We grabbed drinks and I proceeded to fill her in on everything that had happened between me, Rock, and Oscar. I left out the stuff about Neo. I could hardly admit my attraction to him to myself, let alone to someone else, and I definitely wasn't ready to tell anyone about what had happened between us against the Maserati.

As far as I was concerned, it had been a one-off, a moment of delusional weakness brought on by the adrenaline rush of our car chase.

That's what I told myself anyway, and lucky for me, I didn't need those details to entertain Claire. She was more than excited to hear about my steamy altercations with Oscar and my growing attraction to Rock.

I stopped short of telling her about my visit with Nikki. I'd told Claire I just wanted to know more about Emma's life at Aventine, purposefully leaving out the part where I was looking for answers about her disappearance. I didn't want Claire to feel betrayed, but if I was being honest with myself, I was also still feeling cautious on the trust front, at least when it came to Emma.

Sharing the dirty details — emphasis on the word *dirty* — about my makeout sessions with the Kings was one thing. Letting the cat out of the bag that I was actually at Aventine to find Emma, or at least find out what had happened to her, was something else entirely.

I stopped dishing when Alejandro, Claire's crush from the Saints, came over with a few of his friends and started chatting us up. I let the alcohol loosen me up, swaying to the music while I listened to the gorgeous dark-haired cartel boys. The music was too loud for me to pick up all the details, but they didn't seem to mind as I nodded with interest and let my gaze slide around the bonfire.

Alexa was busy batting her eyelashes at George and so far hadn't paid me any notice. Maybe I got a pass because I'd helped the Kings win the game, or maybe she was just too distracted by George, but whatever it was, I was happy to get a reprieve.

I found myself instinctively looking for the Kings, but they were nowhere to be found, and I wondered again what they got up to when they weren't in class. Besides the fights at the Orpheum. Because I was almost positive there was a hell of a lot more they weren't saying.

Eventually, Claire peeled off with the Saints to do shots of some rare, high-end tequila they'd brought to the party. I opted out, already feeling pretty buzzed from the two drinks I'd already consumed.

I was happy, something that surprised me, and even more surprising, I was relaxed. Normally, my mind would have been ringing an alarm that *relaxed* was a mistake at Aventine. But tonight, I just didn't care. It felt good to feel like I belonged, to enjoy drinking and dancing and talking with people my own age without the storm cloud of my father, Emma's disappearance, my stalker.

My eyes were drawn to the cliff over the quarry. I'd avoided focusing on it all night, knowing it had the power to unmoor me, but now I couldn't seem to help it, and I found myself moving toward it as if controlled by an unseen hand.

Standing at the edge, I was filled with all kinds of intrusive thoughts.

Three more steps and I'll plummet to the icy depths below. One leap and it might all be over.

It made me feel crazy. I wasn't someone with a death wish. There was still too much to do and see, too much that could happen that I didn't want to miss.

But I guess that was why they were called intrusive thoughts. They just came out of nowhere, like the impulse to turn your wheel into a guardrail on a curvy road or to stick your hand into a fire.

It was like standing on the edge of an abyss in space, nothing but darkness all around and in front of me, not even lights across the water, because there was nothing out here except the mountains.

Just endless blackness and the thought, again, that Emma might be down there somewhere.

The sky spun above me, my heart dropping into my stomach as the ground seemed to give away. I reached out, trying to grab on to something to steady myself, and felt nothing.

Then, strong hands on my shoulders.

"Wow," Rock murmured in my ear. "Are you okay? You were swaying."

I leaned back against him, relishing the safety of his solid chest. "Yeah, I'm fine. I'm just... scared of heights."

He chuckled, and the sound traveled all the way to the tips of my toes. "Then maybe you shouldn't be standing at the edge of a cliff."

"It's weird, right? The way we're drawn to the things that

scare us?" I wasn't even sure what I was talking about anymore.

"I don't know," he said softly. "I've learned not to question the things I'm drawn to."

I wasn't sure what he was talking about anymore either. I could feel the chemistry between us crackling like a live wire.

"Maybe I should follow your lead," I said.

His hands slid down to my hips. He pressed me tighter against him, leaving no doubt about what he was referring to. His hard dick was impossible to ignore against my ass and a familiar yawn of need opened up in my pussy.

"No maybe about it, kitten." He took my hand and tugged me away from the precipice, then led me toward the trees.

I didn't question where we were going. Wherever it was, it was away from the crowd, into the woods where I could put my money where my mouth was, if that's really what I wanted to do.

And it was really, really what I wanted to do.

Anticipation only amped my desire as he led me down a narrow trail, then off into a stand of trees.

He pulled me behind them and pushed me back against the thick trunk of a giant tree. I was surprised by the force of it. When it came to the Kings, I'd come to think of Rock as the teddy bear of the bunch, but a second later I was ready to reevaluate that opinion.

He lowered his mouth to mine all at once, capturing my lips in a fierce kiss and pressing his knee between my thighs.

I was hungry for him, drunk on both the alcohol I'd consumed and the way his lips felt on mine, his tongue setting my mouth on fire as it swept and demanded. His hand slid up my shirt, kneading one of my tits while he pressed my pebbled nipple between two fingers, just hard enough to ramp up my pleasure.

His thigh between my legs teased my pussy, and I angled for more friction on my clit.

He broke our kiss, and I was gratified to hear his heavy breathing as he kissed his way along my jawbone and down my neck.

"That's right, kitten," he murmured. "Ride my leg."

I didn't need any encouragement. I was grinding on his thigh, an orgasm already within reach. I was beyond any kind of shame or embarrassment, too busy working the rhythm on my clit to care.

"That's my good girl," he coaxed.

I wanted him to fuck me, but it was a distant second to my urgent need to come, and I was already all over that one, release close enough to touch.

He lifted my shirt higher and pulled down one side of my bra. I only had a second to gasp against the cold night air on my sensitive nipple before his hot mouth closed around it.

It sent me over the edge and I came hard, riding against his thigh, trying to stifle my moans as my body shattered from the impact.

He didn't stop sucking until I stopped moving, falling limp against his body, holding me up against the tree as I came back to reality.

He kissed me and started working the button on my jeans. "Fuck, it's fun making you come, but this time it's going to be with my mouth or my cock."

I should have been emptied out after the orgasm he'd just

given me, but his words sent a fresh swell of lust through my body just as a voice cut through the woods.

"Rock!" It was unmistakably Oscar, and it was like cold water on my desire. Rock and Oscar had been seemingly good sports about whatever was between the three of us, but I had no desire to test that theory by having Oscar walk up on me with my shirt up, my tit exposed, and Rock's leg between my thighs.

Rock dropped his head to my shoulder with a groan. "Don't move," he said. "Not an inch."

I laughed, fixed my bra, and pulled down my shirt. "I'm not going anywhere."

I was more than ready to finish what Rock had started, my body already revving for the chance at another orgasm, this time with Rock's big dick.

He turned away and hurried back to the trail, then turned toward the bonfire glowing through the trees. I was plummeted into the sudden quiet, the sounds of the party a distant backdrop to the wind through the trees and the scurry of small animals in the woods.

I was suddenly cold, the absence of Rock's body heat all too noticeable, and I focused on the glow of the bonfire, still faintly visible through the trees.

I rubbed my arms, then froze when a branch snapped from the trees to my right.

The woods were quiet. Too quiet. The rustling of squirrels or whatever had been making noise earlier had fallen silent, nothing but the rush of October wind.

I thought maybe I'd imagined it, but a second later, the

slow crunch of dead leaves sounded from the darkness in front of me. And it was no squirrel — it was a footstep.

Could it be Rock, coming back through the woods to scare me for fun?

No, that wasn't right. I may not have known everything about him, but every instinct I had told me he wouldn't think it was funny to try and scare me, especially after the package that had been mailed to the house.

"Rock?" Calling out was almost a reflex, a way to prove to myself that everything was fine, but my voice sounded scared even to my own ears.

Two more footsteps sounded in the leaves, closer this time.

Fuck this.

I pushed off the tree and hurried back toward the trail, breathing a sigh of relief when I reached it. The light of the fire was clearer here, the sound of the party closer.

I was okay. I'd be surrounded by laughter and music and the Kings again in just a couple of minutes.

I took two steps forward, then froze when someone stepped out of the trees up ahead. They were wearing head-to-toe black, including a ski mask that covered their face, but it was clearly a man, his frame tall and hulking.

I forced myself to speak. "What do you want?"

He started toward me, his footsteps slow.

I looked at the glow of the fire behind him. It was so close, but he was blocking the trail. If I went through the trees, I might be able to circle my way back to the party.

He was walking faster now, and I took a step back. I

couldn't take my eyes off him, like watching his movements would somehow prevent the inevitable from happening.

He picked up his pace, making it even more clear that I was his target, closing the distance between us until I could see the dark glittering of his eyes through the holes of the mask.

That's when I ran.

Chapter 52

Willa

Footsteps sounded behind me, my pursuer immediately giving chase. The trail was almost invisible in the moonlight, but I stuck to it by instinct, afraid to get lost in the woods.

It didn't take long for my pursuer's footsteps to grow closer, louder. Adrenaline shot through my body as panic set in, and I veered to the left, breaking through the tree line into the woods.

As dark as it had been on the trail, it was ten times darker now. My breath fogged the air in front of me, but other than that I couldn't make out anything except the shadows of trees all around.

I didn't have time to hope I'd lost whoever was following me. His footsteps crashed behind me over the dead leaves on the forest floor. I ran like my life depended on it, probably because it did, hardly noticing the branches that snagged my clothes and scraped my arms.

I knew it was foolish to look back, that it would cost me

precious seconds, my footsteps slowing to make up for the distraction, but I couldn't help myself. I dared to look over my shoulder and caught movement in the shadows only feet behind me.

I urged my legs to move faster, then gasped when a low-hanging branch smacked me in the face. Something hot dripped down my cheek and I knew I was bleeding.

I was trying to keep myself oriented, remembering where the bonfire had been when I'd been on my way back to it on the trail, and I made another left, diving into another dense section of the woods that seemed to go on and on. I thought I might have glimpsed a glow in the distance up ahead, but I couldn't be sure.

A cry for help lodged itself in my throat but I couldn't shake it loose, some survival instinct kicking in and telling me that every ounce of energy expended would cost me speed.

I pumped my legs harder, aiming for the space through the trees where I thought I might have seen the fire. Except I was running so fast I didn't have any hope of making out obstacles around me.

My foot caught a raised tree root on the ground, and I went down fast and hard.

A cry was wrenched from my lips as I slammed onto my elbows in an attempt to break my fall. I barely noticed the pain of something slicing into my thigh. I hauled myself up by my arms, crawling as I tried to get to my feet again, knowing my pursuer had to be closer, half expecting hands to close around my shoulders.

Back on my feet, I pushed myself forward again. I raced through the trees, my lungs on fire, my leg and cheek burning.

I dared to hope the fall hadn't cost me too much time, that by some miracle I might make it back to the fire.

Then I slammed into the wall of a man's solid body.

It stopped me cold and I knew I'd been a fool. The man had taken advantage of my fall, not to gain on me from behind but to circle ahead through the woods and meet me from the front.

I kicked and flailed, screaming and shouting, hoping someone at the party would hear me over the music. My body was in full panic mode, oblivious to everything but the immediate threat, which was why I didn't realize that someone was saying my name.

"Willa! Willa! It's okay. You're okay. It's me." I stilled, gasping for breath, and looked up into Neo's face. "It's okay. I've got you. I've got you." He was holding me close, pressed against his chest, his big hands smoothing my hair as he murmured the words, "You're safe. You're safe. You're safe."

It shouldn't have been true, Maybe it wasn't. But right then, it felt like truest thing I'd ever heard.

Chapter 53

Rock

"I can't see a fucking thing." I followed Neo through the woods, our flashlight beams cutting through the trees. "I'm surprised she didn't break her fucking neck out here."

We'd made a point of keeping Willa's near kidnapping from everyone else at the quarry — no point drawing attention to ourselves, especially right now — but the party had broken up soon afterward anyway.

Now the woods were quiet, the faint hint of smoke the only sign of the party that had raged an hour earlier.

"She's tougher than she looks," Neo said, dried leaves crunching under his heavy footsteps.

"That what you tell yourself when you're treating her like shit?"

He stopped in his tracks and turned to face me. "Something you want to say?"

I shrugged. "I said it."

I wasn't scared of Neo. I didn't doubt that he could

pummel me to within an inch of my life. I didn't even doubt that he might do it if the occasion called for it.

But I'd take that beating if it was one he needed to give. I'd do anything for the surly motherfucker, and Drago too, just like they'd do anything for me.

"Careful," Neo said, his voice a clear warning.

"No," I said. "I'm not going to be careful. I'm not one of your groupies. I'm going to tell it like it is, like I always have."

He didn't say anything, and I braced myself to take that beating.

"Where were you?" he asked instead. "You were supposed to be with her."

I stared at him through the darkness. "Where were *you*?"

"I'm the one who found her," he said.

"Exactly. What was that? Luck?"

His expression hardened. "Something you want to ask me?"

"Already did," I said.

"And I'm going to pretend you didn't."

He turned around and we continued through the trees, moving slowly, watching for signs of Willa's pursuer. Whoever it was had known we'd be at the quarry, and those invites had only gone out to Aventine's student body after Willa and I had the medals in hand.

My mind churned as I combed the bushes and trees. I'd known having Willa at Aventine would be complicated, but complicated didn't begin to describe the territory we were in.

She was starting to feel like mine — ours — and there was nothing we wouldn't do, no price we wouldn't pay, to protect what was ours.

"Wait." Neo stopped and held up a hand.

I halted my steps. "See something?"

He bent down and reached toward one of the bushes, then straightened and bent his head to look at something in his hand.

"What is it?" I asked, moving in for a closer look.

He handed a scrap of synthetic black fabric to me. I had no idea where it had come from, but the edges were torn, like it had been ripped away by a stray branch.

"Not exactly identifiable," Neo said.

He was right, but fury coursed though my veins anyway. I was holding proof that someone had dared to chase our girl through the woods, scare her, hurt her.

And when we found him, he was going to pay.

Chapter 54

Willa

I clung to Oscar, plastering myself against his side in my bed and closing my eyes against the memory of my pursuer at my back.

He kissed the top of my head and tightened his arms around me. "You sure I can't get you anything?"

He'd asked more than once since we got home, the house eerily silent. Neo and Rock had stayed at the quarry to launch a search for the man who'd chased me through the woods, although I think we all knew he was long gone.

"And you didn't see anything?" Oscar asked gently. "Even a mark on his hand might help."

"It was too dark." I'd been through this, first with Neo, then with Rock and Oscar. "And he was wearing the ski mask and maybe gloves."

The memory of him was as black as the clothes he'd been wearing. I might have thought I'd imagined him if not for the crystal clear memory of him standing on the trail, blocking my way back to the bonfire.

I sat up, something new suddenly occurring to me. "He must have been following me."

Oscar nodded, the stubble on his jawline making him look both sexy and menacing.

Older.

"I thought about that too," he said.

I lay back down, resting my head on his chest as I turned over the new piece of information. The man had waited to approach me until Rock left. He'd known when I was alone, had known I'd try to get back to the party.

He'd intentionally driven me into the woods, and an icy finger traveled up my spine as I thought of all the reasons he might have had for doing it.

Was that what had happened to Emma? Was this the man who'd taken her, hurt her? Or was this my stalker making good on the threat in the package with the pictures and my earring?

Were they the same person?

My mind conjured images of all the things he could have done to me, all the ways in which I could have been taken or killed, the noise of the party masking my screams, the woods obscuring the crime.

I didn't dare think about what might have happened if Neo hadn't appeared when he did.

Something teased my mind, a thread I couldn't quite grasp, but a few seconds later, the front door opened downstairs, the beep of the alarm arming immediately after.

"They're home," Oscar said. He slid out from under me. "I'll be right back."

I sat up and swung my legs over the side of the bed,

wincing as the skin around the bloody gash on my knee pulled. Oscar had bandaged it up with surprising tenderness, but it still hurt like a mother.

"I'm going with you," I said.

I didn't want to be alone, and I wanted to hear what Neo and Rock had found, if anything. It had happened — I had the scratch on my cheek and the bloody knee to prove it — but I was desperate for confirmation someone else could see, desperate to prove that I hadn't just let my imagination get the better of me on a dark night in the woods, even though no one else had questioned my account.

Oscar nodded.

Neo and Rock were both in the kitchen swigging beer when we got there. Their shoes were off, shirts dirty as they leaned against the counter, but they both looked as delicious as ever, Rock's hair tousled enough to be sexy and Neo's face set in a hard expression that reignited the Neo-lust that always seemed to be simmering in my body.

Rock set down his beer and came toward me. "How are you feeling?"

I walked into his arms like it was the most natural thing in the world, like he was my fucking *boyfriend* or something.

"I'm fine." I pulled back to look at him and Neo. "Did you find something? Or am I losing it?"

"You're not losing it," Neo said. He reached into his pocket, then set a piece of torn black fabric on the island.

I picked it up. "What's this?"

"Can't be sure," Rock said, "but we think it was torn from the clothes of the person chasing you."

I studied it, hoping for something more certain to appear.

Nothing did.

"This could have come from anyone," I said. "At any time."

"Maybe," Rock said, "but we searched the trees where you'd been running. It was off trail, dense."

"It's too much of a coincidence," Neo said. "It had to have come from whoever was chasing you."

I nodded and set the piece of fabric back on the island. "Thanks for looking. I'm sorry you didn't find anything more substantial."

Oscar sat on one of the chairs and pulled me between his legs.

"I shouldn't have left you alone," Rock said, his expression anguished. "I'm sorry."

I reached for his giant hand. "It's not your fault. We were close to the party. I could see the fire through the trees. If the guy hadn't blocked my way on the trail, I would have been with the group in under a minute."

"But he did," Neo said, his voice brittle. "Which is why we can't leave you alone anymore. It's not safe." He rinsed his bottle and set it in the recycling can. He always surprised me with conscientious shit like that. "So don't make plans for Saturday."

"What's happening Saturday?"

"Fight," Neo said, heading for the stairs.

"At the Orpheum?" I asked.

"Yep."

I started to protest out of habit — I still wasn't used to being ordered around by three ginormous guys who acted like prison wardens — then caught myself. I'd been off balance the last time I'd been at the Orpheum. I hadn't made use of the opportunity. Now I knew what to expect, and thanks to Daniel Longhat and his journalism syllabus, I had some questions for the townies.

Oscar shut off the lights in the kitchen while Rock double-checked that the alarm was armed, then we headed up the stairs together.

"Want one of us to stay with you?" Oscar asked.

I did, but I wasn't delusional enough to believe that I'd get any sleep with Rock or Oscar in my bed.

"It's okay," I said.

"We can just sleep," Rock said. "Scout's honor."

I laughed. "You were never a boy scout, and we both know," I looked at Oscar and corrected myself, "make that the *three* of us know, that there won't be any sleeping if one of you stays in my room."

Maybe it was a trial balloon, a way to test whether they'd flinch at the mention of the three of us.

They passed with flying colors. Oscar grinned. "Oh ye of little faith."

I shook my head. "You know I'm right."

He leaned in to kiss me on the lips. "You're definitely right, tiger. As long as you know I'm capable of just being with you if that's what you want."

"Me too," Rock said on my other side. He kissed the sensitive skin under my ear and I shivered. "I can totally just hold you and shit."

I forced a laugh, but right then, standing with my hands on the muscled chests of two different but equally hot guys? I was ready to say goodbye to sleep for the foreseeable future.

"You know where to find us," Oscar said.

Us. I liked the sound of that, and not just because two protectors were better than one.

I raced through the woods, the branches slapping at my naked body, scratching my face.

My pursuer was close enough that I could hear his breath, close enough that I could smell the tang of his sweat.

I tried to make my legs pump faster, but I seemed to slow down instead, the trees tunneling in front of me, receding instead of growing closer. I was running as fast as I could, sweat dripping from my face, but I wasn't moving.

Then the man's arms were around me, lifting me off the ground from behind, his breath in my ear as I kicked and flailed.

A scream lodged in my throat, my vocal cords paralyzed as I fought, panic rising in my chest.

This was it. I was going to die. Like Emma.

A whimper tore from my throat, a far cry from the scream I was aiming for, and then a voice.

"*Shhh... you're okay. I've got you.*"

My eyes flew open and I was suddenly back in my dark room at the Kings' house, sitting up in my bed, strong arms clasping me to a manly chest.

The nightmare receded, and I pulled away to see whether Rock or Oscar had appeared in my room right when I'd needed them.

Except it wasn't either of them. It was Neo.

He looked down at me, his expression unreadable, his eyes liquid in the darkness. "You were having a nightmare."

"I was back in the woods," I said, too stunned by the fact that Neo Alinari was comforting me for the second time that night to say anything else. He smelled like sleep and fire smoke and the faint vestiges of cologne, his chest bare over basketball shorts.

My nipples were hard under the T-shirt I'd worn to bed, and I was all too aware of the fact that I was in nothing but that and underwear, Neo and I as close to being naked together as we'd been since that moment on the road.

My pussy — the fucking bitch — reacted like it always did to Neo, and I fought against the impulse to pull him into my bed.

"You're safe here." There was a promise in his voice, something I was almost willing to take to the bank.

"Was I screaming?" I asked.

He hesitated. "Not exactly."

I pulled away a little more and he dropped his arms. I already wanted them back. "Then how did you know?" I asked.

"I've been sitting." He nodded to the chair against the wall next to my bed. "Over there."

My brain misfired as I tried to make sense of what he was saying. "You were *watching* me?"

"Watching *over* you is more accurate," he said, rising to his feet. "Can I get you anything?"

I shook my head, exhaustion washing over me as the adrenaline from the dream drained from my body.

He started for the door, then looked back at me. "You

look... peaceful when you sleep. When you're not having a nightmare, I mean."

I thought I read something like longing in his eyes, but I couldn't be sure. I was still trying to think of something to say when he slipped from the room a second later.

All the air left my lungs and I flung myself backward on my bed, feeling like I'd dodged another bullet.

Neo was tangled up in my thoughts, my dreams, my recollection of the chase through the woods. I'd been terrified until I'd felt his arms around me, his voice soothing in my ear.

It's me.

Against all odds, the words had made me feel safe. I remembered the way his arms had felt around me when I'd woken up from the nightmare, when he'd saved me in the woods.

And then, I thought of something else, the thread that had been bugging me earlier, the worry I couldn't quite grasp.

How had Neo known I was in the trees? There was no trail there, no way for him to stumble upon me racing through the dense trees in that part of the forest.

Which meant it had either been a coincidence... or he'd been looking for me in a place I shouldn't have been.

I thought back to that night, picturing him, and saw him in black jeans and a black sweater.

Had he brought a ski mask?

My heart thudded in my chest. Had Neo broken through the trees to lap me because I'd been getting closer to the party?

Because he'd been the one chasing me?

Chapter 55

Willa

"You sure you don't want to come sit with us?" Oscar asked in the cafeteria the following week.

"I'm sure," I grumbled.

They were back to walking me to class, and since Rock had exams, Oscar had been my private security detail that day. I was itching to put some distance between us, if only to prove to myself that I hadn't been totally converted by the Kings.

Sitting at another lunch table was starting to feel like my final stand.

"Suit yourself," Oscar said, casually dropping a kiss on my lips. "Offer's always open."

"Thanks." I watched him take a seat next to a petite redhead who blushed when he glanced her way and I started to second-guess myself, then pushed back the impulse to join them.

I didn't need to piss all over the Kings to let everyone

know they were mine. They weren't mine, and I didn't even want them to be mine.

Well, I didn't want Neo anyway.

Liar.

I ignored the whisper in my head, but I couldn't keep myself from looking for him at the table. I found him right away, his dark head a few inches taller than the other guys at the table, a navy T-shirt stretched across his broad shoulders

I couldn't pretend I wasn't happy to see that the blonde wasn't there today.

"Willa!"

I followed Claire's voice to our table and slid in next to her.

"It's okay, you know," she said.

"What is?" I asked.

"If you want to sit with the Kings," she said. "I wouldn't blame you, and it looks like you're definitely on the guest list."

"What do you mean?" I turned to the Kings' table and saw that Neo was staring at me across the cafeteria. I had a flash of memory: his arms around me in my bed, the smooth skin of his bare chest, the smell of cologne and smoke.

It would have been so easy to pull him back onto the mattress with me, to —

Nope. Not going there. My stupid cunt was begging for him, but my brain was in charge.

For now.

"I like it here," I said.

She smiled. "There'll always be a place for you here. You're one of us. And speaking of which," she said, clearly switching gears, "I realized we've never been out!"

I laughed. "That's true. Although we did party at the welcome ball."

"I mean *out*," she said, her eyes shining. "Off campus."

"Ohhh!" I said, like I was finally getting it. "You want to go *out* out!"

"It's October and I haven't even been to Ruby's yet," she said.

"Ruby's?"

"It's a club in town," Quinn said. "They have an awesome DJ on the weekends."

"Sounds fun," I said noncommittally. The Kings wouldn't even let me walk to class alone. They definitely weren't going to let me party with Claire. Unless...

"Saturday?" Claire said. "We can do a girls' night."

"Define 'girls' night,'" I said.

"No boys?" Erin said from across the table.

"It's just that the Kings have been really weird since that thing at the quarry." I felt stupid saying it, both because I hated being the center of attention and because I didn't want to admit how entangled I'd become with the Kings.

"Well," Claire said, "it's not like there won't be other guys at Ruby's."

"Yeah, just tell them to give us some space," Erin said.

"They'll probably be too busy holding court with all the girls who want to fuck them to pay attention to us anyway," Quinn said.

Great.

"I can't Saturday," I said. The guys had made it clear I was going to the next fight at the Orpheum. "But Friday would work."

Claire beamed. "Friday it is!"

I was almost excited to tell the guys. They were going to be furious.

"Miss Russo?"

I turned toward the voice and was surprised to find a slim older woman staring at me intently. "Yes?"

"Dean Giordana would like to see you in his office."

"Um... yeah. Sure." I shrugged at Claire for show, but the blood was roaring in my ears.

Was I about to get pinched for stealing the medals?

I stood and caught Neo's eye. I was sure his expression was impassive to anyone looking, but I was starting to know him.

Starting to read the look in his eyes.

And right now it said. *Chin up, Jezebel.*

I stood straighter and followed the woman out of the cafeteria.

Chapter 56

Willa

"**G**ood afternoon, Miss Russo," Dean Giordana said when the older woman escorted me into his office on the second floor.

"Good afternoon," I said.

It was weird being back in the office during the day. Everything looked a little different, like I'd fallen down the rabbit hole the night of the ball and gotten a glimpse of something that only existed in a slightly parallel universe.

He gestured at one of the chairs in front of his desk. "Please have a seat."

The woman left the room and closed the door behind her. The noise of the building receded.

Dean Giordana clasped his hands in front of him on the big wood desk and peered at me from behind wire-rimmed glasses I'd never seen him wear. His brown hair was mousy and thinning up close, his pale eyes a little watery.

I clasped my hands in my lap to keep them from shaking, every rule-following nerve in my body humming.

"As you may have heard, someone stole the achievement medals from the case in the teachers' lounge last week," he said.

I nodded. "I heard they were returned?"

Rock and I had returned them to the statue in front of the admin building the night after the party at the quarry, placing them around the neck of the ancient founder who'd been carved out of stone.

"That is true," the dean said, "but their return doesn't lessen the crime of their theft."

The logic sounded stupid to me. If something was returned, it was no longer stolen. Technically, you could say it had been borrowed.

But this didn't seem like the time for semantics.

"Which brings me to your presence in my office this afternoon," he said. "The cameras—"

He was stopped short by the ringing of the phone on his desk.

He sighed and picked it up. "I'm in a meeting. Yes... yes." Another sigh. "I'll be right there." He hung up the phone and stood. "Please excuse me for a moment."

"Sure."

He beat a hasty retreat, leaving the door open on his way out, and I breathed a sigh of relief.

It was one thing to play the game in secret, to break into Dean Giordana's office when no one was around. It was something else to lie to his face.

I was not an experienced liar. Just the thought of being grilled by the dean of Aventine made my palms sweat. There was too much at stake for me to get expelled. I had some credibility with the other students at Aventine now, and I knew from Nikki that something weird was going on.

Beyond the usual, I mean.

I needed to be here, on campus, to find out what had happened to Emma, and I silently cursed the Kings and the stupid game for putting me in this position.

I looked around the office, trying to talk myself down. My face was hot, which meant I was probably flushed, and sweat was breaking out on my brow. One look at me, and Dean Giordana wouldn't have to ask questions — my guilt would be staring him right in the face.

I looked at the books lining the shelves and the framed pictures, sinking into the normalcy of it, the sound of students talking and laughing a soothing backdrop beyond the open door.

This was fine. I knew the story I had to tell, had rehearsed it more than once with the guys: I'd been in the admin building because I had a question about the charges for my tuition, but I'd gotten a text reminding me of an appointment and had to leave before I got the chance to go to the bursar's office.

Short, simple. So why did my pulse feel like a freight train barreling through my body? I hadn't even felt this way when we'd stolen the medals.

Because Rock was with you.

I hated the voice in my head, and hated even more that it was right.

The Kings made me feel like I could do anything.

Like I was safe.

Ugh. Where the fuck was Dean Giordana?

I read the titles on his books, but most of them were related to law or business administration — in other words, they were boring af — so I focused on the photographs instead.

There were a lot of them, mostly showing Dean Giordana with various men in suits. The men were always shaking hands. Either that, or they had their arms around each other like they were long-lost pals.

I recognized a younger Roberto in one of them next to the dean on a boat, both of them looking virile and tanned. My stepfather looked mostly the same, but Dean Giordana had a thick head of brown hair in that one, so it had to have been taken a long time ago.

In another picture, a group of guys stood with their arms around each other, all of them wearing some kind of uniform. They couldn't have been more than twenty, and they painted a perfect picture of wealth and privilege, all of them smiling and attractive.

All of them men.

I studied the expression on their faces, trying to place what they all had in common, then realized it was certainty. They all looked *certain*.

Of their privilege. Their entitlement. Their safety.

I drew in a breath as my fear hardened into something else, something still and cold.

The guys in the picture looked certain of those things because they could afford to be. The world wouldn't tell them no. It wouldn't hurt them.

It wouldn't dare.

But Emma had gone to Bellepoint thinking she was safe. Then she'd come here.

Dean Giordana was responsible for the safety of the students on Aventine's campus — all of them — but he looked the other way when the girls from Bellepoint snuck on and off campus. He looked the other way when we played the game. He looked the other way when students like Neo, Oscar, and Rock were obviously involved in some bad shit in town.

And why shouldn't he? It was all about appearances at Aventine, all about making the parents happy so they'd keep writing those fat checks. He didn't care at all about Emma or any of the Bellepoint girls who'd gone missing.

I drew in a breath, my heart beating slow and steady. The sweat had cleared from my forehead, and my face no longer felt hot.

I'd stolen the medals because I had to, because it was the only way to build credibility with my fellow students, and they were the ones who'd last seen Emma. Why should I feel bad about playing a game everyone at Aventine was playing one way or another?

"I'm sorry for the interruption," Dean Giordana said, returning to the office. He sat behind his desk. "As I was saying, we're talking to all of the students who were in the building over the last few days. According to our security cameras, you were one of them, so Miss Russo, I must ask, do you know anything about the theft of the medals from the teacher's lounge?"

I shook my head calmly, the lie flowing off my tongue like water. "No, Dean Giordana. Not a thing."

Chapter 57

Willa

"I can't believe we let you talk us into this," Oscar said as we pulled up to Ruby's Friday night.

His hand was on my bare thigh in the backseat, his thumb rubbing sexy circles on my skin that made me want to forget Ruby's and spend the night fucking him instead.

"I didn't talk you into anything," I said, adjusting the neckline of my drapey gold dress. Its thin straps, plunging neckline, and a back that dipped almost to my ass made it impossible to wear a bra, but I wanted to tease my tits, not give everyone a free show. "I told you I was going out, and you insisted on coming."

"Like you knew we would," Neo grumbled from the driver's seat.

"It's not my fault you've appointed yourselves my personal bodyguards," I said. I was being flippant, but I was secretly glad they'd attached themselves to me like industrial-strength glue.

I was still having nightmares about the chase through the

woods. The truth was, I didn't feel safe when I was alone anymore, but no way in hell was I going to give them the satisfaction of knowing that.

"It's for your own safety," Rock said from the passenger seat of the Hummer.

"It's your call," I said. "But I can't be a prisoner in the Kings' house."

That had been the crux of my argument when I'd told them I was going out with Claire and the girls, that it would start to seem weird if I didn't do normal things with my friends. I wouldn't say it worked — the Kings didn't give two fucks what anyone thought — but after a brief argument about how it would be hard to protect me in a dark club crowded with people etcetera, etcetera, they'd given in and agreed to come with me.

Oscar's hand slid higher on my thigh, lighting a match to the embers he'd been stoking on the ride to Ruby's. He leaned over and murmured in my ear, his breath hot against my neck. "We could just forget this and go home and fuck."

I was glad it was dark in the car and he couldn't see that my nipples were hard under the gold dress. The sexual tension between us was becoming impossible to ignore. If we didn't do something about it soon, we were going to spontaneously combust.

But Claire was waiting, and now that I was dressed, I was ready to party. It had been a long time since I'd cut loose with friends. The welcome ball didn't count. I'd known I was breaking into Dean Giordana's office, and even though I'd had fun dancing with Claire and her friends, it was my first night out at Aventine and I'd been nervous in a million different ways.

Now I felt like I belonged, and I surveyed the crowd lining up outside Ruby's with excitement. "I hope we won't have to wait long."

Rock turned around to grin at me from the passenger seat. "We won't have to wait at all."

I didn't have a chance to ask questions. The car doors flew open and the Kings got out, Oscar taking my hand and pulling me out after him. I teetered a little in the sky-high black boots I'd paired with the dress, and he put a firm hand on my lower back to steady me.

Everyone in line turned to look at them, and I had to say, I didn't blame them a bit. The Kings were looking fine, and it was obvious I wasn't the only one who thought so.

The girls in line looked at them like hungry cats stalking a flock of birds, except the Kings weren't birds, they were falcons, and they would eat every one of those cats alive.

The cats just didn't know it yet.

I was feeling pretty good walking with the three of them to the door of Ruby's. I was the envy of every girl in line and I knew it. I didn't have a lot of experience with the position. Emma had always gotten all the attention. She'd been beautiful and audacious, and every man from fourteen to ninety had fallen all over themselves to catch her eye.

I'd been the quiet one in the back reading a book, happy to be out of the spotlight.

I pushed down my sadness at the thought of Emma. I'd been sad so often in the past two years. My whole life had been obliterated, first by my dad's betrayal and then by

Emma's disappearance. Maybe it was selfish to want something for myself, but right then, I just wanted one night where I didn't think about any of the shitty things that had happened to me.

The door to Ruby's was open but roped off, music beating from inside the club, lights sweeping the room beyond the door. Neo approached the giant bouncer, a bearded guy with cut biceps under a tight T-shirt.

The bouncer nodded at Neo with recognition. "Sup?"

"How's it looking in there?" Neo asked.

Even now, I couldn't take my eyes off him. His thighs barely seemed to fit inside his gray dress pants, and I knew if I looked I'd see the bulge of his big dick, something I was spending more time thinking about than I wanted to admit.

He'd left the top three buttons of his midnight-blue shirt unbuttoned and I tried not to focus on the smooth triangle of skin there that begged for my tongue. He'd combed his hair back with some kind of product, a look that only accentuated his bone structure, so severe it was somehow beautiful.

"All good for now." the bouncer said.

The bouncer unclasped the rope and Neo led the way. Oscar gestured for me to follow him and then fell in behind me, followed by Rock. It was a lot of swagger, a lot of testosterone, and I was loving every second of it.

The music was cranked inside the club, the beat traveling from the floor up through my legs and into my chest. It was a cavernous, industrial place, probably some kind of old factory right on the border of the cute part of Blackwell Falls and the other side of town where the Orpheum was, where Oscar had told me not to go when he'd brought me into town for makeup.

Was that only five weeks ago? It felt like a lifetime.

I needed to find Claire, Quinn, and Erin, but the music was too loud for me to say that to the guys, so I scanned the crowd for my girls instead.

It didn't take long to find Claire, shaking what her mama gave her on one of several pedestals that seemed intended for that purpose in front of the DJ booth. Her emerald-green dress rode so far up she was practically giving everyone a crotch shot, but it was obvious from the glee on her face that she was having too much fun to care.

Quinn occupied the pedestal next to her, moving her ass to some kind of grunge/rap mash-up. They were clearly way ahead of me in the drinks department, something I intended to correct immediately.

Lucky for me, Neo had the same idea. He led us to the bar that lined one entire wall of the massive industrial space. Three bartenders worked the crowd of people lined up for drinks, and Neo worked his way to the front with the single-minded purpose of a bulldozer clearing ground.

A clean-cut bartender with dark hair and eyes took an order I couldn't hear, and a couple minutes later, four drinks appeared on the bar.

I was annoyed that Neo had ordered for us all — as if he knew me — but the music was too loud to fight it. I took the slightly green drink from Rock's hand and sipped, satisfied to find that it was delicious.

Rock leaned down and murmured in my ear. "Just to get you started."

The brush of his cheek against mine did all kinds of crazy things to my body, amping up the need that seemed to hum under the surface of my skin no matter how many times I went to town with my vibrator.

I looked up at him with a smile I could only hope adequately conveyed my current turned-on status.

His grin widened, and this time when he leaned down, his voice was a growl. "Keep looking at me like that, kitten, and we're out of here."

Then we were on the move again, Neo leading the way through the crowd and up a set of suspended metal stairs. We stepped onto a mezzanine area that was clearly for VIPs and he led us to a plush U-shaped booth with a bird's-eye view of the dance floor.

The guys slid into the booth but I downed my drink and set the empty glass on the table.

I hadn't come here to sit with the guys like some kind of diamond under glass.

I lifted my hand in a wave, not wanting to scream over the music, then felt a rush of satisfaction when Neo scowled as I turned away from them to head back downstairs.

They'd insisted on coming, but this was my night out with Claire, Quinn, and Erin. I was going to do me while they did whatever it was they planned to do in the VIP section.

I was halfway down the stairs when I looked up and realized exactly what that was as a flock of beautiful girls descended on the Kings' booth.

It fucking figured.

Chapter 58

Willa

I tried to ignore the jealousy surging through my veins as I searched the club for Claire. It wasn't my business what the Kings did.

Or who they did.

Claire was easy to spot even though she'd moved from the pedestal by the DJ's booth onto the dance floor. Her copper hair was on fire in the sweeping light of the club, and her sequined dress caught the light from every direction. Quinn and Erin danced next to her, grinding suggestively on anyone within a five-foot radius.

They were clearly having a great time and I was more than ready to join them.

Claire squealed when I made my way to them on the dance floor and she pulled me into a sweaty, drunken hug.

"You made it!"

I barely heard her over the music, but it didn't matter. Spirits were obviously high and it was easy to forget about the

Kings as I joined them in shaking, grinding, and swinging our hips to the beat.

I accepted several rounds of drinks from the other girls, and two from a group of guys who were handsome enough but looked more like boys than men compared to the Kings.

I was glad I was too drunk to give that much thought. Instead, I enjoyed the buzz and euphoria that came from the alcohol, the music, and what felt like my first taste of real freedom since I'd returned to the States.

I didn't know how much time had passed when I locked gazes with a familiar set of eyes from across the room. By now I was more than a little drunk, and I angled for a better look to try and place the face, but it was no use, everyone was buzzed and high now, and I was jostled from my position by some guy with a buzz cut and a face full of tattoos.

The person I was trying to get a better look at vanished from sight, and I gave up, surrendering to the high of the moment.

At some point it occurred to me that I really had to pee. Like, really bad. I'd been having so much fun, I hadn't been paying attention to my bladder despite all the alcohol I'd consumed.

I stopped dancing and tugged on Claire's arm, mouthing the word *bathroom*, but she was distracted by a dark-haired boy with kissable lips.

Clearly Claire had a type.

Erin and Quinn had disappeared from sight, so I slithered through the crowd toward the back of the club, assuming that's where the bathrooms were since that's where they almost always were.

I made my way down a long corridor, then swung a left at the end of the hall. There was a line for the women's room, so I took my place at the back and tried not to dance around like a kid needing to pee.

Twenty minutes later, I emerged from the bathroom relieved and ready for a fresh drink. The line had shortened in the time I'd been in the bathroom, and I made way my way past three girls and headed back for the long dark hall leading back into the club. I wasn't even to the halfway point when a familiar face started making his way toward me from the other end of the hall. He was almost on top of me when I realized it was Professor Ryan.

He smiled, and there was nothing teacherly about it. "Hey you! Fancy meeting you here."

He didn't seem all that surprised to see me at Ruby's, probably because there were only a handful of places to party in Blackwell Falls.

I instinctively tried to steady myself and appear less drunk. Call it a lifetime of conditioning and countless attempts to avoid the critical eyes of adults always trying to rain on our parade.

"Professor Ryan. What are you doing here? I mean, you're probably just out having fun right? Because teachers want to have fun too, I guess." I sounded like an idiot, but it was the best I could do in my current not-even-close-to-sober state.

He chuckled, and I had to admit, there was something a little sexy about it. "We do like to have fun on very rare occasions," he said. "I'm just glad you're the one that caught me. I have to insist you call me Joshua now."

We had edged to the side of the hall to let one of the girls who'd been in line pass, and I realized we'd stepped into a tiny vestibule that seemed to lead to some kind of office or supply room.

"You look great," he continued. His eyes shamelessly raked my body, leaving no doubt that he was all too aware we weren't in class.

The attention wasn't necessarily unwelcome. I wasn't sure I was interested, but in my current state, I wasn't *not* interested either.

"Thanks." He didn't look like a professor tonight. In fact, he fit right in with all the other cute, well-dressed guys in the club. "You don't look so bad yourself."

Was I flirting? I didn't mean to be flirting, but a second later, he closed the distance between our bodies. He was standing only a couple of inches away, close enough that I got a whiff of his cologne, something a little too sweet.

"I've been wanting to see you off campus," he confided, leaning in to speak close to my ear.

"Really?" I wanted to leave, to say something socially acceptable that would get me away from him, but my brain wasn't working right, probably because it was swimming in alcohol.

"Really," he said. His hand had migrated over my collarbone and down to my chest, his finger dipping toward my cleavage. "I felt it the second you walked into my class. That... spark. You felt it too. I could t—"

The rest of the sentence was silenced by a high-pitched whine that sounded from his mouth when someone closed their fist around his fingers. It took me a second to gather all the pieces.

Neo and Oscar standing behind Joshua Ryan, looming like angry oak trees while Rock squeezed Joshua's fingers in his enormous fist.

I think Joshua might have been screaming, but it was hard to tell with the music so loud. A second later, I heard the crack of bone.

That wasn't hard to hear at all.

A couple of girls came around the corner, obviously looking for the bathroom. They took one look at the scene playing out in front of them and beat a hasty exit back the way they'd come.

"You're touching something that belongs to us," Neo said darkly, coming around to stand next to Rock, who still held the professor's fingers inside his closed fist.

"I didn't know, I didn't know!" Joshua shrieked.

He didn't know? Wait... I struggled to make sense of what was happening, what was being said, all of it transpiring both too slowly and too quickly.

You're touching something that belongs to us.

That part I got, and a rush of anger rolled through me. I wasn't even into Joshua Ryan, but I certainly didn't belong to the Kings.

"Listen you egotistical, posturing caveman." Was I slurring? I couldn't be sure, but I was definitely jabbing my finger into Neo's chest while he towered over Joshua Ryan. "I don't *belong* to you. I don't belong to anyone." Yep, I was definitely slurring, but I was on a roll. "Just because I'm being forced to live with you, and just because you're all stupid hot — yeah, I said it, you too, Mister Caveman — doesn't mean I *belong* to you." I tried to stand straighter as a demonstration of my autonomy. "So you can just take your supersized ego and shove it up your — "

Neo rolled his eyes. "Drago," he barked. "Get her out of here. Now."

I barely had time to register the words before Oscar's hand closed around my arm. "Come on, tiger. Time for a bowl of milk and a nice nappity-nap."

"What...? You can't just drag me..." I trailed off, because that's exactly what he was doing. Well, not dragging me, but definitely propelling me along the hallway, back into the club, away from whatever Neo and Rock intended to do to Joshua Ryan.

He led me through the dance floor and stopped to say something to Claire. Her eyes widened when she glanced at me, but we didn't have time to talk about what was happening. A second later, Oscar was on the move again, heading straight for the door of the club.

We spilled out into the night air a minute later, and I gasped as the cold hit my skin in the skimpy dress.

"That'll sober you up," Oscar said with a laugh.

I wanted to protest. I hadn't agreed to leave Ruby's, and I definitely hadn't agreed to be dragged out of there by Oscar-fucking-Drago.

But I was suddenly exhausted, all the fight gone out of me. I just wanted to go home and sleep it off.

The next thing I knew, I was being herded into the passenger seat of the Hummer.

"How will Rock and Neo get home?" Now I was slurring both from drunkenness and sleepiness.

"Don't worry about them," Oscar said, reaching over me to grab the seat belt.

He fastened it, his face close to mine, and I took the opportunity to lick the seam of his luscious lips.

He let out a growl and stared into my eyes, his face only an inch away. "You're pushing it, tiger."

"Maybe I want to push it," I said, teasing his lips with the tip of my tongue again.

I definitely did. I wanted to push it so fucking badly.

He sighed and closed his eyes as if for strength, then straightened and shut the door.

Chapter 59

Willa

"We're home."

I opened my eyes to find Oscar leaning over me in the passenger seat, his dark eyes looking at me with something that might have been warmth but might just as easily have been pity.

"What...?" I tried to remember what was going on. It came back to me a second later: Ruby's, too many drinks, Joshua Ryan. "Did I fall asleep?"

He chuckled, low and sexy. "All the way home. Come on, let's get you to bed."

I moved carefully, testing my legs, but I already felt more sober than I had at the club.

I walked with him to the door of the house where he disarmed the alarm, then armed it again.

"Let's go, tiger."

The house was dark and quiet as we climbed the back stairs to the second floor.

He opened the door to my room and followed me inside

where I collapsed onto my bed, flinging myself back on the mattress.

I sighed. "I love bed." I was no longer smashed, but I was still feeling loose.

"I'm sure bed loves you back." He turned on the bedside light and the room was bathed in a soft glow.

I heard the zipper on my boots, then felt him work them off my feet. He rubbed along my arch and I moaned in pleasure.

"Jesus, tiger. I think it's time for me to go," he said, standing.

I sat up quickly, trapping him between my legs and running my hands up his thighs, over his stomach and chest.

"What if I don't want you to go?" I asked, looking up at him.

And I didn't. I really didn't.

He leaned his head back and looked at the ceiling, then took my hands, still on his chest. "You know you're killing me right?"

"I mean it," I said. There was nothing playful in my voice now, and while I wasn't stone-cold sober, I also wasn't hammered. I knew what I was doing. What I wanted. "Stay."

He looked down at me, his eyes liquid. "You're drunk."

I could hear the concern in his voice, not that I was drunk, but that I didn't know what I was doing, that I would regret it in the morning.

"Not anymore. Okay, I'm still a little drunk," I amended, my voice steady. "But I know what I want. I want you."

He stared down at me for a long moment, then crushed me back onto the bed with a groan. He stretched his body out over mine, the weight heavenly as his mouth crashed onto mine.

I moaned and wrapped my legs around his hips, the fabric of his pants weirdly sexy against my inner thighs as I opened my mouth to him.

We'd had more than a few kisses over the past five weeks, more than a few *hot* kisses, but none of them held a candle to this one. It was full of raw hunger, his mouth frenzied and demanding as he closed a possessive hand around my throat.

His dick was big and hard, pressing against my pussy through his pants, lighting my core on fire while his tongue stoked the flame. I was more than up for it, and I met every sweep of his tongue with one of my own, letting my hands trace over the hard plane of his back and down to his tight ass.

And he was doing his own exploring. He loosened his hold on my throat and closed it over one of my tits, half-exposed in the slinky gold dress.

"Too many clothes," he growled. He rose onto his knees and took the dress in both hands while I looked up at him through a haze of desire. I heard the rip of the fabric, felt the air of the room on my exposed flesh as he tore the dress from my body.

"I liked that dress," I said, only half caring that he'd destroyed it in his hurry.

"I'll buy you another one," he said, grabbing ahold of my black thong underwear and tearing them off with a tug.

Now I was really turned on, and I sat up in bed to unfasten the buttons on his shirt. He tore it off himself, sending buttons flying while I worked the zipper on his pants.

His dick sprang free, long and magnificently hard. I wrapped my hand around it and he hissed with pleasure before kicking off his pants.

A lot of the things I'd done with Oscar lived in infamy in my own mind — getting off in the projector room at the Orpheum and letting him eat me out while I sprawled on the pictures he'd taken of me came to mind.

But being completely naked with Oscar Drago in bed was bliss on a different level. I sighed as he lay on top of me, then laughed when he cupped my ass to get me to scoot farther up onto the mattress.

"That's some booty scoop you've got there, Mr. Drago," I panted.

"Just an appetizer," he said, wedging himself between my thighs. "I can't wait to squeeze your glorious ass while I fuck you."

The words were a lightning bolt of heat to my cunt, and I reached down and took his pierced dick in my hand while he crushed my lips under his in a blistering kiss. He was like a deranged animal, his hands roaming my body like he wanted to be sure I was real while his tongue staked a claim on my mouth.

His shaft was velvety, the piercings at the base and tip smooth and cool in comparison to his hot skin.

"Did they hurt?" I asked between kisses.

"Pain is just weakness leaving the body," he said, kissing his way down my neck.

"Are you quoting a Nike ad right before you fuck me?"

He dropped his head against my chest and laughed. "I've never done this before."

"You're a virgin?" I was kidding, obviously. If Oscar was a virgin I was Miley Cyrus.

He snorted. "I've never laughed in bed. Not in a good way anyway."

Now I was the one who laughed. "I'm happy to be your first... something," I said, running my fingertip over the moisture beading the tip of his cock.

"Don't worry, tiger. You're going to be my first for a lot of things."

I didn't know what that meant, but he sounded serious.

"Will it hurt?" I asked, playing with the two barbells that formed an X at the tip of his dick. I wasn't really scared — I was too desperate for that — but I was curious.

His laughter was dark. "More like hurt so good."

My pussy, already pulsing with need, clenched tighter in anticipation.

He took one of my nipples in his mouth and sucked while he slid a hand between our bodies. I sighed when he slipped two fingers inside me and stroked my clit with his thumb.

I stroked my hand down his shaft and ran my thumb over the ring at the base. "And this?"

He lifted his head. "That's going to make you scream — in a good way — when it rubs your clit."

"What are you waiting for?" I asked. I was dripping for him, and I wrapped my legs around his hips to pull him closer only to feel him laugh against my tit.

"Greedy little thing, aren't you?" he murmured against my skin.

"Are you complaining?"

"Not on your life." He rose on his knees and positioned

himself between my thighs. "In fact, I've been waiting to hear those words come from your pretty mouth."

The sight of his muscled body between my legs, his perfect dick jutting proudly, was enough to make me beg.

"There are condoms in the nightstand," I said, twisting onto my stomach to reach for them.

He grabbed my ass and squeezed, and another rush of wet heat shot to my cunt.

I fought with the seal on the box, cursing myself for not doing it ahead of time, and fished out one of the foil packets.

I tore it open and he snatched it from my hand.

"What if I want to fuck you bare?" he asked.

"I'm not on birth control," I said.

"What if I don't care?"

I looked for the teasing glint in his eyes, but it wasn't there. "Don't be crazy, Oscar. Put the condom on and fuck me already."

He hesitated, then rolled it over his shaft. He grabbed my calves and put them on his shoulders, a move that lifted my hips off the bed.

I was no virgin, but I'd never been so exposed to a man. Most of my hookups had occurred in dark rooms, and more than a few had been hurried encounters in places that didn't lend themselves to full nudity.

His eyes raked my body appreciatively, leaving no doubt that he was more than happy with what was on offer.

He positioned his dick at the entrance to my pussy, then ran the tip through my folds, slicking it with my juices. The metal piercings on his tip were delicious: cold against heat, smooth metal against damp skin.

I closed my eyes with pleasure and lifted my hips.

I wanted more.

His chuckle was low and dark. He grabbed my hips and pulled me closer, then drove into me hard and slow.

I moaned into the room and opened my eyes. He was looking at me with something like possession, and I didn't mind it a fucking bit.

He withdrew slowly, then slammed into me again, picking up a rhythm that I matched, our bodies working in time. The barbells on the tip of his dick stroked the walls of my pussy as he sank into me, pushing against my cervix when he was fully seated.

The sensation was one just shy of pain, and an orgasm built at my core.

Then he lowered one of my legs, keeping the other one on his shoulder as he pushed into me from another angle.

I gasped as the piercing at the base of his dick hit my clit on the downstroke.

He chuckled. "Told you."

"Fuck... that feels incredible."

I felt like a bundle of kindling to Oscar's match, sensation overwhelming my body, sending shivers up my spine as my orgasm threatened to spill over.

"Oh my god..." I closed my eyes and gave myself over to the insane pleasure.

"That's right, tiger. Come for me."

He stroked faster and I moved my hips to the rhythm, meeting him halfway, climbing the peak of my orgasm until it shook loose, like a tether breaking, setting me free.

I screamed as my body shuddered, tremors rolling over and through me, light exploding behind my eyelids.

He groaned as he came with me. "Fuck yes. Fuck..."

He didn't stop until he'd wrung me dry. Then he took my leg off his shoulder and leaned down to kiss me.

He lowered himself to the bed next to me and pulled me into his arms.

"You're perfect, Willa."

I didn't have the energy to say anything in return. I was drifting into sleep when it occurred to me: he'd called me Willa.

Not *tiger*. Not *beautiful*.

Willa.

Chapter 60

Willa

I woke up suddenly the next morning, sitting up in bed with my tits exposed and Oscar sprawled out naked next to me. It took me a second to realize the door was open, Neo standing in its frame, glaring at us.

I could tell he was pissed, although I didn't know whether it was because of the obvious sexual attraction we'd both been fighting or the fact that I'd dared to sleep with one of his best friends. I prepared myself for his wrath, or at the very least a few well-placed jabs, but when he opened his mouth it wasn't to lob another insult my way.

"You need to come downstairs. Now." The words were softer than I'd expected, minus the usual undercurrent of hatred.

It didn't make sense, but he was gone a second later, leaving the door wide open.

Oscar sat up and took my face in his hand. "Dammit, I was really hoping for a repeat of last night. Or better yet, multiple repeats."

I trailed a hand down his chest. "I will definitely take a rain check. Or several rain checks."

He got up, giving me a full view of his perfect ass as he hunted around for his pants. He tucked his dick inside without underwear and tossed me his dress shirt from the night before.

"There are no buttons remember?" I asked.

His grin was wicked. "It's coming back to me."

I padded naked to my dresser and pulled out a T-shirt and some underwear, all too aware of his eyes combing my body.

A headache had started at the back of my skull, an unpleasant reminder of what had turned out to be a fucking amazing night, in spite of what had happened with Joshua Ryan. I wondered what had happened to him after Oscar and I left, but that was a question for another time.

"Let's go, tiger," Oscar said, holding out his hand.

Neo was waiting with Rock in the kitchen, both of them looking typically perfect even though it was before eight a.m. the night after we'd all partied at Ruby's.

There was a heavy vibe in the air, one that immediately sent alarm bells ringing in my mind. Rock didn't even make a crack about that fact that I was wearing a T-shirt that barely covered my ass, or the fact that Neo had found us naked in bed together, something I had no doubt Neo had shared.

That's when I knew something really bad had happened.

I headed for the coffee machine. "I'm going to need a coffee for this, whatever it is."

A knot formed in my stomach while I made myself a cup

of coffee, then started one for Oscar. Neo and Rock already had cups in front of them.

No one said a word, and I resisted the urge to skip the coffee and tell them to get to it. The headache had expanded from the back of my head to my temples. I definitely needed a coffee and some industrial-strength Advil.

I slid one of the cups to Oscar and took mine to the island. "Okay," I said, "spill it."

Neo handed me a folded newspaper.

I opened it and looked at the headline, my mind trying to make sense of what I was reading. It only took a second for the shock to wear off as I read the headline.

Bellepoint Student Found Dead
Homicide investigation underway

And then, the name of the student jumping out at me from the first paragraph of the article: **Nikki Wells.**

Nikki. Emma's roommate.

I looked at Neo. "Nikki's dead?" I expected him to give me some smart-ass retort about the article being self-explanatory.

"They found her body last night," he said instead.

I picked up the paper to read, trying to stop the shaking of my hands. A source close to the investigation said Nikki had been strangled. They didn't know yet how long she'd been in the woods around the Falls before she'd been found. More details would be released.

I set the paper down and looked at the steaming mug of

coffee. It had looked appealing a couple minutes ago. Now my stomach turned over at the sight of it. "It's because of me."

"We don't know that," Rock said.

"We do. Nikki's dead because I went to see her, because I asked questions about Emma."

Rock came over and rubbed my back. "You can't blame yourself because of the actions of some psychopath. The only person to blame is the one who did this."

He meant well, but the words fell flat. Nikki had been alive and going to school at Bellepoint for two whole years after Emma's disappearance. I'd gone to see her and now she was dead.

I looked at each of the guys. "Someone followed me."

Neo nodded, and I was glad that on this at least, no one was fighting me.

There were only two ways someone could have known I'd talked to Nikki: she'd told someone or someone had seen me visit her dorm.

I didn't believe Nikki would have told anyone about my visit. She'd lied to the police to protect herself after Emma's disappearance and had been cagey with me when I'd visited. Somehow I didn't see her shouting from the rooftops about it.

I thought about the roommate — I couldn't remember her name, the one with the takeout bag — but that seemed far-fetched. Nikki hadn't introduced us, and I hadn't seen the flash of recognition that I'd gotten used to while I'd been at Aventine.

That meant someone had been watching me. Us, since Neo had been with me.

Shame heated my face when I thought about the torrid

makeout session I'd had with Neo on the road. Had my stalker — or whoever was watching me when I'd visited Nikki — seen that too?

No wonder Neo's expression was grim.

"I've already called Rafe," Neo said to no one in particular.

"Rafe?"

"Security guy," Oscar said, sitting next to me and taking my hand. "He installed the system here at the house."

"I've asked him to beef it up," Neo said. "Install more cameras, give us a couple of guys to keep an eye on the road until we can have a gate installed."

I looked at him. "A gate? Because of me?"

I didn't even know if I'd still be at Aventine next year. It didn't make sense to turn the Kings' house into a fortress to protect me.

"It's overdue," Neo said, heading for the front of the house. "We've been lazy. And despite what you might think, this isn't all about you, Jezebel."

The nickname lacked its usual bite, like he was just going through the motions.

My stomach roiled, bile rising in my throat, and I knew I had about four seconds to get to a bathroom. I pushed back from the island and stood.

"Where are you going?" Oscar asked.

"I'm going to be sick."

I took two steps toward the stairs and knew it was too late. For a couple minutes all I could do was be sick on the kitchen floor. It was only after I was done, when I'd stopped dry-heaving and my stomach stopped spasming, that I realized Rock was holding back my hair.

"I'm sorry." It was all I could say. I was mortified, but also too mentally and emotionally exhausted to think too much about it.

"It's okay," Oscar said, rubbing my back gently. "Don't even think about it."

"I'll clean up this mess," I said, starting back for the kitchen.

"No, you won't." Rock guided me toward the stairs. "We'll take care of this."

I waited for Neo to make some cutting remark about how I'd soiled the pristine floors in the Kings' house, but he was silent behind me.

I let Rock guide me up the stairs, but all I saw was Nikki's scared face the day I'd gone to see her at Bellepoint.

And now she would never be scared again. Because she was dead.

It would be stupid to think I wasn't next.

Chapter 61

Willa

I brushed my teeth, scrubbed my tongue, and took a hot shower. Then I put on my softest lounge pants and T-shirt and crawled into bed.

Rock had asked if I wanted him to stay, but I really just wanted to be alone.

And not just alone. I wanted to be asleep.

And not just asleep. For a while at least, I wanted to be dead to the world.

I fell into a fitful sleep with dreams of dark woods, glittering water, and dead girls with tangled hair.

When I woke up hours later, the quality of light in my room had changed, and I knew it was afternoon. I lay in bed for a long time staring at the ceiling, listening to the low, almost inaudible hum of the house around me, thinking about Nikki and what her parents were going through.

I didn't know exactly. We'd never gotten the worst of the worst news. My mom might have been convinced Emma was dead, or so she'd said, but we'd never been confronted with her battered body. We still had a sliver of hope that she was out there somewhere, alive — or I did anyway.

There were people who said that was worse. People who whispered it to each other and some who even said it to our faces. But those were people who'd never had someone they loved disappear from their lives. If they had, they would know that any hope, however excruciating, was better than the finality of knowing you would never see the person you loved again.

Nikki's parents were faced with that finality now, and my whole body ached with it, with the knowledge that I might have been responsible for it.

I thought I should cry. It made sense — I felt absolutely miserable, like I might shrivel up and drift away — but tears wouldn't come. Maybe I'd used them all up over Emma. Maybe I'd never cry again. I didn't know. All I knew was that Nikki was dead, and my mind started turning over what that meant, how someone — probably whoever had taken Emma and the other girls — had been desperate enough to remove Nikki with such finality.

They hadn't packed her things and made it look like she'd left on her own, and they hadn't made her disappear into thin air like Emma. Whoever had killed Nikki had been desperate enough to murder her and leave her in the woods with obvious evidence of that murder.

It meant something. I just didn't know what yet.

A knock sounded at my bedroom door and I lifted my head. "Come in."

Oscar eased the door open and entered carrying a tray.

When he got closer I saw that it held a covered dish, a mug of steaming tea, a plate of little cookies, and a stack of books.

"Rock made you some food and tea in case you're hungry," Oscar said.

He set the tray on the nightstand and handed me the mug of tea, then lowered himself to the mattress next to my legs.

Now that some time had passed, I was even more horrified that I'd puked all over the kitchen floor and left the Kings to clean it up.

Not exactly a sexy end to the hot night I'd shared with Oscar.

I took a careful sip of tea. "Hmmm…"

"Ginger," Oscar said. "Rock said it'll calm your stomach."

I cradled the mug in my hands. "I'm sorry about the mess."

He tucked a piece of hair behind my ear. "Don't be." He grinned. "Neo cleaned it up."

I almost spit out my second sip of tea. "Neo? Did you have to promise him the blood of my firstborn child?"

Oscar shook his head. "He offered."

I frowned. "I just... I don't get it."

"Get what?"

"He's *such* a bastard sometimes. Most of the time," I said. "It really seems like he hates me, but then he goes and does or says something nice and I start to feel like I'm crazy."

Oscar smiled. "You're not crazy, but Neo doesn't hate you. I told you that already."

"Right, but his attitude toward me contradicts you every day."

"Neo is just... complicated." Oscar hesitated, like he was choosing his words carefully. "He's been through a lot."

Roberto Alinari was an asshole, no doubt about it. I had a vague memory of hearing that he'd abused Neo, that the abuse was why Neo's mom had left when he was little, and I had no doubt that having Roberto for a father had been no picnic.

But the rest of us hadn't had it easy either. No one did in our world.

I thought about Rock's mom, who'd died of cancer, and Oscar's brother, whose suicide was considered such a sign of weakness that the family had made up a lie to explain his death.

"He can join the club," I said. "That doesn't give him an excuse for being a dick."

"There's more to it," Oscar said.

"So enlighten me," I said. I was tired of feeling one step behind the Kings.

"Not my story to tell, tiger." He stood and kissed the top of my head. "Text us if you need anything else."

I set the mug down and picked up the stacks of books — three that were on my wish list. "Wait... How did you know I wanted these? How did you even know I like to read?"

I hadn't been reading as much since I'd arrived at Aventine, and definitely not in front of the Kings.

"You posted pictures of the books you read on social media," he said like it was obvious. "And the books were easy, I just looked at your wish list online."

He was almost out the door when I thought of something else. "What time are we leaving for the Orpheum?"

It was Saturday. That meant Neo had a fight, and I'd already been told in no uncertain terms that I'd be attending so the Kings could keep an eye on me.

"We're not," Oscar said. "Fight's been canceled."

I raised my eyebrows. "Neo must be taking that well," I said, my voice thick with sarcasm.

Oscar shrugged. "He's the one who canceled it."

Chapter 62

Willa

I spent the rest of the afternoon in bed reading. I ate the soup and was relieved when it stayed down, then nibbled on the cookies while I read. I was trying to distract myself, both from the disturbing image of Neo cleaning up my puke and the fact that he'd canceled tonight's fight.

I didn't know for sure it was because of me — and even if it was, it might have been because he didn't want the hassle of going to the Orpheum with someone who had a giant target on her back — but I couldn't think of another reason.

I'd only been to one of the fights, but it was obvious that image was a big part of the whole thing. Neo wouldn't have canceled lightly, not when it might have made him look weak.

Had he canceled because of me? Because I was sick?

But that didn't make sense. He'd probably cleaned up after me to protect the kitchen floor. Maybe he'd even done it to be *nice* — although that was hard to imagine when he was still calling me Jezebel and sneering at me every chance he got — but actually caring that I was sick was way too much of a fantasy.

He was more of a mystery now than when I'd first moved into the Kings' house, and that was something that made me deeply uneasy. Things were supposed to be getting clearer, not more complicated.

Which brought me to the other thing, the thing I was trying to avoid thinking about: whether or not to stay at Aventine.

The package from my stalker had been disconcerting, but by itself, it wasn't enough to make me consider leaving. I'd be an idiot not to consider it now that Nikki Wells had turned up dead.

My shock over Nikki had faded to sadness, then morphed into real fear. I had no idea who might be next, but I was definitely at the top of the list.

Did I want to find out what had happened to Emma badly enough that I was willing to risk my life? My mom and I had our differences, but I wasn't sure she'd recover from another loss, not even with Roberto Alinari paving the way with designer handbags and hundred-dollar bills.

The questions echoed through my mind until my phone buzzed with a text from the group chat I shared with the Kings.

Feeling good enough for *Love or Money*? Oscar had texted.

I'll heat up some more soup, Rock added.

My stomach grumbled. I was suddenly starving, and I

knew exactly what I needed. **No more soup, but I'd kill for some greasy lo mein.**

I wondered if Rock would be offended, but a few seconds later four emojis showed up: a bowl with noodles and chopsticks.

Coming right up, he added.

I waited, wondering if Neo would contribute, but I wasn't surprised when he didn't. He hardly ever spoke to me — in person or otherwise — unless it was to say something snide, and he seemed annoyed as fuck by my relationships with Oscar and Rock.

Oh well, what was it Nana Russo had said? Don't look a gift horse in the mouth?

Oscar and Rock were on offer, plus trashy TV and lo mein. It was enough of an incentive to make up for having to deal with Neo

I got out of bed, brushed my teeth again, and applied deodorant. I was brushing my hair when my phone rang, Mara's face lighting up the screen for a FaceTime call.

I answered, then propped up the phone while I brushed.

"Hey," Mara said. She wasn't smiling, and I knew why: word about Nikki was out beyond Blackwell Falls. I would need to call my mom. "I just heard. Are you okay?"

I paused my brushing to lean my elbows on the sink. "I'm okay."

"She was Emma's roommate right?" Mara asked. She was on her bed in the dorm, her curly hair pulled into a messy bun on top of her head. "I saw her picture on the news."

I nodded. "Same Nikki."

"Oh my god..." Mara's eyes were wide. "What's going on up there, Willa?"

I considered telling her about the envelope from my stalker and my visit to see Nikki, but it only took me about half a second to nix the idea. There was no point worrying Mara. She was hundreds of miles away. She couldn't do anything to help me, and knowing what was going on would only make her worry.

Plus, I was starting to feel like anyone I talked to was in danger, and I was *not* doing that to Mara or to anyone else. Not after what had happened to Nikki.

"I don't know," I said. "It's definitely weird."

I felt like a total asshole for playing dumb, but it was for Mara's own good.

"You should go home, Willa. I don't like this."

"I don't have a home." I didn't realize how true it was until I said it. Our house had been sold when my mom moved into Roberto Alinari's garish mansion.

Not exactly a welcome refuge.

"Come stay with me then," Mara said, her eyes pleading.

"At the dorm?" I shook my head. "No offense, but no thanks. I'm fine here. Really." I forced a smile even though it was the last thing I felt like doing. "Believe me, if you saw how protective the Kings are, you wouldn't be worried."

"Really?"

It had worked. Now she was interested.

"Really," I said. "They won't even let me walk to class alone."

"All of them?" she asked with a suggestive lift of her eyebrows.

"They take turns," I said. "Well, Rock and Oscar take turns. Neo still hates me."

Oscar's words drifted through my mind. *He's the one who canceled it.*

Mara grinned, and I suddenly missed her fiercely. "Two out of three isn't bad. And you're calling Drago by his first name now. What, pray tell, does that mean?"

I straightened and fluffed my hair. "I've been calling him Oscar almost since the beginning," I said innocently.

"So you haven't slept with him? Or Rock? Or both of them?" she asked.

I looked at my phone. "I didn't say that."

"Oh my god, you *bitch*!" she said. "Tell me everything."

"I'd love to but they're waiting for me with dinner," I said. "Let's just say if you ever want to know what if feels like to get fucked by a gorgeous guy with a shitload of dick piercings, I'm your girl."

She squealed. "I knew it! Good for you. And also, you lucky bitch."

I laughed. "I was definitely feeling pretty... lucky. Among other things."

"Is Rock on the menu too?" she asked. The pierced dick detail had made it clear I'd slept with Oscar.

"He is very definitely on the menu," I said. "I just haven't had a chance to partake. And it's kind of... *weird* living in the same house with all of them."

"I say sample every course, girl!" Mara said. "When in Rome right?"

My phone buzzed with a text from Rock.

Food will be here soon gorgeous.

"I have to go," I said. "Dinner's almost here and I'm starving."

I hadn't had time to tell her about getting hammered last night and then being sick in the Kings' kitchen.

"Fine," she sighed. "Go back to your exciting life of luxury with the three hottest guys in the family."

"But we didn't talk about you," I said. "What's new? Seeing anyone?"

She rolled her eyes. "These Columbia boys are all trust fund babies. Either that, or they're the opposite of trust fund babies and spend all their time studying."

"Well, you're in New York City," I said. "No one said you have to stick to campus right?" She bit her lower lip, a Mara tell for holding something in. "What's up?"

"It's not the same without you," she said. "I don't really have any, you know, *friends*."

"Are you serious?" Mara was the best friend — and the funnest — I'd ever had.

"It's just weird," she said with a sigh. "I'm not really connecting with the people here. Maybe it's me."

"It's not you," I said. "You're amazing. It's only been a few weeks. You'll find your people."

I thought about inviting her up to Aventine for a weekend, but the way things were, I didn't want Mara within a hundred miles of Blackwell Falls. We weren't just talking about unexplained disappearances anymore.

"Thanks, girl," Mara said. She suddenly looked tired. "You're right. You should go have your dinner."

I didn't want to leave her, but I really was starving, my

stomach emptied out after being sick followed by a day of hardly eating. "You sure?"

She smiled. "Hell yes I'm sure. Go eat with your hot Kings so I can live vicariously through you. I have homework anyway."

"Okay," I said, "but I'm going to check on you later."

"Deal," she said.

I gave my mom a quick call — straight to voice mail, but I'd tried — then found the guys downstairs in the living room. Neo was queueing up *Love or Money* while Oscar and Rock argued over how much it would take for Jennyfer, one of the finalists, to take the money instead of continuing with Maxx (yep, he spelled his name with two *X*es).

"You're looking better," Rock said when he saw me.

"I feel better. Thanks for the food. And the books." I looked at Neo, because I didn't want to assume he had no part in it.

He scowled. "Don't look at me, Jezebel. Thank these two cunt-whipped losers."

I swallowed my disappointment. Whatever reason Neo had for cleaning up after me and canceling the fight, it had nothing to do with his feelings for me.

"Where should I sit?" I asked Rock.

"Your usual spot," Rock said.

"I have a usual spot?"

"You do now." Rock took one end of the couch and patted the spot next to him. "Next to me."

"I think you mean between the two of us," Oscar said, taking the other end.

The doorbell rang and Neo opened the drawer on one of the side tables in the living room and withdrew a gun.

"That's the food." He tucked the gun into the back of his jeans and headed for the front door.

"We're answering the door with weapons now?" I asked.

"Just until we get the gate installed," Oscar said. "Neo has a rush on it."

Maybe I should have objected, or at least been unsettled by it all. But the truth was, I found it comforting. Someone was kidnapping and killing girls, maybe the same someone who'd been following me around, taking pictures of me and scratching my eyes out in them.

Maybe the same someone who'd taken Emma.

Living with three guys who carried guns and knew how to use them wasn't a bad insurance policy. The world tilted on its axis as I realized I was slip-sliding into the same world I'd grow up in, the one I'd sworn I'd escape.

And I was liking it.

I pushed the thought away and settled into a night of TV and food, cocooned on the sofa between two gorgeous hulking guys who were more than capable of protecting me.

It was only when I looked over at Neo, watching me from the chair across the room, his eyes dark with something fierce and unnamable, that my fear returned. But this time, it wasn't fear for my safety that was front and center, but fear of myself.

Of what I might do if I stayed in the Kings' house much longer.

Of what I wanted.

I woke with a start as I was lifted into the air. Struggling was instinctual. "What...?!"

"Shhh... it's me," Oscar said, kissing the top of my head. "I've got you."

I calmed down, sinking against his strong chest. "Did I fall asleep?"

He chuckled and I felt the vibration of it against my body. "About an hour ago."

The living room was dark, and I could see Neo and Rock moving around, checking the alarm system and getting ready for bed as Oscar carried me toward the front staircase.

"I can walk," I said.

"Why would I let you do that when I can carry you?"

I gave in with a sigh. It felt good to let go, to be taken care of.

He carried me past the Kings' rooms to my own and lay me down on the bed, then tucked my feet into the blankets and pulled them up around my neck.

He bent to leave a lingering kiss on my lips. "Night, tiger."

I reached for him. "Can you stay until I fall asleep?"

"I can stay as long as you want," he said, lowering himself to the chair next to the bed.

Forever.

I closed my mouth against the word that had jumped into my mind. I was tired, that was all, and I drifted quickly into sleep.

The next time I opened my eyes, the room was dark. I lay

under the warmth of my blankets and let my eyes adjust to the darkness.

At first I thought Oscar was still in the chair next to my bed, that he'd stayed long after I'd fallen asleep, but as my vision cleared, I realized it wasn't Oscar.

It was Neo.

He was awake and looking right at me, eyes blazing, mouth turned down in an expression of anguish.

"Neo?"

He took so long to answer I thought maybe I'd imagined him sitting there, that he'd started haunting my dreams the way he haunted me when I was awake.

Then he spoke, his voice strangely tender. "Go to sleep, Jezebel."

Chapter 63

Willa

I watched the people milling around on the sidewalk in town as Rock pulled the Audi next to the curb, but all I saw were Neo's glittering eyes, staring at me through the darkness in my room last night.

He'd been gone when I woke up, the chair across from my bed empty.

Had I imagined it? Dreamed it?

I didn't believe either of those things. I could still see him, could still hear his voice.

Go to sleep, Jezebel.

It had been real.

"Wanna talk about it?"

I looked over at Rock. "About what?"

He grinned. "Whatever's on your mind, kitten."

My heart dropped into my stomach. The bulge between his thighs was all too obvious in his jeans, and I remembered what it had felt like to grind against him in the car outside the Queens' house. It always looked like his T-shirts were a size too small — in a good way — and I could almost feel the sensation of his smooth bare skin under my palms.

I hadn't seen him naked yet, but I hadn't spotted any tattoos so far, and there were no signs of piercings either. I was eager to explore the differences between him and Oscar, and I had a feeling fucking both would be a very sexy study in contrasts.

My body responded to the thought right on cue, my pussy clenching with desire.

Jesus. What a thirsty bitch I'd become.

"I'm good," I said, because the alternatives were to tell him I'd been thinking about fucking him and Oscar at the same time, or that before that, I'd been thinking about Neo in my room.

He reached for my hand. "There's a lot going on. It's okay if you're feeling off balance."

I'd been feeling off balance for so long I wasn't sure what the alternative felt like. Maybe this was my new normal — everything going to hell in a handbasket, as Nana Russo would say.

I squeezed his hand. "I'm definitely a little off balance, but I'm okay. Thanks for yesterday, and for this."

This was a trip into town for pastries and coffee at Cassie's Cuppa. I'd needed the Saturday in bed, and ending it with trashy TV and greasy takeout was the cherry on top, but I had cabin fever.

I'd expected the Kings to fight me when I'd said I wanted to go into town for coffee, but Rock had just grabbed the keys to the Audi and ushered me to the garage.

"I'll text you my order," Oscar said as Rock closed the

door behind him.

Neo had been quiet, expression tight, no sign of the moment that had passed between us the night before (it had been real, I knew it).

"It's not a problem," Rock said, opening his door. "Your wish is my command. Besides, I could do with one of Cassie's bear claws."

"You?" I laughed getting out of the car. "What about the additives? What about the grease? What about the *white sugar*?"

He smiled as he took my hand. "Make fun all you want, but someday when we're old and gray, you're going to thank me."

Old and gray. Why did I like the sound of that?

Cassie's was hopping, a long line forming at one end of the counter with people waiting to place their orders, a small crowd standing at the other end while they waited to pick up their coffee.

We got in line and I scanned the pastry case, my mouth watering over doughy eclairs, fried bear claws, and chocolate croissants.

"What's good?" I asked Rock.

"Literally everything," he said. "Cassie makes everything fresh every morning."

"She makes everything herself?" The case was stuffed full of pastries that looked every bit as good as the ones I'd sampled in Paris.

He shrugged. "She might have a kitchen team, but everything is made here."

"Wow," I said as we inched closer to the counter.

Kings & Corruption

There was only one person in front of us now — a guy about my age with a faded blue backpack — and I could see Cassie bustling behind the counter, her copper hair shining in the morning sun that streamed in through the cafe's big windows.

Two guys worked the line, ringing up orders and making coffees, while Cassie straightened and refilled metal cans labeled with different kinds of coffee.

When it was finally our turn, I ordered a latte and a chocolate croissant, then waited while Rock ordered for himself and Oscar. I'd make Rock promise we could sit and enjoy our coffee at Cassie's, so Oscar wouldn't get his eclair until later, but beggars couldn't be choosers.

Cassie turned when she heard Rock's voice and her face broke into a smile. "Surprised to see you here," she said warmly. She was somehow both adorable and gorgeous with freckles dancing across her small nose, sparkling hazel eyes, and perfect skin. "Neo have a break between fights?"

Right. Neo didn't eat junk when he was preparing for a fight.

"Nothing for Neo today," Rock said. "Our girl here needed some caffeine and sugar."

Our girl. It had a nice ring to it.

If Cassie thought the choice of words was surprising, there was no indication of it in her expression when she looked at me with a smile.

"Good morning, Willa. Nice to see you again. The Kings taking care of you out there?" It was an innocent question without a hint of innuendo, like it was perfectly normal for a woman to live with three men she wanted to bang who weren't at all opposed to the idea.

"Good morning," I said. "They're feeding me chocolate and sugar on a Sunday morning so I can't complain." The guy who'd taken our order set our pastries down and turned away to make our coffees. Perks of being a friend of Cassie's, I guess. No waiting with the other customers at the end of the counter. "These look amazing, by the way," I said, eyeing the pastries.

"Thank you," she said. "It's a labor of love. I hope you enjoy them."

"I'm sure I will." I liked her and hoped I'd get to know her better while I was at Blackwell Falls.

The barista returned with our coffees and we said our goodbyes before moving out of line.

"She's so nice," I said.

I made my way to an empty table by the window, then felt Rock's arms on my elbow guiding me to one in the back. "Yeah, but we can't say the same about your stalker, so no window for you."

Right. My stalker. I'd seen the gun under Rock's jacket — something I now realized the Kings always carried off campus, except at the Orpheum where it wasn't allowed — but that didn't mean I wanted to make it easy for some creep to take pictures of me enjoying a coffee at Cassie's.

"Fine," I said as we settled into a table at the back of the restaurant. I wasn't going to complain. The cafe was full of light, even in the back, and at least I was out of the house for a couple of hours.

I'd just taken a blissful sip of one of the best lattes I'd ever had when Claire appeared next to Rock. I knew right away something was wrong. Her eyes weren't lit with playfulness, and her mouth was drawn into a frown.

"Hey!" I got up to give her a hug. "What are you doing here?"

"I was just making a coffee run, but I'm glad you're here." She glanced nervously at Rock, then back at me. "Can I talk to you for a minute?"

Rock stood, obviously getting the message. "I'll be right there," he said, gesturing to an empty table next to the window."

Claire took his seat, and my stomach knotted with nervousness. I knew what this was about.

"You talked to Nikki, didn't you?" she asked. There was no accusation in her voice, just a calm certainty I didn't have the heart to refute.

"I did. I'm sorry. I just couldn't..." I looked down at my latte, the weeping willow that had been drawn in foam by the barista fading into a blob. "It's killing me not knowing what happened. I can't just walk away."

As I said it, I knew it was true. Whatever options I'd been entertaining since Nikki's murder, I couldn't leave Aventine without knowing what had happened to Emma. My internal debate had raged only because I knew staying was stupid and dangerous.

But that didn't mean I could leave.

"I get it," Claire said. "I don't love it, because I think you see now what I meant about Emma and why you shouldn't talk about her. And I know I don't have to tell you, especially now, that continuing to talk about her or ask what happened to her puts you in a lot of danger. But if something happened to one of my brothers or sisters, I wouldn't stop asking questions until I had answers."

I exhaled the tension I'd been holding while I'd been waiting for Claire to denounce me as a liar. "Thanks. I'll be okay. The Kings are looking out for me." I didn't really know what that meant, and I still wasn't 100% sure I could trust them, but I couldn't lie about the fact that I felt safe with them.

It didn't make sense. None of this did, but there it was.

"I'm glad," Claire said. "That makes me feel a bit better."

"But Claire..." I lowered my voice. "You know something right? That's why you knew it was a bad idea for me to ask about Emma."

Her face turned a shade paler. "I don't. Not really. Just... you know... *rumors*."

"What kind of rumors?" I didn't want to push, especially now, but it was as safe as it was going to get. We were out in public, no different from eating together in the cafeteria every day. We could be talking about anything.

"That the guys at Aventine liked to fuck with the Bellepoint girls," Claire said. "But I've never seen it. Not once. I would have reported it if I had."

I nodded, wondering what it meant. "I wouldn't blame you if you wanted to keep your distance," I said. I'd finally made a friend, a real friend, and now I was going to tell her to stay away from me. "I'm poison right now, and the last thing I want is to put a target on your back. It's better if you steer clear of me for a while."

Claire reached across the table for my hand and looked into my eyes. "No way. Friends don't abandon each other when things get tough. Besides, if someone wants to fuck with me, I welcome them to try. My family would have their heads on a pike."

Her certainty did nothing to calm my worry for her. Emma had been a member of the Russo family, one of the oldest and most powerful Mafia families in the region, and it had done nothing to keep her safe. True, my dad had been MIA by that point, something that might have made whoever took her feel more confident, but I still wasn't big on gambling with Claire's life.

"You're a good friend," I said. "Actually, you're the best friend I have here. Make that the only one."

It was true, but it was also a deflection. Claire could opt out of steering clear of me, but I would do my best to avoid being alone with her until I found out who was trying to stop me from asking questions.

'Are you kidding? School is so much better with you here," she said. "You have no idea how bored I was before you came. I mean, Erin and Quinn are great and everything, but I've never met two people who can talk about absolutely nothing for so long."

I laughed. I loved hanging with Erin and Quinn, but I knew what Claire meant. It wasn't hard to tune out their endless chatter.

"What are you up to the rest of the day?" I asked, eager to move on to a less stressful topic.

She rolled her eyes. "Research for the Bad Ball. I think I'm going as Charlotte Corday."

"Who's Charlotte Corday?" I knew it was tradition for Aventine's student body to dress up as notorious criminals for the Bad Ball on Halloween, but the name didn't ring a bell.

"She was an assassin during the French Revolution, and not on the good side," Claire said. "She stabbed the leader of the revolution to death in his bathtub."

I laughed. "Nice."

"Have you decided on a costume?" she asked.

"Ugh. No. I kind of forgot about it with everything else that's been going on."

The Bad Ball was the last thing on my mind, but it was less than a week away, so I needed to figure something out.

"We've got that covered," Rock said, reappearing next to Claire.

I looked up at him. "Great, but I'm guessing I need a costume too."

"That's what I mean," he said. "We've got your costume covered."

I had to force myself to frown at him, just to prove the Kings couldn't boss me around. He didn't make it easy. He was so fucking beautiful, so easygoing, like some kind of cheerful god. "What if I don't like the costume you picked for me?"

"You will," he said. He turned his smile on Claire. "No offense, but you're in my seat."

I rested my forehead in my hand. "Oh my god, Rock. Rude."

Claire laughed and stood, obviously feeling better after our talk. "It's all good. I have to go anyway." She leaned down to give me a hug, then spoke softly next to my ear. "I'm here for you, girl. Text or call if you need anything. And I do mean anything."

"Thanks."

"Everything good?" Rock asked, his brow furrowed with concern.

I hesitated. I hadn't told the Kings that I'd talked to Claire, that she'd been the one to point me in Nikki's direction. I hadn't trusted them enough to tell them.

But I was tired of balancing on the knife's edge of trust with them — telling them enough to get what little information I could out of them without fully trusting them. Now, I knew Emma's fate wasn't the only thing at stake. Other girls had gone missing, and Nikki was dead.

I needed allies. Real ones. The Kings had told me they were on my side, but I hadn't fully believed it, and to be fair, they hadn't given me much to go on.

Then again, trust had to start somewhere.

"I talked to Claire about Emma," I said before I could change my mind. "She's the one who told me about Nikki, that Nikki had been to Aventine with Emma."

"Why didn't you say anything?" Rock asked. "We could have gone with you to Nikki's. Without the car chase, I mean."

My cheeks got hot. There had been no way to keep my theft of the Maserati from Oscar and Rock, but I hoped with a vengeance that Neo hadn't told them about how close we'd come to fucking on the road. "To be honest, I wasn't sure I trusted you."

"Why?"

It was such a simple honest question that it took me a second to come up with an answer. "You said you'd help me find out what happened to Emma, and you haven't told me much that I don't already know."

"And?" he prompted, his blue eyes piercing.

"And... you're part of it."

"Part of what?" he asked.

"Aventine, the parties, all the shady shit that goes down at school," I said.

He sat back in his chair and rubbed the scruff on his jawline. "You're not wrong."

"I'm not?"

He shook his head. "We haven't given you enough. I see that now. But listen, kitten, you don't have to steal a car or put your life in jeopardy if you're pissed or suspicious or whatever. Just talk to us."

I took a deep breath. "Okay, I will. But you have to talk to me too. Tell me what you know about Emma, about what happened to her."

"That's... complicated, but it's not because we were involved," he said. "Do you trust me. Do you trust us?"

I swallowed the fear in my throat. Lust was one thing.

Sex was something else.

But trust? Well, trust was my kryptonite.

Still, I wasn't going to find out what had happened to Emma by myself from the luxury prison of the Kings' house while they watched me like sexy hawks.

"I trust you," I said. I had to force the next sentence out of my mouth, Neo's face swimming in my mind. "All of you."

His smile lit up his face. "Good." He stood and held out his hand. "Now come on. We have to go."

"Why?" I asked, taking his hand. "It's Sunday."

He pulled me up. "Yep, and that means training day."

Chapter 64

Willa

"I didn't agree to this."

I was in the gym at the Kings' house with Oscar, arms folded over the pink tank top I'd thrown on over a sports bra. Rock had explained on the way home from town that Oscar would be teaching me some basic self-defense maneuvers. They didn't plan to leave me alone anytime soon, but they didn't want to leave anything to chance.

"Can you really come up with an argument against it?" Oscar asked. "This is basic stuff. Honestly, every woman should learn it."

I glared at him. "Maybe it wouldn't be necessary if we didn't have to worry about men killing us."

"I agree," he said. "I fucking hate that you have to think about this shit, that any woman has to think about this shit, but I'd rather deal with that reality and keep you safe."

His easy agreement threw me off balance. I was still getting used to the fact that the Kings — Rock and Oscar anyway — weren't quite the sexist dickheads I'd assumed them to be.

Plus, he looked hella hot in gray sweats and a black tank top that showed off his bulging biceps and gave me a peek of the perfect chest I'd been aching to run my hands over since we'd had sex Friday night.

Sometimes I forgot how big he was, not as big as Neo — no one was as big as Neo — but still huge, looming over me by at least seven inches.

"Fine," I said grudgingly.

"Good," he said. "Let's start with something simple. You'll be the asshole trying to hurt someone the first time, then we'll switch." He stepped closer and held out his arm. "Grab my arm."

I took hold of it and a second later found myself on my knees, my arm twisted behind my back. I tried to get up, but the downward pressure on my arm prevented me from moving. "What the *fuck?*"

He chuckled behind me. "Again, and I'll explain."

I stood and he held out his arm. "You don't think I'm going to be stupid enough to hold out my arm so some douchebag can grab it, do you?"

"Don't be a smart-ass," he said, flipping a lock of silky dark hair out of his eyes. "You could be swinging your arms while you walk, or someone could just grab one of them to get you into an alley or something. If someone wants to grab you, they're most likely to grab your hair or your arm. Let's do it again, but slower."

He showed me how it worked — clamp my hand down on the attacker's hand on my arm, sweep upward, put my other hand on their forearm to drive them to the ground — and we did it twice more.

"Your turn," he said, grabbing my arm.

I repeated his moves and he went to his knees on the ground, although it was obvious he was working with me.

"You were a very compliant attacker," I complained.

He laughed and got to his feet. "You're learning. The goal is for these things to become second nature. We'll move faster as you get more confident."

We did it a few more times, then worked through several other basic movements — how to bring someone down if they grabbed me by the shoulders, how to twist away if someone grabbed my hair, and even how to drop someone if they grabbed me from behind.

By the time we were done, I was sweating and breathing hard, but I had to admit, I felt empowered.

"What if someone has a gun?" I asked.

"We'll work on that next week," Oscar said. "And Rock is going to take you to the shooting range and make sure you know how to fire a weapon."

Three months earlier, I wouldn't have wanted anything to do with a gun. Now, I had to ask myself if I would have fired a gun to save Emma. To save Nikki. To save any of the girls who'd gone missing.

It was an easy answer: in a fucking heartbeat.

"Are we done?" I was desperate for a shower.

"Not quite," Oscar said. "The last thing I want you to do is scream."

I lifted my eyebrows. "Scream?"

"Yes, scream. Women are told to scream, and they'll claim they'd scream if faced with an attacker, but their programming prevents them from doing it when it counts," he said.

"Programming?"

"Being told to be nice and all that shit," he said. "It's one of the things that compels women to get in the car with a stranger when they know they shouldn't or help some psycho asshole who says he needs directions right before he stuffs her in his trunk."

He wasn't wrong. Would I scream if someone tried to grab me in public? I wanted to think so, but I wasn't arrogant enough to be sure.

"Okay," I said. "What do you want me to scream?"

He shrugged. "*No? Get your hands off me?* Whatever you want." I hesitated, because it turned out, even thinking about screaming for no reason made me feel self-conscious. "Would it help if I pretend to grab you?" Oscar asked.

"Maybe," I admitted.

He stepped forward and grabbed my arms.

"Leave me alone!"

It wasn't exactly a scream, so I wasn't surprised when he shook his head. "Louder."

He tried again.

"Leave me alone!" Better, but Oscar didn't seem impressed.

His expression turned angry. "Someone is trying to hurt you, Willa." He moved fast, stepping behind me and wrapping his arm around both of mine, pinning them at my sides and locking me in a backward embrace as he spoke low and menacingly in my ear. "They're trying to take you, like they took Emma."

"Leave me alone, motherfucker!" My scream echoed through the room, vibrating through my body as my adrenaline spiked, the bloodcurdling scream sending all kinds of freaked-out messages to my body.

I used one of the maneuvers he'd taught me to break the hold of his arms, then slammed my heel down on one of his feet.

"Fuck," he grunted, stepping back.

I turned to face him, aware that I was breathing fast, that I was ready to defend myself even though the only other person in the room was Oscar.

"That was better," he said. "How do you feel?"

I analyzed the question. How did I feel? I felt pissed. Hearing Emma's name in the middle of the exercise had made what happened to her real in a way it hadn't been before.

Sure, I'd imagined it. I hadn't been able to help myself. Imagining all the ways she might have been taken — kicking and screaming, drugged before she could know what was happening, lured by someone she knew — had been the stuff of my nightmares for two years.

But feeling Oscar's arms close around me, being momentarily powerless in the face of his greater size and strength, had unleashed something raw and animalistic in me.

Something that was determined to *survive*.

And also, maybe it was just the adrenaline, but I was fucking turned on.

"You okay?" Oscar asked.

His skin was covered in a faint sheen of sweat that only made his powerful body sexier, his nipple piercings faintly visible through the thin fabric of his tank top, his dick an obvious bulge in the gray sweats.

I was on him before I was conscious of making the decision.

"Fuck," he groaned as I wrapped my arms around his neck and slammed my mouth against his.

He reached for my ass and lifted me into the air, and I wrapped my legs around his waist as the smooth metal of his tongue piercing teased my mouth.

I was already soaked for him, my pussy clamoring for his cock.

He stalked toward one of the weight benches and set me down, then tugged off my tank top and sports bra.

I lifted my ass so he could pull off my shorts and underwear, and I reached for his shorts and tugged them down, licking my lips at the sight of his pierced dick, wide and hard.

He pulled off his tank top and I closed my hand around his shaft, then took him in my mouth, stroking his balls as he slammed into the back of my throat.

"Fuuuuuck..." he moaned.

The piercing at the base of his shaft teased my upper lip, the metal crisscrossing his tip oddly erotic in the back of my throat.

I released him a little at a time, then went to work stroking his shaft while he fucked my mouth.

He took a fistful of my braid in his hand and tugged. "You're such a fucking good girl, tiger. Such a good bad girl."

The words only intensified the inferno raging at the center of my body. I was on the verge of coming and he hadn't even been near my dripping pussy. I reached down to finger myself as he slammed into my mouth again and again.

"Uh-uh," he said when he noticed me stroking myself. "As much as that fucking turns me on, that's my job. You can make yourself come later, and I'll be more than happy to watch, but right now you're going to come on my face."

He withdrew from my mouth and knelt between my slick thighs, his cock jutting between his thighs.

He spread my legs and breathed a sigh. "Every part of you is fucking gorgeous, tiger."

I leaned back on the bench, propping myself up on my forearms as he ran his tongue through my folds from one end to the other.

"Oh my god," I moaned, dropping my head back.

"Not fucking close enough," he grunted, yanking me down by the legs and putting my calves on his shoulders. "I want to be buried in your sweet pussy."

His piercing did crazy things to my clit when he circled it slowly with his tongue. I didn't think it could get any better until he sank two fingers inside me.

I moved my hips to the rhythm of his fingers as he finger-fucked me, working my clit with his tongue, climbing the peak of an orgasm that promised to rock my world. I was lost in sensation, totally blissed out — which was probably why I didn't notice that Rock was standing in the doorway.

Chapter 65

Willa

"Jesus fuck," Rock groaned.

I lifted my head and saw that his eyes were locked on my naked body, Oscar's face between my thighs. I was barely coherent, only vaguely conscious of the fact that I should probably cover myself or tell him to leave or something.

Except I didn't want to do either of those things. I just wanted Oscar to never stop what he was doing.

"Ever hear of knocking?" Oscar asked. "Can't you see I'm trying to make our girl come?"

"I can go," Rock said, except he didn't look eager to leave, and I could see the outline of his erection through his jeans.

Oscar looked you at me. "It's your call. Want him to leave?"

"No." This was definitely not the time for lies. "I want you to keep eating my pussy."

A slow smile lifted the corners of Oscar's luscious mouth. "Want him to join?"

I laid back on the bench and looked over at Rock, but before I could invite him, he shook his head. "I'm going to have her to myself before I share, but I'll watch if it's all the same to you."

He addressed the question to both of us, but his penetrating gaze made it clear he was asking me.

I reached between my legs in answer and threaded my fingers through Oscar's hair, then tugged. "I hope you don't think you're finished."

He laughed and closed his mouth around my clit, resuming the pace of his fingers as my hips moved to meet his thrusts.

When I looked over at Rock, he was leaning against the wall, jeans unzipped, stroking his magnificent cock. He was rock-hard and huge, and the coil of my impending orgasm tightened another notch.

"How does our girl taste?" Rock asked, a little breathless.

Oscar lifted his head and used his thumb to take over where his tongue had left off. "Like fucking paradise with a side of nirvana. You're going to love it."

Their banter only made me more turned on, and I locked eyes with Rock, watching as he stroked his sleek shaft, blue eyes hooded with desire.

I was on erotic overload — Oscar's tongue working magic on my cunt, his fingers deep inside, Rock getting himself off on the display — and finally closed my eyes and let myself step to the precipice of release.

Oscar seemed to sense it, and he picked up the pace on my clit, the soft click of his tongue and lip piercings a backdrop to my heavy breathing and the low moan that was torn from my throat as I leapt over the edge.

The orgasm was less wave and more freight train slamming into my body.

"Don't stop," I panted, blind to everything but extending my pleasure as long as possible. "Don't you fucking stop."

He kept up the pace on my clit, his fingers still working my pussy until every last tremor had been wrenched from my body and I lay, sweaty and gasping, on the weight bench.

"For the record," Oscar drawled, "I don't need the instruction. I won't stop until you beg me to stop."

He stood and swore.

I lifted my head in a daze. "What?"

"Condom." He felt around behind him until he found his shorts and withdrew a foil packet from the pocket.

"Were you seriously thinking this would happen *here? Now?*" I asked with a laugh.

He tore it open and smiled while he unrolled it onto his shaft. "Tiger, I'm not passing up a single chance to fuck you, here, there, or anywhere. Now stand up and give me that sweet ass."

I'd never scrambled so fast for some dick, although in my defense, this was some world-class dick.

I turned around and he grabbed my neck from behind, pushing my upper body forward onto the bench.

"You might want to hang on," he said.

I gripped the sides of the bench and turned my head to look at Rock through all the hair that had fallen out of my braid. His eyes were glazed over, his cock engorged as he stroked, his gaze locked on me and Oscar.

I felt Oscar's tip at the entrance to my pussy and a second later he slammed into me hard.

"Fuck!" The pleasure was almost too much to bear.

His fingers dug into my hips as he dragged himself out of my channel and slammed into me again. The barbells on the head of his cock stroked the walls of my cunt, heightening my pleasure, and I let out a long, low moan as he picked up a rhythm.

I moaned, pushing back against him as another orgasm built at my center.

He slipped a hand over my hip and down to my clit, then worked circles around it while he pounded me from behind. He was so big his head was hitting my cervix, but I was nowhere near complaining.

I looked over at Rock and saw that he was stroking faster, his cock even bigger and harder than it had been when he'd started. I picked up the pace, my movements becoming more frenzied as I became more desperate for release.

"This is so fucking hot," Rock grunted. "I'm about two seconds from coming."

The words ratcheted up my own pleasure and I leaned into the coming explosion.

Oscar sensed it. "That's right, tiger. Come again. Show Rock how you scream."

The words were like a floodgate on my orgasm and it tore through my body like a hurricane. I closed my eyes, then heard Rock bark out an order.

"You better look at me while you come, kitten."

I did, and it was just in time to see him come, semen

streaming from the head of his cock as he jerked his shaft, a guttural growl torn from his lips.

"Fuck yes," Oscar said, coming behind me, slamming into me with long, fast strokes that extended my orgasm, the waves rolling over me like an earthquake that wouldn't stop shaking.

When he finally stopped, I was left panting, trying to catch my breath, aware that sweat was dripping down my back toward my shoulder blades, my hair damp with it. The room was filled with our collective heavy breathing while we all came down from whatever the hell *that* had been.

Finally, Oscar slapped my ass. I yelped, surprised to feel my sexual hunger roar to life all over again.

"Best fuck of my life," he said, bending over to kiss my back.

He helped me up and stroked the hair back from my face.

"This time or last time?" I asked.

"Every fucking time." He kissed me, his tongue moving in languid strokes. "Let's go shower."

I looked over at Rock, who'd grabbed a workout towel from the rack on the wall and was cleaning himself up. "You coming?"

"Fuck no," he said. "I can't handle the temptation of you wet and naked."

"You don't have to," I teased. I thought I might be getting the hang of this sharing thing. "I'm sure Oscar would be happy to watch this time."

Rock groaned and ran a hand through his shaggy blond hair.

He shook his head and stalked toward me, sliding a hand

into my hair and kissing me deeply, his tongue staking claim over my mouth while Oscar stood naked on the other side of me.

"Don't fucking tempt me, kitten," he said when he broke the kiss.

Oscar laughed. "You have balls of fucking steel. I don't know if I'd be able to resist."

"Yeah, well, you've had your fun." Rock looked at me, his expression deadly serious. "Soon, I'm going to have mine."

Chapter 66

Willa

Despite the fact that I was a marked woman, I was feeling pretty good by Monday morning. Partying with the girls Friday night, followed by the hottest sex I'd ever had (twice) and a lazy Saturday night lounging with the guys, had been just what the doctor ordered.

I didn't even mind when Rock walked me to class after Oscar planted a steamy morning kiss on my mouth in the parking lot. Neo was long gone by then, not to class, but in the Hummer, like he was our dad dropping us off at school, and I wondered again what he was really up to.

Rock took my hand as we made our way to my psych class. We hadn't spoken about the erotic encounter in the gym, but I could feel it sitting between us. I hoped he didn't regret watching, because I got turned on every time I thought about him stroking himself while Oscar fucked me senseless in the same room. It had made me even more excited to go to bed with both of them, and I was really hoping it hadn't changed Rock's mind.

We'd reached the walkway leading to the lecture hall when he pulled me off the sidewalk and under the branches of a tree lit orange and gold by the October sun.

He pulled me against him and took my face in his hands, then branded me with a kiss that made me weak in the knees.

"I've been wanting to do that since watching you come with Drago in the gym," he said. "Actually, I've been wanting to do a lot more, but this will do for now."

I looked up at him, very aware of his hard dick between us. My cunt was a rabid animal clamoring for his cock.

"I wouldn't object," I said. "Although I have to say, it was pretty hot watching you get off while I got off with Oscar."

His eyes seemed to darken to a deeper shade of blue, raw hunger reflected in their depths. "It was more than hot. I haven't been able to think about anything else."

"You could have joined us."

There, I'd said it. I'd made it abundantly clear that I was completely available for the opportunity to fuck both of them at the same time.

He flashed me a lazy grin. "That is an offer I will definitely take you up on." He leaned in, running his nose along the sensitive skin of my neck to murmur in my ear. "Right after I fuck you within an inch of your life myself."

My breath hitched as he pressed a kiss to my neck. "I can't wait."

"Come on." He grabbed my hand and led me back onto the pathway. "We better go before we do it like animals right here in front of everybody."

I'd been too turned on to notice, but several people were giving us curious glances as they headed for the lecture hall.

No doubt the rumor mill was in full swing — and possibly very confused, since I'd been seen in various states of affection with both Oscar and Rock.

Then again, Aventine was an upside-down world, one where the usual rules didn't apply. Maybe everyone assumed the Kings all slept with the same girl. If the rumors were true, I wasn't the first girl they'd shared.

The possibility sent a howl of jealousy through my body. I didn't know what this was between me, Oscar, and Rock — and I wouldn't even try to figure out my relationship with Neo — but I knew I hated the thought of them with anyone else.

Fuck.

I didn't think about Professor Ryan until we hit the door of the lecture hall. Then it all came back to me — Joshua Ryan touching me at Ruby's, Rock breaking his fingers, Rock and Neo telling Oscar to get me out of there.

I had no idea what had happened after I'd left, and I'd been too shaken by the news of Nikki's death to care about some pissing contest between the Kings and my professor.

Now my whole body crackled with nervousness.

"Don't worry about him," Rock said, as if reading my mind. "He knows better than to fuck with you now."

I didn't have time to ask questions. Rock pushed the door open and we stepped into the lecture hall, already half full of students thanks to my little interlude with Rock under the tree out front.

I breathed a sigh of relief when I spotted Joshua Ryan standing in front of the giant chalkboard. I hadn't realized until then that I'd been worried the Kings might have killed him.

But there he was, looking down at something on his laptop. It wasn't until we got closer to the front of the lecture hall that I saw the bruises that shadowed his face. His nose was bandaged (broken?), his lip was split, and it looked like he might have taken a few stitches up by his left eyebrow.

He moved carefully to pull down the screen he used to project information while we took notes, like it was painful for him to walk and reach.

"Fuck," I muttered. "What did you and Neo do?"

"Don't you dare feel sorry for him," Rock said. "You think you're the first student he's preyed on? He's lucky he's alive. That wasn't a given."

I shivered a little as Rock turned to me. "Thanks for looking out for me at Ruby's."

He touched my face, and I spotted several of the other students turn to watch us in my peripheral vision. "Always. Everyone at this school needs to know you're ours. They fuck with you, they meet with us."

Four months ago the words would have made me roll my eyes and assert my independence. The fact that I now felt a flush of warmth was proof that I'd really fallen down the fucking rabbit hole.

He kissed me on the lips, then turned to give Professor Ryan a meaningful look before turning back to me. "See you after class, kitten."

I slid into one of the rows, taking a seat on the end, and pulled my laptop out of my bag. I was not looking forward to staring at Joshua Ryan for an hour and a half. I didn't trust myself not to feel sympathy, and if Rock was right, he didn't deserve it.

I hadn't gotten around to telling him "no" exactly, but the power dynamic between teacher and student was all kinds of fucked up, and it was clear from Joshua Ryan's confidence at Ruby's that this wasn't his first rodeo.

I thought maybe he'd avoid looking at me during class, that we'd just pretend the incident at Ruby's hadn't happened, but when I looked up from my stuff, he was staring right at me.

And he didn't look scared. He looked furious, his face drawn with rage, eyes blazing with accusation.

I was still unsettled when I made my way to the cafeteria that afternoon. I hadn't expected Joshua Ryan to be cowed exactly, but I definitely hadn't expected the kind of open defiance he'd shown after getting beaten bloody by the Kings.

I debated saying something to Rock or Oscar, then decided against it. Professor Ryan was entitled to be pissed, even if he'd crossed a professional boundary, and I didn't want to be responsible for a broken arm or leg.

Or worse.

Did I really believe the Kings were capable of murder? So far I'd only seen them beat the shit out of two people — Enzo and Joshua Ryan — but they carried guns with them everywhere.

And it wasn't just the guns that made me think they were capable of murder, it was the easy way they handled them, the way they didn't hesitate to put the hurt on any man who displeased them.

Would they kill if someone went too far?

Maybe.

The admin building was buzzing, students huddled in the halls and making their way to and from the cafeteria. It took me a minute to realize why it was so much more crowded, then I remembered the Bad Ball.

Everyone was showing pictures of their costumes to friends, careful to hide them from the general population to avoid being copied. I wondered again what the Kings had in mind, then decided it didn't matter. They could literally dress me in a paper sack for all I cared, although given Neo's taste in gowns, even a paper bag would be emblazoned with the Dolce logo.

I waited in line to grab a prepared sandwich — turkey and avocado, my favorite — and a bottle of water, then wound my way through the crowd. It was so packed I had to hold tight to my sandwich as I was jostled and shoved.

I sighed with relief when I made it to my regular table.

"There you are!" Claire said.

"Wow, it's crazy in here today," I said.

"Everyone's psyched for Saturday," Quinn said from across the table. She looked gorgeous as always, her curly hair pulled back from her forehead by a colorful scarf.

"Plus it's getting colder," Erin said.

"True." I shrugged off my jacket and glanced at the Kings' table, then wished I hadn't when I saw that the blonde was back and draped over Neo's lap.

"What are you going as?" Erin asked. Her wide, elfin eyes

always made it seem like she was super eager to hear the answer to any question.

"Couldn't tell you," I said, cracking the cap on my water.

"I don't blame you for keeping it a secret," Quinn said. "Some of these bitches would copy every look in your closet if you told them where you'd bought it all."

I laughed. "No, I mean, I can't tell you because I don't know."

"The Kings have chosen for her," Claire said with a suggestive lift of her eyebrows.

Quinn smiled her approval. "Brave. I like it."

"But what if you don't like the costume?" Erin asked. "Like, what if it's ugly or something?"

Claire rolled her eyes. "We're talking about the Kings. It's not going to be *ugly*."

Erin looked wounded, and I hurried to smooth things over. She was definitely the downer in the group, but she also lived for Claire's approval, and Claire, god love her, could be a real bitch.

She was *my* bitch, but still.

"It's definitely a risk," I said to Erin. "But honestly, I've just had so much going on. I'm relieved to let someone else deal with it."

Erin smiled gratefully and cut a glance at Claire. "It makes sense when you put it like that, and Claire's right, the Kings have amazing taste, and you're, like, one of them. They're going to make sure you look hot."

"But not too hot," Quinn said knowingly. "I heard a rumor that Professor Ryan's face had a run-in with Neo's and Rock's fists at Ruby's."

Claire bit her lip, trying to hide her smile. "I heard the same rumor." She looked at me. "Care to comment?"

I shook my head. "I think I'll pass."

Claire laughed. "Good girl. Anyway, Quinn's wrong."

Quinn balled up her sandwich wrapper and tossed it onto the table. "Seems to be my forte. What am I wrong about now?"

"I'm just giving you a hard time," Claire said. To her credit, she sounded like she meant it. "But the Kings aren't going to play Willa down. They'll make sure she's the hottest girl at the dance, then kill anyone who dares to look at her."

Everyone laughed like it was a joke, but I was starting to wonder if it was the truth.

We talked some more about the Bad Ball — Quinn and Erin were going as a couple of the Manson girls, which was dark even for me — and then moved on to midterms.

We left together for our next classes, shoved through the masses, and parted ways outside the admin building. Erin was right, it was getting cold, and I shoved my hands into the pockets of my jacket on my way to English 101, then felt my fingers brush up against a piece of paper.

I pulled it out, expecting to find a long-forgotten receipt, and saw that it was a folded piece of white printer paper.

I stopped cold when I opened it and saw the words printed on its surface.

Meet me at the old hunting cabin at midnight during the Bad Ball if you want to know what happened to your sister.

YOU CAN'T TRUST THE KINGS.

I looked around, like I might see whoever had stuck the note in my pocket skulking away, but no one stood out in the crowd of students making their way to and from the admin building.

I looked back at the note. This was the first time I'd worn this particular jacket at Aventine, which meant someone had slipped it in my pocket in the past three hours.

I thought back over the first half of the day: walking to class with Rock (no one would dare), sitting in Professor Ryan's class (no one had sat on either side of me), and meeting Claire, Quinn, and Erin for lunch.

It had to have been lunch, probably on my way to the cafeteria or on my way out, or maybe when I'd been pushing through the crowd to get to the lunch table.

The question was, who was it? And what did they mean about the Kings?

Chapter 67

Willa

I stood in my underwear and stared at the dress hanging over one of my closet doors with suspicion, trying to figure out what the Kings had gotten me into. Short and black with long sleeves and a cutout from the collarbone almost to the waist, it might have been a dress made for any slutty occasion.

This was what I got for leaving my costume for the Bad Ball to them. I'd had plenty of time to insist I'd come up with my own costume. I'd taken the easy road, and now it was time to pay the piper, another of Nana Russo's favorite sayings.

I turned to the bag of accessories Rock had brought to my room, but it wasn't much help. I took everything out one at a time and set it all on my bed: a retro-looking purse, a pair of sheer black thigh-high stockings with black seams up the back, a pair of basic black stilettos (if Jimmy Choo was basic), a hat that looked almost like a beret, a delicate vintage watch, and a pack of cigarettes with a note taped to the front with Rock's handwriting: *Don't you dare light one of these.*

I snorted out loud. I'd never met such a hot nerd.

Taking a deep breath, I got to it. I had exactly two hours before we had to leave for the Bad Ball, and I didn't want to be rushed, especially since I was also psyching myself out for the meeting at the hunting cabin.

I'd been instructed to do my makeup however I wanted and to braid my hair, and I ran through my plan while I went to work in front of the bathroom mirror.

First, steal the gun from the console by the front door. Rock hadn't had time to teach me how to use it, but my dad had been a Mafia don. I wasn't squeamish about guns, and I'd rather have it and risk firing it wrong than need it and not have it.

The next part was harder: I'd have to hope the Kings weren't watching me every second so I could sneak away. Not exactly a foolproof plan, but there wasn't much else I could do.

I'd figure something out.

The scariest part of all would be getting to the hunting cabin. I'd had no idea what the note meant, but an online search had turned up several articles about abandoned cabins in the woods surrounding Blackwell Falls. Some of them had been used by the workers and foremen when the quarry had been in production. Others had been used for hunting.

I'd been nervous about finding the right one, but it turned out there were a lot of weird people out there who liked to hunt for abandoned places, and a couple of them had posted maps of the various cabins.

Only one of them was close enough to walk to from

Aventine, and I'd mapped it about a mile from the admin building and ballroom.

A mile wasn't an easy walk through the woods, especially in the dark, but it was doable, and I'd stashed a pair of boots and a jacket behind one of the ceiling panels in the women's restroom closest to the ballroom.

I could do this.

I looked at myself in the bathroom mirror. "You can do this," I whispered.

My makeup looked good. I'd taken a chance on both a smoky eye and a red lip — a combo that was usually too much — reasoning that any famous female criminal was probably a historical figure, and makeup was almost always heavier back then.

Besides, the dress screamed skanky. It was clear what the Kings wanted. Who was I to disappoint?

Anyway, it worked, and I thought about the next part of the equation while I braided my long hair.

The Kings. I hadn't told them about the letter, and I didn't plan to. It was a gamble. The person who'd slipped the note into my pocket was more than likely an enemy — but it played on my biggest fear about the Kings: that I couldn't trust them.

My conversation with Rock at Cassie's had left me feeling sure we were on the same side, but it had been a fragile trust based on desperation.

What choice did I have?

Now I had another choice. It sucked, but it was still a choice.

If the note was right and I told the Kings about the

meeting, I might never get the promised information about Emma. If it was wrong, I might end up fighting for my life.

In the end, I was willing to risk my life for Emma's. The only way to find out if the note was right about the Kings was to meet the asshole who'd written it.

Finished with my braid, I went back to the bedroom, pulled on the stockings, and slipped into the black velvet dress and shoes. I was glad I still had the coat Neo had sent for the welcome ball, because the dress didn't stand a chance in hell of keeping me warm.

The hemline barely covered my ass, the lace top of the stockings peeking out when I moved, and my tits were in serious jeopardy of falling out of the cutout neckline. When I turned around, I saw that the dress plunged almost all the way to my ass, leaving precious little fabric to actually cover it.

"So much for leaving something to the imagination," I muttered, returning to the bathroom.

I dug around in my stuff for some fashion tape, taped the neckline to prevent a nip slip, and put on the shoes and hat. I finished with the vintage watch and stood back to take in the effect.

I still didn't know who I was supposed to be, but I had to hand it to the Kings: it looked great, definitely someone historical, probably from the early 1900s.

My phone dinged with a text from Oscar in the group chat.

Our life of crime awaits.

It was close to home, but I laughed out loud anyway.

In other words, get your ass down here. We're not waiting.

I blinked in surprise when I realized the last one came from Neo.

Interesting.

He speaks for himself, Rock texted. **I'll wait forever.**

I laughed again and got the gorgeous Fendi coat out of my closet. I'd wait to put it on so I could get the Kings' approval on the way I'd put the costume together. Then I grabbed the purse and dropped a few things inside, including the pack of cigarettes, and a small flashlight I'd found in the garage.

I used the front staircase this time, because what was the point of having a staircase worthy of *Architectural Digest* if you couldn't use it to make grand entrances on special occasions?

The Kings were standing in the foyer, and I knew immediately I'd nailed the time period on the costume. They all wore similar wing-tip shoes, baggy pants, dress shirts, and suit coats with wide lapels. Oscar and Rock looked elegantly old-school in fedoras, while Neo had slicked his dark hair back with something that made it shine under the light.

Rock whistled as I made my way down the stairs. "Jesus fuck," he said, his mouth hanging open as he watched me descend the staircase. He looked like a movie star from the 1940s. "You look good enough to eat."

The innuendo was clear in his voice, and my pussy throbbed at the idea of Rock's face between my thighs.

I hit the foyer and gave a little curtsy. "I'm glad you approve."

Oscar's eyes raked my body from head to toe. His tongue darted out to tease the ring in his lip, and I was instantly wet thinking about the way it felt when he used the stud on my clit.

"I don't know if we're going to make it out the door with you in that dress, tiger." I wasn't sure whether his voice held a threat or a promise, but I was down for either.

"After all this," I said, gesturing to the costume, "we are definitely making it out the door. Besides, you all look amazing too. Might as well show it all off."

I made a point of including Neo in my gaze, just to be nice, but he didn't seem to care one way or the other.

Rock slung an arm over my shoulders. "Know who we are yet?"

His expensive cologne went right to my pussy. I was dying for him to make good on the promise to fuck me, although I doubted tonight would be the night if (when) they found out I'd given them the slip at the ball to meet a stranger in the woods.

"Not a clue," I said.

He reached under the console and pulled out three retro cardboard rifles. "Bonnie and three Clydes." He handed one to Oscar and Rock. "Not as cool as the real thing, but you know..."

"Yeah, kind of frowned upon to have real weapons on campus," I said.

"Exactly," Rock said, as if they weren't all carrying all the time.

I reached into Oscar's jacket and felt around the smooth cotton of his shirt for the holster, the one holding a real gun. "Doesn't seem like you're too worried about the rules."

Oscar leaned down to give me a lingering kiss. "Not when it comes to protecting you, tiger."

Neo stalked toward the garage door. "Jesus you're pathetic."

Rock helped me with my coat and I sighed as I sank into the thick wool. Then we were filing into the garage and heading for the Hummer.

I forced myself to stay calm while I waited for everyone to get in the car — Neo driving (of course), Oscar in front, Rock and I in back. I made myself wait a few more seconds until Neo started the car.

"Wait!" I said. Neo's eyes found mine in the rearview mirror. "I forgot something."

Neo sighed. "Hurry up or you'll be walking."

I knew he was bluffing but there was no point biting back. I slid from the car and hurried back into the house. I disarmed the alarm, then hurried to the console table by the door, praying my instinct was right and the gun was still there.

I opened the small drawer and breathed a sigh of relief at the sight of the handgun.

I didn't know a lot about guns, but I knew they were personal, at least in our world. No man went around sharing his weapons, and the ones they carried were like trusted friends.

This was an extra, one kept by the door for emergencies, and I took the risk of an extra second to look under the console, unsurprised to find a bigger badder weapon attached to the underside of the table. My dad had kept one there too, and others around the house.

Just in case.

I straightened and stuffed the gun in my purse. At first it wouldn't close, the gun too big for the clutch.

I removed my phone and stuck it in my coat pocket, then tried again.

This time the gun fit. Barely.

I breathed a sigh of relief and armed the alarm before heading back to the garage, my purse heavy with the weapon inside.

"Ready?" Rock said when I slid into the back seat.

I forced a smile. "Ready."

I didn't know if it was true, but one way or another, I was about to find out.

Chapter 68

Willa

The dance was in full swing when we got there, the ballroom floor packed with bodies dancing to music spun by a DJ at one end of the room. The setup was familiar, complete with a full bar, but this time it had been decorated for Halloween, the walls covered with floor-to-ceiling canvases splattered with red paint to look like blood.

A fog machine or three funneled mist from somewhere in the room, giving the whole scene a hazy quality that would be perfect for my escape into the woods.

Neo scowled, then leaned over to say something to Oscar, and I wondered if he was thinking about how hard it was going to be to act as my prison warden with the fog swirling in the air.

The only downside was that I didn't see Claire and hunting through the fog could take hours. I needed to meet up with the girls, do the whole wow-you-look-great thing, and get everybody onto the dance floor stat.

Kings & Corruption

One thing I'd learned about the Kings — at least so far — was that they didn't dance at these things. They were too busy in their role as jailers, or protectors, depending on how I was feeling about it at any given moment.

I scanned the room, hoping for a glimpse of Claire's vibrant hair. I didn't see her, but I landed on the bar, and if there was one thing I could be sure of, it was that one of the girls would end up at the bar sooner rather than later.

I pointed and mouthed the word *drink* to the Kings, not bothering to shout over the music.

They moved into formation like a squad of soldiers, Neo taking his usual position in front while Oscar and Rock stepped in behind me. I wondered if this was what celebrities felt like with all their security and if they ever had to plot an escape from their own team.

I got to the bar and ordered a Huckleberry Twist, which had become my drink of choice since coming to Aventine. I raised a questioning eyebrow at the Kings, and they ordered shots of whiskey.

I wasn't surprised. It was hard to imagine the Kings, who were always wound so tight when they were on guard duty, nursing a cocktail.

The bartender set our drinks down and I took a sip of mine, trying to relish the unique taste of huckleberries. If I wanted to be alert for the meeting at the cabin, I wouldn't be able to finish it.

Shame.

Less than a minute after I'd taken my first sip, Claire came barreling toward the bar with Erin and Quinn on her heels.

"There you are!" she said, clearly many drinks ahead of me. She threw her arms around me. "I thought you'd never get here!"

"You look amazing!" Quinn shouted over the music.

Claire pulled back from our hug to give me a once-over. "You do!" She looked at the three Kings, lined up at the bar like sexy Italian statues. "Bonnie and Clydes!"

I smiled. "You got it. And look at you! What a great costume!"

Claire's dress was full of ruffles and flounces, clearly inspired by the French Revolution, but the details were where the inspiration ended. This was the XXX version, with a hemline that didn't even try to cover her ass and a deep neckline that made me hope she'd used some tape.

Her makeup was over-the-top Marie Antoinette, and her red curls had been piled onto her head in an elaborate style that must have taken hours.

She turned around to give me a look at the back, showing off ruffled, petticoat-inspired panties that barely covered her exposed ass cheeks. She wore white, thigh-high stockings, complete with a sheathed knife tucked into the lace. I hoped it was fake, but knowing Claire, it probably wasn't.

"Wow," I said. She really did look incredible, and the best part was the blood she'd splattered all over the costume. "You look unbelievable!"

"Thanks," she said.

Erin and Quinn looked appropriately creepy as Manson girls, both wearing long brunette wigs and flowery, 1970s-style dresses. They'd taken a different tactic with the fake blood, smearing it over their necks and arms and leaving bloody handprints on their dresses.

We exchanged a few more compliments and I waited while they ordered another round of drinks, holding up my nearly full Huckleberry Twist when they tried to include me. Then I turned around and blew a kiss to the Kings, leaning against the bar and looking like three bronze gods.

Rock grinned and Oscar looked like he wanted to have me for dinner, but Neo obviously wasn't amused by my playfulness. His features were drawn into his trademark scowl, his eyes dark with the hatred I sometimes saw there.

I didn't understand him, but tonight was definitely not the night to try.

I squeezed my way onto the dance floor with Claire and glanced at my phone as we started moving. It was almost 10:30 p.m., and it might take me up to an hour to get to the cabin. One of the people who'd posted a map to it online had said there were old markers on the trees, but apparently they were faded and the trail was mostly overgrown.

I'd printed the map, but I had no way of knowing exactly how dense the woods would be leading to the cabin, or how hard it would be to find the markers at night.

I needed to be out of here by eleven at the latest.

I smiled and laughed with Claire and the girls while we danced, but a ticking clock was running in the back of my mind, my gaze constantly pulled to the Kings. I tried to play it cool, to look like I was just casually glancing around, but I needed to know when it was safe to make a break for it.

I was sweaty from dancing when one of the Knights, an enormous blond with shoulders as wide as a barge, approached Neo. They conferred, heads bent together, for about a minute. Then, Neo spoke to Oscar, who glanced in my direction, and left the room with Rock and the big Russian.

Two jailers down, one to go.

It was as good as it was going to get.

I shouted that I was going to the bathroom, not that Claire and the girls cared given their current state of drunkenness, and headed that way. I didn't doubt that Oscar would follow, but it would take him time to move through the crowd, and even more time for him to find it suspicious when I didn't leave the bathroom.

Then, he'd have to find Neo and Rock to report my absence before the three of them tried to sniff me out like hunting dogs.

Well, good luck with that boys. I didn't know how I was going to make my own way through the woods, and I at least had a map of where I was going.

The thrill of victory didn't last long. What I was doing would be a reckless, too-stupid-to-live moment in any horror movie, but this wasn't a horror movie. It was my life. Emma's life. If there was something to know about my sister's disappearance, I would risk anything to hear it.

There were only two other girls in the bathroom when I got there. I walked into one of the empty stalls and waited until they left, then moved to the one closest to the wall.

Standing on the toilet, I reached for the ceiling panel where I'd hidden my boots and jacket — my Fendi coat had been handed over to the coat check — and pulled them down.

I shoved my feet into the boots, laced them in a hurry,

and slipped on the jacket. I removed the map and gun from my bag and hesitated over my phone. Once I left campus, it would be the only link I had to the Kings. If I left it behind, I'd really be on my own, but if I took it and the Kings managed to find me before I got information about Emma, I might lose my only chance to know what had happened to her.

I put my phone in the bag and stored it with my heels in the ceiling. Then I slipped the map and gun into my jacket pocket and hoisted myself up to the window.

Chapter 69

Willa

The bathroom window was harder to get through than I'd expected, mostly because it was smaller than it looked. I had one moment of sheer panic when I thought I might be stuck, but a little wiggling shook me loose, and I dropped to the ground with a thud and started running before Oscar could come looking for me.

There was no trail on this side of the building. The tree line was so dense I wasn't sure where to step through to find the path that was allegedly still marked on the trees leading to the cabin.

But the clock was ticking, so I looked at the map and took my best guess, then started tramping through thick stands of trees and the dry leaves that blanketed the ground.

It was so dark I could only see a couple feet in front of me. It was weird not having my phone, but I was relieved to have the tiny flashlight. Without it, I wouldn't have stood a chance in hell of finding my way to the cabin.

I was starting to get nervous that I'd made a mistake, that I'd stepped into the woods in the wrong place. Despite carefully watching the trees, I hadn't seen anything resembling a marker, and I was debating whether to change course when my flashlight landed on something out of the ordinary on one of the tree trunks up ahead.

I was grateful for my boots as I stepped through the leaves to get a better look.

And yep, there it was. Up close with a flashlight, I could barely make out a faded smear of orange paint on the white trunk of a birch tree. I felt a surge of triumph, then realized it could be a marker for anything.

Still, I badly needed the win, and I kept going, holding my breath until I spotted another marker about five minutes later.

After that the markers came regularly, painted on oaks, maples, and birch trees along the trail depicted on the map in my hands.

I wondered about the Kings, who were probably going batshit right about now. It wouldn't have taken long for Oscar to realize I'd snuck out of the bathroom. After that, he would have texted Neo and Rock.

I could only hope they wouldn't think to follow me into the woods right away. Maybe they would check the rest of the admin building first, or even drive back to the house in case I'd decided to leave without them for some reason.

I couldn't be sure what they would do, but I didn't hear them in the woods behind me.

Not yet anyway.

Other than the occasional weird sound coming from the darkness of the woods, it was terrifyingly quiet. I'd never been so utterly alone.

It was easy to lose track of time without my phone. My hands and face were cold, and I cursed myself for not thinking to bring gloves. Eventually I came to a small fork. Not a path exactly — the woods were too dense for that — but the smaller bushes and trees had been pushed down in two directions, like someone had stepped on them or crashed through them.

I tried not to think about that last possibility, about Emma or someone like her running through the trees just like I had when I'd been chased at the quarry party.

I consulted the map and looked at the arrow that had been drawn just before the little square representing the cabin. It was the only thing on the map besides the winding trail of ink that represented the barely marked trail and the cabin at the end of it.

And the arrow pointed right.

Was this what it meant? I held the flashlight between my teeth and rubbed my hands together to keep them warm while I considered my options. It didn't take long because I didn't have many of them: turn back, go left, or go right in the direction of the arrow.

I stepped to the right and continued through the trees.

On the plus side, I was almost there, and I slowed down a little, keeping my eyes peeled for the cabin. I'd already decided I would wait in the trees when I found it. I had no way of knowing whether the person who'd given me the note would already be inside or if they would arrive after me, but I preferred to get a look at them before I was trapped with them in a cabin in the middle of the woods.

I stuck my hand in my jacket pocket, the cold steel of the gun a reassuring talisman.

A glimpse of light through the trees halted my forward motion, and I stood still, blinking to make sure I wasn't imagining it.

But no, it was there, a faint gold light up ahead. A fire maybe, or one of those camping lanterns.

Another minute and it came into view, a tiny wooden cabin with a hole in the roof and a partially caved-in porch. The glow came from one of two broken windows that flanked a rough-hewn door hanging askew on its hinges.

The whole thing gave me the heebie-jeebies. It looked like it had been there for two hundred years and had been unoccupied just as long.

I shivered, looking around for a tree big enough to hide behind. I'd taken two more careful steps toward a giant oak with a trunk twice as wide as my body when I heard the snap of a branch to my left.

I froze and turned off the flashlight, then waited to see if I would hear it again. I didn't, and I continued forward, assuming it had been a deer.

It was a mistake, and one I realized a moment later when strong arms grabbed me from behind. I struggled, panic rising in my body, threatening to black out everything else.

I remembered my gym session with Oscar and opened my mouth to scream. "Get the fuck off —"

Sadie Hunt

I hand came down over my mouth, followed by a string of curse words.

And then, the cold barrel of a gun against my head.

Chapter 70

Oscar

I tapped my foot on the floor of the hall, my eyes on the door to the women's restroom. I'd watched Willa snake her way out of the ballroom and had immediately done the same, pushing and shoving in order to keep her in my line of sight.

I fucking hated this. I hated that she couldn't have one night to dance and have fun with her friends without a security detail.

But I also knew it was necessary, and as much as I hated it, the alternative was un-fucking-acceptable.

I was in way too deep. Thinking about something happening to her, about the light that fucking lit up my world leaving her eyes, sent me into a panic unlike anything I'd ever felt.

I'd had loss in my life. Plenty of it. But I didn't know if I would survive losing her.

And I wasn't the only one. Somehow this girl had us all by the balls and she didn't even know it.

I pulled out my phone and checked the time. What the *fuck* was she doing in there? I wasn't one to time a lady in the bathroom — I mean, it took how long it took — but she'd been in there for ten minutes, presumably alone since two other girls had exited almost as soon as Willa went inside.

Finally, I pushed off the wall. Fuck it. She would be pissed, but she was adorable when she was pissed.

And sometimes, a little scary, which was just as much of a turn on.

I pushed open the door. "You alive in h— "

I froze, my eyes drawn to the open window over the last stall, a ceiling panel slightly displaced just above it.

"*Motherfucker.*"

I was already running for the weapons we'd stashed in the Hummer when I opened my phone to text Neo and Rock.

Chapter 71

Willa

There were two of them, something I only realized when I'd been dragged into the cabin and the second man closed the creaky door, shutting us inside.

The first man was stronger than me, but he still grunted as he hauled me backwards, resisting my attempts to struggle against him until he finally shoved me against one of the cabin walls.

"Bitch!" he snarled.

I went sprawling, smacking my face against the wall of the cabin as I tried to regain my footing.

I backed against the wall and tried to get my bearings. I'd been right about the lamp inside the cabin, except it wasn't a modern camping lamp, it was one of those old-fashioned ones that used oil or kerosene. Its flame cast strange shadows on the walls, like a scene straight out of a horror movie where I deserved to die because I'd left my phone and come without the Kings.

The cabin was small, a single room with a tiny bathroom visible beyond the half-open door across from where I stood. There was a decrepit table and a couple of chairs, a ratty old soda, the stuffing coming out in tufts, and a stained mattress on the floor I didn't want to think about.

The first man stood facing me, the gun pointed at my face, his eyes wide behind a ski mask like the one that had been worn by my pursuer in the woods. The other man was wearing a ski mask too, and I flinched when he walked toward a shovel leaning against the wall.

"Hurry up," the first man said.

"Do you want to do it?" the other man hissed.

"Just get it done," the first man said, turning to face the other man. There was something familiar about his voice, but it sounded artificially deep, like he was trying to disguise it. "You know what he said."

I carefully felt around in my pocket while the two men exchanged words and was relieved that the gun was still there.

"Yeah, I know what he said." The second man's voice didn't sound familiar, and he clearly didn't give two fucks about trying to disguise it. He turned to look at me and a shiver ran up my spine. His eyes were so dark they were almost vacuous. He was bigger than the first man, towering over him by at least a few inches with big arms and broad shoulders. "I'm just saying, if you'd rather dig, I'd be happy to keep our little friend here company."

"I'm not digging." There was a note of finality in the first man's voice that said he thought he was in charge, but of the two of them, it was the second man I most didn't want to be alone with. "Just make it quick."

"Ground's fucking cold," the second man said. "I'll work as I fast as I can."

That's when it hit me — they were talking about digging. In the woods.

They were going to kill me out here and bury my body where no one would ever find it. I'd be just another missing girl people talked about years from now.

Like Emma. Was this what had happened to her?

I forced myself not to think about it. I couldn't find Emma if I let these men kill me, bury me in the woods.

I had to get out of here.

The second man left the cabin, slamming the door behind him. It groaned on its hinges, but I knew there was no hope of anyone hearing it. We were in the middle of nowhere and I hadn't told anyone where I was going.

In my desperation to find out what had happened to Emma, I'd gambled and lost.

The first man stared at me, breathing heavily, like he was trying to figure out what to do next. I was struck again by the familiarity of his eyes, but they weren't familiar enough.

I had no idea who he was.

"Who are you?" I said. "What do you want with me?"

"You were warned," he said in that weird, abnormally low voice.

I had the crazy thought that he might be one of the Kings, that they were pulling out all the stops to get me to stop asking questions because they were involved in Emma's disappearance.

But I rejected the idea almost immediately. Would I put it past the Kings to teach me a lesson? Even a hard one?

Hell no.

Would they hurt me doing it? Throw me against a wall? Scare me? Make me think I was going to die like Emma?

Also a hell no.

This was someone else.

"Did you hurt my sister?" I asked. "Did you... did you kill her?" I almost couldn't bear to say the words, but they'd been stuck in my throat for two years. I couldn't carry the question around anymore, not when I had the chance to ask it.

He started pacing, muttering to himself, or maybe to me. I couldn't be sure. "I knew you were going to be trouble, knew this was a mistake..."

"Okay, listen," I started, trying to keep my voice calm. The man outside digging my grave had acted like he was going to pick up milk from the store, but it was obvious this man — whoever he was — didn't want to be here. Maybe I could still get out of this alive. "You don't have to do this. I just... I just need to know what happened to Emma, okay? I can't see your face. I have no idea who you are. I just need to know. Just... just tell me, and I'll stop asking questions, I promise."

"Do you think you have bargaining power here?!" he roared, stepping closer and resting the gun against my temple. "Does it feel like you have any power? Any leverage?"

I raised my hands, my heart beating so fast I was afraid it would jump out of my chest. "No! No... I'm sorry. You have the gun. You have all the power."

The pressure of the gun against my temple eased up and

he stepped back, putting a few feet of space between us again.

"You always think you have the power," he muttered, pacing the cabin. "Like you deserve something because of what you have between your legs, like *you* get to make all the decisions, all the choices."

Okay, now I knew who — what — I was dealing with.

"I'm sorry," I said again. "You're right. You're in control here. You're going to kill me and bury me in the woods and no one will ever find me. I get it." Fear galloped through my body as I said the words. It was so powerful, my vision started to recede, a buzzing coming from inside my brain like I was going to pass out.

No. I would *not* faint like some weak-ass heroine. I would not.

I thought of Emma, saw her face, the way it lit up when she laughed, and then, the last face I thought I'd conjure in a moment like this one — my mom. I saw her the way she'd looked when I'd been little, when she'd been happy and full of laughter, telling jokes to make me giggle on the way to school, lying next to me in bed when I was sick.

I was not going to let her lose another daughter. I just had to keep this fucker talking long enough to figure something out.

"I just... I'm begging you to tell me what happened to my sister," I continued. "I accept that you're going to kill me, okay? I just want to die knowing what happened to her."

I didn't know what I expected, but it wasn't the bitter laughter that erupted from his mouth. "You don't get it, do you? We want you to suffer. All of you. That's the *point*." He was pacing again, walking back and forth in front of me while he ranted like some kind of fucked-up preacher in some kind of fucked-up church. I slowly — so slowly — slipped my hand into the pocket of my jacket and wrapped my hand around the gun. I'd never fired one before, but I'd seen it in movies and stuff. I'd figure it out. "It's the only way you'll learn. It's for your own good. That's how things change, that's how — "

I pulled the gun out and fumbled with what I thought was the safety and his head spun up to look at me.

Time seemed to slow down as my brain tried to process what was happening.

The safety clicking off on the gun in my hand.

The man in front of me raising his weapon.

The feel of the trigger giving way under my finger as I fired, the force of my arm jerking back, the sound exploding in my ears.

The man grabbing his thigh, a scream pulled from his lips as blood darkened his pant leg, blood dripping onto the floor.

The realization that I'd hit him, not enough to drop him, but enough to wound him.

Enough to buy me time.

And then, the crack of gunfire just outside the door before it burst open, Neo filling its frame.

Chapter 72

Willa

The masked man turned toward the door, his eyes wide with shock as Neo burst into the room, Rock and Oscar on his heels like avenging angels, all of them with weapons drawn.

I didn't have time to wonder how they'd found me. A round of gunfire exploded, the sound overwhelming in the confines of the cabin. It was impossible to tell who was firing where as wood splintered from the cabin's walls, jars and glasses shattering on the makeshift shelves.

I ducked instinctively, the gun still in my hands, and watched as the man swayed on his feet, then went crashing to the floor, knocking over the table and one of the chairs on his way down.

The old-fashioned lamp went flying, and a second later an ominous *whoosh* sounded through the cabin as the fire spread from the lamp to the wood floor, which was dry enough to act as kindling.

The fire was between me and the Kings, its flames licking higher as it reached for more fuel.

"Stay there, Willa!" Oscar had to yell the command, and I was aware as if from a distance that I hadn't expected fire to be so loud. "I'm coming!"

I was still holding the gun, the metal welded to my hand as I tried to take in the scene. My gaze landed on the man I'd shot in the thigh, still and sprawled across the floor in front of the fire.

I should have been happy he was dead, but all I could think about was Emma.

Now I'd never know what had happened to her.

The fire grew louder as it consumed more fuel, smoke filling the room. I coughed, remembering a statistic I'd heard somewhere along the way, that more people died in fires from smoke inhalation than from the actual flames.

Glass shattered from all sides, the heat blowing out what was left of the cabin's windows.

Then Oscar was there, crouched in front of me, his expression so still he might have been made of stone. It was only his eyes that gave away his worry.

"Come on, tiger. We have to get out of here. This whole place is going up."

The fire was growing at an alarming rate, creating an insurmountable obstacle between us and the door. I could only vaguely make out Rock and Neo on the other side of it.

I coughed and Oscar helped me to my feet, prying the gun from my hands. "We'll have to go out the window."

He stripped off his shirt and wrapped it around his arm,

then used it to sweep what was left of the glass out of the frame.

Gunfire sounded from the front of the cabin and Oscar looked over his shoulder, a stricken expression on his face. "What the fuck?"

The second man. Everything had happened so fast, I'd forgotten he was out there.

"There's another one," I shouted, too late obviously.

"Just one?" Oscar asked after another round of gunfire had subsided.

The fire was everywhere. I couldn't see a thing beyond the space where Oscar and I stood. "I think so."

He was digging my grave. They were going to kill me and bury me out here.

Like Emma.

The words drifted through my mind like the smoke filling the room.

The gunfire sounded again, farther away this time, maybe outside. Oscar got down on his knee and threaded his hands together. "You first."

I put my foot in his hand and he boosted me to the window. Without the glass, it was bigger than the bathroom window in the admin building. I slid through it with no problem, dropping onto my hands in the dirt outside the cabin, coughing as the cold air hit my smoke-filled lungs.

Oscar followed a second later, just as Neo and Rock ran around the side of the cabin, their faces and clothes smeared with soot.

"Thank god," Rock said, grabbing me and pulling me against him. He pulled back and held my face, running his hands down my neck and over my shoulders and arms. "Are you okay? Are you hurt?"

I shook my head. "I'm fine. The other man..."

"He ran into the woods," Neo said.

"We wanted to make sure you were okay," Rock said.

A loud crash broke thought the night as the roof caved in on the cabin, sparks rising into the darkness. It would have been pretty if I hadn't come so close to being killed.

"We have to go," Oscar said, taking my hand.

He pulled me along the side of the cabin after Neo and Rock, and we rounded the corner to the front and headed for the trees where I'd been kidnapped and dragged into the cabin.

I looked back and understood why some people were captivated by fire. Flames licked from the cabin's window frames, reaching for the doorway like a living thing, a fiery beast consuming everything around it.

I thought of the man inside, the one who'd pointed the gun at my head.

"Wait!" I tugged my hand loose from Oscar's. "The man..."

"Come on!" Neo shouted at me. "We don't have time for this. We need to get out of here and call the fire department before this fire burns down the whole forest."

I looked from him back to the cabin, then back at him, Oscar and Rock. "I'm sorry."

Then I ran.

"What the *fuck*!" I heard Neo yell behind me.

The heat hit me like hellfire as I approached the door but I didn't stop.

I had to know.

The fire was almost to the door, the smoke tearing a round of hacking coughs from my lungs, sanding my throat raw as I edged into the cabin. It took me a second to find him, just in front of the wall of flames gaining ground inside the structure.

He hadn't been consumed yet, but I probably had less than a minute before he was swallowed by the fire.

I hurried toward him, dropped to my knees by his feet, and ripped the mask off his face.

Dean Giordana stared up at me, his watery eyes wide and sightless. Bullet holes riddled his forehead and chest, making it clear his cause of death wouldn't be the fire.

It had been the Kings.

Then I was being pulled to my feet by Neo, dragged out of the cabin almost the same way I'd been dragged into it.

This time not toward death this time. Toward life.

Chapter 73

Willa

I let loose a round of coughing, and Oscar tightened his arm around me. "You okay? Need more water?"

I rested my head back on his chest. "No, I'm good."

I'd downed about a gallon of water when we got back to the house — we all had — and then taken a shower. The water swirling the drain had been black from all the dirt and soot on my body, and it had never felt so good to put on sweatpants and a long-sleeve T-shirt.

They'd insisted on staying with me, climbing into my bed on either side of me like two beautiful, muscly bookends.

"I can get you some tea with honey," Rock offered on the other side of me. It was after four in the morning, the room dark around us. "It'll soothe your throat."

"Maybe later," I said. "I think I'm finally getting sleepy."

He picked up my hand and kissed it. "Then you should sleep."

"What about you guys?' I asked, snuggling deeper into

the covers, relishing the safety of being surrounded by them both.

Oscar kissed the top of my head. "Don't worry about us, tiger. We're all good."

"Do you think they got there in time to put out the fire?" I asked.

Rock had called the anonymous tip line for Blackwell Falls PD to report seeing flames in the woods and we'd heard sirens ringing through town less than a minute later.

"I don't know," Rock said. "I'm sure there will be something about it in the news tomorrow. Right now, all I care about is you."

I sighed. "I'm sorry," I said for the hundredth time. "I should have trusted you."

Rock squeezed my hand. "We can talk about that later. Just sleep."

My eyelids were heavy, the events of the night spinning through my head. We hadn't been able to talk about the fact that Dean Giordana had almost killed me, that he'd obviously had something to do with Emma's disappearance, and maybe the other girls too.

Maybe even Nikki's.

Oscar was convinced I was still in shock, that it would hit me later, after I'd slept, once my body knew it was safe for me to feel feelings again.

I closed my eyes with a sigh. There was no safer place for me to be than with the Kings. I knew that now. Turns out they'd put a tracker in the vintage watch that had been part of my costume. I'd be mad about it later, probably even royally pissed, but right now I could only be grateful.

If they hadn't done it, there was very little doubt in my mind that I'd be dead. Sure, I'd gotten off a shot with the gun, but it had hit Dean Giordana in the thigh. He probably would have put a bullet in my head before I had the chance to fire the gun again.

I hadn't even been able to think about the second man yet. Dean Giordana was dead, but there had been another man willing to bury my body where no one would ever find it, and I had no doubt they hadn't acted alone.

There had been too much uncertainty in Dean Giordana's voice, too much resignation in the other man's attitude.

They'd been taking orders.

Once I slept and coughed all the black shit out of my lungs, I'd start thinking about who that might be.

For now, I just wanted to sleep, and I closed my eyes, letting sleep come for me.

I was drifting off when I heard a soft tap at the door.

I lifted my head as Neo opened the door. He stood in the doorway for a long moment, his expression unreadable in the dark room.

"Mind if I sit?" he asked.

I shook my head, and he entered the room and took the chair next to the bed, the one I'd found him in the night I'd fallen asleep on the couch in the living room.

He looked comically large in the chair, which had clearly been picked out with me in mind. I stifled a smile and laid back down on Oscar's chest.

This time, sleep came fast. The last thing I saw was Neo,

staring at me from across the room, his features distorted with the familiar anguish I didn't understand.

Chapter 74

Willa

"You really don't have to do this," I said to Reva as she gathered the ingredients for chocolate chip cookies on the counter.

Behind her, Rock put his hands together in a gesture of prayer and mouthed the word *please*.

"Don't be silly, darlin!" Reva said. "You've been through so much. You need some homemade cookies and milk. The chef here," she said, hooking a thumb at Rock, "should know that."

I still didn't understand her relationship with the Kings, but she seemed to know everything that had happened on the night of the fire. I would definitely be digging into that mystery at some point.

"Oh, wow," Oscar said, entering the room and eyeing the ingredients lined up on the island, "are you making cookies?"

His voice squeaked a little on the last word, and I stifled a snort of laughter.

"I am!" Reva said happily. "And I'm happy to do it."

"You're... too good to us," Oscar said weakly, giving her shoulders a squeeze.

"It's the least I can do after what Willa went through last weekend," Reva said, all business as she bustled around the kitchen.

The fire department had put out the fire with minimal damage to the forest, thanks to Rock's call. An investigation was under way to determine the cause, and so far the police hadn't released anything about a body being found inside.

It was only Tuesday. Dean Giordana hadn't even been reported missing yet, or if he had, it was being kept quiet.

It wouldn't last. The Kings had prepared me for shit to hit the fan.

And soon.

The fire department would find human remains, an investigation would be launched into the cause of death, and they would eventually discover his identity. After that, it would only be a matter of time before they discovered he hadn't died from smoke inhalation or the fire but from several gunshot wounds.

The Kings had told me not to worry about it when I'd asked a bunch of questions about ballistics and evidence — not that I was an expert in forensics, but I'd followed enough true crime to get the gist of an investigation.

I'd let it go. For now, I was just happy to be alive.

That wouldn't last either. There was still at least one person running around out there who'd intended to kill me, and I still didn't know what had happened to Emma.

"Willa, can you go to the garage and get me a new bag of flour?" Reva asked.

"Sure," I said. Rock and Oscar had left, probably hoping to avoid sampling Reva's cookies straight out of the oven when they'd be forced to lie and smile and say they were delicious. "Where is it?"

"There's extra everything on the wire shelves in the first room on the right in that little vestibule," she said. "The flour should be on the bottom."

"What vestibule?" I had no idea what she was talking about.

She laughed. "I'm not surprised you haven't seen it. The garage is bigger than my entire house. The supply closet is in the back corner, by the motorcycles."

Now it made sense. I'd only admired the bikes from afar. I'd been too busy salivating over the cars. "You got it."

I opened the door to the garage and walked past the gleaming cars and motorcycles. Reva was right, there was a small dark hallway near the back corner that I'd never noticed before.

I entered it hesitantly and lights came on overhead, obviously activated by my presence.

I looked at the door on the right, then noticed another door across from it.

One with a keypad that glowed red.

I mean, come on. No one could blame me for wanting to see what was behind it, including the Kings.

Probably.

I thought about it and tried the code for the front door. Nothing happened, so I tried the code for the alarm next.

The red light turned green, and a click sounded from the door.

I turned the knob and stepped into a dark room filled with display screens. I closed the door behind me and stepped closer, trying to get my head around what I was seeing.

It didn't take long. It was the security feed from cameras around the property.

And they were everywhere.

Six screens displayed live images from the front door, the back patio area, the kitchen, the living room, the second-floor media room, the gym.

I looked at the display showing the kitchen where Reva was stirring something in a mixing bowl and saw a drop-down menu from the room labeled *Kitchen*. I clicked it, and several more rooms showed up as options.

Foyer.
Staircase (front).
Staircase (back).
Neo's Room.
Drago's Room.
Rock's Room.
Willa's Room.
Willa's Bathroom.

Motherfuckers.

Every single room in the house was covered, the Kings' bathrooms included.

And then: *Driveway (house), Driveway (trees), Driveway (road).*

I clicked on *Driveway (house)*, not even sure what I was looking for, and got a view of the driveway near the house.

The top of the screen displayed the current date and time, but there was a dropdown menu there too.

I used it to choose the date Emma had gone missing, starting around eleven p.m.

It was stupid. I'd been suspicious of Oscar after I'd gotten the pictures from my stalker, and I'd been suspicious of Neo after he'd found me in the woods the night of the quarry party, but the Kings had proven themselves when they'd pulled me out of the burning cabin.

Hadn't they?

I let the feed from the night of Emma's disappearance play.

I might have thought it was a static image if not for the clock ticking at the top of the screen: 11:00, 11:10, 11:20.

Nothing changed, and I was almost ready to turn it off — Reva would be waiting for her flour, and I didn't want the Kings to think I still doubted them — when something moved into frame at the top of the driveway.

A second later, Emma spilled out into the parking area in front of the Kings' house.

My heart stuttered in my chest, and I had to force myself to keep breathing as I watched her walk unsteadily toward the house, her face getting clearer as she neared the camera.

I felt like my chest was being gripped by an unseen hand. I'd looked at Emma's pictures thousands of times since she'd disappeared, had even looked at some of the videos I had of her on my phone, but those things were part of a past that hardly seemed real.

This was Emma on the night she'd gone missing, possibly

the last image ever captured of her, and it felt like it was shattering my heart into a million pieces.

She hesitated as she got closer to the door, and then, from behind the camera, I saw the broad shoulders of a man I would recognize anywhere, even from behind.

Neo.

She stopped when she saw him. He bent to say something to her, his profile coming into view, expression stern, then grabbed her arm. There was no audio, but she winced from the force of his grip.

A moment later she was pulled forward, her image disappearing from the screen.

I wound it back to the moment Neo had grabbed her and paused the video to get a better look at her expression. It was an easy one to identify, probably because it was one I'd so rarely seen on Emma's face: fear.

Looking at my sister's face on the screen, I had absolutely no doubt that she was scared.

No, not just scared.

Terrified.

I stared at the screen, feeling like I was in a never-ending nightmare as the truth crystalized in my mind.

The Kings had told the police they hadn't seen Emma that night, but that had been a lie.

They'd been lying all along.

Epilogue

Neo

I jogged in place in the corner, my eyes on my opponent (Julio?) across the sparring ring, my mind on someone else.

Willa.

It was always her. Always Willa Russo.

It always had been.

She didn't know that. Could never know that.

I'd seen the way she'd watched her sister, like Emma was a star, like Willa had been nothing more than a shadow passing behind her. It had been that way for as long as I could remember, Emma front and center, everyone acting like she was the fucking second coming while Willa stayed in the background, reading her books.

Watching.

That was the thing about Willa, one of the things I'd noticed about her a long time ago: she saw things.

She *noticed*.

Everyone else was too busy thinking about themselves.

How does the world see me? What do I look like? Am I getting enough attention? Enough appreciation? Am I getting everything I'm owed?

Myself included. I was the most self-involved motherfucker out there.

Except when it came to her. Because once upon a time, Willa Russo had stepped in to face the biggest baddest wolf of them all.

And she'd done it for me.

She'd been just a little thing back then. I don't even know if she remembered it.

But I did. I remembered every second of that day. Would go to my grave with it seared into my memory.

It was the day I'd been bound to Willa forever.

The day we all had.

"Okay, you guys know the rules," Mick, the sparring ref, said, moving into the center of the ring. He looked from me to the other guy. "Neo, Julio, keep it cool."

Right. This wasn't the Orpheum. It was the Gym — a seedy warehouse on the bad side of town with no official name. There were rules here, and one of them was Don't Kill Your Sparring Partner.

Note to self.

The ref moved out of the way and I rolled my shoulders and moved into the center of the ring, my mind still on Willa as my sparring partner and I began our dance.

I landed a right hook to Julio's face first, just to show him who was boss. He shook it off, then danced to my left.

My feelings — I fucking hated that word — for Willa were... inconvenient.

What did feelings matter? The world was what it was. The people who should protect you were usually the ones who'd stick a knife your back, then use it to cut a sandwich.

I fucking hated that Willa was learning that lesson, that she'd had to see that loser Giordana as Exhibit A. I wanted to kill that animal again for what he'd done to her, for fucking daring to manhandle her, to point a gun at her head.

The memory of it sent a shot of fury through my body, and I feigned right, then moved left and landed a vicious kick to Julio's solar plexus.

It felt good, and I jogged on my feet while he gasped, staggering backward to put some distance between us while he caught his breath.

Go ahead, Julio. Catch your breath. I'm not going anywhere.

I'd just about lost my fucking mind when Oscar told us Willa had given him the slip. We were on it pretty fast, but she didn't know how fast things could turn bad, how quickly you could go from being perfectly safe to being dead.

Especially at Aventine.

Especially if you were someone I loved.

I wanted to save her that misery, save her from meeting the same fate as her sister, but she wasn't making it easy.

Julio moved back into the center of the ring looking pretty pissed off. He tried to land a jab, but I ducked and ended up behind him, then gave him a kick in the ass.

He went sprawling and I got a warning from Mick that I barely heard.

Julio moved back into the ring fast, his eyes blazing. I let him land a punch and gave him a second to feel victorious, then I moved in for the kill, advancing fast, throwing punches with both hands, one after the other until he was stumbling back toward the rope.

I was all over it. What did this fucker think? That the rope was a safe zone?

I punched hard and fast, thinking about the one thing I really wanted but could never have, thinking about what I would do, what I would burn, who I would kill to protect her.

I was barely aware of the fact that I was still throwing punches, that Julio had slumped to the ground, his eyes already swelling closed while the ref tried to pull me off his limp body.

There were a million reasons I could never get close to Willa Russo, and she didn't need to know any of them. She just needed to stay away from me, and I needed to make her stay away, even if that meant treating her like shit.

Because in our world, feelings were a liability. All that mattered was staying focused on the goal.

On the prize.

And the prize for all of us — whether Willa knew it or not — was motherfucking vengeance.

Thanks for reading Kings & Corruption! Read Kings & Chaos, book two in the Aventine University series, and find out what happens when Willa steps into unexplored territory (*snerk*) with more than one of the Kings — and uncovers the shared history that bonds them forever.

Did you enjoy this book? Please help other readers find it by leaving a review.

Want freebies, book news, and exclusive Aventine U content? Sign up for the Sadie Hunt newsletter and learn more about Blackwell Falls and the swoon-worthy Kings: https://mailchi.mp/1986196a4e5c/sadie-hunt

Find me online:
Instagram: @authorsadiehunt
TikTok: @authorsadiehunt
Facebook: authorsadiehunt

Share Kings & Corruption and tag me on Instagram and/or TikTok for a like, comment, and share!

Made in the USA
Middletown, DE
20 September 2025